D1707033

BOOKS BY LYNETTE NONI

The Medoran Chronicles

Akarnae
Raelia
Draekora
Graevale
Varadesia

The Medoran Chronicles Novellas

We Three Heroes

The Whisper Series

Whisper
Weapon

AКА

AKARNAE

THE MEDORAN CHRONICLES

BOOK ONE

LYNETTE NONI

PANTERA
PRESS

PANTERA
PRESS

First published in 2015 by Pantera Press Pty Limited.
www. PanteraPress.com

Please send all permission queries to:
Pantera Press, P.O. Box 1989, Neutral Bay, NSW, Australia 2089 or
info@PanteraPress.com

A Cataloguing-in-Publication entry for this book is available from the National Library of Australia.
ISBN 978-1-925700-79-4 (Hardback)
ISBN 978-1-921997-51-8 (eBook)

Cover and Internal Design: Xou Creative www.xou.com.au
Editor: Deonie Fiford
Proofreader: Desanka Vukelich
Typesetting: Kirby Jones
Author Photo: Lucy Bell
Printed and bound in the United States by Bang Printing

Pantera Press policy is to use papers that are natural, renewable and recyclable products made from wood grown in sustainable forests. The logging and manufacturing processes are expected to conform to the environmental regulations of the country of origin.

For anyone brave enough to believe in the impossible.

Embrace the wonder.

One

"Honey, if there was any other way, your mother and I would take you with us in a heartbeat."

Alexandra Jennings stared out the car window into the dense forest and sighed deeply into her phone. "I know, Dad. But it still sucks."

"I'm sorry, sweetheart," came her father's reply. "But the International Exchange Academy is one of the best schools in the country. They'll take good care of you."

Alex only just managed to hold back the words that tried to leap from her tongue straight down the phone line.

Take me with you! she wanted to scream. *Don't abandon me!*

That was what it felt like her parents were doing, even if it wasn't their fault. They'd been offered the opportunity to study under a famous archaeologist—a once in a lifetime invitation— but there was a catch. They couldn't take anyone with them, which meant Alex was being shipped off to a boarding school for the rest of the school year—*eight whole months.*

And it got worse. Not only were they leaving her behind, they were also headed to some middle-of-nowhere dig-site in Siberia—as in, *Russia*—which was in a complete communication dead-zone. No phone coverage. No Wi-Fi signal. Not even a *postman.* After today, Alex wouldn't be hearing from them again until they returned at the beginning of June for the summer holidays.

"I just hate that I won't be able to contact you," Alex said, not for the first time. "What if I get bitten by a tick and end up with Lyme disease?" Her eyes scanned the thick woodland. "It's a definite possibility. And don't even get me started on how many wild animals Wikipedia says are in the forest up here. What if I get eaten by a bear? Or a cougar? I won't be able to call you and tell you what happened!"

Her father's amusement rang clearly through the connection. "In the unlikely event that you're mauled to death by the wildlife, you won't be able to call *anyone*."

"But no one else will be able to call you on my behalf, either," Alex pointed out. "That means you'll miss my funeral and you'll never get any closure about my death. You'll always wonder if it was a wolf or a bobcat that enjoyed *Alexandra à la carte*."

Her father chuckled. "I'm going to miss your sense of humour."

"Dad, I'm being serious here. Carnivorous animals are no laughing matter."

He wisely ignored her and instead said, "Your mother's making weird hand gestures at me. I'm guessing the Valium have finally kicked in. I made her take a double dose—you know how much she hates flying—so I think the peacock-bobbing and flapping arms mean she wants to talk to you. I better put her on before she takes someone's eye out."

Alex smiled into the phone. "Probably a good idea."

"I love you, sweetheart. The time will pass quicker than you realise."

Before she could respond, a crinkling noise sounded through the earpiece as he handed the phone over.

"Alex?" came her mother's somewhat slurred voice. Another ten minutes and she'd be out cold—which was for the best, since she *really* didn't do well on planes.

"I'm here."

"I don't have long, they've just started boarding our—*hic!*— flight," she said. "But I wanted to say—*hic!*—goodbye, again."

Alex frowned at the back of the seat in front of her. "Are you all right?"

"Fine, fine," her mother said, hiccupping again. "I just had a little drink to help wash down the sedative. *Hic!*"

"I'm pretty sure you're not supposed to mix alcohol with those drugs, Mum," Alex said, failing to keep the humour from her voice. "And you know, statistically speaking, you're more likely to get kicked in the head by a mule than to die in a plane crash. You're going to be fine."

"Of course I will be." Her mother's words became even more slurred as the medication continued taking effect. "And you will be, too. I know you wanted to come with us, but this is really for the best. *Hic!* You've been stuck following us around the globe for your entire life—it's time you settled in one place and had a chance to make some friends your own age."

Her mother had a point. Moving countries every few months while her parents chased the next big archaeological discovery hadn't helped Alex's social development. She didn't have any friends—she wasn't even sure how to *make* friends. High school politics were beyond her understanding; she had no idea what to expect from her new school. It wasn't like she could just go and sit beside someone in the sandpit, eat dirt with them, and declare a state of 'besties forever'.

"You're right," Alex said, mustering up as much optimism as she could. "I'm sure everything is going to work out great."

"That's the—*hic!*—spirit," her mother replied. "Now, I better go before the purple monkey eats my last banana. *Hic!*"

Alex pulled her phone from her ear and looked at it quizzically before returning it once more. "What did you say?"

"I said—"

She was interrupted by Alex's father in the background. *"Time to board, Rach. Say 'goodbye'."*

"I have to go, Alex," her mother said. "I know you're going to have a fabulous time at the—*hic!*—academy. We'll see you in June. Not long now!"

Clearly the meds were doing their job, especially if eight months equalled 'not long now'. But Alex didn't want to ruin her mother's happy buzz, so she kept her mouth closed.

"I love you, baby. Be careful, but have fun!" And with those final words, a quiet *click* disconnected the last phone call they'd share for a long, long time.

Feeling disheartened, Alex turned to look out the car window again, noticing that there were many more trees surrounding them now than before. It was clear evidence of just how easily a few hours of driving had transported her from her most recent home in Cannon Beach, Oregon, to somewhere on the outskirts of Mount Hood National Forest. The change in scenery from the rocky coastline to the thickening woodland was startling, and Alex couldn't help but feel like she was already a long way from her comfort zone.

"Miss? We're here," her driver finally said.

They'd stopped in a private driveway barricaded by two massive, wrought-iron security gates. A sign woven into the steelwork spelled out the words: 'International Exchange Academy'.

The driver spoke quietly through the intercom and a moment later the gates opened without so much as a creak. They moved slowly up the narrow, tree-lined path until they reached the academy itself.

"You've got to be kidding me," Alex muttered at the view out the window.

The academy really wasn't all that different from the stereotype she'd envisioned—big, ostentatious, gothic even. But the students?

They looked miserable. All of them wore tight, uncomfortable-looking uniforms despite the fact that it was Sunday afternoon and there were no classes until the next morning. And they didn't appear to be *doing* anything; they were just loitering aimlessly. It was as if they had nothing better to do than wait for someone to come along and break into the monotony of their boring existence. Looking at them, Alex seriously doubted she'd be able to follow her mother's advice to 'have fun'.

When the car pulled to a stop, she noticed a group of students mingling near a gaudy, medieval-styled water fountain. They weren't smiling. They weren't laughing. They were barely even talking amongst themselves. All Alex could think was that she would be more likely to make friends with a rock than any of the students scowling in her direction.

Don't judge by appearances, she told herself. First impressions weren't always accurate, right? Alex might not like being abandoned at the academy, but she was determined to at least try and make the most of her stay. And that meant keeping an open mind, regardless of the unwelcoming vibes coming from her new classmates.

"I'll take your bags," her driver offered, interrupting her thoughts. "You should head into the administration building and speak with the headmaster."

Alex grabbed the enrolment papers from her bag and handed the rest of her luggage over. She wasn't an official student yet since her parents hadn't had the time to properly enrol her before leaving.

"Which way do I go?" she asked the man as he started to walk away with her belongings.

He pointed to the closest building and left her standing on her own while the zombie-like students just stared at her.

Right, let's get this over with, she thought, gathering her courage. She wasn't an animal in a zoo, and she didn't appreciate all the speculative glances directed her way. Nevertheless, she held her head high and headed towards the administration building.

As she walked around the fountain she flicked through her paperwork once more—partly to avoid looking at the creepy gargoyle statues around the water feature, partly to avoid making eye contact with the other students, and partly to make sure everything that needed to be signed was, in fact, signed.

Alex was so distracted by her papers that she barely heard the whispered, "Fish out of water, think we should help her?" and the corresponding, "Absolutely. We wouldn't want her to choke."

Before she could properly register the words, something slammed into her, causing her to stagger forward. She managed to regain her balance just in time to avoid a messy fall into the grungy-looking water.

"Oh, I'm *so* sorry!" a girl around Alex's age said. "I'm so clumsy sometimes."

"It's okay," Alex assured her, straightening. "No harm done."

"Brianna! You're always getting in the way! You almost sent the new girl into the fountain. What kind of a welcome would that have been?" said another girl who stepped up beside them.

"Really, it's fine," Alex said again. She didn't want to cause any problems before school even started. It was bad enough that she was transferring mid semester.

"It's fine?" the newest girl repeated with a toothy grin. "Hear that, Brianna? She said it's fine."

Alex wasn't sure what to make of their exchange. Their identical beaming smiles put her on edge, so she quickly excused herself. "I have to go and see the headmaster, but I'm sure I'll see you both around."

"Oh, allow us to help," the non-Brianna girl said. "It's the least we can do. You wouldn't want to go to the wrong place and cause a—"

Her timing was perfect, really. When Alex stepped forward, Brianna 'accidentally' tripped over her own feet again. She bumped hard into Alex who had nothing to hold on to and no room left to find her balance. With her arms cartwheeling uselessly, Alex fell straight into the fountain.

The moment her head broke through the surface of the water, she heard non-Brianna gleefully finish the last word of her sentence.

"—splash."

The previously quiet courtyard erupted into laughter.

"Welcome to the academy, Newbie."

Alex scowled at the two girls as she swiped her sopping hair out of her eyes and pulled herself out of the fountain. She ignored the continuing laughter and marched towards the administration building, determined to put as much distance between her and the uniformed—and *mean*—zombies as possible.

Barely five minutes had passed since she'd arrived at the academy and already she knew her parents had been wrong. Judging by her classmates' welcoming committee, there was no way she was going to have an enjoyable time, nor was it likely she'd make any friends. Not a single person had tried to help her out of the fountain—they'd all been too busy laughing at her. That told her all she needed to know. She would just have to grit her teeth and get through the next eight months, and once her parents were back, she would never have to return to the academy again.

She trudged forward with bitter resolve and tried to air out her enrolment papers, but there was nothing she could do since they were just as soaked as she was. At least the ink hadn't run, that was something.

Alex entered the building and paused when she caught sight of her reflection in a mirror just inside the doorway. Her clothes were stuck to her shivering body, her long dark hair was stringy and wet, and her normally warm brown eyes were darkened by her turbulent emotions.

She shook her head and turned away from her bedraggled appearance. So much for making a good first impression.

Dripping water all the way, Alex headed over to the reception desk.

"Can I help you?" asked the lady seated there, without so much as a glance upwards. It was probably for the best since Alex was leaving a small lake on the pristine floor.

"I'm here to enrol," Alex said. It didn't take a genius to hear the misery in her voice.

"Name?" the woman asked.

"Alexandra Jennings."

"Take a seat, Miss Jennings."

Alex shuffled over to a line of chairs and sat down with a *squelch*. She still couldn't believe what had transpired outside. She wondered if it was too late to try and call her parents one last time—and convince them to find a way to smuggle her away with them—but she knew it was useless. Their plane had probably already taken off; they were likely long gone. She was on her own.

"The headmaster will see you now," the receptionist said, still not bothering to glance up. "Down the hallway, third door on the right."

Alex rose from her seat and headed down the brightly lit corridor, soon losing sight of the reception area.

If only things could be different, she thought sadly, knocking on the headmaster's door. There was no answer, so she tried again, louder. When still no call came to enter, Alex shrugged and turned the handle.

It was dark inside the room. Pitch-black, in fact.

"Hello?" she called out from the doorway. "Is anyone in here?"

Just as she was about to retrace her steps and go back to the reception, the room exploded with light. Alex had to hold her hand up to shield her eyes from the sudden brightness. When she was able to lower her arm again, she stared in shock at the sight before her.

"What the...?" she whispered.

I must have hit my head when I fell into the fountain, she reasoned. It was surely the only explanation for the view in front of her.

The doorway opened into a small forest clearing. Sunlight streamed through the canopy of evergreens and their shadows dappled the mottle-coloured forest floor. The surrounding trees continued further than her eyes could see, with no school buildings in sight.

"It must be some kind of optical illusion," Alex muttered to herself. She glanced behind her and took in the sterile walls of the corridor before she turned to face the forest again. She couldn't wrap her head around the different scenery, but something about the dense woodland captivated her attention.

I'll just have a quick look around, she thought. *No one will know. Then I can come back and meet the headmaster.*

Decision made, Alex quickly stepped through the doorway before she could change her mind. She expected to hear the crunching noise of dried leaves under her feet, but instead the ground disappeared and suddenly, impossibly, she was catapulted through the air. The wind rushed past her, whooshing by her ears as she flew along at what felt like the speed of light.

Just when she thought she might throw up, everything stopped.

Alex's heart thumped wildly in her chest. She lay spread-eagled on the ground but had no idea how she'd landed. Her eyes were shut tight, but she could feel the leafy forest floor underneath her; she could smell the woody scent of pine cones in the air; and she could hear noises—branches creaking, birds singing, wind whistling through the trees.

Hesitantly, she opened her eyes and looked around, finding herself lying in the middle of the forest clearing she'd seen through the doorway. But the doorway itself—and the administration building—was nowhere in sight.

The good news was that her airborne journey had mysteriously dried out her sodden clothes and hair. She wasn't even damp anymore. The bad news was that she had no idea where she was or how she was supposed to get back.

Alex sighed and threw her arms out to the sides, sending leaves scattering. "This new school *sucks*."

Two

"That was quite the entrance."

Alex jumped to her feet, but she had to wait for the resulting dizziness to pass before she was able to look up and find the owner of the unexpected voice.

"Hello," he said when he had her attention, a slight smirk playing at the corners of his mouth.

Alex had to blink a few times before she could fully appreciate the picture in front of her. He was, without a doubt, the most staggeringly attractive man she had ever laid eyes on. Almost unnaturally so. She guessed him to be in his late twenties or early thirties, and he had honey-coloured hair and bronze skin. He wore black from head to toe, the material finer than anything Alex had ever seen before. The tailored long-sleeved shirt was open at the collar and tapered by a belt at his waist, meeting a pair of leather-like trousers. The contrast between his tanned skin and dark clothing was breathtaking. But more than anything else, it was his strange golden-coloured eyes that captivated her attention and clouded her mind.

"Forgive me for startling you," he said formally, gesturing towards himself. "My name is Aven."

"Aven?" she repeated, sounding as dazed as she felt. Seriously, he was practically inhuman with his Greek god-like beauty. It wasn't her fault she was distracted. "That's an interesting name."

"Yes," he agreed, his tone pensive. "I suppose it is."

He looked at her like he was waiting for something.

Oh. Right.

"I'm Alex," she said. "Alexandra Jennings, really, but most people just call me Alex."

Aven offered his hand and she tentatively took it, expecting a firm shake, but he surprised her by bowing slightly and pressing a tender kiss to the back of her wrist.

"Charmed," he said, his eyes smouldering.

That's right, *smouldering*. It was something she'd only ever read about in books before, not actually witnessed. Alex was surprised when her legs managed to keep her upright. She desperately hoped he wouldn't notice her blushing. Or swooning.

Alex pulled her hand back and tried to clear her foggy brain. She couldn't figure out why she was so affected by his presence, even if he *was* on a whole new level of gorgeous.

It was only the observation that he seemed to know exactly how he was affecting her that allowed Alex to regain some of her composure. She moved a step away from him, hoping the distance would help. His brow furrowed slightly at her less than discreet movement, but his expression cleared quickly.

"Any chance you can explain what just happened to me?" she asked.

He raised one perfectly sculpted eyebrow. "What do you mean?"

"Well..." Alex gestured to the forest around them. "I just walked through a doorway in the middle of the administration building and then, uh, kind of *flew* here. Where is 'here', by the way?"

Aven was looking at her with a curiosity that bordered on incredulity. "You walked through a doorway and ended up somewhere completely different?"

Alex was fully aware of how crazy it sounded. If she hadn't

experienced it herself, she never would have believed it. "I know it sounds mental, but it's the truth."

After a lengthy silence where he stared intently at her, Aven said, "That is… most interesting. Tell me, Alexandra, where do *you* think we are?"

She had to hold back a shiver at the sound of her name falling so gracefully from his lips. Clearing her throat, she looked around the forest again. "Honestly? I have no idea. I can't even see the academy from here."

A slow smile began to stretch across Aven's face, transforming him from beautiful to radiant. But even as Alex struggled to maintain her slipping composure, she felt like there was something not quite right about him. Sure, he oozed charisma and charm, but it almost seemed… tainted.

She shook her head and focused on the leaves under her feet rather than his appearance, trying to clear her mind. "Look, I guess it doesn't really matter where we are. But I need to get back to the academy and enrol, so do you mind pointing me in the right direction?"

Aven didn't answer. Instead, he began to circle her like a lion tracking its prey.

Alex couldn't help but think of all the horror stories she'd heard about psychopaths dragging young women into forests to murder them. There was something decidedly dangerous about this Aven guy, of that she was certain.

"Tell me, Alexandra," he said, completing his circle and returning to face her, "do you find it at all strange that I happened upon you the moment you arrived here? In the middle of the Ezera Forest, of all places?"

Alex blinked at the unfamiliar name. "The what forest?"

Aven cocked his head slightly. "You've never heard of the Ezera?" At her quick negative shake, he asked, "Then tell me, Alexandra, how is it you know of Akarnae?"

"Akarnae?" Alex repeated, mimicking his pronunciation. *Ah-kar-nay*. How strange. "Never heard of it, sorry."

"Then to which academy do you seek directions?"

She frowned. "The International Exchange Academy, of course."

"I'm afraid the only educational institution nearby is Akarnae Academy," Aven said. "Are you *sure* you haven't heard of it?"

"Positive," Alex said. "But are *you* sure that's what it's called? Because, despite my... flying experience... I can't be that far from the building I was thrown out of. The International Exchange Academy must be around here somewhere."

"Oh, Alexandra, you have no idea how pleased I am to have found you," Aven said, his eyes alight.

Alex took another step away from him as her inner Creep-O-Meter spiked out a warning.

He stepped forward, and she stepped back again. But he just kept moving towards her, his golden eyes glowing from within, trapping her in his gaze.

"I found you here," he said, "just as it was foretold I would. *'A chance meeting in the forest of greeting, their destinies will be bound as one...'* Don't you see, Alexandra?"

She was still trying in vain to put some distance between her and the beautiful yet clearly deranged man, but her retreat ended when she backed into a tree, unable to go any further.

"See what?" she said, her voice quieter than she would have liked.

He stopped directly in front of her and reached out to gently trace his fingers down the line of her cheek. "You are to be my salvation."

Alex's eyes widened and then narrowed at his ridiculous statement. Just as she was debating whether to laugh hysterically or knee him hard enough that he'd never reproduce, he took a step away from her and tilted his head as if hearing something in the distance.

He stood like that for a moment before he moved back towards her, even closer than before, and leaned down to whisper in her ear, "I'll give you some time to settle in and learn how to use your power, and then I shall come for you, Alexandra. Together we will rule all of Medora."

He flashed his disarming smile again and stepped back, casually walking away and disappearing into the dense forest.

Only when he was completely out of sight did Alex breathe a sigh of relief. What a whack-job!

"Hey, what are you doing out here?"

Alex spun around at the new voice, and in her haste she tripped over a bulging tree root, lost her balance, and sprawled face-first onto the forest floor. She heard the sound of suppressed laughter and groaned quietly into the leafy cushions surrounding her before pushing herself to her feet. In front of her were two guys, both around her age. Unfortunately for her humiliated self, both of them were uncommonly attractive, too.

"Maybe it's some kind of gene therapy," Alex muttered.

"What was that?" asked the guy on the right, his blond hair mussed by the wind and his bright blue eyes sparkling with mischief.

"Nothing," Alex said. "Who are you? And where did you come from?"

"I'm Jordan Sparker," said the blond, before pointing to his friend. "And this is Bear."

Bear grinned at her, and it was such a genuinely friendly expression that she unconsciously returned it. Just like Jordan, he also had a mischievous look about him, but his shaggy dark hair and warm brown eyes helped him seem less... devil-may-care.

"And you're from...?" she prompted.

"The academy," Bear said. "Where else?"

Alex almost wilted with relief. Finally, some students who could show her the way out of the forest. Never mind that she still had no idea how she'd come to be there in the first place.

"Your turn," said Jordan. "Same questions."

"I'm Alexandra Jennings," she answered. "I'm supposed to be enrolling at the academy today but I was thrown through a doorway and ended up out here. Then this guy came along and went all weird on me, saying that together he and I would one day rule some place called 'Medora'. That was a fun conversation, let me tell you."

Both boys looked at her with amusement and she abruptly stopped her rambling.

"I think we're going to get along really well, Alexandra Jennings," Jordan said with a grin.

"Alex," she told him.

He shrugged. "Sure. Now tell us more about what happened with this doorway?"

She repeated the story as best as she could, watching them both for signs of understanding. If anything, they looked more and more excited, though she had no idea why.

"All I really want to do is hand in my enrolment papers, find out where I'm sleeping, and put this whole day behind me," she concluded.

Jordan turned to Bear and asked, "Are you thinking what I'm thinking?"

"No question about it," Bear agreed. "It'll be a shock for her, but the best way is just to show her."

"'Her' is standing right here, you know," Alex said pointedly.

"Sorry, Alex," Bear said. "You've just given us a lot to think about. If we're right, then you're the first Freyan to come to Medora in thousands of years. If not more. This is huge."

"Epic," Jordan said.

Alex looked from one of them to the other and asked, "What's a Freyan?"

Bear turned to Jordan who cleared his throat and said, "Freyan is the name we use for someone who comes from Freya, the Original Earth. Medora is our world, which is Second Earth—kind of like a parallel Earth, but different. If we're right about what's happened to you, then you're from another world."

Alex stared blankly for a beat, waiting for them to jokingly cry, 'gotcha!' but their earnest expressions didn't falter.

"Right," she deadpanned. She was *so* not in the mood for any more first-day-at-the-new-school pranks. "I'd say it's been great chatting with you, but… well, nope. Falling into the fountain was bad enough, you don't need to continue this 'let's punk the newbie' charade. So, thanks for the welcome, but I'll just find my own way back."

Alex chose a direction at random and headed straight into the trees. She half-expected Jordan and Bear to try and stop her from leaving, but they let her walk away without argument. She heard them following her and whispering to one another, but she didn't deviate from her onward mission.

It took less than five minutes before the density of the forest began to lessen. The boys moved up beside Alex and together the three of them stepped out from under the canopy of trees.

"But—What—*How?*" Alex stared incredulously at the view, speechless.

Directly in front of them lay a beautiful lake, glistening in the late afternoon sunset. The forest where they stood led straight down to the water's edge, and both the trees and the lake continued on to her right, much further than she could see. To her left, the forest cleared out into a grassy field which bordered the curve of the lake. Alex could even see a few horses grazing in the distance, adding to the picturesque image.

Further on from the fields and resting atop a small hill were a cluster of buildings, each one different from the next. Some looked like they were from the Dark Ages, while others looked as if they'd been built just yesterday. Two in particular stood out to Alex, if only because of their contrasting forms: one was a multi-storied U-shaped complex that was almost futuristic in design, and the other was a tower-like structure in the middle of the campus that looked like it belonged in a *Medieval Weekly* magazine.

"Welcome to Akarnae, Alex," Jordan said.

"What *is* this place?" she managed to say. "Where's the International Exchange Academy?"

"We need to tell you some things that you're not going to believe," Bear said, "but you have to hear us out before you decide to ignore us, okay?"

She nodded absentmindedly, distracted by the picture in front of her. Where *was* she?

"Alex, *focus*," Bear said firmly, turning her to face them.

Seeing their serious expressions, she hesitantly said, "Okay, I'm listening."

They led her over to a fallen tree and made her sit down while they spent the next few minutes describing an impossible reality. When they were finished, she looked at them apprehensively, torn between laughter and tears.

"Let me get this straight," she said. "According to you, I'm from another world, a world that was once identical to your own—this 'Medora' place—but over time the two places changed and became... different places?"

Yeah, that was really articulate. But they nodded, so she continued, "And people from my Earth—sorry, 'Freya'—don't know about Medora or how to get here?"

When they nodded again, she asked, "Then how do you explain me?"

"No idea," Jordan said, grinning widely. "But I reckon we'll have fun trying to figure that out."

Alex looked from him to Bear and asked, "Are you aliens?" When both boys burst out laughing, she frowned at them. "Different worlds? Hel-*lo*! It's not that strange a question, especially considering I feel like I'm the leading character in some kind of alternate reality movie. And you've just told me that there are all kinds of different beings in your world, not just humans. Give a girl a break, would you?"

"Sorry, Alex," Bear said, still chuckling. "Rest assured, we're as human as you are."

Alex let that settle before her brain skipped a million miles ahead. "If I'm in another world, how can I understand you, and vice versa? How do you know English if there's no England here?"

Even Alex had to admit that she was beginning to sound a little hysterical, but it was still a valid question, and one of many that were swirling around her head. Perhaps she should have asked something more pressing, though. Like, if she truly *was* in a different world, how was she going to get home again? Especially since she didn't even know why—or *how*—she'd arrived to begin with. And her parents... Well, at least there was something good to be said about their inability to be contacted, since they would totally freak out if they learned she was missing. Alex shuddered just thinking about their reactions—or perhaps she shuddered because she was beginning to understand the gravity of her situation.

"English, England... I don't know what you're talking about," Jordan said. "We're speaking Medoran, or the common tongue, and since you seem to understand it just fine, then I guess we can presume there's some kind of cross-world comparison. Let's just be thankful that we don't have to mime this entire conversation to each other, and leave it at that."

Alex figured she couldn't expect much more of an explanation, so she decided to move on. "Let's talk about this school of yours," she said, thinking over everything they'd told her in their 'welcome to our world' speech. "You mentioned something about Akarnae being a school for the gifted. What does that mean?"

Bear motioned for her to look at Jordan, so she turned to the blond boy. He smirked at her... and then disappeared into thin air.

She gaped at the empty spot in front of her. "How—?"

"It's my gift," Jordan said, reappearing again and laughing loudly at the gobsmacked expression on her face.

"Your gift?"

"Transcendence," he said. "I can transcend—meaning I can disappear from sight and move through solid objects while invisible."

"That is..." Alex was lost for words, so she settled on, "very cool."

Jordan chuckled and squeezed her shoulder. "It's okay. You'll get used to it here. Everyone at Akarnae has a gift. Bear's is pretty handy too, especially when we want to get out of detention."

"What can you do, Bear?" Alex asked, even if in the back of her mind she was totally flipping out.

"I'm a charmer," he said with a wink.

She felt her lips twitch. "I bet you say that to all the new girls."

He laughed at that before explaining, "I can use my speech to convince people to do things. I literally charm them into action."

"That sounds kind of dangerous," Alex said. If what he said was true, then he had a gift that could cause a lot of damage in the wrong hands.

"It might seem that way, but it's really not," Bear said. "My charms are more like suggestions, you can either act upon or dismiss them depending on how much you like or don't like the idea."

Alex thought about that and said, "Can you show me?"

Bear shared a sneaky glance with Jordan before turning back to her and saying, "You must be hungry, Alex. I doubt you've eaten for hours, right?"

His voice sounded the same, but there was an almost hypnotic quality to his tone. Before she even realised what she was doing, Alex nodded in agreement.

"You're probably so hungry that you would eat anything just to feel relief."

Alex's stomach clenched painfully. She was *starving*. What had she last eaten? A piece of toast for breakfast? She couldn't even remember what it had tasted like, it seemed so long ago.

"I wonder if there's anything around here that we can give you to eat?" Bear continued in that same mesmerising tone.

"Please," Alex said, her own voice sounding strained. "I'll eat *anything*."

"Here, this will help." Bear scooped up a handful of dirt and handed it to her. "It's just like chocolate. It'll taste delicious and you'll feel so good afterwards."

Alex reached her hand out and Bear passed the dirt over. Part of her was desperate to pour the chocolate-like goodness straight into her mouth, but another part was beginning to scream from deep within her subconscious mind. She paused in the act of moving her hand towards her mouth, her thoughts warring with each other.

It's dirt, Alex thought to herself. *Why would I ever eat* dirt*? Gross!*

She threw the handful of earth to the ground and then turned to glare at Bear. "What did you just do to me?"

He and Jordan burst out laughing.

"You should see your face right now!" Jordan gasped between guffaws.

She placed her hands on her hips and narrowed her eyes further.

"Oh, come on Alex," Jordan said once he'd calmed somewhat. "Admit it, that was funny!"

She tapped her foot impatiently and asked Bear again, "What did you do?"

"You asked me to charm you, so I did," he said. "I wanted you to see how it feels when it works, but also how when I press too far, your natural reasoning comes back into play."

"So, you managed to convince me I was starving, even though I'm actually not?"

He nodded and continued for her, "But when I tried to get you to eat dirt, the suggestion was too different from anything you would normally agree to, so you snapped out of my influence."

She shook her head in amazement. "That's... Yeah, I have no words for what that is."

"I just wanted you to understand that while it's pretty cool, it's not a dangerous gift because I can only do so much before you realise you're being manipulated. So, no freaking out about me becoming some kind of tyrannical ruler bent on world domination, okay?"

"That particular scenario hadn't actually crossed my mind," she told him dryly.

"I kind of like the sound of it, though," Jordan mused.

"Fortunately, it's me with the gift, then," Bear said with a grin.

Alex found herself enjoying their easy banter, but her mind was also distracted by the events of the last half hour. It was only just beginning to sink in that she was really, *illogically*, in another world.

"You look like you're going to pass out, Alex," Jordan said, gently grasping her elbow to offer support for her swaying body.

"You try looking okay when you've just had your entire world turned on its axis—*literally*," Alex said, rubbing at her temples. "What am I supposed to do now? How do I get home?"

"Don't worry about that," Jordan said. "Marselle will get you home, no problem."

"Who's Marselle?" Alex asked.

"He's our headmaster," Bear answered. "If anyone can get you back to Freya, it's Professor Marselle. He can do anything."

"Sounds like a regular Einstein," Alex muttered, too low for either of them to hear. Louder, she said, "All right, let's go see this headmaster of yours."

Three

Alex wasn't sure where to look as Jordan and Bear led her out of the forest, around the edge of the lake and up through the grassy fields. When she turned to glance back over her shoulder, she had to stop walking to truly appreciate the postcard-perfect sight behind her. The lake and the forest were beautiful enough on their own, but they were overshadowed by a massive snow-capped mountain not too far off in the distance. It was a spectacular view, made even more so by the colours from the setting sun. Alex had a hard time tearing her eyes from the landscape, at least until the serenity was broken by a loud voice.

"SPARKER!"

Alex spun back around at the noise. What she saw caused her to swallow nervously and back up a step.

The man was possibly the most intimidating person she'd ever seen, and he was walking their way. Tall and burly, he had short-cropped hair which added to his military appearance. But it was his clothes that really caught her attention, since he was wearing some kind of leather armour and… was that a sword strapped to his belt?

Alex turned her attention towards the man's face and found that, while his clothing and bulky physique certainly emphasised his formidable presence, it was his expression that truly made her fear for her life. He looked beyond furious, with icy blue eyes glaring out from under narrowed eyebrows. Even his lips were curled in anger.

When the glowering man was just a few steps away, Jordan smiled and said, "What's up, Karter?"

Alex wondered if Jordan had a death wish, since his words seemed to have the same effect on the man as poking a rattlesnake with a fork.

"You were supposed to report to detention with me after breakfast this morning," the man—Karter—said. "Since it evidently slipped your mind, you'll make up for your lapse in judgement next weekend—*all* weekend—with Finn."

Something about the last two words caused Jordan to pale. Karter seemed pleased with the reaction.

"That'll teach you to waste my time," he finished.

"Aw, come on, Karter," Jordan pleaded. "The only reason I had detention was because I skipped Marselle's speech. It's not like I haven't heard it all before."

"Attendance was mandatory, Sparker." Karter frowned and shook his head. "Your arrogance will be your undoing if you don't watch yourself."

Jordan seemed to wilt by Alex's side. Despite all his bravado, she sensed that he truly respected the man in front of them.

"Yeah, I know." Jordan looked down as he spoke. "Sorry, Karter. I won't do it again."

"Of course you will," Karter huffed. "Just don't get caught next time. Understood?"

When Jordan glanced back up again, he appeared to be fighting a grin. "No problem, sir."

Karter nodded brusquely. "Good."

Just as he began to turn away, he seemed to notice Alex and Bear for the first time.

"Who are you?" he demanded, looking directly at Alex.

"Uh…"

He turned his glare from her to Bear then back to Jordan. "You know you have to register visitors. What's the meaning of this?"

"Ease up, Karter," Bear said. "She's no ordinary visitor."

"She's new here," Jordan added. Then he lowered his voice, making his next statement sound overly dramatic. "And she's from *Freya*."

Karter's eyes widened a fraction before they narrowed again. "Don't be ridiculous, Sparker."

"I'm right here, you know," Alex interrupted, fed up with them all talking about her as if she was invisible. "I can speak for myself."

"What's your name then, girl?" Karter asked, and she instantly regretted opening her mouth.

"Alexandra Jennings," she said, before adding on a quick, "sir."

"Follow me, Jennings," he ordered. "We'll find out where you're really from and what you're doing here."

He didn't wait for her to acknowledge his order, he just turned around and marched back towards the buildings.

Jordan smiled encouragingly at her. "Shall we?"

"I'd rather not," Alex mumbled.

Jordan and Bear chuckled at her words and she smiled back at them before they hurried to catch up to the strange, leather-clad man.

Alex remained silent as the three of them followed Karter across the academy grounds. She saw students walking around, playing games, talking and laughing with each other and she knew that *this* was what a school was meant to be like. There were no stuffy uniforms or miserable expressions here.

Karter led them straight towards the large tower-like building and motioned for them to enter. As they walked through the medieval archway, Alex noticed a bronze plaque attached to the stone wall with the inscription, 'Akarnae Academy'. In smaller letters below were the words: '*Kailas en freydell. Vayla en karsis. Leali en nexar.*'

"Strength in weakness. Victory in surrender. Life in death," Bear translated before she could ask. "It's kind of like our school motto."

"I see." She didn't. Exactly what kind of school was this?

The archway led to an empty room. On one side was a winding stone staircase leading up, and on the other side a similar staircase led down, underground. Karter motioned for them to follow him over to the upwards staircase, and they hastily began their ascent.

Step after step they climbed until they finally left the staircase at the eighth floor and moved into a small waiting room. Karter instructed the three of them to stay there while he walked across the room and knocked on a closed door.

The moment he disappeared into the room beyond, Alex puffed out, "Fill me in—what's going on here? Where are we? And seriously, haven't you guys ever heard of an elevator?"

"It was only eight floors," Jordan said, and she turned incredulous eyes to him.

"There's no such thing as 'only' when it comes to eight floors, Jordan. That's practically a small mountain."

He shook his head, amused, and answered her other questions. "This is Jarvis's office, but I'm not sure why we're here. I thought Karter would take us to see Marselle."

Before he could say more, the door opened and a middle-aged man with neatly combed hair and rectangular glasses walked out. His expression was warm and his smile genuine when he said, "We've been expecting you, Alex."

She looked at him uncertainly, perplexed by his comment and his familiar use of her name.

"I'm Administrator Jarvis," he continued. "Please, follow me and we'll sort out your paperwork." He beckoned her into his office, but she remained where she was, unsettled by his words.

"I'm sorry, my paperwork?"

"For your admission," he clarified.

"For my... admission?"

"I was told you'd have your enrolment papers with you," Jarvis said, looking at her hand pointedly.

Alex tightened her fingers around the crumpled papers that were still miraculously clenched in her grip despite everything that had happened between the doorway and the forest. "I think there's been some kind of mistake, Administrator Jarvis. I'm meant to be enrolling at the International Exchange Academy."

Jarvis smiled at her kindly. "And yet, here you are at Akarnae. Headmaster Marselle mentioned you might be arriving today, and he said you'd likely be confused. He had so hoped to meet you before he left, but unfortunately you just missed him." Jarvis motioned for her to enter his office once again. "Please, come in and take a seat."

Realising she would have to enter the room to get some answers, Alex began to follow him, pausing after a few steps to look back at Jordan and Bear.

Seeing her hesitation, Jarvis said, "Your companions are more than welcome to join us, if you'd like?"

Alex nodded and Jordan and Bear stepped up beside her. Together they entered the room and sat in front of a large mahogany desk. Jarvis took a seat opposite them, while Karter glowered at them all and left without another word.

"Perhaps we should start by getting your questions out of the way," Jarvis offered, watching Alex fidget nervously. "You seem a tad... overwhelmed."

"Overwhelmed doesn't quite cover it," Alex said. "I've just been told that I'm from a different world. That's not exactly normal, you know."

Jordan chuckled quietly beside her. At least someone was amused.

"Oh, good," Jarvis said, pleased. "That saves us a lengthy explanation."

"I think I've had all the explanations I can handle," Alex said, feeling suddenly tired. "I'm ready to go home now, if that's okay with you?"

On the off chance that her parents were able to sneak a phone call in between their connecting flights, she really didn't want to risk them discovering her missing once they landed. She needed to get back, pronto, even if it meant she'd have to put up with the zombie-like students at the International Exchange Academy. They might have been mean, but at least they weren't from another *world*.

Jarvis shifted uncomfortably at her question. "Unfortunately, that's not going to be as simple as it sounds."

Alex stilled. "What do you mean? I have to get home. Right now, before someone realises I'm gone."

There was no way he could have misread the urgency in her voice. And yet, if anything, his expression turned pitying.

"I'm afraid that's impossible at the moment," Jarvis told her. "Headmaster Marselle is the only person who can help you return to your world."

Alex felt her heart rate increasing. "Well, where is he, then?"

"I don't expect to see the headmaster for a number of months," Jarvis said. "He's on a scouting tour—something he does every five years."

Months? Did he say *months*?

"But—But—" Alex didn't even know what to say. "What am I supposed to do until then?"

"You'll remain here and attend classes as one of our students," Jarvis said, as if it was obvious.

Alex could feel a panic attack coming on. "I can't stay here! I have a life to get back to—a *world* to get back to! My parents... my new school..." Admittedly, she wouldn't be completely devastated to miss out on the International Exchange Academy experience, but the rest was a definite cause for concern. "I can't just become a student here and go to classes like it's normal. Not for *months*. Not even for a day!"

At his apologetic look, she quickly grasped for another argument.

"Akarnae is a school for the gifted, right? Well, I don't have a gift. I'm completely ungifted. I can't stay here—I don't *belong* here!" she said. "Can't you get a message to this Marselle guy and ask him to come back sooner?" *Like, tomorrow*, she added to herself.

"I'm sorry, Alex," Jarvis said, sounding like he truly meant it. "If it's any consolation, the headmaster was adamant that you *do* have a gift, and that it will present itself in time. He assured me that you would find your place here at Akarnae."

"How kind of him," Alex muttered. She wasn't thrilled to have some random guy making decisions on her behalf, but she also couldn't suppress a tendril of curiosity. She had a gift? What did that mean? Would she be able to turn invisible, like Jordan? Maybe she'd be able to fly or move things with her mind; that'd be pretty awesome.

Realising that there were some possible advantages to staying at Akarnae—not the least of which was that she could avoid the awful International Exchange Academy—Alex wondered if perhaps it wouldn't be so bad to hang around for a little while. And it wasn't as if she had any better ideas.

"All right, I guess I can wait here until he returns," she hesitantly agreed, hoping that her parents stuck to their original plan and wouldn't try to call her one final time. Judging by the alcohol-Valium cocktail her mother had ingested, Alex figured she was probably safe. Her dad would have his hands full keeping her mum conscious and out of trouble, so it was unlikely that either of them would even think about contacting her when they landed. Once again, Alex found herself feeling grateful for their inability to communicate over the next few months. If she had any luck at all, she'd be back to her world without them ever realising she'd been missing.

"Excellent," Jarvis said, genuinely happy with her decision.

"You're going to love it here," Jordan promised, his eyes sparkling. "Just wait, you'll see."

Bear nodded his agreement, and their enthusiasm was so contagious that Alex couldn't resist offering a tentative smile in return. At least she already had two friends in this strange place—that was more than she'd ever had in her world.

"Now we've settled that, may I please have your enrolment papers?" Jarvis asked.

"They're not for here, you know," Alex pointed out as she handed them over.

"I just need some basic information to create your personal file," he said, skimming the forms before placing the paperwork into the top drawer of his desk. He closed the drawer and a moment later opened it again, pulling out an entire folder. Alex's eyes widened when she read the label: *Alexandra Rose Jennings*.

Jarvis withdrew a document out of her newly created file and handed it over.

"How did—?" She shook her head, realising that it was probably best if she didn't ask about the apparently magical file. She was in another world—anything was possible.

"Just sign on the line and you'll be officially enrolled," Jarvis said.

She skimmed the paper quickly, taking in the rules and regulations of enrolment. Everything seemed pretty normal until she read four words at the bottom of the page: '*Alexandra Jennings: Potential Untested*'.

What did *that* mean?

"Wonderful," Jarvis said after she'd signed her name and handed the document back. "Now all that's left is to see which classes you'll be attending. I think the best way to go about this is to test you and explain the results afterwards."

"Test me?" Alex repeated. "Test me for what?"

"For your potential, of course."

"And that means…?"

"Before I explain, I need to tell you a little more about the academy," Jarvis said. "We have five years of official education, with two additional years for students who are chosen to continue on as apprentices in specific subjects. Due to the demanding nature of the classes, the youngest enrolments we have are fourteen years of age, meaning that students graduate at eighteen—or twenty for the apprentices."

"Ooo-kay," Alex said, drawing the word out. None of this was really going to affect her since she'd be leaving as soon as the headmaster returned. "That still doesn't explain what you mean by potential."

"I'm getting there," Jarvis promised. "Our classes are split into two categories: age-based and potential-based. There are five subjects for each. Core Skills, Medical Science, Species Distinction, History, and Studies of Society and Culture are all age-based classes; while Combat, Archery, PE, Chemistry, and Equestrian Skills are all potential-based."

Combat? Species Distinction? Alex wondered if she'd heard right.

"You had your sixteenth birthday recently, correct?" Jarvis asked, glancing quickly at her file.

"Yeah, in July," she answered, not sure if that meant anything to him. Was the calendar year the same on Medora as on Earth—err, Freya?

"That works out well then," Jarvis commented. "Despite your lack of previous experience in the age-based subjects, you'll still have to join with the third year class. Jordan and Bear are also in that class, so I'm sure they'll help bring you up to speed."

"Go team!" Jordan said, holding his hand up for a high-five.

Alex chuckled at his boyish expression before asking Jarvis, "How do you test for the potential subjects?"

Jarvis handed her a lollipop and she looked at it dubiously.

"Go on," he urged. "This is the potential test."

"That makes absolutely no sense," she said, but she took the candy and unwrapped it, sticking it in her mouth. She swivelled her tongue around the foreign object, surprised at the different flavours it produced. Apple, cherry, grape, pineapple, orange. Every swirl brought a different fruity flavour to her mouth.

"Now," Jarvis started again, "the potential-based classes are divided into five different levels of difficulty—Alpha, Beta, Gamma, Delta and Epsilon. The level you train at is based on your potential for that particular class. The potential-based subjects also tend to be the most physically demanding."

"Like Combat?" Alex asked around the lollipop. "Is that even legal?"

"Akarnae abides by a unique set of laws," Jarvis answered sketchily. "Our instructors are given free rein to do what they must in order to help bring out the best in our students."

Well… that didn't sound daunting at all.

"I can assure you that Combat is a favourite subject for many students," Jarvis pressed on. "Very demanding, but educational nonetheless. Karter is the instructor for that class."

Why was she not surprised? Big man. Leather costume. Sword. Total no-brainer, really.

She swirled the shrinking candy around her mouth, waiting for Jarvis to continue talking about the classes, but his attention was elsewhere.

"Where did I put that thing?" he muttered, rustling through the papers on his desk.

As she watched him, Alex unconsciously crunched down on the remaining sweet, chewing until only the stick remained.

"Aha!" Jarvis exclaimed, withdrawing a small, resealable bag. He indicated to the stick poking out of her mouth. "All done?"

She nodded and he motioned for her to drop the stick inside the bag. Alex did as directed and, after he sealed it and placed it on his desk, she watched in amazement as the bag disappeared, replaced by a single piece of paper.

"How—?"

"New world, new rules," Jordan said, laughing at the gobsmacked expression on her face.

Right. She'd have to remember that in the coming days.

"Well, this is certainly a surprise," Jarvis mumbled to himself as he read the words on the paper.

"What's wrong?" she asked.

"Some of your results are… unexpected."

He handed over the sheet of paper and Jordan and Bear leaned in to read with her.

Potential Test: Alexandra Rose Jennings

Combat ~ Epsilon

Equestrian Skills ~ Epsilon

PE ~ Delta

Archery ~ Gamma

Chemistry ~ Gamma

After reading the page, Alex looked up to find her friends staring at her with shocked expressions.

"What?" she asked.

Jordan looked like he was about to burst out laughing. "This is going to be a *great* year."

She frowned slightly when Bear smirked and nodded his agreement. What was up with them? She turned back to Jarvis to see his countenance still unchanged from before. "Why do you look so... apprehensive?"

"I'm just surprised by your results," he said again. "Particularly for Combat."

"Why?" Alex asked. "Epsilon is the lowest grade, right?"

The three of them stared at her with varying degrees of pity.

"Epsilon is our most advanced ranking, Alex," Jarvis corrected. "It's the highest level of training we have on offer here. Despite all our students being re-tested each year, very few manage to rate at an Epsilon level for anything. Ever. Often the students in Epsilon classes are the apprentices who have been chosen to remain behind for specialised training, or those students who have the aptitude to become apprentices after their fifth year."

Alex felt the blood drain from her face. That couldn't be right.

"At present," Jarvis continued, "I believe there are only five other students in the Epsilon class for Combat, all of whom are at least a year older than you. As for Equestrian Skills, there are only six other students in your Epsilon class. One of them is your age, but the rest are older again."

Alex considered his words before finally saying, "Perhaps the lollipop was wrong?"

Jarvis shook his head. "The testing is foolproof, I'm afraid."

"You can change it though, right? You can put me in a lower level?" Seeing his regretful look, she cried, "No way—I don't know the first thing about offensive fighting!"

"I understand your unease," Jarvis said soothingly, "but if the results say you're at this level, then that's what you are. The testing doesn't ascertain how capable you are at the subjects, but rather, it judges how good you'll be if you apply yourself to the training. According to your results, you have a tremendously high level of potential for these subjects."

Alex scowled at the piece of paper. "Lucky me."

"Hey, at least you'll have Bear and me in PE," Jordan said, reading her results again. "And me again in Chemistry. That's something to look forward to. We can blow stuff up together."

"Whoopee," she responded dryly.

He nudged her playfully and she smiled despite herself.

"It's getting late. I think we've all had enough for the night," Jarvis said, covering a yawn. "Unless you have any other questions?"

"Dozens, but none I can articulate right now," Alex admitted.

Jarvis looked at her with understanding. "My office is always open if you need to talk. Rest assured, everything you require for your stay will be provided for you. Your dorm room is ready and waiting, and your classes will begin first thing in the morning."

He handed her a new sheet of paper which showed her class schedule.

"Any problems, you know where to find me," Jarvis said, before turning to Jordan and Bear. "Do you mind showing Alex to the dorm building since you're going there anyway? She's on the third floor, room seven."

Jordan made a choking noise. "Are you serious? Room seven?"

Jarvis appeared puzzled. "Is there a problem?"

"You've put her in with D.C.?" Bear asked, his eyes wide. "Is that... wise?"

"I'm sure they'll get along splendidly." Jarvis covered another yawn with his hand. "Eventually."

Jordan snorted. "If you say so."

Alex wasn't sure what to make of their reactions. What was wrong with her roommate?

"Oh, and one more thing before you go," Jarvis said. "It's probably best if you keep where you're from and how you came to be here between us."

"Why?" Alex asked.

"Being from another world is quite the anomaly. There could be... certain complications if your story was to become well known. Only tell those whom you trust will keep your secret."

"All right," Alex said, accepting his judgement on the matter.

"I'm sure we can count on your friends to help you out as needed," Jarvis added.

"Definitely." Jordan smiled at Alex. "We can say you're the queen of some forgotten civilisation who demands that we all bow down to you. Except for me—I found you first so I get to be your right-hand man."

"You'd make a better court jester," Bear said with a grin.

"Perhaps something closer to the truth," Jarvis suggested, "such as Alex being a transfer student?"

Jordan's face fell. "That's just boring."

"But so much easier to remember," Alex said. "And besides, you can still be my right-hand man if you want."

"I suppose I'll take what I can get," Jordan happily agreed.

"It's almost curfew, so you better all get along now," Jarvis said, dismissing them. "Let me know if you have any problems settling in, Alex, but I'm confident you'll be fine."

Alex barely had the chance to call out a quick, "Thanks, Jarvis!" before Jordan and Bear pulled her from her seat and dragged her out of the office.

Four

"Allow us to be your tour guides," Jordan offered once they were outside again.

The sun had long since set during their time with Jarvis, and now that her adrenaline had worn off, exhaustion was beginning to seep into Alex's mind and body. Nevertheless, she nodded her agreement.

"The academy is made up of eight main buildings," Jordan said. He then pointed to the medieval-inspired building they'd just left. "This fine construction is called the Tower. Most of the professors have their offices and sleeping quarters inside, so if you're trying to sneak around after curfew or anything, stay away from this area."

"Noted," Alex said.

"There's also the Stable Complex, which is pretty self-explanatory; the Arena, which is where Combat classes are held; the Clinic, for Species Distinction; the Sir Carsus dorm building, where first through to fifth year students live; the Lady Omar dorm, for the apprentices; and then there's Gen-Sec—the General Sector building—which is where most of the boring classes are held."

"By 'boring', Jordan means they're intellectually challenging rather than physically demanding," Bear cut in. He pointed off into the distance, but it was too dark for Alex to see anything. "Gen-Sec is the massive U-shaped building you probably saw earlier. One length of the 'U' is for Chemistry-related labs and workrooms, and another length has normal classrooms for History, Core Skills and SOSAC. The middle part of Gen-Sec is for the Medical Science labs and other research rooms."

"The Med Ward is also in the middle section," Jordan said. "It's like our very own hospital, and it covers the entire ground level. You'll probably be a frequent visitor there, especially with your high potential classes."

Alex sighed. "Yay."

Jordan grabbed her arm and pulled her forward. "We won't show you around the entire campus tonight because it's late and you look like you're about to drop on your feet. But as long as you know the most important building, I think you'll be all right."

Bear snorted and Alex wondered where they could be taking her. When Jordan brought them to a stop in front of a large square building, she couldn't help but roll her eyes when he said, "This is the food court. It's a very important place that will see to your nutritional needs for breakfast, lunch and dinner. Don't forget where this building is and you'll be fine."

"You're such a dork." She smiled at him to take the sting out of her words.

"I'll have you know that I am no such thing," Jordan argued. "I am the epitome of all things awesome."

"I can't believe you just used the word 'epitome' in a sentence, let alone in that context," Alex marvelled dryly as they started walking again.

Before Jordan could offer a comeback, Bear jumped in and said, "Can you tell us about Freya, Alex? We already know the basics, since our technology is much more advanced than yours and we have people who spend their whole lives studying your world. But I want to hear it from your point of view. What's it like there?"

Surprised by what he'd just revealed, instead of answering, Alex asked her own question. "There are people here who study my world? Could they have a way to get me back home?"

Bear shook his head. "They can only look into Freya through a viewing screen, they can't physically travel there. As far as I know, all they do is watch other worlds and glean information about the inhabitants, geography and technology—and whatever else they can see. There's no interaction, and definitely no visitation. Multi-world transportation is beyond the scope of even our most advanced tech, at least for now. Maybe in another decade or so—who knows?"

Alex's hopes deflated again and she resigned herself to the fact that she really would just have to wait for the headmaster to return. "Okay, what do you want to know about my world?"

While she answered their questions, Bear and Jordan slowly led her to the Sir Carsus dorm, where they took up their roles as tour guides again.

"All students except for the apprentices live in here," Bear said, heading through the doorway. "Jarvis said you're on the third floor, same as us. There are two students per room; Jordan and I have been dorm buddies since first year."

That explained their brotherly friendship. Alex wondered if she'd find that kind of close relationship with her own roommate.

She followed them up an attractive winding staircase in the middle of the building. When they reached the third floor, she was led down a hallway filled with doors until they reached one labelled with the number seven. There was no handle or lock on the door, and she wondered how she was supposed to get inside.

"It's touch-activated," Jordan explained before she could ask. "It'll open when it reads your bio-signature, which Jarvis should have uploaded by now. You and D.C. are the only ones who can open your door from the outside. Give it a go."

Alex pressed her hand to the door and it automatically clicked open.

"That's pretty cool," she admitted.

"Do you want us to come in and introduce you?" Bear offered, albeit hesitantly.

Alex peeked through the doorway. It was dark inside, but a large window on the opposite wall allowed some moonlight to spill into the room. In the dim light she could just make out two beds; one was already occupied.

"I think she's sleeping," Alex whispered. "I can introduce myself in the morning."

"Good idea," Jordan said. "And hey, how about we stop by on our way to breakfast? We can all go down together, if you want?"

Alex smiled. "That'd be great, thanks."

"No problem," he said, before they both wished her goodnight and headed further down the hall to their own room.

Alex quietly entered her dorm and the door sealed shut behind her. She tip-toed over to what she thought was the bathroom, and once the door was closed she turned on the light. It was nice, if simple. There was a toilet, a shower and a basin with a large bench—half of which was covered with her roommate's toiletries. Alex opened the drawers on what she presumed was her side and she was pleased to find a new toothbrush and toothpaste ready and waiting for her.

When she was finished, she turned the light off and crept back into the room, tripping over only once before reaching her bed and crawling under the covers. She would be able to explore more in the morning... and hopefully find a change of clothes.

While lying in the dark, Alex reflected over everything that had happened that day. Somehow she'd been transported to an entirely different world, and she was now stuck there for an unforeseeable amount of time. It was insane, yet she'd clearly seen evidence of it being true. People in *her* world didn't disappear at the drop of a hat—nor did lollipop sticks, for that matter. Of course, it was possible that she really *had* bumped her head after falling into the fountain at the International Exchange Academy, but she doubted that was the case. If so, her hallucination was certainly lengthy—and detailed.

No, it looked as if the impossible truth was her new reality, as illogical as that might be. But on the positive side, she'd somehow managed to gain two friends without even trying. Jordan and Bear had already formed a solid bond with her and she felt comfortable around them, almost like she'd known them for years, not hours. She had no idea how that had happened— she hadn't even had to resort to eating dirt in a playground with them. Though, Bear's gift *had* almost caused her to eat dirt, come to think of it. Hmm.

Another interesting development that she couldn't quite get her head around was the possibility that she had some kind of gift. There had never been anything special about her before—surely she would have noticed if she could shoot laser beams out of her eyes. That kind of thing was hard to miss, right? Perhaps they were wrong about her, perhaps she was just as normal as she'd always considered herself to be. Only time would tell.

Alex had no idea what the next few days, weeks, possibly months had in store for her. All she could do was hope for the best, and to do that, she knew she would have to fully embrace her new world, no matter how surreal it was. Acceptance was the key, even if nothing made sense to her. If need be, when she finally made it back home, she'd make sure to find a seriously good psychiatrist.

On that thought, Alex smiled wryly to herself and snuggled deeper into the bed. It was surprisingly comfortable, and it wasn't long before her overwhelmed and exhausted brain quieted enough for her to drift off to sleep.

Alex woke suddenly, startled by the sound of a door slamming.

Where am I? she wondered, sitting up and blinking sleep from her eyes. Memories from the day before flashed across her mind as she took in her surroundings and, realising that it hadn't all been some kind of head-trauma-induced hallucination, she collapsed back onto her pillow and groaned loudly.

A knock at the door caused her to bolt upright again.

"Alex?" Jordan called. "You up?"

"Rise and shine!" Bear added.

She scrambled out of bed, tripping over the blanket in her haste and falling heavily to the floor.

"What was that noise?" Bear called through the door. "You okay?"

"I'm fine," she answered, rubbing her stinging elbow and pushing herself back up to her feet. When she opened the door, Jordan and Bear took one look at her and burst out laughing.

"What?" she cried indignantly, running her hands through her bed hair.

"Not a morning person, huh?" Jordan observed between laughter.

She crossed her arms. "What gave me away?"

"Just your sunny disposition," Bear said, still chuckling.

"It's early," she told them. "I only just woke up."

"We can see that," Jordan said, his eyes still alight with humour. "Classes start in less than an hour, so you'd better hurry up or else we'll miss out on breakfast."

"How long does it take you to eat?" Alex grumbled, but she headed to her closet. It was full of clothes, all in her size. She wasn't sure whether to be creeped out or grateful. Jarvis had mentioned that everything would be provided for her, and so far he was right.

Alex marvelled briefly at the strange assortment of clothing—was that a cape?—before she grabbed a pair of jeans and a fitted green T-shirt. Jordan saw her selection and shook his head, taking the jeans away and pulling out a pair of stretchy black yoga-style pants instead.

At her questioning look, he said, "We've got PE first up and denim chafes. Trust me, you'll want something you can move comfortably in."

She shrugged and moved into the bathroom for the fastest shower ever. When she came back out, Bear was standing by the window and Jordan was sprawled across her bed, clearly bored.

"Finally," Jordan muttered. "I'm starving."

She didn't bother pointing out how quick she'd been. "Do I need to take anything with me to breakfast? Textbooks?"

"What classes do you have today?" Bear asked.

She looked at her timetable. "Um... after PE it's Archery, Medical Science, and then Combat."

"Med Sci is the only one you need stuff for and you can grab everything after lunch," Bear told her.

Jordan held out a pair of running shoes and some socks. Seeing Alex's amusement, he defended, "I know what girls are like when they have to figure out clothes. I'm about to die of hunger, so just put them on already so we can leave."

She laughed and did as he said before pocketing her timetable and following them out of the room. On the walk through the dorm building, many students called out to Jordan and Bear and sent curious looks in her direction. The boys returned the greetings but didn't stop to talk to anyone, much to Alex's relief.

She still wasn't sure how she was supposed to fit in and not draw attention to herself.

"Hey, guys?" she said as they stepped outside and into the crisp morning air.

"Yeah?" they answered in sync.

"How are we going to do this?"

"Do what?" Bear asked.

"This whole, 'I'm new here but I'm really just from out of town, not from another world'? People are going to notice that I don't know how things work around here."

Jordan didn't look concerned. "Don't worry about it, Alex. I doubt anyone will care if you say or do something strange, but even if they do, you already have an excuse because you're new. Everyone will understand that you need time to settle in."

His words made her feel better.

"And besides, if it all blows up in your face…"

"Yes?" she prompted when Jordan didn't continue. "What then?"

"Well… we'll cross that bridge if we come to it."

Alex sighed. "That's reassuring."

Upon entering the food court she discovered tables and chairs of different sizes, colours and shapes scattered throughout the room. With no logic to the set-up, she felt as if she'd stepped into a grown-up version of a kindergarten play area. She shook her head and followed her friends over to a triangular table, taking a seat between them.

"I'm starving," Jordan said, again. He picked up what looked like a menu and motioned for Alex to do the same. She glanced over the list of options, surprised by the variety. Everything from a continental breakfast to toast and cereal was available for selection.

Alex looked around the food court. People everywhere were eating but she could see no sign of where the food came from. She wondered where she had to go to place her order and turned to ask when her question died in her throat.

Jordan pressed his finger to a circle beside one of the menu options and almost immediately a plate full of scrambled eggs and bacon appeared in front of him, complete with knife and fork. He then pushed on another circle and a stack of pancakes arrived. A third press brought a glass of orange juice. Apparently satisfied, he placed the menu to the side and looked up, taking note of her wide-eyed expression.

"What?" he asked.

Bear chuckled and slapped Jordan on the back.

"You'll have to forgive Jordan. He's a bit clueless sometimes, especially on an empty stomach." Bear indicated to the menu. "It's a TCD—a TechnoConnectivity Device. Just press the circle beside what you want and it'll be transferred here through the connection."

Alex touched the separate circles for blueberry pancakes, maple syrup, and a glass of apple juice. Her selection appeared immediately, steaming hot and smelling delicious.

"This seems kind of… impossible," she said. Nevertheless, she spread the syrup over her pancakes and took a bite. Mmm. Sugary heaven. "How does it work?"

"No idea," Jordan said around a mouthful of food.

"Helpful," she mumbled, taking another bite.

"Bear can explain," Jordan said after swallowing. "He's a complete whiz at Chemistry. Epsilon level—unnaturally smart."

"Why do you always manage to make what should be a compliment sound like an insult?" Bear grumbled.

Jordan shrugged and started on his massive stack of pancakes. "It's a gift."

Alex cleared her throat and looked at Bear, waiting for an explanation.

"Firstly, you have to remember that everything is different here, Alex." Bear spoke quietly, careful not to gain the attention of those seated near them. "Our technology is really advanced. Most of the cool things we can do are because of the different kinds of TechnoConnectivity Devices we have. Some TCDs are readily available to the public, like ComTCDs, which we use for instant holographic communications."

He paused to pull a small black object out of his pocket and placed it into the palm of his hand before touching the screen and saying Jordan's name. A chiming noise sounded, and Jordan pulled out a similar Device, his coloured silver. Alex wasn't sure what he did next, but she gasped when a miniature real-time hologram of Bear rose up out of the screen Jordan held—as did a live version of Jordan appear above Bear's Device.

"Awesome," she breathed, watching the holograms mimic Jordan and Bear's movements perfectly.

"Pretty neat, huh? ComTCDs also make it easy for us to check in with our families—and anyone else—while we're here at Akarnae," said both the actual Bear and the miniature version of him. He ended the connection and both boys pocketed their Devices again. "Other TCDs can do all kinds of things—I could spend hours talking about some of them—but to keep it simple, this one here—" he pointed to the menu on the table "—is linked to an offsite food station where people are employed to prepare meals for residents of Akarnae. When we make our selection, they place the food into an out-tray of sorts, and the networked connection transfers it through to our end."

After seeing the hologram Devices, Alex had kind of expected something more... *detailed*. "That's your explanation?"

"Pretty much," Bear answered. "Add to that some intellectual Techno-babble about particle transference and regeneration, and you've got the answer you're after."

She took a sip from her juice and said, "It sounds an awful lot like magic to me."

"Don't be ridiculous," Jordan said, his amusement clear. "There's no such thing as magic."

Alex looked at him incredulously. "I beg to differ." She pointed to herself and raised her eyebrows. "Exhibit A."

"You're a special case," Jordan replied, and her eyebrows just rose higher. "Not special–special," he amended quickly. "Just, you know, uh, special."

Alex had to fight a grin at the uncomfortable look on his face.

"What Jordan means is that you're an anomaly," Bear interjected. "But you being here is still not magic."

Alex looked between the two of them. "Well, I'm sufficiently confused. But whatever. If you say it's not magic, then I'll believe you. New world, new rules. We'll leave it at that."

Both Jordan and Bear smiled at her.

"You're taking this pretty well," Bear said.

She shrugged. "It's not like I have a choice. I'm stuck here for better or worse until your headmaster gets back from wherever he is. I just have to deal with this as best as I can until then. And once I get home, I'll book myself in for what I anticipate to be some much-needed therapy."

"Don't worry, Alex," Jordan said. "We'll make sure you have an unforgettable time while you're here. That therapy will be well worth it."

Alex had a hard time trusting their matching grins, but before she could warn them that she didn't want any trouble, a loud gonging noise filled the food court.

"Time to see what you're made of, Jennings," Jordan said, pulling her from her seat and dragging her towards the doors. "If you can survive the next two hours, you can make it through anything."

She looked sideways at him as she followed them both outside. "Care to explain?"

"You've heard of PE, right?" Bear answered for him. "Physical Education?" At her nod, he continued, "Well, here we call it Physical Exhaustion, mostly because of the instructor, Finn. You'll understand why soon enough."

Wonderful, she thought.

When the three of them stopped at the outskirts of the large grassy field they had trekked across the day before, Alex noticed a group of students already waiting around. Most of them were in stretching positions. She counted thirteen people; sixteen including her trio. By the looks of the others, Alex guessed they were around her age or older. Two of them might have been slightly younger.

A few of the students glanced up in curiosity as they approached, but before any introductions could be made, a loud voice trumpeted nearby.

"Up! Up! Up! No dawdling! You're on my time now!"

Alex looked around until she found the man who was shouting. He was of medium height with stringy, dark blond hair pulled back into a ponytail. His thin body was wiry, with skin straining over his taut muscles. If there was such a thing as 'too fit', then he was it.

Alex looked into his eyes as he approached and she couldn't help but notice that he looked a little... *wild*.

"You know the drill; get started on your warm-up laps. *Go!*" he yelled, sending the students scattering. Bear and Jordan took off with the others, but Alex hesitated, unsure of what she was supposed to do.

The instructor—presumably Finn—noticed her now that she was alone.

"Who're you?"

She stepped towards him. "Alexandra Jennings, sir," she said. "I'm new here."

"That doesn't explain why you're still standing here," he snapped. "Ten laps. Get to it!"

She gaped at him and turned to look out over the enormous field. It had taken them ages just to walk across it the day before. How was she supposed to fit ten whole laps into the two-hour class, let alone whatever else he had planned?

"What are you waiting for, Jennings? Move!"

There was nothing for it but to follow his instructions. She set out after her classmates—who were now way ahead of her—and focused on putting one foot in front of the other.

To her dismay, she had company.

"You call that running? My grandmother can run faster than that!"

She looked over her shoulder to see Finn jogging along behind her with some kind of metallic stick in his hand.

"Faster!" he barked.

She picked her pace up to a near-sprint, disgruntled by his pushiness.

"I said, *faster!*"

"I'm… going… as… fast… as… I… can!" she panted out.

"Not good enough!"

Alex felt a stinging sensation on her backside. It wasn't until she felt it a second time, more painful than the first, that she realised what it was. Finn had zapped her with the metallic stick.

She stopped dead and turned to face him, breathing heavily.

"What do you think you're doing?" she shrieked.

"Not running, that's for sure," he retorted. *His* breathing was perfectly controlled. "Now pick up the pace; I want to make it back by nightfall."

"But—you just zapped me!" she spluttered. "Like an animal!"

"What? This?" He shocked her with his stick again, this time by whacking her on the hip.

Alex gasped from the stinging pain and rubbed her side. "*Ow!* Stop that!"

"I'll stop when you start running," Finn told her, reaching forward to zap her again, but she took off before he had another chance to make contact.

The man was insane. There was no way he could treat students like this. It wasn't ethical. It wasn't moral. And it certainly wasn't legal. At least, not in her world.

Unfortunately, she could only keep running at a sprint for so long, and soon enough she had to drop her pace or risk breaking an ankle. The moment she slowed, Finn was waiting for her, zapping stick at the ready.

Five

Two hours later, Alex was lying on the field, moaning. Everything ached, including parts of her body that she hadn't previously known *could* ache.

With the psychopathic Finn hot on her heels, Alex had soon caught up to her classmates, but even that hadn't been enough to please the deranged PE teacher who had continued to zap her forward. She had never run as far or as fast before in her life. And now she wondered if she'd ever be able to walk again.

"You survived, at least. That's more than some can say."

Alex didn't have the strength to open her eyes and acknowledge Jordan's comment. She could hear the amusement in his voice—she didn't need to see it as well.

"You should stretch, you know," he told her. "If you don't, you'll regret it later."

She pried her eyes open. Even *that* hurt. "I doubt it'll make much difference now." She knew that he was right though, so she forced herself into a sitting position, grimacing as her muscles pulled. "Ow."

"You're lucky," he said, not even trying to hide his grin. "Finn was easy on us today."

She paused mid-stretch. "You're kidding, right?"

"You should see him on a bad day," Jordan said, and he offered Alex his hand. She couldn't hold back a groan of pain as he pulled her to her feet.

His mouth quivered but he managed to suppress his laughter, sending her a look of sympathy instead. "You've still got a full day ahead of you yet. Including Combat."

She grimaced. "Don't remind me."

"You have Archery next, right?" he asked, turning away and motioning for her to follow.

She pulled her timetable out and scanned it as they walked. "Good memory."

He nodded. "Bear had to take off for Chem, but I still have a few minutes to get to the stables. I'll show you where to go."

They didn't get far before Jordan noticed her discomfort and mercifully slowed his pace.

"It'll get easier," he said. "Just give it a couple of weeks."

Weeks? She wasn't even sure she would last the day!

"Delta PE and Epsilon Combat will be your toughest subjects," Jordan continued, "but with such high potential levels, that's not surprising." He scratched his chin. "You're Epsilon for ES too, aren't you? That'll be demanding as well."

He really wasn't making her feel any better.

"ES?" she repeated.

"Equestrian Skills," he clarified. "Tayla's the instructor. She's great—as long as you respect her horses."

They rounded the crest of a hill that looked out over another large grassy area. It was sectioned off into three segments by thick, bushy hedges that bordered the edge of the forest.

"That's where you need to go." Jordan pointed to the segment closest to the main school campus. "See those people over there? They'll be your classmates."

She spotted the group and nodded.

"Meet you in the food court for lunch?" He waited only long enough for her to agree before he turned and jogged back up the path.

Alex mustered her courage and descended the hill, arriving at the same time as her instructor. For the next two hours she was thrilled to play around with a bow and arrow, even if she missed the target every time she made a shot. In her defence, she was somewhat distracted by the elf-like teacher, Magdelina Llohilas—or Maggie—who looked like she'd stepped straight off the set of a fantasy movie. Seriously.

When Alex wasn't watching the graceful teacher, her attention was caught by one of her other classmates. The girl had thick auburn hair and the most interesting eyes Alex had ever seen; they were as blue as the sky, changing into a vivid green towards the middle. The colour was startling, made even more so by the frequent, menacing glares the girl directed towards Alex.

When lunch time finally arrived, Alex was relieved to leave the class behind. She had no idea what the other girl's problem was, and she was glad to put some distance between them.

"Hey, Alex!" Bear called as she entered the food court and made her way over to him. "How was your class?"

She sent him a wry grin as she took her seat. "I'm still alive."

Bear copied her expression. "I wasn't sure you were going to make it, you know. Not after PE."

She grimaced before laughing with him and admitting, "It was touch and go for a while."

Jordan arrived a moment later and slumped into the chair beside her. "I'm starving."

"You're always starving," Alex observed. "I've known you less than a day, but the common theme is that you're hungry— *all the time*. Maybe you have worms?"

Bear had just taken a sip of water and, hearing her words, he spat his mouthful out, choking on a laugh.

Jordan sent them both an unimpressed look and picked up his menu, grumbling about being 'a growing boy'. When his meal arrived, it was accompanied by a glass of something purple and bubbly.

"What's that?" Alex asked, pointing to the unnatural-looking drink.

"Dillyberry juice," he answered, sliding the glass towards her. "Have a taste."

She sniffed it and took a tentative sip, her eyes lighting up with delight. The juice might have looked funky but it was delicious. It reminded her of wild berries mixed with lemonade and coated with icing sugar. It was very sweet, but it also had a tangy aftertaste. She picked up her menu and ordered a glass for herself.

"Be careful not to overdo it," Jordan warned when she drank half of her juice in one go.

"What do you mean?"

"It's an energy drink," he explained. "Very concentrated."

Alex wasn't too concerned. How bad could it be? The taste was well worth the consequences. She'd probably just have to make a few extra trips to the bathroom, no big deal. It might even be a blessing in disguise if it got her out of some of her dreaded Combat class later that afternoon. Bathroom breaks were a basic human right, after all.

She drained the rest of the glass as she skimmed through her menu, settling on a chicken salad wrap and another glass of dillyberry juice. Both appeared instantly and her used glass disappeared with the arrival of the new.

"Hey," Jordan said, speaking through a mouthful of food. "I forgot to ask you earlier. How was D.C. this morning?"

Alex shook her head. "I woke up to a slamming door, no roommate in sight."

"That explains it, then," Jordan said, seeming satisfied. He sipped his juice before taking another bite of food.

"Explains what?"

"Why you haven't asked Jarvis for a new room yet," Bear answered for him with a knowing grin.

Alex looked between the two of them. "Is she really that bad?"

Both boys just smirked and continued eating.

Alex picked up her purple juice, sipping thoughtfully. It didn't take her long to finish the second glass, but she was still surprisingly thirsty, so she ordered another. All that running in PE must have dehydrated her.

A few minutes—and another emptied glass—later, Jordan stopped her from ordering more of the delicious juice. Only then did she realise just how odd she felt. Kind of light-headed and, well... *buzzy*. The whole room was jumping up and down. Was there an earthquake? Just as she was about to ask what was going on, Jordan pressed his hand down on her shoulder. All motion ceased and she realised that she must have been physically bouncing in her seat.

Bear pointed to her empty glass. "How many of those have you had?"

"I dunno," she said giddily, her voice slurring the words. "But they taste *really* good!"

The boys looked at each other with unreadable expressions. She tried to remember how many glasses had arrived and disappeared over the course of the lunch break and she felt tremendously pleased with herself when she was able to recall the number.

"THREE!" she yelled triumphantly. "I'VE HAD THREE!"

Jordan and Bear jumped at her exclamation and heads turned in their direction from all corners of the court.

"Oops. Sorry," Alex apologised, whispering this time. Then she giggled.

Wait, *giggled*?

She did it again.

Uh-oh.

She looked at Jordan, horrified. "What's wrong with me?"

"Come on," he ordered, rising from his seat. "We'd better get you over to the Medical Ward."

Alex tried to stand but found her legs were made of jelly. She crashed noisily down to the floor, gathering even more attention than before.

"My legs are angry at me. Too many runnings." She giggled again as her vision flickered in and out of focus. "That's not right. Too much running. Better."

She nodded to herself and looked up at Jordan and Bear who were standing over her. "You're really tall," she observed, squinting at them. She cupped her mouth with both hands and yelled, "Helllllllooo up there!"

The boys shared another glance before reaching down to help her to her feet.

"All right, up you get," Jordan said, steadying her as she swayed on her feet. "Easy there."

"Wheeeeee!" she squealed, watching the room spin around her. "That was fun! Can we do it again?"

Jordan's mouth twitched and Bear couldn't hold back a snort of laughter as he reached out to grab her free arm. Together they hauled her out of the food court, carrying most of her weight between them.

Once they were outside, she glanced from one boy to the other before tucking her legs up underneath her. "Look at me! I'm *flying!*"

Jordan and Bear grunted as they were forced to shoulder the additional weight of her whole body.

"There must be an easier way to do this," Bear mumbled as Alex bounced around in their arms, throwing her weight up and down and laughing hysterically. What a great game!

"There is," Jordan replied, and in a single motion he swept Alex up into his arms, bridal-style.

"Much better," Bear said, untangling her arm from around his neck.

"For you, maybe," Jordan muttered.

Alex looked up at her new mode of transport in wonder. "You're *really* strong!"

Jordan raised an eyebrow. "Don't get used to it."

"I wish I could do that!" she squealed, pointing to his face.

"Do what?" he asked.

"The one-eyebrow thing! I can never do it right! It makes me look like a demented monkey."

Bear laughed and turned to Jordan. "She's going to be *so* mad at you when she comes down from this."

"How is this *my* fault?" Jordan demanded.

"You should have told her about the juice," Bear answered.

"I really like that juice," Alex said with a longing sigh. "It's yummy. Tastes like happiness in a cup."

"I *did* tell her!" Jordan said to Bear. "I told her to take it easy, she just didn't listen."

"I did too listen. I'm a good listener. I'm the best listener who'll ever listen," Alex said, trying to catch a butterfly fluttering across their path. Such pretty colours!

"All I'm saying is, you probably should have told her *why* she shouldn't drink so much," Bear said. "But then again…"

They both looked down at Alex who, unsuccessful in her butterfly-catching attempt and bored of their conversation, was wiggling her eyebrows up and down over and over again, trying to raise one without the other. Why was it so difficult?

"… there's nothing like first-hand experience," Bear finished.

Six

Sometime later, Alex opened her eyes to a bright blue-coloured ceiling. She was lying on a bed under a crisp white sheet in the middle of a large, well-lit room.

"Hello?" she called out, sitting up.

"Ahh. You're awake. Excellent."

A man was walking towards her, clipboard in hand. He looked to be in his mid-forties, and he had a kind face with intelligent green eyes. There was a stethoscope draped around his neck, and his white lab coat had a pocket embroidered with the name *Dr. Fletcher Montgomery*.

"How are you feeling, Alex?" he asked, picking up her wrist to check her pulse.

"Okay," she replied uncertainly. Her memories were hazy; she had no idea where she was, or how she'd arrived in the blue-ceilinged room. It *looked* like she was in some kind of hospital— which only served to heighten her anxiety, since she'd always had an irrational fear of doctors.

He nodded and pulled out a silver instrument. "Follow the light, please."

She blinked when he aimed the beam at her eyes and did as he asked.

"Your vitals are looking much better. I think you'll be fine to go now." He scribbled something onto the clipboard and started to walk away.

"Uh—Doctor Montgomery?" she called out, hoping the name was right.

He paused and turned back to her, his expression amused. "So formal, Alex? I'm hurt."

She looked at him strangely. What was he talking about?

"After all," he continued, "it was only an hour ago that you told me I was the nicest doctor you'd ever met and if I didn't agree to marry you, then you had no reason to continue living."

Um... What?

He grinned at her. "I'm flattered. Truly. But it would be highly unprofessional of me to accept your proposal. I hope you don't take it personally? I know how difficult it must be, especially considering your thoughtful—and creative—love song."

Alex felt her cheeks burn. She'd *sung* to him? How humiliating.

The doctor chuckled and sat down at the end of the bed. "If you think what you said to me was bad, just wait until you catch up with your friends again."

Alex groaned, not sure she even wanted to know.

"What happened to me?" she asked. The last thing she could remember was eating lunch in the food court.

"Nothing too serious," he answered. "Just a slight overdose of dillyberry juice. According to your friends, you had a few too many glasses, not knowing about the side-effects."

"Side-effects?"

"Similar to those of someone under the influence of alcohol or narcotics," he explained. "You were essentially on a sugar-high. Dillyberries contain large doses of glucosamine, with a glass of juice holding roughly the equivalent of a glass of sugar."

Alex felt like slapping herself. Why hadn't she listened to Jordan's warning? "How did I end up in here?"

"You don't remember?"

"I can't remember *anything!*"

"No need to shout," he said with a calming gesture. "I'm not deaf."

"Sorry, sir," she mumbled.

"No matter," he said, waving her apology aside. "And none of that 'sir' business. Call me Fletcher."

She nodded and waited for him to continue.

"Memory loss is common after a dillyberry overdose," Fletcher told her. "I've treated you with some medication to dissolve the excess sugar in your bloodstream, and your nap should've taken care of the rest. As to how you ended up here, you'll have to ask your friends."

Yeah, there was no way she was going to do that. She would be keeping what little self-respect she had left by repressing the entire episode.

"You should be fine to head off to class now," Fletcher added. "We're halfway through third period. Plenty of time for you to catch up."

"Thanks so much for your help, Fletcher," she said, jumping off the bed. "And sorry for the, um, marriage proposal. I don't suppose we can forget that happened?"

"Consider it eliminated from my memory, Alex," he said with a warm smile as he escorted her out of the Ward. "I'm sure we'll see each other again soon." At her confused expression, he sent her a wink and explained, "Your friends mentioned that you're in Epsilon Combat."

Alex groaned. Just how bad was that class going to be?

She decided not to respond to his statement and instead pulled out her timetable to find that she was meant to be in Medical Science, her only age-based class that day. "Fletcher, any chance you can tell me how to find Laboratory Three?"

Following his directions, Alex headed up two flights of stairs and down a long corridor before she reached the solid door labelled 'Lab. 3'. She hesitated outside, wondering whether she should knock before entering. But the decision was taken out of her hands when the door sprang open.

"Are you going to stand there all day, Miss Jennings?"

Startled, Alex quickly entered the classroom. She was surprised to discover that—for some inexplicable reason—the door was transparent from the inside, like a one-way window.

"Are you done with interrupting my class?"

Alex turned away from the see-through door and searched for the owner of the sharp voice. It took her a moment to move her gaze past the curious glances from her classmates—and the amused looks from Jordan and Bear—but when she found the short woman close to the front of the room, Alex had to clamp down on a burst of laughter. It looked like a washing machine had thrown up a rainbow and plastered it all over the woman's lab coat.

Alex blinked a few times in the hope that it would help fade the sight—which it didn't—and then she hesitantly stepped forward. "I'm—"

"I'm well aware of who you are," the woman interrupted, levelling her strict gaze on Alex. "I'm Professor Luranda, head of Medical Science, and tardiness is unacceptable in my class."

"I didn't—"

"Fortunately for you, your friends explained your absence," the professor interrupted again. "Since it's your first day, I'll be lenient. In the future, arrive on time or face the consequences."

That was hardly fair. It wasn't as if Alex had deliberately planned to end up in the Medical Ward. But she would have to let her indignation go, since the professor appeared to be waiting for a response. "Uh, sure thing, ma'am."

"*Professor.*"

Alex jerked. "Pardon me?"

"The correct response is, 'Sure thing, *Professor*'. Lack of respect is something else I will not tolerate in my class, Miss Jennings."

Alex nodded, not wanting to further aggravate the short, crazy-coated woman.

"Well, what are you waiting for?" Professor Luranda said. "Go and find a seat so I can continue my lesson."

Unfortunately, the only spare seat was next to the red-headed glaring girl from Alex's Archery class.

Alex waited until the professor disappeared into the storeroom before she turned to quietly introduce herself. Sure, the entire class already knew who she was thanks to her late entrance, but she hoped striking up a polite conversation with her moody desk partner would ease some of the weird tension between them. "Hey, I'm—"

"I don't care," the girl interrupted, not even looking up from her textbook.

Alex's eyes widened. Talk about rude. But even so, she tried again, "I'm—"

"I still don't care."

"But, I—"

"Is there something wrong with you?" The girl marked her page, turning to Alex with narrowed eyes. "Let me make myself clear: I. Don't. Care. Who. You. Are."

Alex stared at the other girl in shock and then turned her attention to the front of the class when Professor Luranda stepped back into view carrying a box of glass containers.

"Now, class," the professor said, continuing on with the lecture that Alex had missed, "while the toxicity of Faenda venom can cause damage to internal organs over extended periods of time, in a life or death situation its paralytic effects can provide an adequate—if unorthodox—stabilisation treatment."

Professor Luranda proceeded to walk around the room, placing a container on every table. Each jar held a black flying insect with glowing green wings and a painful-looking stinger.

"In your pairs, I want one of you to reach into the jar and provoke the creature to sting you," the professor instructed. "The paralysis will only last for a few minutes, and in that time the non-paralysed student will ensure their partner does not fall and hurt themselves while under the effects of the venom. You will then switch roles. Begin as soon as you are ready."

Alex looked up to find her partner smirking at her.

"After you," the other girl challenged.

Alex grit her teeth and reached for the jar. Once her hand was inside, it didn't take long for the little black and green Faenda to feel threatened and sink its stinger into her flesh. And, wow, it hurt a lot more than she'd expected. Or maybe her added pain was a result of her head thumping onto the lab bench as the paralysis took effect. So much for her partner keeping her from harm.

It took maybe three minutes for Alex's limbs to start tingling, indicating that she was coming out of her immobility. In that time it was impossible for her not to wonder about the ethics of her new school. From the relentless PE teacher with his Taser-stick, to being purposefully stung by a venomous insect, Alex couldn't figure out how any of it was acceptable. Once again she had to remind herself that she was in a new world and that she just had to go with it.

When she was finally able to lift herself up from the bench, Alex shook her tingling hands and looked over at her partner. "Your turn."

The other girl buffed her fingernails on her shirt and said, "Can't. I'm allergic."

Yeah, right, Alex scoffed internally. She opened her mouth to object, but someone else cut in first.

"What's going on over here?" the professor asked, seeing that neither Alex nor her partner were currently under the effects of the venom.

"Jennings was just about to have her turn," the other girl said, shaking her hands out as if she was the one recovering from the paralysis.

"What?" Alex blurted. "But, I—"

"You've already disrupted my class once, Miss Jennings," Professor Luranda said, turning away. "Hurry up and complete your task, or else you'll find yourself with a detention."

Alex gaped at the professor's back before slicing her enraged eyes to her partner.

"Maybe you should start with your head already on the bench this time," the other girl suggested, trying unsuccessfully to keep a straight face. "That must have hurt."

"What's your problem?" Alex demanded.

Seeing the professor's eyes on her from the front of the classroom, Alex angrily shoved her hand into the jar once again. As she felt the sting and the accompanying paralysis overcome her for the second time, all she heard was her partner's whispered, "You are, Roomie," before she thumped onto the desk again.

Did she say 'Roomie'? Alex wondered with a sickening feeling, while she waited for her newest bout of paralysis to wear off. *That's just my luck.*

She didn't get the chance to talk to the girl further because Luranda jumped straight back into her lecture, demanding the attention of the entire class.

When the gong finally rang, the other girl—who Alex now presumed was D.C.—took off without a word, and Jordan and Bear bounded over.

"How're you feeling?" Bear asked.

Alex grimaced. "Do you mean after the dillyberry disaster, or because of the two paralysis-induced face-plants into my desk care of my oh-so-loving roommate?"

Bear bit his lip to keep from smiling but Jordan didn't bother trying to hide his amusement. "Um, both?"

"Well, it's so nice of you to ask," Alex said, leading the way out of the room, "but I really don't want to talk about it."

"Fair enough," Jordan agreed for them both, still grinning as he stepped up beside her. "You ready for Combat?"

"Nope," Alex answered. "But I don't think I have a choice, so lead the way."

A few minutes later, Alex found herself staring in awe at the intimidating structure in front of her. The aptly named Arena was a mammoth colosseum-like construction that looked as if it was straight out of the gladiator era.

Seriously, what was with this school?

Jordan and Bear had to physically pull her forward as they rounded the hill leading to the magnificent site. Alex couldn't deny that the view was spectacular, but she wasn't able to appreciate it fully since she was too distracted by her fear of what went on inside those sandstone walls.

"You'll be okay," Bear said, seeing the queasy look on her face. "Karter might be a piece of work, but he knows what he's doing. He won't let you die, not on your first day."

Jordan nodded his agreement. For some reason they both seemed to think those were reassuring words.

"Thanks, guys," she said, to keep them from saying anything else 'encouraging'. "I'll—uh—hopefully see you later."

She tried to muster up a smile, but it probably looked more like a grimace.

Jordan clapped her on the shoulder and Bear gave her the thumbs-up, then they both took off for their Delta Archery class.

Alex forced herself to move forward and she soon discovered that the inside of the Arena was almost as magnificent as the outside. There was no roof, instead the thick walls stretched straight up to the sky. Dotted around the sandstone perimeter were archways that led into large, sheltered rooms. For some reason, Alex doubted they were used for wet-weather classes.

"You lost, Jennings?"

Karter was scowling at her from halfway across the Arena. Once again he was dressed in his weird leather ensemble, the sword still belted to his waist.

Alex counted five other students stretching on the ground near him, all of them male. She held her head high as she walked over to the small group, trying to ignore the feeling of her feet sinking into the dark, sand-like powder that covered the entire floor of the Arena.

"No, sir," she said as she approached. "I'm in this class."

Karter looked at her incredulously before he threw his head back and burst out laughing. A few of the others in the class also snickered at her words. She frowned and dug her timetable out of her pocket, shoving it under Karter's nose. His eyes widened as he read the slip of paper and his laughter ceased.

"This is a joke, right? There's no way *you*"—he made it sound like there was something wrong with her—"could be in this class."

Alex just shrugged. She wasn't about to argue with him since she felt the same way. Stupid lollipop.

"What an... *interesting* turn of events," Karter hissed. His formidable arm muscles were flexed in tension and the veins in his neck looked like they were about to pop right out of his skin.

Alex swallowed nervously but held her ground.

"All right, then," he said, eyeing her thoughtfully. There was a dangerous glint in his icy gaze. "Let's see how this plays out."

Seven

Alex woke a few hours later to the sound of drums banging inside her head. She winced as she reached back and felt the egg-shaped bump just behind her ear.

"Twice in one day," came a familiar voice. "Lucky me."

"Fletcher?" she asked, confused. She tried to sit up but the room swam around her and she was forced to lie back down again. "Eugh," she groaned.

"Easy there, Alex. You've got quite the concussion." Fletcher walked into view, clipboard in hand once more. He pulled out his flashlight and aimed it into her eyes, just like he had earlier in the day. She ducked away from the beam, squinting from the pain caused by the bright light.

"Sorry about that." He scribbled onto his clipboard. "Just had to check."

She started to nod but stopped when it felt like a knife was stabbing into her brain.

"What happened?" she asked, trying to ignore the throbbing.

"Why don't you tell me what you remember?"

Alex thought back over the afternoon's events. After Karter had agreed to let her stay in the class, he'd ordered her to stretch before pairing everyone up. She'd been partnered with Declan Stirling, a hulk of a boy easily twice her size.

Karter had instructed them to spar with each other,

practising 'easy' hand-to-hand combat and progressing to harder levels of difficulty.

Alex hadn't known where to begin. She'd tried to tell Karter that she had no fighting experience, but he'd just shrugged and walked away, claiming that it wasn't his problem.

She'd looked at her massive partner, certain he wouldn't fight a defenceless girl. Her confidence had vanished the moment his massive arm had come flying towards her. She'd practically watched her life flash before her eyes.

Surprisingly enough, Alex had managed to duck the first blow, and the second as well. Her reflexes had mapped their own instinctive, adrenaline-fueled reactions, and without even knowing how, she'd ended up kicking her leg out towards his torso.

The massive boy had grunted in surprise when her foot connected with his abdomen, but that hadn't stopped him from latching onto her ankle and twisting her leg away from him. Her whole body had spun through the air, leaving her to slam head-first onto the ground.

She couldn't remember anything after that, so she figured she must have been knocked unconscious.

Fletcher listened and took notes as she described the details to him.

"That sounds about right," he agreed. "At least there's no memory loss this visit."

Alex bit back a sarcastic retort and watched as the doctor walked over to a medical supply cabinet and pulled out a glass vial. When he handed it to her, she eyed the bright green liquid warily.

"It'll help with the pain," he told her.

Trusting him, Alex downed it in one go. She was pleasantly surprised by the minty taste, and even more delighted when the throbbing drums disappeared almost immediately, along with her splitting headache.

"Wow," she marvelled, sniffing the glass container. "What was that?"

"Standard issue pain reliever," Fletcher answered. "You'll learn how to make a batch in your Medical Science class so you can look forward to hearing about it from Professor Luranda. I'm sure you don't want the lecture twice." He winked at her and she smiled back in gratitude.

"So," she started, looking around the now familiar room, "when can I get out of here?"

Fletcher chuckled. "Not a fan of hospitals?"

She smiled at him to show that she didn't have anything against him specifically.

"She lives!"

Alex turned at the interruption and found Jordan and Bear standing in the doorway.

"Way to go, Alex! Your first day here and you've already been to the Med Ward twice!" Bear called out. "That's got to be some kind of record. Right, Fletch?"

"One day the two of you will learn to appreciate the sanctity of this Ward and not disrupt my patients." Fletcher spoke sternly to the boys, but Alex could see a hint of a smile behind his strict expression.

"One day," Jordan mused, "we just might." He grinned at Alex. "But not today."

Fletcher mock-sighed and motioned for them to enter the room.

"As I was saying before I was rudely interrupted," Fletcher threw a warning glance at the two boys who perched themselves haphazardly on the end of Alex's bed, "I suppose it will be all right if you leave, so long as you wait a few hours before sleeping."

She nodded and was pleased when she felt no stabbing pain this time.

"Jordan, Bear, you're responsible for making sure she remains awake. Think of it as punishment for disturbing my peace and quiet."

Bear snorted. "This place is like a morgue, Fletch. The disruption can only be good for you."

Alex crossed her arms, waiting for someone to come to her defence and say that spending time with her wasn't a form of punishment.

Jordan must have caught her expression since he hastily said, "But, err, if we *had* wrongly disturbed your peace and quiet, you should know that asking us to look after Alex isn't a punishment."

Bear looked at his friend in confusion before finally catching on. It was probably the elbow to the ribs that did it. "Right," he agreed, wincing a little as he rubbed his side. "It's like giving a kid candy instead of broccoli after he breaks your favourite porcelain vase."

Alex, Fletcher and Jordan all looked at him with varying expressions of bemusement.

"What I mean is," Bear continued, trying to explain himself, "you're not punishing us, but rewarding us. We'd be hanging out with Alex anyway."

"You don't say?" Fletcher said, his tone dry.

Both boys nodded and Alex concealed a smirk, knowing the doctor was barely refraining from rolling his eyes.

"Then on that note, it's time for you three to leave," Fletcher said, shooing them off the bed and towards the door. "Try to wait a few days before visiting me again, Alex."

"I'll see what I can do," Alex promised with a wave as she followed her friends outside.

After they left the Med Ward and had a quick dinner, Jordan and Bear decided to give Alex a more complete tour of the academy to show her where all her other classes were held. It didn't take them long, and the three of them soon headed back to the dorm building.

"There's one more place we need to show you," Jordan said as he and Bear guided her down the staircase and into the basement.

"Welcome to the Rec Room," Bear announced, leading her through a doorway and into the room beyond.

Alex glanced around with wide eyes. "What *is* this place?"

"It's our Recreational Room," Jordan answered. "It's where we come if we want to just chill out for a while, or if we don't want to study in our rooms. As you can see, it's pretty well equipped."

Alex *could* see that. The Rec Room had everything from a roaring fireplace surrounded by comfortable couches, to study tables with supportive-looking chairs. There was even a mini dining area up the back of the room.

Bear saw where she was looking. "You can order food just like in the food court, but the menus are limited to snack food."

Alex nodded as she took in the rest of the room. She was pleasantly surprised to note the relaxed atmosphere as students chatted easily with one another. Some looked like they were working on their homework together, some were snacking on a late-night supper, and some were even roasting skewered marshmallows in the fire.

"Come on," Jordan said, leading the way over to a doorway in the far wall.

The room she followed him into was an entertainment area. Lounges, cushions, beanbags and every other comfortable object imaginable filled the space. There was also a huge screen covering the wall, offering their very own mini cinema.

Jordan walked over to a touch-screen panel and scrolled through what looked like a menu before pressing an option on the list with a satisfied smile. Almost immediately the screen came to life.

"Here," he said, handing her a silver ring.

She looked at him quizzically and slid it onto her finger. The moment she did, her world turned upside-down and then, amazingly, she was *inside* the movie that was playing on the screen.

"No way!" she cried, glancing around in awe.

"Virtual reality at its finest," Jordan said as he stepped up next to her.

Bear appeared a moment later and the three of them stood side by side amongst the ruins of an abandoned castle. It was half-overgrown by the encroaching forest, with the stone foundation crumbling in places all around them.

"This is amazing!" Alex exclaimed, trying to take in everything at once. "What can we do in here?"

As she spoke, a scream sounded from somewhere to her left and a woman dressed in a bloodied wedding gown ran in from the woods, seeking refuge in the ruins.

A wolf the size of a small horse hurtled out of the trees, chasing after the bride as she disappeared further into the crumbling castle. The creature jerked to a halt only a few steps away from Alex, and it was so real, so lifelike and so *close* that she actually gasped and flinched away from it.

"Jordan, buddy, what setting do you have it on?" Bear asked, his voice much quieter than normal.

"I didn't check," Jordan said. "Why?"

For some reason the wolf seemed to have lost interest in chasing the woman. Instead, it remained where it was, staring intently at Alex and her friends while growling low in its throat.

"Didn't you hear about the upgrades?" Bear whispered, backing up a step and pulling Alex and Jordan with him.

"Is something wrong?" Alex asked, watching a glob of bloodied saliva drip from the wolf's snarling mouth.

Talk about high definition. The quality of the scene was incredible.

"We need to get out of here," Bear said urgently.

The wolf snarled in their direction and dropped back on its haunches as if preparing to launch through the air. If Alex hadn't known any better, she would have thought it was about to try and attack them. But they weren't really there; it was called *virtual* reality for a reason.

"Take your rings off!" Bear yelled. "*Now!*"

Hearing the panic in his voice, Alex didn't hesitate to follow his order. Just as the landscape faded and the world turned upside-down again, she saw the wolf spring directly towards the three of them, bloodied saliva flying from its open mouth.

Back in the Rec Room once more, she stared at the screen on the wall. The enraged wolf was pacing around the castle ruins in agitation. She would have been more curious about what was going on in the 'movie' if she hadn't been so freaked out by the wet, bloodied drool sliding down her arm.

"What just happened?" she whispered, staring at the drool and turning to take in her friends' white faces.

Jordan clearly had no idea and he looked at Bear in question.

"You *really* shouldn't have skipped Marselle's meeting the other day," Bear said wearily to Jordan, as if that explained everything.

Jordan's face cleared with understanding, but Alex was still in the dark.

"Excuse me, but can someone explain why I have wolf slobber on my arm?" she demanded, somewhat hysterically, as she wiped the offensive goo off using the hem of her shirt. "Were we nearly just eaten?"

"We're okay, Alex," Bear said soothingly. "It was a close call, but we're okay."

"Close call?" she repeated, incredulous. "I almost became a doggy treat!"

"You wouldn't have been hurt," Bear said. "There's a security measure that pulls you out of the virtual world if you so much as get a paper cut while you're in the system."

She calmed slightly. "So, we wouldn't have been eaten?"

"No, definitely not."

"I don't understand," Jordan said, frowning at the wolf still pacing across the screen. "It used to be just plain virtual reality. We couldn't interact with it or anything."

"Upgrades," Bear said simply. "Marselle told us that they're still working out the glitches." He paused for a moment and then added, "Apparently censoring appropriate viewing material is still on the to-do list."

"You think?" Alex muttered.

"I'm sorry," Jordan said sheepishly. "I had no idea about the upgrades."

He sounded truly remorseful, so Alex decided to let him off the hook.

"Well, we definitely don't have anything like that where I'm from," she said with a shake of her head. "Let's chalk this up to one of those 'live and learn' experiences and never mention it again. Agreed?"

"Sounds like a plan." Jordan seemed grateful that she wasn't about to rail at him.

"Do you want to try that again?" Bear asked. Seeing Alex's expression, he quickly added, "On a lower setting—virtual reality without interaction?"

Jordan looked to Alex for her answer and she hesitantly nodded. It really had been incredible before they'd realised something was wrong.

"Pick a different movie, though," Alex pleaded. "No wolves."

"You got it," Bear agreed.

They spent the next two hours wrapped up in an epic science fiction adventure, travelling across the universe in spaceships and discovering life on other planets. All in all, Alex thought it was the perfect ending to such a memorable first day in her new world. But as she headed to bed that night—and was completely ignored by her moody roommate—she wondered how long she would have to wait for the headmaster's return. Medora wasn't her world. She couldn't get attached. If she did, she would only be dooming herself for heartache.

Eight

The rest of Alex's week continued in much the same way as her first day. Every morning she awoke to the sound of her door slamming as D.C. left the room, and every evening she collapsed into bed, exhausted. Her classes were insane, with the taser-wielding Finn being the least of her worries.

Well, almost.

Much to her relief, Combat didn't cause her any more problems because when she walked into her second class, Karter immediately benched her, ordering her to sit down and not touch anything. Really, what was she—five? But when she watched her classmates proceed to attack each other with wooden staves and, later, actual swords, she couldn't help but be relieved by her enforced time-out.

As for her other classes, she actually had to participate in them. To say they were 'strange' didn't even begin to come close to the truth.

Chemistry was taught by a complete wacko of a professor, Fitzwilliam Grey, who only answered to 'Fitzy'. He fit the stereotypical description of 'crazy scientist' so well that Alex wondered if he had inspired the cliché. Almost laughably, he greatly enjoyed blowing things up—the more explosive, the better. The subject itself was also nothing at all like what she expected. Apparently 'Chemistry' was an ambiguous term in Medora, where they dealt with the formulaic creation of what

Alex still considered to be magic, despite her friends' arguments to the contrary. Nothing they did in their class should have been possible, and yet, to Alex's unending confusion, it was.

The Core Skills teacher, Professor Astrid Marmaduke, was the polar opposite of Fitzy. She was also extremely frustrated by Alex's inability to exhibit any kind of gifting. Since Core Skills focused on controlling one's gift, Alex found herself in a predicament. But her anxiety turned to awe when Marmaduke demonstrated her own gift—a combination of low-level mind arts, including moving objects telekinetically and reading surface thoughts from another person's mind. It was kind of freaky, but also pretty awesome. Alex wondered again what her own gift might be—if she did actually *have* one. Until it presented itself, Core Skills was going to be a waste of her time.

Alex's History class turned out to be much more interesting than expected. The enigmatic teacher, Doc, kept his students entertained with his worldly tales of adventure. He was easily the smartest man Alex had ever met, as evidenced when he randomly broke into other languages. Apparently he was fluent in twenty-seven different dialects—twenty-six of which Alex had never heard of before.

The Equestrian Skills instructor, Tayla, was just as great as Jordan had promised. But despite her friendliness, Tayla still told Alex that she would have to prove herself before joining the Epsilon class proper—a class that, to Alex's annoyance, included her still-incensed-for-no-apparent-reason roommate. Fabulous.

As for Alex's Species Distinction class, the teacher had contracted some kind of rare influenza from one of the creatures in his care, which left him quarantined and his students with a free period. Alex wasn't one to complain—she had a *lot* of homework and was grateful for the added free time—but she was still curious about the subject and looked forward to seeing what it was all about once the teacher was better.

Easily the strangest class she had was Studies of Society and Culture—or SOSAC—but not because of the subject itself. Professor Caspar Lennox was the teacher and one glance had left Alex wondering if he was a vampire. His skin was a mottled grey colour, and his long hair and eyes were the blackest black she had ever seen. Even stranger were his feet—or rather, where his feet should have been. It seemed as if he walked on a swirling mass of black cloud. Every step the man—*vampire!*—took wrapped his feet in the dense black substance. It was downright creepy. Add to that his long, hooded cape, made out of some kind of shimmering black material, and he was officially on Alex's list of people who she never wanted to meet down a dark alleyway at night.

Fortunately, Jordan was seated next to Alex in her first SOSAC class and he took pity on her wide-eyed stare and whispered, "He's a Shadow Walker."

Was that a code word for vampire? Probably not. Akarnae had some admittedly questionable teaching staff, but she doubted that a lean, mean, blood-drinking machine would be allowed to educate students on a daily basis.

Despite Caspar Lennox's disturbing appearance, his voice was melodious and soothing as he delivered his lecture about the dignitaries of Tryllin—Medora's capital city—and the governing monarchy. Alex learned that King Aurileous Cavelle was the current ruler, and he lived in Tryllin with his wife, Osmada Cavelle, and their only child. Apparently the entire royal family was beloved by the people—or so claimed Caspar Lennox.

When the SOSAC teacher moved on from the royal discussion, Alex quickly lost concentration. How was she ever supposed to remember that Samson Graver, the one-eyed juggler from Dupressa, was related to Preston Ballantyne, the current High Court judge of a place called Mardenia? And really, who cared?

All in all, the classes at Akarnae were different to anything Alex could have imagined. Without Jordan and Bear, she never would have survived her first day, let alone her entire first week. And her continued existence truly *was* a miracle, since half of her teachers were slave-driving psychopaths, her subjects ranged from unethical to downright deadly, and her roommate, D.C., made her feel like a walking disease.

Jordan and Bear were Alex's anchors; if not for them, she would have left the academy and searched for the headmaster on her own despite having no idea where he was. But the three of them had become rock-solid friends and Alex was willing to keep on waiting for Marselle's return as long as they continued to cheer her up at the end of each increasingly difficult day. She'd met a few of her other classmates, but everyone was so focused that they barely paid her any attention. Jordan and Bear, though... well, they made the effort. And she was beyond grateful.

Another thing she was grateful for was the meeting she'd had with Jarvis mid-way through the week. The administrator had called her to his office and explained more about Medora, telling her that the world itself was similar to Earth—Freya— in that it had started out as one massive supercontinent, but instead of the land breaking apart into smaller continents, natural disasters had ripped Medora's coastlines to shreds and submerged whole chunks of land under the ocean. In the end, what was left was one single land mass which was given the same name as the world—Medora. It was separated in the middle by the Durungan Ranges, a collection of mountains that spread from the eastern shore right across to the western sea cliffs. For the sake of simplicity, anything located north of the mountains was called the Northland, and anything located to the south was the Southland.

The names were completely lacking in creativity, but whatever.

She'd also learned that Akarnae was located in the south of the Northland, right in the heart of Medora. And, even better, the seasons were exactly like what she was used to back on Freya—with the Northland being like the Northern Hemisphere of Earth, and the Southland being like the Southern Hemisphere. Even the dates matched up, including the school year which was from August to June, when the academy broke up for summer holidays. So weird. But it simplified everything for her, at least. Which meant that, once more, she decided just to accept the strangeness.

Sometimes that was easier said than done, and by the end of the week when Friday evening finally rolled around, Alex was exhausted. Classes had finished for the day and she, Jordan and Bear were sitting in the Rec Room with Connor and Mel, two of their age-based classmates who happened to be cousins. The five of them were finishing up with their Med Sci homework, and Alex was struggling to keep her eyes open.

"What do you think, Alex?"

She looked up from her work, trying to clear the cobwebs from her mind. "Huh?"

Her friends laughed at her deer-in-the-headlights confusion, until Mel took sympathy on her and said, "You look wrecked. Maybe you should call it a night?"

Alex nodded in agreement. "Yeah, I think I might. This week has been insane. I'll see you all later."

After a round of goodnights, Alex retreated upstairs to her dorm. D.C. was already in bed reading a book and her startlingly blue-green eyes narrowed in displeasure when Alex stepped into their shared space.

"You can glare at me all you want, but it's not going to change the fact that this is my room too," Alex said, too tired to care if she sounded rude.

"Maybe I'm hoping that one of these days you'll get the hint that you're not welcome," D.C. said, her gaze moving back to her book.

Alex snorted. "Trust me, I've been reading you loud and clear all week. But this is me not caring."

With that, Alex settled into bed for the night. The week's events caught up to her the moment her head hit the pillow and she was sound asleep before her roommate could even voice a snarky reply.

Nine

Crunch, crunch, crunch.

A strange noise woke Alex the next morning. It was so out of place in her otherwise quiet room that she snapped her eyes open and bolted upright in a panic. Her quick movement almost caused her to smack straight into the smirking face of Jordan, who was sitting on the edge of her bed, eating from a bowl of cereal.

"Wakey wakey, Sunshine."

Alex groaned and collapsed back onto her bed, shoving her pillow over her head. "Wha-re-oo-ing-ma-oom?" she asked, her words muffled by the material.

Jordan prised the pillow out of her sleep-weakened fingers and pulled it away from her face.

"Pillow talk, huh? Didn't know you felt that way about me," he said, winking at her.

She glared back at him. He was way too chirpy in the morning.

"I said," she repeated, ignoring his attempt to embarrass her, "what are you doing in my room?"

He shrugged and took another mouthful of cereal. *Crunch, crunch, crunch.* "I was bored."

Alex looked at the clock beside her bed and groaned again. "Can't you be bored somewhere else? It's Saturday!"

"I know, but you missed breakfast," he told her, like it really mattered. "Caring friend that I am, I brought you some."

Jordan handed her the half-eaten bowl of cereal like it was a prized treasure. She scrunched her nose up at it and shook her head, so he moved the spoon to his mouth once more.

"Your loss," he said.

Alex sat up and leaned against the headboard. "How did you get in here? I thought you said only D.C. or I could open our door?"

"Yep," he said, scooping up more cereal. "But you forget what my gift is."

Jordan wiggled his eyebrows and she remembered that he could move through solid objects while invisible.

"How long have you been sitting here?" she asked, slightly creeped out by the idea that he'd been watching her sleep.

"Not long," he said. Something about the twinkling of his eyes warned her that she shouldn't have asked. "But long enough to know that you talk in your sleep."

"I do not!" she spluttered, her face growing warm.

"Yeah, you do." He grinned knowingly and scraped the last of the cereal from the bowl.

Alex desperately wanted to ask what he'd heard, but most of her dignity had already flown out the window. She was determined to keep the little that was left, so she pushed Jordan aside and headed to the bathroom. After washing her face and cleaning her teeth, she wandered back into the room to find her friend exactly where she'd left him.

"Tell me something," she said, sitting down again. "Do you sneak into all the girls' dorm rooms?"

He laughed "I don't need to *sneak* in, Alex."

Seeing the face she pulled, he laughed again.

"Okay, okay," he said, relenting. "I can tell that you're going to freak out about me being some kind of pervert now, but there's no need since I can't transcend through these doors. The security features protect against any gift-related tampering. At a school for people with special skills—not to mention teenage hormones—I guess they figured it was better to be safe than sorry. I have to get in and out like every other person."

"Then how did you get in here?" Alex asked again.

He looked at her like it should have been obvious. "D.C. let me in."

"What?" she asked, bewildered. Why would her malevolent roommate have let Jordan into the room? That would have been considered *nice*.

"D.C.," Jordan repeated. "Also known as the grumpy red-head with terrible people-skills."

"How unexpected," Alex muttered, accepting that miracles apparently *did* happen. "Right, moving on. What are we doing today?" It was her first weekend in this strange new place and she was excited to see what sort of things they could get up to.

"About that…" Jordan fiddled uncomfortably with a fraying thread on her blanket. "I got a message last night reminding me about my detention with Finn this weekend."

Alex had forgotten all about the punishment Karter had given him when she'd first arrived at the academy. "That sucks, Jordan. But you don't have to look so worried—I'm sure Bear will keep me entertained until you're free again. Where is he, anyway?"

Jordan looked even more uncomfortable. "Actually, Bear's doing some extra credit Chemistry project with Fitzy. He only found out last night after you went to bed early, but he's going to be locked away in a lab all of today, and probably tomorrow too."

"Oh." Alex tried not to show how disappointed she felt. "Well, maybe Connor and Mel will be free to hang out. They seem pretty cool." Granted, Alex hadn't spent much time with the cousins, but they'd acted friendly enough on the few occasions she'd been with them.

Jordan winced. "Uh, they're not here, Alex. They take off home every weekend for some kind of family thing."

Feeling disheartened, Alex only said, "I guess that means I'm on my own, huh?"

"I'm really sorry," Jordan said. "But if it makes you feel any better, I'll be free after dinner. Bear, too. We can all hang out in the Rec Room or something."

She smiled weakly at him. "Yeah, that sounds good."

"I'd better get going if I don't want Finn to give me any extra work," he said, nudging her knee affectionately. "But I'll see you tonight, okay?"

"Sure thing," she said, watching as he stood and walked to the door.

The moment Alex was alone again, she sighed and looked around her room. She had been in Medora for less than a week, but she was so used to having either Jordan or Bear—or both—around that she wasn't sure what to do now that she found herself facing a large amount of time without them. She was surprised by her newfound sense of reliance, since she'd never been a clingy person before; she'd always maintained a strong sense of independence. But there was just something *nice* about having friends—something she'd never personally experienced. She loved her parents, for sure, but she was only just beginning to realise how much she'd missed out on because of their career-driven lifestyles. Her upbringing had caused friendships to seem so overrated, but she knew that wasn't the case anymore. It was just annoying that now, when she actually *had* friends, she still had to spend the weekend alone.

But then again, perhaps it was a good idea to create some distance between her and the boys. Eventually she would be going home, and it wasn't like she'd be taking either of them with her. They belonged in Medora, and Alex belonged in Freya. It was as simple as that.

"Enough of this," Alex muttered, scrunching her face up at her turbulent thoughts. She didn't have to make a choice between having friends and not having them—it was already done. She would be foolish not to enjoy her time with them while she could, even if it meant that she would miss them when she was back in her world. Better to have loved and lost, and all that.

With a nod to herself, almost like she was mentally sealing her decision, Alex moved to her wardrobe, determined to make the most of her day regardless of who she was—or wasn't—spending it with.

Alex was ravenous when lunchtime arrived. She'd successfully whittled her morning away by completing her pile of homework—mostly from Medical Science, surprise, surprise—and she planned to spend the rest of the afternoon reading through her Core Skills textbooks to research the topic of giftings. Despite seeing Jordan use his transcendence gift and Bear use his charm, she still found the concept difficult to grasp.

After eating a quick meal, Alex hurried back to her dorm room and deliberated which of her three textbooks she should start with. They all sounded interesting: *Unwrapping Your Gift: How To Grow Your Talent And Better Your Skills* by Miranda Crotchett; *A Comprehensive Study Of Personal Giftings* by Phillippe R. Brandon; and *So, You Think You're Gifted?* by Laurence Tillman.

In the end, Alex decided on the comprehensive study. She didn't think she was gifted, so that eliminated the third option, and since she didn't have a gift to unwrap, she skirted away from the first.

Heading outside, she settled underneath a tree by the lake. It didn't take long before she was mesmerised by the book in front of her. Hours passed as the sun slowly moved across the horizon. A late afternoon breeze stirred up the grass and whistled through the trees. And still, Alex kept on reading:

> While some scholars claim that only a minority of individuals have the ability to access personalised giftings, notable theorist Fredérike Von Duffé suggests otherwise. Von Duffé believes that every single human being has the potential to use and develop their own personal gift, but it is only the minority who have the natural biological and psychological connection to their gift that allows for easier access. Von Duffé writes in his book, *For Richer or Poorer: Gift Equality for the Common Man*, "Why would one person be given such great power and another not? Perhaps the better question is, why would one person be able to *access* such power and another not?"
>
> While the theorist's beliefs are stirring, especially for those desiring such gifts, Von Duffé's research lacks supportive data and empirical evidence, and thus is generally discredited by other professionals in the field…

The feeling of hot air blowing against her ear startled Alex. Standing directly behind her was Monster, a shaggy little pony Tayla had assigned Alex to care for in her Equestrian Skills class. He was only the size of a large dog, barely coming up to her hip, but he had more than enough personality to cover his diminished height and he'd quickly found his way into her heart.

"Hey, little fella," she cooed, scratching behind his ears. "What are you doing sneaking up on me?"

Looking out at the setting sun, Alex realised just how late it was. She'd been so caught up in her reading that she hadn't noticed how fast the afternoon had passed.

Alex picked herself up off the ground and gave Monster one last pat before heading off to her dorm building. She was surprised when he followed along beside her like a shaggy pet dog.

"Looks like you've made a friend."

Alex glanced up to find Bear leaning casually beside the entry to the dorm.

"It wasn't hard," she said. "I gave him an apple the other day. We're best friends for life now."

"If only it was always that easy," Bear said.

Monster chose that moment to nudge Alex with his rather solid head, causing her to stumble forward. Bear laughed at the display and Alex turned her glare from the pony to her friend.

"What are you doing out here, anyway?" she asked, trying to shoo Monster away.

"I was waiting for one of you guys to get back so we can go for dinner. Have you seen Jordan yet?"

Alex shook her head. "Not since this morning. How long do you think Finn'll keep him out?"

Bear shrugged. "I don't—"

"SPARKER! GET BACK HERE!"

Alex turned to see Jordan sprinting towards the dorm building with Finn hot on his heels. The PE coach was waving a pitchfork in the air and looked like a rabid farmer chasing after an errant cow.

Jordan quickly reached the entryway and ducked behind them. "Hide me!" he whispered to their backs.

Alex thought his request was a bit ridiculous since it was clear that he was standing there, but she stayed where she was nevertheless. It was still difficult to resist taking a step backwards when Finn approached them, waving his pitchfork madly.

"Where's he gone? I know he came this way!"

Alex looked at Finn as if he was crazy. Couldn't he see Jordan standing behind them?

She could have slapped herself for being so obtuse. Of *course* Finn couldn't see him. Jordan was probably using his gift and playing the invisible man. Thankfully, Alex had enough sense to keep her mouth closed. Bear, however, took a step towards the enraged teacher.

"Who are you looking for, Mr. Finneus?" he asked, his voice mesmerising.

Finn blinked at him a few times, as though he had to gather his thoughts. "Eh? Oh. Sparker. Jordan Sparker. He was doing detention with me and I haven't finished with him yet."

"Sir, it's nearly dinner time," Bear said, again using the smooth and captivating voice. "Surely you don't want to miss dinner?"

Alex found herself nodding. Bear could have said anything in that voice and she would have agreed. It seemed like Finn was facing the same predicament, since he shook his head as if to clear it.

"But—But I'm not done with him yet!" Finn valiantly tried to keep himself composed, but his blazing anger had already cooled enough that he lowered the pitchfork to rest on the ground. "There's still plenty of light left for work."

"But surely *you* don't want to work anymore tonight?" Bear continued. His words were so hypnotic that Alex wondered if Finn would want to work ever again, let alone tonight. "It's such a beautiful evening. I'm sure you have plenty to do without having to worry about babysitting a student. There will be enough time for that when he joins you again tomorrow."

Finn rubbed his stubbly chin thoughtfully. "I suppose you're right. Plenty of time tomorrow. And I *am* a bit peckish." His stomach gurgled and Alex saw Bear smile triumphantly.

"If you see Sparker, tell him he'd better get a good night's sleep, 'cause he's gonna have a big day tomorrow."

"Certainly, Mr. Finneus," Bear said, still using his charming voice.

Finn nodded to himself and walked away from them.

When he was out of earshot, Bear turned to Alex and said, "And that's how it's done."

Before she could respond, Jordan re-materialised beside them and clapped a hand on Bear's shoulder. "Thanks, mate. I totally owe you one."

Bear huffed out an amused breath. "You owe me way more than one, Sparkie."

"Good thing we're not keeping count then, huh?" At least Jordan had the grace to look sheepish.

"I can't believe you just charmed him like that," Alex said, amazed anew at Bear's gift.

"I told you it comes in handy," Jordan said.

Alex massaged her temples. "This place is so insane. Nothing makes sense here."

It wasn't the first time she'd longed for the simplicity of her own world. Earth—Freya—*whatever*—might have been lacking on the technological advancement scale, but at least it offered a what-you-see-is-what-you-get reality. There were no unexpected surprises, no strange abilities. Her world made *sense*, which was much more than she could say about Medora.

"It might be easier if you just embrace the senselessness," Bear said with a compassionate look.

"After everything I've seen and heard this week, that's all I really *can* do," Alex agreed.

"Are you really okay with all this?" Jordan asked, and she was surprised by the genuine concern in his gaze. "Most of the time you seem to be handling it well, but other times..." He trailed off, not needing to finish his sentence.

"I'm not going to lie—it's messing with my head a bit," Alex admitted. "I know you said there's no such thing as magic here, but that's still what it seems like to me. Where I come from, we don't have supernatural gifts, let alone all the other stuff.

It's a lot to take in. But people also don't jump from one world to another through disappearing doorways, so I figure that if I can accept where I am and where I'm from, then I have no reason to deny all the other crazy stuff that happens here. And besides, it's not like I can just close my eyes, stick my fingers in my ears, and chant 'la-la-la, I'm in my happy place' for the next few months until the headmaster arrives. That's impractical. Not to mention, just plain weird."

Jordan and Bear had seemed impressed through most of her response, at least until she'd segued into the potential chanting—then they'd just looked entertained.

When she finished, there was a moment of silence before Bear grinned and said, "Supernatural gifts? Really?"

"What else am I supposed to call them?"

"Fair enough," he accepted. "But for the record, there's nothing magical about our abilities. It's just biology."

"If you say so," Alex said, stepping forward to lead the way inside. "But if that's the case, I still think I'm missing that strand of DNA."

"We'll see," Jordan said. "You never know what the future might bring."

Ten

The weeks passed surprisingly quickly and soon enough almost a whole month had disappeared. Alex's lessons continued in much the same way as her first week—they were still completely insane. Her weekdays were filled with classes, classes and more classes, while her weekends were spent catching up on her endless pile of homework and hanging out with Jordan and Bear. Despite knowing that she didn't belong in Medora, Alex soon began to enjoy the absolute randomness of Akarnae, as well as the people who inhabited the school.

Four weeks after her arrival in Medora, Alex sat in the food court deliberating what to eat for lunch when someone sat down beside her.

"I heard about what happened this morning. Are you okay?"

Alex looked up from her menu to see Mel's concerned expression.

"It was a bit of a shock, but I'm all right now," Alex said, recalling the near-catastrophic events of the morning. Compared to what might have been, Alex's sore throat and chest were nothing to complain about.

Their PE class had been held in the massive Lake Fee that morning so Finn could test their 'water survival skills'. In the act of trying to save one of her classmates from what she'd thought was an actual drowning, Alex had nearly lost consciousness under the water. Finn had pulled her to the surface at the last second and thumped what had seemed like the entire lake out of her lungs before she'd been able to breathe freely again. Then he'd asked her if she was an idiot, because *of course* the entire exercise had been a set-up and her classmates had never been in actual danger to begin with.

Mel leaned in closer. "I heard you nearly *drowned*." She shuddered. "I'm so glad I'm only a Beta for PE. Finn's a real pain in the you-know-what, but he doesn't make us do anything *dangerous*."

"It's not so bad," Alex said weakly, trying to convince them both.

Jordan snorted from across the table and she realised how untrue her statement was. He and Bear had been beside themselves with worry when she hadn't resurfaced for so long, but they'd both been too far away to do anything. She was just lucky that the PE teacher had been nearby, otherwise... well...

Just as she decided to change the topic, she felt a tap on her shoulder and turned to find Fletcher standing behind her.

"Finn told me about your class this morning, Alex," the doctor said. "How're you feeling?"

"I'm okay," she answered, fidgeting under his watchful gaze. He must have heard the strained tone of her raw vocal chords, since his eyes narrowed with disbelief. Thankfully, he didn't press the issue.

"Very well, then," Fletcher said after a pause in which Mel quietly excused herself to go and find her cousin. "If you're at all concerned, please drop in to see me."

"I will," she promised.

Fletcher nodded and began to walk away, calling over his shoulder, "By the way, Maggie asked me to tell you that if you ever skip her class again, she'll give you detention for a month."

Alex groaned as soon as Fletcher was far enough away not to hear, and she looked up to see Jordan and Bear's amused expressions. Neither of them had known she'd skipped her Archery class in favour of a hot shower and some warm clothes after PE.

"Don't tell me that Miss Goodie-Two-Shoes skipped class?" Jordan teased.

She shrugged, trying to downplay the situation.

"Our little girl's growing up," he said, wiping away a fake tear.

"You're one to talk, mate," Bear said with a laugh. "It's not like you've never skipped before."

"It's hardly the same," Jordan said, "since I get permission first."

"Permission?" Alex asked. "How can you get permission to skip class?"

They both looked at her pointedly, waiting for her to catch on. When she didn't, Jordan leaned in to whisper in her ear. "When your best friend is a charmer, it's easy. Remember Finn?"

Alex's eyes widened in realisation and she looked at Bear. "I can't believe I forgot! I didn't even think to ask for your help."

Bear just grinned and said, "Don't worry—there's always next time."

She nodded in agreement and continued to think about the possibilities as they stood and headed to Medical Science.

Professor Luranda spent the first half of the lesson droning on and on about the properties of Silver Cloverfoot, a beautiful—and deadly—purple and silver flower. Just when Alex thought she might drop off to sleep, an alarm sounded. It wasn't the usual gong noise that signalled a class change or meal times. Instead it was a wailing, keening, high-pitched siren that caused Alex and her classmates to clutch their ears and cry out in confusion.

"*Silence!*" Professor Luranda shouted from the front of the room, her rainbow robe contrasting with her rapidly paling face.

Everyone froze at her command and all noise ceased until the only sound left was the screaming of the alarm.

Alex watched, ears ringing, as Luranda picked up her Communications Globe. It was a black, glassy sphere about the size of a tennis ball with swirling white mist inside. When Alex had first seen one in her History class, Bear had explained that the Globe allowed the academy staff to contact one another immediately in the case of emergencies. Sort of like an intercom or a phone, but with both visual and audio output. Plus, they all had built-in Bubbledoors for instant transportation to… somewhere.

Bubbledoors, Alex had learned early on, opened up wormholes that worked like teleportation devices. When she'd first heard about them, she had asked her friends why the headmaster couldn't just use one to zip back to the academy and send her home. They hadn't been able to answer her, other than to say that Marselle must have his reasons for staying away. Whatever those reasons were, Alex struggled to believe they were good enough to excuse his negligence, not when he could just come and go in the blink of an eye. Like everything else in Medora, his continued absence didn't make any sense.

Luranda spoke quietly into the Globe with her back turned to the students. Over her shoulder Alex could see the faint outline of Jarvis's face inside the swirling mist of the sphere.

Eventually the professor lowered the Globe and turned back to her students. "We are to wait here until further instructed."

That's it? Alex wondered. She knew better than to question the strict professor, but she shared a glance with Connor who was seated beside her and she could see he was thinking the same. What were they waiting for?

To her surprise, the professor didn't continue teaching. Instead, Luranda took up a position next to the transparent door at the front of the room.

Alex leaned in to ask Connor about the purpose of the one-way visual doors. "Why are—?"

She stopped because two things happened. First, the siren ended, trailing off into a ringing silence. And second, the room instantly blackened.

Alex heard her classmates scraping their chairs away from their benches and standing. Once again there were exclamations of surprise, and in some cases, fear. While uneasy herself, Alex didn't think it was wise to get up when she couldn't see anything. They were in a medical laboratory, after all. The last thing she needed was to stumble in the dark and fall onto a scalpel.

A moment later the lights in the classroom came back on. Alex blinked away the stars in her vision and noticed that the corridor on the other side of the transparent door was still an inky black, thick and gritty.

"Please take your seats, students. There's nothing to worry about," Luranda said. "It's just the Lockdown procedure."

Her words weren't convincing. Luranda was clearly anxious about something, and she continued to gaze out into the dark corridor.

Alex turned around to see how Jordan and Bear were faring, and she felt better when she saw them calmly reading their textbooks. She tried to get their attention, but they were too caught up in their work.

She turned back around to the front of the room before her brain registered what she'd seen and she snapped back to look at them again. Jordan and Bear *never* did schoolwork unasked.

Alex narrowed her eyes and peered closer at her friends. She gasped in surprise when, as Bear moved to turn a page of his book, she could see *through* his arm to the wall behind him. Even the book was partly transparent.

Without thinking, Alex started to rise from her seat, but a hand pressed down on her shoulder and pushed her back onto her chair.

"Don't move," Jordan whispered in her ear.

He must have been using his gift, but she had no idea why—nor did she know how there was a semi-opaque copy of him doing homework up the back of the room. And she couldn't ask, because Luranda chose that moment to take her eyes off the door and glance around her classroom, making sure everything was still in order.

Alex held her breath as the professor's cool gaze swept over her. She could still feel Jordan's hand on her shoulder and she prayed that Luranda wouldn't notice her not-completely-solid friends up the back. She released her breath only when the older woman seemed satisfied enough to return her attention to the door.

Alex didn't dare speak, but she pulled her paper close and wrote four words:

What are you doing?

It was the weirdest thing ever when her pen vanished and writing appeared on the paper, letter by letter.

INVESTIGATING. YOU COMING?

Alex kept her eyes facing the front of the room but gave a quick nod. There was no way she was going to miss out on whatever he had planned.

She flinched when a different voice spoke in her other ear.

"Drink this," whispered Bear, and a vial was pressed into her hand under the table. "It will feel a bit weird, but try not to move much."

Jordan being invisible—*transcendent*—she could understand, but Bear too? She decided to worry about that later and instead knocked her pen off the bench, giving her an excuse to bend and retrieve it. While she was under the table she quickly swallowed the contents of the small vial—which tasted faintly of strawberries—before sitting back up in her seat and holding as still as possible.

It only took a few moments before she was overcome by the oddest sensation. Her flesh began to tingle as if she had pins and needles, while her heartbeat throbbed loudly in her ears. Her temperature spiked feverishly and the warmth expanded slowly outward from her body, growing like a tangible presence as it pulsed in time with her heart. Even her clothes were pulsing outward, only stopping after they had risen about half a centimetre above her actual self. As she looked closer, she realised that her expanded figure wasn't completely solid, but it was still convincing enough to get by. Just like the copies of Jordan and Bear studying up the back of the room, Alex now had her very own copycat illusion.

"Are you ready for this?" Jordan whispered once the pulsing finished.

Alex nodded again and his grip tightened on her shoulder. One moment she was grounded, sitting in her seat, and the next she felt like she was soaring through the outer atmosphere. She closed her eyes as the feeling washed over her, enjoying the floating sensation.

A moment or two passed before the feeling began to fade. She still felt like she was soaring on a cloud or floating in water, but she also had a better idea of where her feet were and how to use them. She opened her eyes and blinked a few times, trying in vain to clear her vision. It was like a shower screen covered her eyes; she could still see everything, but it was all slightly blurred around the edges. No matter what she did, her sight wouldn't clear, and she realised it must be a result of whatever Jordan had done to her.

"Let's go," Jordan said quietly, keeping a tight hold on her arm and pulling her up from her seat.

She was about to protest—surely Luranda would notice the movement—but she snapped her mouth closed as she stepped out of the replica, leaving the copy in her seat. Her decoy didn't move much; she just stayed looking towards the front of the room, blinking.

No one noticed that there were two of her in the classroom, and since she could now see Jordan and Bear perfectly while everything else around them was still blurred, she guessed that Jordan must somehow be covering her with his gift.

"How—"

"Shh!" Jordan interrupted. "I'll explain outside."

With one hand on her shoulder and the other gripping Bear, Jordan led them straight towards the wall.

"Jord—" Alex didn't even get a chance to finish whispering his name before he thrust all three of them into the wall.

Or rather, *through* the wall.

Oh. Right. She'd forgotten he could do that. Instead of slamming into the solid barrier, she felt as if her body had been sucked into a vacuum and spat out the other side. Real pleasant.

Steadying herself, Alex looked at her new surroundings. All she could see was, well, nothing. It was still pitch-black.

"Let's try and get outside," Bear said from somewhere to her left.

She couldn't see either of the boys, but she was comforted by Jordan's hand which was still on her shoulder. He pushed her forward once again, and all she could do was trust that he knew which direction they were heading in—or that they'd again be able to move through anything solid in their path.

Walking blindly through the dark hallway was eerie, and Alex was relieved when she felt the vacuum sensation again, which meant they were moving through another solid object. Light soon pierced her eyes, and even though her surroundings were still blurry, she could easily see that they'd entered another classroom. A Chemistry lab, to be specific, and one that was currently in use.

Alex crept with her friends towards the other side of the room, hoping neither Fitzy nor any of his students would sense their invisible presence.

"But why is it necessary?" one of the boys in the class asked. Alex recognised him from her Equestrian Skills class, but she couldn't remember his name.

Fitzy either didn't hear him or didn't care to respond. Unlike Professor Luranda, the Chemistry teacher wasn't staring out the door of the lab into the dark corridor beyond. Instead, he was at the head of the room, writing frantically on his board.

"Fitzy?" the boy tried again.

The wacky man turned at the sound of his name and seemed to realise that he still had a classroom full of students.

"What's that, Wilson?"

"The Lockdown, Fitz," the boy—who she now remembered was named Ryan—seemed exasperated. "You were telling us about the Lockdown, remember? Why is everything dark out there?" He indicated with his hand towards the corridor.

"Oh! Lockdown, you say?" Fitzy straightened his glasses and squinted towards the corridor. "That's not good! Why didn't anybody tell me?"

He hurried over to his desk to pick up his Communications Globe, but Alex didn't find out what happened next because she was pulled through another wall into the darkness beyond.

And then another.

And another.

Eventually they reached the outer wall of the Gen-Sec building where, without warning, Jordan's hand disappeared from Alex's shoulder and she fell like a dead weight to the ground.

Eleven

The drop was only short, but her breath was still forced from her lungs with an "*oomph!*" when she landed on some kind of bushy hedge.

After rolling off it and onto the grass, Alex looked up and realised firstly that her vision was clear again, and secondly that the three of them had just fallen from the second floor of Gen-Sec. She rubbed her shoulder and turned to glare at Jordan.

"Sorry about that," he said, offering her a hand up. "I didn't want to risk finding some stairs to get to a lower level. And I knew this bush would break our fall."

Alex thought it best not to respond.

"What's a few bruises, hey?" Bear said, clearly excited by their escape.

"How did we get out here?" Alex asked, brushing leaves and twigs out of her hair.

They looked at her as if she had a few screws loose.

"We walked. Then we fell," Jordan said carefully. "Did you hit your head when you landed?"

"No, Jordan," she huffed. "What I meant is... You used your gift on us, right?"

"How else do you think we got out without being caught? And walked through walls?"

"I just—I didn't know people could do that. Share their gifts, I mean."

"Some people can't," he said, "but since mine is a physical gift, I can make it work for other people too."

"That's… really handy," Alex said, impressed.

"It has its limitations," Jordan admitted. "It only works with physical contact, which is why I had to be holding onto you the whole time."

"So, I'm not transcended anymore?" Alex asked. That would explain why her blurred vision had cleared—and where it, and the earlier anti-gravity sensation, had come from to start with.

"No," Jordan confirmed. "But we should be okay out here since everyone else will be stuck inside with the Lockdown."

"What *is* the Lockdown?" Alex asked.

Jordan looked at Bear and they both shrugged. "No idea."

"That's what we're investigating," Bear said, practically bouncing with anticipation. "Let's go see what we can find out!"

"I think we should head to the Tower," Jordan said. "That's where Jarvis'll be, and if anyone knows what's going on, it'll be him."

Decision made, the three of them headed towards the centre of the grounds, carefully keeping to the sides of the buildings and staying as sheltered as possible. When Alex asked why Jordan didn't just keep them all invisible, he explained that it was tiring to use his gift on other people. But even so, whenever they had to cross an expanse of uncovered ground, he grabbed onto them and hurried them invisibly towards the next building.

The Tower wasn't too far from Gen-Sec, but they took the long way around the apprentices' dormitory and the food court so that they'd have more cover if anyone was looking out at the grounds. When they eventually reached the entrance to the Tower and stepped inside, their journey became more complicated.

"Did anyone bring a torch?" Alex asked into the darkness. Like the building they'd just left, the entire Tower was pitch-black.

"No need," Bear said from somewhere ahead of her. "We've got Jordan."

Before Alex could ask what he meant, Jordan spoke. "I know my way around this place better than my way to the food court."

"You'd have to," Bear replied. "This is basically your second home, what with all the trouble you get into."

"It has its uses," Jordan said, and Alex felt him grab her hand and pull her forward.

"Wait! Jordan!" she cried. "How can you see where you're going?"

"I can't," he said, still moving her through the inky blackness. "But I don't need to. The stairs are over here."

Sure enough, a few steps more and Alex heard a *thunk* when his foot collided with the staircase. He cursed quietly before muttering out a grumbled, "Watch your step."

With only those words for warning, Jordan continued to pull Alex forward, and she concentrated on stepping up the stairs without falling on her face.

They continued upwards for so long that Alex wondered if they were climbing to the moon. The darkness was so disillusioning that she felt as if they'd ascended much higher than the Tower stood.

"We're almost there," Jordan whispered as he finally led them onto a flat surface. "Just like our dorm rooms, Marselle's office is warded against unidentified entry, so I won't be able to use my gift to get us inside. But I should be able to get us into his antechamber. We might hear something from there."

"Why do we want to get into the headmaster's office?" Alex asked, panting from the climb. "I thought we wanted to find Jarvis?"

"Jarvis will be in Marselle's office," Bear explained. "It's the only way he could have communicated with the other teachers, since only the headmaster has primary access to all their Globes."

"I'll try and get us into the antechamber but, whatever you do, don't let go of me," Jordan said. "And don't make any noise."

Alex gripped his hand tighter when he started forward again. She felt the sucking sensation as they walked through a wall, and once more she found herself blinking stars from her shower-screened eyes as she adjusted to the light of the new room, one that must have also been separated from the Lockdown's darkness.

"What's taking so long?"

Alex nearly jumped out of her skin at the sound of Karter's voice, and Jordan squeezed her fingers in warning, reminding her to stay silent.

"When the Lockdown was activated, it shut down the Tower's identification protocol. I have to reset the system before we can enter the room," Doc said. He was standing beside a panel in the wall, fiddling with some wires. "I'm working as fast as I can, but please remember that I'm a historian. Technology doesn't always agree with me."

He seemed frazzled as he worked methodically at separating the wires and pressing buttons on the touch-screen panel.

"Take all the time you need, Doc," Finn said in a tight voice, pacing near the doorway. "We'll just wait here while *he* walks around the campus like he owns the place."

"We don't even know he's behind this," Doc murmured into the panel, casting a quick, anxious glance towards the door of the antechamber. "And besides, it's not like he could get very far out there," he added, tilting his head towards the inky blackness shown through yet another transparent door.

"Bah!" Finn grunted, aiming a kick at the wall. "That's just what he'd want us to think! Not that it even matters—we all know what he's here for. I don't see why Jarvis called us up here when we should be out there stopping him, especially since this Lockdown is just making his job easier! I say we should just go and get the—"

"Might I recommend we continue this conversation when we're certain no one else is listening?"

Alex hadn't realised anyone else was in the room and she turned so fast that her neck cricked. Leaning against the wall on the other side of the chamber was a man she'd never seen before. He was very handsome, in a rugged kind of way, with dark hair and a strong jawline showing a hint of stubble. He was dressed all in black, with a cape similar to the shimmering one that Caspar Lennox always wore. A dagger was belted to his waist, but Alex doubted it was the only weapon he carried. Despite his relaxed position, he looked... *dangerous*.

And he was staring straight at her.

"You can never be too careful," the man added, his dark eyes locked onto hers.

She shivered and gripped Jordan's hand hard enough to bruise.

"Calm down, Ghost." Finn waved his hand at the other man dismissively. "There's no one here but us."

"Hunter's right, Finn," Karter said, his eyes darting around the room. "We should watch what we say until we know what's going on."

Finn mumbled to himself but it was clear he was outvoted so he slumped against the wall to wait.

The silence was unbearable. The dangerous man—Hunter? Ghost?—still hadn't taken his eyes off Alex. She could feel sweat beading on her forehead and she was sure everyone could hear her frantic heartbeat. She squeezed hard on Jordan's hand again, hoping he would get the message that they needed to get out of there.

Before he could respond, Alex was pushed back as the room began filling with people who appeared out of thin air. All of her teachers arrived within seconds, along with some other people Alex had seen around the campus but didn't know.

She pressed herself closer to the wall when everyone in the cramped room began speaking at once.

"What's happening—"

"Is it—"

"Why haven't we—"

"Does anyone know if—"

"SILENCE!"

Like most people in the room, Alex jumped at the unexpectedly loud noise. Who would have thought that the quiet historian had such a powerful set of lungs?

"Unless anyone else here knows how to override the Tower's security system," Doc said, "I would greatly appreciate it if you could keep the noise down. I'm finding it rather difficult to concentrate."

The new arrivals mumbled their apologies and started up quiet conversations. Since no one seemed to know anything, Alex decided to focus on the people closest to her, much like it appeared Jordan and Bear were doing. From what she gathered, Karter had just asked Tayla and Maggie why everyone had arrived at the Tower all at once.

"Jarvis called us," Maggie said, waving her Communications Globe. She still held a bow in her free hand and had a quiver of arrows strapped to her back. "He asked us to come straight away to discuss the situation."

"I guess he didn't realise we'd be locked out of the office," Tayla said. "I had a spare period and was in the staffroom so I don't know what happened outside. Were you in the middle of a class, Mags?"

Maggie nodded. "When the Lockdown first activated, the entire campus was blacked out; even the sun couldn't pierce through the darkness. I was teaching an Alpha class—it was pure luck that no one got shot. But when the secondary protocol kicked in, the Lockdown dispersed back into the buildings only. I moved my students to the nearest lit classroom and waited with them until I was called here. How long has Doc been at the control panel?"

"Not long," Karter said. "He'll have it figured out soon enough."

"All done," Doc called out, as if on cue. "We just have to wait for the system to reboot."

Alex noted the teachers' relieved expressions but her attention was caught by one man in particular. Or rather, it was caught by the fact that one man was *missing*. The man who had been staring at her the entire time was no longer leaning against the wall.

She glanced frantically around the room before she found him standing beside Professor Luranda. Wondering if she'd imagined the whole staring incident, Alex moved her gaze away from him, but she froze when she heard him speak quietly from across the room.

"That boy, the one whose gift can make him invisible," he said to Luranda, "did you have him in your class just now?"

Alex felt her heart skip a beat.

"Jordan Sparker?" Luranda straightened her multi-coloured coat. "Yes, I had the entire third year class."

"Was he in your lab when you left?"

"Of course he was," Luranda said. "All my students were accounted for. Sparker in particular, since I know all too well his penchant for troublemaking. When I left, he was sitting up the back of my room with his head bent over a textbook."

"I see," the Hunter man said, his eyes flicking over to Alex and her friends for a fraction of a second. "That *is* a relief."

He almost looked amused.

"We're in!" Doc called when the door finally opened.

"Well done, Doc," Jarvis's voice carried in from the next room. "I forgot that you'd be locked out, but well done indeed."

Alex took a step forward and tried to get a glimpse inside the headmaster's office as the teachers streamed through the door. From her limited view, she could see that it looked like a boardroom, with a large rectangular desk spanning the length of the room. The best part was the far wall which was completely transparent and looked straight out over the entire academy.

"All right everyone, please take a seat," Jarvis called as the teachers continued to pour through the door. "We have a delicate situation on our hands and we must deal with it immediately to ensure the safety of everyone residing on the academy grounds."

Alex took another step forward, not wanting to miss anything he said.

"As many of you might have guessed, we had an unauthorised visitor arrive just after lunch." Jarvis's voice was deep and serious. "We can't be sure, but we believe the intruder was here on a scouting mission. We have no evidence indicating he is aware that what he's after is here at Akarnae, so it could have been a simple coincidence. But coincidence or not, had his mission been successful, I can't begin to describe how catastrophic the consequences would have been. Thankfully, the Lockdown procedure impeded his search, and he has since fled the grounds."

There was a loaded silence before Jarvis continued. "While earlier I was unsure, I can now confirm that our intruder was—"

The last person stepped into the office. The door clicked shut.

"Of all the rotten timing," Bear whispered. "We were just about to hear—"

"I think you've heard quite enough, Barnold," interrupted a quiet voice that froze Alex and her friends to the spot.

Oh, they were in *so* much trouble.

Twelve

Fear quickly overtook Alex when she saw the Hunter man standing near the door and staring straight at their 'invisible' faces.

"I believe it's time for you three to return to your class," he said, before he opened the door to the headmaster's office and slipped quietly inside.

Alex didn't know if her knees would be able to hold her up much longer, shaking as much as they were. She had only a second to take in her friends' equally shocked expressions before Jordan yanked on her hand, pulling her forcefully after him. She barely felt the sucking sensation as they moved through the wall, and then they were sprinting off down the staircase, intent on getting as far away as possible.

The Lockdown must have deactivated while they'd been snooping, since the corridor outside the antechamber was no longer filled with darkness. Knowing that all the teaching staff were in conference upstairs, Alex let go of Jordan's hand so they could move easier and faster down the Tower staircase.

Only when all three of them had sprinted the entire way back to Gen-Sec did they stop and gasp for breath.

"That was intense!" Jordan said, exhaling with a laugh.

"Who *was* that man?" Alex asked, panting. "And how did he know we were there? He was staring at us practically the whole time!"

"That was Hunter," Bear said, also trying to catch his breath. "Some people call him 'Ghost' since you never know where he is or what he's doing unless he wants you to know."

"He's brilliant," Jordan added. "We'll hopefully have him next year for Stealth and Subterfuge. I can't wait. Bear and I have been counting down ever since we first heard about his class."

Alex shuddered at the idea of having that man as a teacher. "Why next year?"

"SAS is restricted to fourth years and up," Jordan explained. "Even then it's very exclusive, since Hunter only picks a handful of students who he thinks will be worth his time."

That was good news for Alex. It was unlikely she would still be in Medora for the next school year, but even if she was, she couldn't think of any reason why Hunter would consider her to be 'worth his time'.

"But how did he know we were there?"

"Not much gets past Hunter," Jordan said. "He probably heard us breathing or something."

"From across the room?" Alex asked in disbelief.

"If there's one thing you need to remember about Hunter," Bear said, "it's this: never underestimate him."

"Is that so, *Barnold?*" Alex couldn't help it. Despite the seriousness of their conversation, teasing Bear about his name was just too good of an opportunity to pass up.

"Uh, yeah, about that..." He tugged on the collar of his shirt. "I really do prefer Bear."

Jordan snorted. "So would anyone whose parents had named them Barnold."

Bear didn't seem bothered by the ribbing. "At least I came with a ready-made nickname."

"What do you mean?" Alex asked.

"My full name is Barnold Eustace Arthur Ronnigan," he explained. "B-E-A-R."

Alex cocked her head to the side. "That works well."

"I don't know about you guys," Jordan interjected, "but I think we should take Hunter's advice and get inside before Luranda comes back."

Alex and Bear agreed, knowing that with the professor at the meeting, the danger of being caught had lessened significantly. Well, caught again. Alex still wasn't sure why Hunter hadn't punished them when they had to have broken a heap of school rules.

As she followed her friends along the now lit but still empty corridors, Alex was painfully reminded of her aching chest. During the adrenaline-filled Lockdown she'd managed to forget all about her near-drowning in the lake, but now her body was screaming in discomfort. She hadn't exactly been taking it easy, what with falling out of a building and running all over the campus. If anything, she'd probably done more damage to herself.

By the time they reached their lab room, Alex was taking shallow breaths and trying to resist the urge to cough. While she wanted to ease the pain, she knew coughing would only make it worse; especially now that her sore throat had also returned with a vengeance.

"How do we get back in there?" she asked, wincing as her voice caught on the words.

"It's just like when we pulled you out of the illusion, but the opposite," Bear said, retrieving three vials from his pocket and distributing them. "Drink this, and when you're back in position, your illusion will fade away automatically."

It sounded easy enough, so Alex drank the liquid and gave him back the empty glass tube. It was lime-flavoured this time, and the tangy citrus stung her raw throat.

"What is this stuff?" she asked as the tingling sensation began again.

"Its most common name is Desert Oasis," Bear said. "It's named after the illusion people see when they're lost and hallucinating. When they're far away it looks real, but up close it's not."

"But it's not foolproof, is it?" Alex said. "I could tell you weren't real before we left the class. Why didn't Luranda notice?"

"She was a bit preoccupied with the Lockdown," Jordan said. "And it probably would have only caught her attention if our illusions did something unusual."

"Like studying?" Alex asked, smirking.

"Yeah, well, we didn't have a lot of planning time," Jordan defended. "And besides, it worked. Luranda thought we were still in class. That's all that matters."

Alex bit back her retort and took his offered hand. She felt his gift wash over her as he pulled her through the wall and back into their classroom.

It was a simple enough matter to join with her illusion, just as Bear had said. All she had to do was sit back down and merge into the image of herself. The moment she was in place, Jordan released her hand and she became visible again. The illusion slowly shrank back into her skin, and when she couldn't see any trace of her replica, the tingling sensation disappeared.

Alex turned around to look at Bear and Jordan, who grinned back at her, indicating that their illusions were gone as well. She heaved a sigh of relief.

They'd really done it.

Alex could have laughed, but she decided against it. Not only would it aggravate her chest, but her classmates would probably think she was unstable. Instead, she leaned over to see what task Luranda had set in her absence.

"I take it you're back?" Connor whispered.

Alex quickly nodded. She supposed it would have been concerning if Connor hadn't realised he'd been sitting next to an illusion for almost an hour.

He smiled and handed over a sheet of paper which turned out to be a copy of his notes. "You owe me one," he whispered. "And I expect to hear *all* about it later on."

Before Alex could reply, a Bubbledoor opened at the front of the room and Professor Luranda appeared in a swirl of colourful light that quickly faded like mist. Her face was alarmingly pale and pinched with anxiety.

"Classes are cancelled for the afternoon," the professor told them. "In an hour there will be an assembly in the food court where Administrator Jarvis will address today's events. Attendance is mandatory, but you're free to do as you please with the rest of the time."

Luranda walked over to her desk and placed the Communications Globe back onto its holder. When she turned around to discover them all still in their seats, she made a shooing gesture. "Go on, then. Class dismissed."

Still no one moved.

Alex fidgeted in her seat, feeling as uncertain as the rest of her classmates looked. The moment she shifted, a stab of pain spasmed in her chest, reminding her again of all the lake water she'd inhaled earlier that day—and just how hard Finn had thumped on her back to get it all out. She sucked in a sharp, burning breath and immediately felt as if a thousand fire ants were stinging the back of her throat while a herd of elephants played football with her lungs. All she wanted was to get out of the classroom and find some relief for her pain, but like everyone else, she was hesitant to leave just yet.

One of the girls in the front row— Kelly Gleeson—tentatively raised her hand. "Excuse me, Professor, but you haven't set any homework."

Kelly had just verbalised what everyone else was thinking. Luranda *never* failed to set homework, and that was the reason why no one had moved.

The professor snorted, and Alex thought it was perhaps the most undignified sound that she'd ever heard the strict woman make.

"I'm sure you can manage for one night without it, Miss Gleeson," Luranda said. "Now, off you all go before I change my mind."

Her words were enough to motivate them all to hurry out of the classroom.

"How good is this!" Bear said, joining Alex and Connor in the corridor.

"Yeah, not only did we skip class *and* not get busted for it, but we've got no homework! Plus, we get the afternoon off!" Jordan said, doing a happy-jig that should have looked lame but he somehow managed to pull off.

"Skip class?" Mel asked, having just joined the group.

Alex knew that she, Jordan and Bear were in for a long explanation. Unfortunately, all she wanted to do was curl into a ball until she felt better.

"Let's head back to the Rec Room and we'll tell you guys there," Bear said as he started to lead them away.

Jordan tugged on Alex's elbow to keep her from following. "Are you all right? You look like you're about to throw up or something."

She grimaced. "I'm not feeling too good."

"I'm not surprised," he said. "You've had kind of a rough day."

She chuckled at his understatement and winced at the pain it caused.

"Why don't you go and see Fletcher?" Jordan suggested, his concern evident. "Whatever's wrong, he'll be able to fix you."

Alex found herself nodding in agreement.

"I'll cover for you," Jordan said. "Come meet us when you're done and we'll all go to Jarvis's assembly together."

Alex thanked him and he hurried to catch up with the others while she headed down to visit the doctor.

When she reached the Med Ward, Fletcher was nowhere to be seen, so Alex pulled herself up onto one of the hospital beds to wait for him. She closed her eyes, wondering if a quick nap would alleviate some of her discomfort.

It was only when she started to drift off that she heard the voices.

Alex cracked her eyes open and raised her head to look down the long stretch of the uninhabited Ward. On the far side of the room was a door labelled 'Contagious Infections' and it was slightly ajar.

Alex lay back down and closed her eyes again, figuring that Fletcher was probably in there with a patient. She was ready to try and sleep once more, when an unfamiliar voice broke through the haze of her mind.

"Who raised the alarm?"

Alex snapped her eyes open and quietly slid off the bed, tiptoeing closer to the door.

"It was automatically activated," came Fletcher's muffled response.

"Automatically? How?" The unknown voice was deep and masculine, and sounded too old to belong to a student.

"Jarvis told us that the headmaster placed stronger security wards around the academy before he left," Fletcher said. "The only people who can visit while he's gone are those who have been welcome here previously—students, faculty and alumni. Other people can visit only if they're in the company of a current academy resident. Otherwise they won't be able to enter the grounds."

"If no one unwelcome can enter the grounds, then why were we on Lockdown?"

Fletcher hesitated before replying, "The Lockdown was activated because the wards were breached."

There was a pause after his words, as if the other man couldn't believe what he'd heard.

"The wards were *breached?* Marselle's wards? How is that possible?"

Fletcher sighed. "I don't know, Varin. I really don't know."

They were silent for a moment.

"Is Jarvis sure it was him?" the other man asked so quietly that Alex had to lean in closer to hear.

"Yes." Fletcher sounded weary. "He's sure."

The man cursed, and Alex wished they would reveal more. Who was this person that everyone seemed so worried about? And what was he after?

"Fletch, you've got to get me out of here soon," the man pleaded. "I'm no good to anyone like this. I need to be out there helping. Especially now."

"Just a bit longer, Varin," Fletcher said. "You'll be back to normal by the time classes resume in the New Year."

The other man groaned. "That's almost a month!"

Alex heard Fletcher murmur something soothing before the sound of a chair scraping across the floor caused her to back away from the door. She didn't want to get caught eavesdropping so she quietly scrambled back to her bed. The moment she lay down and closed her eyes, she heard the door squeak as it was fully opened. She blinked and sat up, schooling her face into an expression of surprise.

"Fletcher?" she asked, playing the innocent card. "I didn't realise you were here."

He pulled the medical mask off his face. "How long have you been waiting, Alex?" he asked, glancing nervously towards the room he'd just left.

"Not long," she replied, telling the relative truth. "I hope you don't mind, but when I realised you weren't here, I decided to wait." Also the truth. "I was going to try and have a nap." Again, the truth. She'd just left out some other details.

Fletcher relaxed at her words and excused himself for a moment. He left the room—presumably to wash his hands, or so Alex hoped—and returned with her file.

"Now, what can I help you with?"

"I—uh—" She felt foolish now, knowing that she should have come earlier. "You mentioned at lunch that Finn told you what happened this morning?" He nodded and she continued, "Well, I was just wondering if you might have something to help me—um—feel a bit better?"

His gaze softened. "Why don't you tell me how you're feeling, and I'll tell you if I have something that will help, hmm?"

She swallowed, and then winced again at the pain.

"Sore throat?" Fletcher asked, watching her reaction.

She nodded. "Really sore. And my chest hurts."

"Hurts how?" he asked, scribbling on his chart.

"Like it's burning," she responded.

"All the time?"

"Only when I breathe," she said dryly.

Fletcher chuckled. "Well, we'll want to fix that then, won't we?"

"That would be nice," she agreed.

"Lie down on your stomach for me," he said, all professional again. At her questioning look, he explained, "Finn mentioned that he gave your back quite a thumping in order to expel the water from your lungs. I just want to make sure he didn't crack a rib. He can be rather... enthusiastic."

Enthusiastic? Alex could think of better descriptions, none of them anywhere near as complimentary. But Finn *had* practically saved her life, so maybe she should cut him some slack.

Fletcher whistled through his teeth when he got his first look at her back and Alex remembered *why* she had such negative descriptions for her PE teacher.

"Is it bad?" she asked, her voice muffled by the pillow.

Fletcher pressed on a few tender spots before letting her sit up again. "It looks worse than it is," he told her. "Nothing appears to be broken. You just have some impressive bruises."

He bustled over to his medicine cabinet and returned with two vials. Alex scrunched her face up at the unappealing brown colours.

"Don't give me that look," he said. "It wouldn't have been so bad if you'd come in earlier."

She looked at the ground. "I know. I'm sorry."

He patted her on the shoulder. "Don't worry about it, Alex. But in the future, try to remember that prevention is often better than a cure."

She nodded in agreement and took the vials from him. Holding her nose, she raised the first one to her mouth and swallowed as quickly as she could. Her eyes widened when she recognised the taste. "Chocolate!"

"What did you expect?" Fletcher laughed. "It's like you're disillusioned to believe medicine is disgusting."

"Before I met you, medicine *was* disgusting," she murmured, raising the other vial to her lips. It tasted faintly of cinnamon.

Within seconds Alex was feeling immensely better. Her throat no longer scratched and her lungs had stopped burning. She took a deep breath, relieved when she felt no pain, and she smiled at the doctor. "Fletcher, you're brilliant!"

He waved away her praise and handed her another two vials. "You might not be saying that tomorrow morning if you wake up in pain, so make sure you take these before bed tonight," he said. "You should be fine after that, but if you experience any further discomfort, please come and see me straight away."

"I promise," she said, meaning it.

"Good," he replied. "Now, off you trot. You're due to be in the food court soon for Jarvis's meeting."

"You're not coming?"

"No. He's already spoken with the faculty members. The assembly is just for the students' peace of mind."

Fletcher seemed surprised when Alex didn't ask him any questions, but she couldn't think of anything that wouldn't give away what she'd already heard. Instead, she jumped off the bed and straightened her rumpled clothes.

"Thanks again, Fletcher," she said, motioning to the two vials she held.

"Any time," he replied, escorting her to the door.

She smiled and waved goodbye as she left the Med Ward and slipped outside into the chilly air.

Thirteen

As Alex walked away from Gen-Sec she wondered about the conversation she'd overheard between Fletcher and the mysterious Varin, but her thoughts were interrupted by an unexpected voice.

"Hello, Alexandra."

She spun around to find a man standing directly behind her, a man she recognised from the day she'd first arrived in Medora.

"Aven," Alex gasped, stumbling backwards in an attempt to put some space between them.

"I didn't mean to scare you," he said, looking amused.

"You didn't," she lied.

If anything, he seemed even more amused.

Alex was conscious of the fact that not so long ago there had been an intruder upon the academy grounds. She glanced to her right and left and was dismayed to realise that there was no one else around. She'd been in the Med Ward for a while—most of her classmates were probably already at the food court, getting ready for the assembly.

Her heart picked up speed as she turned back to Aven. For all his startling beauty—and he looked even better than she remembered—she would never forget how he'd acted during their forest meeting. He was not someone she wanted to be left alone with.

"What are you doing here?" Alex asked.

"Why, Alexandra, if I didn't know any better, I'd say you're not pleased to see me."

"What makes you think you know better?" she asked, crossing her arms defiantly. "You kind of weirded me out the last time we met. I'm not looking forward to a repeat performance."

Aven chuckled and the sound was so charmingly pleasant that Alex felt herself subconsciously relaxing.

"You have nothing to worry about," he said, still smiling indulgently. "I'm no threat to you."

"And yet, you still haven't told me why you're here," she pointed out.

He shrugged, and the normally careless motion was carried out with more grace than she thought possible. "It's been a while since I last visited the academy. I sought to reacquaint myself with memories long buried."

"Memories?"

"I was a student here myself, once upon a time," Aven told her.

That helped Alex feel more comfortable. He wasn't the intruder then, at least. Alumni were welcome at Akarnae, or so Fletcher had told the other man in the Med Ward, which meant Aven must not have been the reason for the Lockdown.

"When did you graduate?" she asked, her curiosity taking over.

"It feels like forever ago," he answered, a smile curling the corner of his mouth.

That was an odd answer considering his relatively young age, but he didn't notice her questioning glance since he was looking around the campus.

"Tell me, Alexandra, is Headmaster Marselle in residence at present?"

Her internal alarm bells started ringing and she looked at him suspiciously. "Why do you ask?"

Aven's golden eyes blazed with suppressed emotion until he blinked, leaving her to wonder if she'd only imagined the fire in them.

"We've not caught up for a while," he said. "I merely wish to pay my respects."

It seemed like a normal enough answer to Alex. Figuring there was no harm in telling him, she said, "Then I'm sorry, but the headmaster is away at the moment. We're not sure when to expect him back."

Something unidentifiable flickered in his piercing gaze but it was gone before she could process it. Presuming it was disappointment, Alex hurried on to say, "Administrator Jarvis is here. I'm sure he would be happy to greet a former student."

"No doubt you are correct," Aven agreed, "but perhaps another time."

She opened her mouth to argue but was distracted when his mesmerising eyes caught hers. He spoke again before she managed to form any words. "Are you enjoying your stay here?"

She blinked, but still she was trapped in his gaze. "I—uh—huh?"

He moved closer, stepping deliberately into her personal space. "Have you discovered your power yet?"

"Do you mean my gift?"

Aven shook his head. "Not your gifting; I couldn't care less about whatever insignificant ability you possess. I'm speaking of the power you wield. Has it yet been confirmed? Have you learned how to control it?"

Okay, what? Alex had no idea what he was talking about, and from the near-fanatical look in his eyes, she wasn't sure she *wanted* to know. What she did want was to get away. Especially because she was finding it difficult not to answer him. It was almost like she desperately wanted—no, she *needed*—to please him. Like it was out of her control. It was different to how she'd felt when Bear had used his gift on her, but she still wondered if Aven was attempting to manipulate her in some way.

He raised an eyebrow, prompting her to answer. Despite her battling thoughts, she couldn't help but notice that his eyes were blazing again, like molten gold.

"I—" she started, not able to keep her mouth shut any longer. But before she could say anything, she was interrupted.

"Jennings! What are you doing out here? The meeting starts in five minutes!"

Alex tore her eyes away from Aven and looked up the path to see her roommate standing there, hands on her hips.

"Well?" D.C. called. "What are you waiting for? If you're late they'll blame me for not getting you, so hurry up!"

Alex sighed and waved in acknowledgement.

By the time she turned around again, Aven was gone.

Later that night, Alex collapsed onto Jordan's bed after telling him and Bear about the events of her afternoon. The three of them had retreated to the boys' dorm straight after the assembly where Jarvis had assured the students that there was nothing for them to worry about as the Lockdown had been merely a precaution. A precaution for what, he hadn't said. And despite his reassurances, Alex had noticed his pale complexion even from the back of the room.

"Let me get this straight," Jordan said. "You ran into the same guy who you first met when you arrived here, talked with him for a while, and then watched as he disappeared before your very eyes?"

Alex shook her head. "I didn't see him disappear. He was just gone when I turned back around."

"Right," Jordan said, sounding sceptical.

"Is that so hard to believe?" she asked. "And anyway, his disappearing act wasn't the important part of the story. It's obvious he must have opened a Bubbledoor. The more important questions are, who is he and what was he doing here? And why is he so interested in me?"

"Come on, Alex, any guy with eyes would be interested in you," Bear said, scooping up a handful of popcorn that they'd taken from the Rec Room earlier.

She choked out a startled laugh. "Excuse me?"

"Bear's right," Jordan agreed. "He'd have to be blind not to be interested."

Alex felt distinctly uncomfortable at the turn in the conversation and had trouble making eye contact with either of her friends.

"Chill out, Alex," Jordan said, nudging her with his elbow. His amusement showed all over his face when he said, "I never took you for someone who would get embarrassed so easily."

"You know we think of you like a sister," Bear said, also clearly amused. "You better not get all weird around us just because we can agree that you're—"

"Okay, this conversation is *so* moving along now," Alex interrupted, feeling heat blossom across her cheeks. "We were talking about Aven, remember?"

Jordan nodded. "Yeah, you're right. And there's something you need to know about his 'disappearing act'."

"What's that?"

"You can't just use any old Bubbledoor to enter or leave the academy grounds," Jordan said. "It has to have been authorised by a senior faculty member in order to get through the wards. This Aven guy couldn't have Bubbled away without a regulated, legitimate Bubbledoor."

"Plus, Jarvis told us that until they know what caused the Lockdown, academy security has been increased and the wards won't allow *anyone* to enter or leave the grounds without a faculty member," Bear added. "Not until our holiday break in two weeks."

"*Just a precaution*," Jordan said, mimicking Jarvis. His tone emphasised just how unnecessary he thought the idea was.

Alex, however, was unsure. The more she thought about Aven, the more apprehensive she became. Uneasiness churned in her stomach and she wondered if she should let Jarvis or one of the other teachers know about his visit. But if he really was who he said he was, then there was nothing to report. So, she had to figure out if he was telling the truth first.

"Okay. Let's work on what we can verify before we try to figure out the rest," she said, redirecting the conversation. "We need to confirm his identity."

"Did D.C. recognise him?" Bear asked.

Alex hesitated, wishing he'd asked a different question. After Aven disappeared, Alex had asked D.C. if she'd seen him vanish, but the other girl had looked at her as if she was insane and claimed that there hadn't been anyone else with Alex. Then, in true D.C. fashion, she'd stormed away while mumbling about Alex being a complete wacko.

"Uh… no," Alex said, choosing not to share D.C.'s opinion. "She didn't recognise him."

"But he claimed to be alumni, right?" Jordan said. "So we can just look him up in the Archives. Every student who ever attended Akarnae is listed."

Alex jumped to her feet. "Great! Let's go!"

"Not so fast," Jordan said, pulling Alex back onto the bed. "It's already past curfew. We won't be going anywhere tonight."

Alex looked out the window into the dark and realised it was later than she'd thought.

Jordan must have noticed her disappointed look, because he threw an arm over her shoulders and said, "First chance tomorrow we'll go and have a look at the Archives. Promise."

Stifling an unexpected yawn, Alex nodded. "It's been a long day. I should get to bed."

After saying goodnight to her friends, Alex headed up to her room, thankful that D.C. was nowhere to be seen. The last thing she wanted after the day she'd had was to deal with her hostile roommate.

She changed into her pyjamas and swallowed her medicine as per Fletcher's instructions, before pulling back her blankets and sliding into bed.

Despite her exhaustion, she was excited about visiting the mysterious Archives. What little she'd heard about them intrigued her, especially since she knew they could only be reached through the library—which was another place that had fascinated Alex ever since her first visit with Jordan during her second week at the academy.

Like everything else in Medora, the library was far from what she would call 'normal'. For one thing, it was located underground. Beneath the Tower, to be precise, which at least offered an explanation for the descending staircase in the medieval building.

The stairs led down to a foyer of sorts; a vast room that spread much further than should have been possible, lit with flaming torches and a huge chandelier which hung from the centre of the space. Paintings and tapestries decorated the walls, showing notable events, people and places from the course of Medoran history. The strange thing was, those paintings and tapestries *changed* at randomly timed intervals, which Jordan had claimed was because there was too much history to show for the artwork to remain stationary.

Alex had been transfixed until Jordan had pulled her into the centre of the room to meet the librarian, an odd little man with mousey hair like a ball of fuzz on the top of his head and spectacles so thick with glass that his eyes goggled owlishly from behind them.

"I'm surprised to see you here, Miss Jennings," the man had said to her. "I expected you much sooner than this, thinking you would be teeming with questions about your world and ours."

Alex had gaped at him. "How do you know who I am?" she'd asked. "And where I'm from?"

He'd blinked at her with his enormous eyes. "I'm the librarian. It's my job to know."

Offering no further answers, he had pulled out a stumpy wooden cane and led them—at a hobbling pace—to yet another set of stone stairs which spiralled downwards once again. They had opened at the bottom to a massive room, packed full of cascading books.

After showing Alex how to use the touch-screen technology to navigate the library's maze-like layout, the librarian had started to walk away, but Jordan had stopped him, claiming he hadn't told Alex about the full extent of the library.

The librarian had looked at Jordan with narrowed eyes for a moment before he'd murmured, "I suppose she of all people should know." He'd then caught Alex's confused gaze and explained, "Legend claims that the library spans over many levels, that it goes deeper than you could possibly fathom, and that each level holds more information than you could ever imagine."

Alex had glanced back at the staircase which had led them into to the cavern-like library room, then she had turned to look at Jordan and the librarian quizzically. "But the staircase ends here. It doesn't go any further."

The librarian's owlish eyes had remained locked on hers, but he'd only shrugged dismissively. "Like I said, it's only a legend."

Jordan's response had been to roll his eyes and say, "You don't always use a staircase to get to the lower levels. I'll show you some time."

And that was all either of them had said on the matter.

Since that day, Alex had frequented the library a number of times each week for study purposes, but she'd yet to venture any further than the main book level. That was all about to change with Jordan's promise of visiting the Archives.

Because the Archives, Alex knew, weren't on the main level.

Fourteen

Alex had to wait until classes finished the next afternoon
before she could visit the Archives. Unfortunately, she and her
friends hadn't been very discreet about their plans, and Mel
and Connor had overheard them talking at lunch. The cousins
had invited themselves along, claiming they knew a short-cut—
whatever that meant.

When they finally entered the library, Alex wished she'd
found a way to dissuade Mel and Connor from joining them,
since they hadn't stopped squabbling with each other and she
was starting to get a headache.

"Hurry up, would you!"

"I can't move any faster than this!"

"Then you shouldn't have come!"

"Ha! Like you would even know where to go without me!"

"What are you talking about? I found this place first!"

"No you didn't! I showed you how to get in!"

Alex sighed and rubbed her temples when they halted for the
fifth time.

"You guys need to keep your voices down if you don't want
to get us caught," Jordan said. Despite his cautious words, he
was leaning haphazardly against a bookshelf, not caring that he
was disobeying rules himself by eating a pastry he'd managed
to sneak past the librarian's keen gaze.

"What's the problem anyway?" Bear asked, stealing the

pastry from Jordan and tearing off half, handing the rest back. He graciously divided his own portion to share with Alex, who smiled at him in gratitude.

As she chewed on the apple and custard goodness, she was able to tune out the incessant arguing that started up again with Bear's question. But it only took a few bites before the pastry was all gone and she was once again aware of the bickering.

"If you hadn't forgotten how to—"

"Me! It was you who said that you'd—"

"Don't blame me for this! I'm the one who—"

They were wasting too much time and drawing too much attention. Alex still wanted to get back to the food court for a quick dinner once they were done, so she decided to intervene.

"*Enough!*" she said, in a not-so-quiet library voice. She immediately lowered her tone, realising that a few students had stopped what they were doing to stare at them. "Remind me again why we're all here?"

Mel blinked at her. "To visit the Archives. Remember?"

Alex felt the remainder of her patience begin to dissolve. "Not why we're *here*, but why we're *all* here. I only need one person to show me how to get down there."

The others all looked at each other before turning to eye the pastry Jordan was still eating. Like clockwork, every one of their stomachs growled as they realised they could bail on Alex and go eat a proper dinner.

All at once, they began to make their excuses.

"I've just remembered—"

"I told Fitzy I'd—"

"I'm supposed to be meeting—"

The only person who failed to come up with something fast enough was Jordan, who was unable to speak since he'd just taken the last bite of his food when they'd all decided to abandon Alex. He swallowed the considerable mouthful with a grimace and said, quite unconvincingly, "Um, I think I can hear someone calling my name?"

Alex grabbed his arm, leading him forward. "Come on, Sparkie. Just show me where to go and you can leave me there."

He grumbled something about how unfair his life was and pulled her in the opposite direction. "This way."

She followed him around a number of shelves, twisting and turning through numerous aisles, before he finally came to a stop. They waited in silence for a few minutes, and the quiet was so uncharacteristic of Jordan that Alex began to worry he was annoyed at having to stay back with her. When she finally looked up at him, she didn't find the frustrated expression she expected. On the contrary, it seemed like he was fighting a grin.

"What—" She jumped and only just managed to bite her tongue on a squeal when a hand came to rest on her shoulder a second before Bear stepped into view.

"Took you long enough, mate!" Jordan said, laughing at Alex's shock.

"I had to make sure they didn't follow me," Bear explained. "I actually had to go with them to the food court before doubling back."

"What are you doing here?" Alex asked, confused by his presence.

Bear looked at Jordan. "You didn't tell her?"

Jordan laughed again. "Nah. I was having too much fun watching her worry about whether I was mad at her for missing dinner."

Alex's mouth dropped. "I was not!"

"Yes, you were," Jordan said. "You're so easy to read. You'd think by now you'd be used to the idea that we actually enjoy your company." He looked at her with a mixture of amusement and exasperation. Then, in a brotherly gesture, he pulled her in for a rough hug. When he let her go he reached a hand upwards and messed with her hair.

Both her friends laughed at her indignant expression, which was highly ineffective since she now looked as if she'd just fallen out of bed.

"Ha ha ha," she drawled. Annoyed as she was, she still couldn't keep the smile off her face.

"You weren't actually worried, were you?" Bear asked seriously. "About us not wanting to hang out with you?"

The thought *had* crossed her mind, but she only shrugged, feeling embarrassed.

"You should talk to us about that stuff, you know," he told her. "We're guys, so you have to clue us in from time to time."

Jordan nodded his head in agreement. Alex didn't think she'd ever seen either of them so serious before.

"Okay," she said quietly.

Jordan reached out to tilt her head up, so she had no choice but to make eye contact. "Promise you'll talk to us whenever you're worried about something? No matter how big or small you think the problem is?"

"I promise," she said, looking at them both.

"Good." He released her chin. "That's what friends are for."

"They're also good for sneaking into secret levels of the library," Bear said to lighten the mood. "We only have a couple of hours left before curfew, so we should get moving."

"Right," Jordan agreed. "What we need is around here somewhere…"

As Jordan thumbed through the collection of books on the shelf closest to them, Alex turned to Bear and said, "I'm still not sure why you had to make sure Connor and Mel didn't follow you back?"

"Because where we're going is secret," Bear replied.

"But they said they know where the Archives are."

Jordan snorted while he continued looking through the books. "Everyone knows where the Archives are. They're the most non-secret secret ever."

Non-secret secret? There was definitely something wrong with his grammar but she let it go. "What's the problem, then? Why couldn't they come?"

"You'll see," Bear said.

Before she could object, Jordan interrupted. "Now, pay attention because you'll need to remember this for next time."

He pointed at the book he'd located on the shelf and Alex read the title out loud. "*The Encyclopedia of Current Events?* That doesn't make sense," she said. "How can current events be written in an encyclopedia? They'd be out-dated by the time it was published!"

Jordan ignored her and said, "Pull out the book."

She looked at it with mistrust. "This isn't going to be one of those totally clichéd pull-out-the-book-and-a-trapdoor-will-appear deals, is it?"

Jordan rolled his eyes. "Just pull out the book already."

Alex reached for it, her muscles tense and ready to react. She clasped her hand around the spine and took a deep breath, quickly yanking the book off the shelf.

Nothing happened.

Jordan and Bear burst out laughing.

"It's not funny!" she told them. She couldn't keep the corners of her mouth from twitching though, and she easily gave into her own laughter.

"All right, all right," she said, trying to regain her dignity. She looked at the book in her hands and flicked through the pages. "Now, seriously, how do we—" Before she could finish her question, the floor disappeared under her feet, leaving her to slide down a chute in complete darkness.

"JORDAAAAN!" she screamed as she slid faster and faster. "BEAAAAAR!"

Echoing laughter drifted down from above, along with a faint "*Wheeeeeeee!*"

Before she could scream at them again, the slide began to level out and she slowly came to a stop in a well-lit room. There was a flaming torch mounted on the wall beside a sealed wooden door, but otherwise the chamber was empty.

Alex's head was spinning but she didn't want to get trampled by her friends, so she quickly got to her feet and steadied herself against the nearest wall. A moment later the still-laughing Jordan slid into view, and Alex didn't hesitate before hitting him with the heavy encyclopedia she was still holding. He only laughed harder, and when she went to attack him again, he reached out and trapped her hands. It was only then that she realised he was holding a book, too. She squinted at the cover, making out the title: *The Encyclopedia of Current Events*.

"What—"

"Wheeeeeeee!"

Bear came sliding down the chute, interrupting her question. Jordan quickly stumbled to his feet to make way for their friend.

"What a ride!" Bear said, and he laughed as he took in Alex's harried expression.

"You could have warned me!" she said to them.

"You'd already guessed about the 'clichéd trapdoor'," Jordan said, repeating her words with a smirk. "What was the point in warning you when you'd already figured it all out?"

Alex chose to ignore him and turned her attention to Bear just as he was getting to his feet. She noticed that he was also carrying an encyclopedia.

"What's with the books?" she asked.

"Isn't it obvious?" Jordan said, waving the tome in his hands. "The *Encyclopedia* is the ticket down here."

"But why are there now three of them?"

"It's also the ticket *out* of here," Bear answered. "We each need our own because the books activate a single-use Bubbledoor that goes from this level back up again."

Alex's mouth opened in an 'O' shape before her curiosity took over once again. "But there was only one copy on the shelf. Where did your copies come from?"

Both boys looked at each other and shrugged.

"No idea," Bear said. "That's just the library for you."

Alex didn't bother to point out that his reasoning made no sense. It was hardly the craziest thing she'd heard since arriving in Medora.

"Let's go see these Archives, yeah?" Jordan said, walking over to the sealed wooden door and motioning for Alex to come closer. "Open your book to page seventy-four and press it against the door."

Alex did as instructed and waited for the door to open. As the seconds ticked by, she wondered why it was taking so long. Maybe she'd opened the wrong page? She double-checked and tried again.

Still nothing. No movement. No noise. No indication whatsoever that the door was preparing to open.

Alex looked up to see a purple-faced Jordan who, at that moment, finally released the laughter he'd been holding in. Bear quickly joined him. They'd tricked her—again.

"What did you expect to happen?" Jordan asked once his laughter died down.

She kept her tone flat when she answered, "I expected the door to open, obviously."

"Did you think to try knocking?"

Alex wasn't sure if he was being serious or not. She didn't want to fall for another prank, but before she had the chance to decide what to do, Bear reached around her and rapped his knuckles three times on the wooden surface. The latch clicked softly and the door opened wide enough for her to see into the room beyond.

"Wow."

In all honesty, the room itself wasn't that impressive. It was just like stepping into a computer lab, with independent cubicles and comfortable-looking chairs facing touch-screen panels. The space was large, but certainly not as large as the entire level of the Tower they were under.

The reason Alex was so shocked was due to the number of *people* in the room. She took in the faces—most of them adults— and asked the obvious question: "If this place is so secret, how do so many people know about it?"

"Like Jordan said before, 'secret' is a bit of an overstatement," Bear said. "We're not really sure what the secret is—whether it's how to get down here, or the fact that there's a *here* to get down to. Either way, most people know about the Archives, and if they don't, it's a good bet that someone they know can tell them."

"It just seems weird that the librarian acted so strangely about the 'legend' of the library if everyone knows about it," Alex murmured.

"Truth is, not many people know about the entrance we took, as far as I'm aware," Jordan said. "That's another reason we wanted to get rid of Connor and Mel—just in case they don't actually know. It's not something we're supposed to share, strictly speaking."

Alex looked around the room in confusion. "Then how did all these people get in here?"

"There are other entrances to the Archives all around Medora," Bear said, "but they're access points only. Bubbledoors transport people directly here from wherever they start. But, like us, they can only ever get back out the way they came in."

"Very few people would know that the Archives are actually a part of Akarnae's library," Jordan said. "Any other students who have used the entrance we took would most likely believe the encyclopedia acts just like the other access points. But we know differently—we're still underneath the Tower."

"How do you know?" Alex asked.

"We'll show you later," Bear promised.

"Come on," Jordan said, stopping her from questioning them further. "Let's get this search for your disappearing stranger out of the way."

Alex dutifully listened as Bear explained how to use the touch-screen panels, and after making sure she understood what she was doing, he and Jordan took off to give her some quiet research time. Once they were gone, she brought up a page listing Akarnae's yearbooks from the past fifteen years and touched the 'search' tab. She then eased back into her seat and waited for the new screen to open.

She almost fell out of her chair when the results appeared. Not only were past students listed, but so was everything else about them, including their relatives, friends, neighbours—*everything*. Each individual's entire history was listed and available for public perusal. There was just too much information for her to look through, so she found the task bar and typed in 'Aven', hoping to refine her search. The page loaded instantly:

There are 0 matching results. Similar listings include:
1. Avette
2. Aeina
3. Arianne
4. Astella

The list continued down the page, but there was no listing for Aven. Alex returned back to the yearbooks and sighed as she took in the overwhelming amount of data that she would have to sift through in order to find the mysterious stranger.

Better get started, she thought to herself as she opened up a random year, *because it's going to be a long night.*

"You've been here long enough, Bookworm. It's time for some fun."

Alex looked up at Jordan and Bear's expectant faces and said, "But I haven't found anything yet!"

"That's too bad," Jordan said, without much sympathy. "But you can come back tomorrow. It's almost curfew and there's more for you to see before we leave."

Alex consented without further arguing. They'd given up their night for her, after all. And their dinner.

"Now, in the future when you come down here, to get out again you just have to go back into the room with the slide, open the encyclopedia to the last page, and press your hand to the paper," Bear explained. "You'll see a door appear in the wall and when you go through it you'll find a Bubbledoor that'll take you straight back to where you first picked up the encyclopedia—which will also disappear during transport, by the way."

"Why are you telling me and not showing me?"

"Because we're not leaving that way," Jordan answered with an excited gleam in his eyes.

She rose from her seat and stretched the kinks out of her back. "How are we getting out of here, then?"

"Keep up and you'll see soon enough." That was all Jordan said before he spun on his heel and walked away, jerking his chin as an indication that she should follow.

She glanced at Bear and he winked before heading in Jordan's footsteps.

Alex trailed after them, shaking her head. *Boys.*

The Archives had cleared out significantly of people in the hours that she'd been researching, but there were still a few stragglers lingering around. Because of this, Alex wasn't surprised when Jordan and Bear led her towards a corner at the back of the room that was out of sight.

"Have a seat here and we'll tell you what we're going to do," Bear said.

The moment Alex's backside touched the ground, she was airborne. It was a completely unexpected sensation, especially since she was moving *upwards*, and at an incredibly fast speed.

Alex gasped and glanced down to find that she was still sitting on the floor, but only a square metre of it which was acting as her express elevator—'express' being the key word.

She didn't even have time to scream before she slammed into the ceiling.

Fifteen

I'm dead, Alex thought. *Squashed like a cockroach. What a way to go.*

Only, she wasn't squashed. And she wasn't moving upwards anymore, either.

Alex opened her eyes—not even sure when she'd closed them—and carefully looked around. She was sitting on the floor still, but the Archive terminals were nowhere in sight.

She realised that she must be on another level of the library, and she hurried to move off the ground in case her friends came up after her. The instant she moved aside, the square metre of elevator floor vanished into thin air and Bear was propelled into view.

He grinned at her.

She glared at him.

Then the floor disappeared again, causing Bear to scramble quickly to the side.

"That is such a safety hazard," Alex mumbled as Jordan appeared on his own carpet square.

"Nothing to it," Jordan said, standing and brushing off invisible dirt.

"Feel free to tell me the next time something like that's about to happen," Alex said pointedly.

Jordan and Bear looked at each other and chorused: "That would've ruined the surprise!"

She shook her head with amused exasperation. "Where are we?"

"Another level of the library," Bear answered.

Alex sent him a look. "Obviously."

He chuckled and added, "Another *secret* level, I should say. One we doubt many people know about. It's how we realised the Archives are part of the library itself, otherwise there wouldn't be a way to get in here. Pretty clever, really."

Jordan was nodding in agreement. "We found the entrance in our first year, completely by mistake. It was a busy day in the Archives and there was a queue of people lining up to access the TCD panels. So we walked over to the corner to get out of the way and sat down to wait."

"I still remember the look on Jordan's face when he flew into the air," Bear said, smiling at the memory. "Absolutely priceless."

"Of course, Bear followed straight after me," Jordan added. "Even with the forewarning, he was still green-faced when he crashed into me."

"Crashed into you?" Alex winced. "That sounds painful."

"I hadn't moved off the entry square since I was a bit, uh... dazed by the experience," Jordan said. "So, really it was me who crashed into him, since the floor disappeared with me still on it. Luckily there wasn't far to fall because the squares move so fast. It was more of a smack in the face than a crash, but whatever."

Hearing his words, Alex was glad she'd thought to move off the square before it had disappeared under her. Rather than linger on what might have happened, she spun around and squinted into the darkened room. "There's nothing in here."

The only light source came from two flaming torches, one on a bracket near where they were standing and another on the other side of the room. Both flames were bright enough to illuminate most of the large space, but there wasn't anything to see.

"Are you sure?" Bear asked.

She looked around again, squinting into the firelight. But nope, still nothing. The only thing that was even slightly out of place in the room was the carpeted floor. It was patterned into different coloured squares, each about the same size as the express elevator floor.

Alex felt her stomach tighten with unease as she looked down. She was standing on a wooden square, which was odd since the rest of the floor was carpeted. No, that wasn't quite right, she realised. A number of the squares around the room were also wooden, including the ones that Jordan and Bear both stood on. In fact, all the squares directly beside the area they'd entered from were wooden, along with a few others splattered across the floor at random intervals.

"We call this the hopscotch room," Jordan said. "We come here when we're bored."

"Hopscotch?"

He nodded. "It took us a long time to figure out how the room works and how to get across it—"

Bear mumbled something into his hand that sounded suspiciously like, "Without serious injury," and Alex glanced at him sharply.

"—but we managed to work it out," Jordan continued loudly, ignoring Bear's interruption. "We had to, since the only safe exit is over there and there's no other way out." He pointed to the flaming torch on the other side of the room.

Alex gulped. It was a lot further away than she'd originally thought. And she didn't even want to know why he had used the word 'safe' before 'exit'. Were there *unsafe* exits?

"What's with the floor?" she asked.

"Wooden spaces are safe," Jordan explained, tapping his foot on the floor he was standing on. "Grey carpet takes off upwards into the air and vanishes within five seconds."

Alex realised that they'd all arrived on the grey-coloured carpet, which explained why the floor had vanished before the next person's arrival.

"Blue carpet is okay to stand on if you have no other choice," Jordan continued, "but your body goes numb if you stay there for too long. Black carpet isn't actually carpet at all—it's just empty space, so avoid those squares."

"What happens if you fall down one of them?" she asked.

Jordan just looked at her. "Don't."

Bear noticed her expression and said, "We dropped a torch down one once. It just kept going and going until we couldn't see the light anymore."

"Right," she said, feeling slightly ill. "Avoid the black squares. Got it."

They nodded at her.

She looked at the floor again and realised that there was one colour left. "What about the red carpet?"

The boys exchanged glances and Jordan said, "Trust me, you're better off not knowing. Just steer well clear of any red squares."

Seeing that Jordan wasn't going to explain, Alex sneaked a glance at Bear. He mimed a quick action with his hands coming together before snapping his fingers out and mouthing a single word: 'BOOM'.

Jordan hadn't seen their interaction, but he must have noticed the panicked look on Alex's face because he hurried to reassure her. "It's fine, Alex. We've done this hundreds of times."

She looked at the red squares dotted across the room and simply said, "You're crazy."

"It's a piece of cake," Jordan promised. "You'll love it."

"Yeah," Bear agreed. "And besides, the red squares aren't the problem. The real challenge is that all the squares change colour."

Alex gaped at the boys before turning her attention back to the floor. Sure enough, within a few seconds a number of the squares changed colours. They pulsed for three warning beats before the change took place. One red square became grey, while another red square turned to wood. A black square turned red, while a blue square turned black. There was no sequence or order to the colour changes—they were completely random. And there didn't seem to be a set time, either. Some of the squares changed within seconds; others weren't changing at all.

It was a death-trap, but according to her friends it was also the only way out of the room.

"All right, let's do this," she said, causing both Jordan and Bear to whoop excitedly.

"I'll go first, then you follow me, Alex, exactly where I step. Bear will come behind you," Jordan said. "And remember, only one person on a square at a time."

She hadn't been told that before. "Why?"

Jordan grimaced and said, "They're kind of... booby-trapped."

"Booby-trapped," she deadpanned.

He looked at her innocently and shrugged as if to say it wasn't his fault.

"You know what?" Alex muttered. "I don't even want to know how you know that."

Jordan's smile widened when he realised she wasn't going to yell at him. "Ready, then?"

He took her terse nod as an affirmative and turned his attention to the square closest to him, waiting for it to change from black to a safer colour. The moment it became a wooden surface, he jumped.

I can't believe I'm about to do this, Alex thought, as Jordan moved to the next square over, leaving her to jump after him.

The first jump was the hardest, but it became easier after that. She continued following Jordan around the room, only glancing back occasionally to make sure Bear was still following them. Both boys frequently asked how she was doing, but she was so focused on not tripping onto the dangerous squares that she couldn't say much more than "fine" or "still here" or "I'm going to kill you later" without losing her concentration.

The further they travelled across the room, the more her confidence grew. It really wasn't so hard. In fact, she could almost understand the thrill that both Jordan and Bear seemed to get from the experience. She felt a distinct sense of accomplishment every time she narrowly avoided a dangerous square or made a particularly impressive jump onto a safe one. It was... exhilarating.

"Still with us back there?" Jordan called, glancing over his shoulder.

Seriously? Where else would she be? Alex looked down at the ominous black square to her left and realised that perhaps he wasn't enquiring just to annoy her. She felt tingly all over as she looked into the empty space.

"Yeah, I'm still—" Alex broke off when she realised that something wasn't right, since her tingly feeling was escalating. Glancing down, she saw that the wooden square she'd been standing on had changed to blue. She hadn't even noticed it pulsing, but now her legs were quickly turning numb.

"Jordan, move!" she called, hurrying him along.

"I can't—I'm boxed in!"

She looked ahead. Sure enough, all the squares around his safe wooden one were either black or red. He wouldn't be moving on until they changed colour, and none of them were pulsing yet.

"Alex," Bear called urgently from behind her. "Move to your right."

"But I—"

"NOW!" he ordered.

Trusting Bear, Alex jumped awkwardly off her square just as it turned a dangerous red colour. Her semi-numb legs almost sent her careening right over the other side of the new floor, but she managed to balance herself just in time. Unfortunately, she'd landed on another blue square, increasing her discomfort. The space diagonally opposite her was wooden so she leapt for it, but her wobbly legs couldn't hold the landing this time and her momentum carried her onto the next piece of carpet.

Jordan and Bear screamed out her name as her numb body fell onto the grey surface. She was instantly airborne, clinging on for dear life and flying upwards at a devastating speed.

Five seconds, she willed her brain to comprehend. *I've only got five seconds before it disappears and I'll fall.*

The realisation shocked her body to respond and her adrenaline to kick in, pumping blood to her numb extremities. She didn't have time to think about anything but survival as she pushed herself up and threw herself over the side of the carpet, just as it disappeared beneath her.

It was remarkable how high she'd been tossed in only a few seconds. And it was just as remarkable how quickly she fell. She couldn't bring herself to scream as the patterned floor moved closer and closer. Irrationally, she worried about which square she would land on, before realising that it wouldn't matter since she was about to become like a bug on a windscreen.

She had only a moment to glimpse the horrified expressions on her friends' faces as the floor rose to meet her.

"ALEX!"

"NO!"

Alex never heard the *crunch* of her body slamming against the ground. Nor did she feel the accompanying agony. She was surprised, really, to learn that dying would be so quick and painless.

But then a new kind of surprise filled her when she realised that the reason she didn't feel any pain was because she hadn't hit the ground. She was still falling.

Only then did Alex scream, as she plummeted down the black square and into the darkness below.

Sixteen

*"**She wove him a hat made from** a melody*
He wondered how to fix his calamity
If she'd known how to sing
He'd have worn it with a grin
But instead he preferred it a parody."

Alex stirred into consciousness, slowly making out the quiet voice of someone singing.

"She sewed him some socks made from a happenstance
He wondered why they looked just like his pants
If she'd known how to sew
He'd have worn them with a bow
But instead he hoped she'd ignore their absence."

Not yet ready to become fully awake, Alex lay listening to the soothing baritone.

"She knitted a coat made from a memory
He wondered about her sense of propriety
If she'd known how to knit
He'd have worn it in a jiff
But instead he worried about atrophy."

That doesn't even make sense, Alex thought.

She waited to hear the next verse, but the voice stopped singing and asked, "Are you ready to wake up yet, my young friend?"

"Not really," Alex mumbled. She was warm and comfortable. She felt safe for the first time in recent memory. Why would she want to wake up?

The voice chuckled lightly. "Come now, you'll feel much better once you've had something to eat."

Alex's stomach grumbled at the mention of food and she opened her eyes hesitantly, afraid of what she might see.

"Where am I?" she asked, sitting up to look around the room. She was lying on a cushy couch in what seemed to be a study of some kind. Flaming torches illuminated overflowing bookshelves that lined the room, and there was a single wooden desk wedged in the corner. Seated behind the desk was a man facing away from her. He was writing with an old-fashioned calligraphy quill, feather and all.

"And who are you?" she added, when the man didn't answer her immediately.

"Just a moment, please," he said. A candle on the desk flickered shadows over the side of his face when he turned slightly in her direction. His short, silvery-grey hair—the only feature she could distinguish from her angle—glowed with the light of the flame.

The man continued scribbling for another minute before he signed off with a flourish and placed his feathered pen on the desk. When he turned around, the first thing Alex noticed were his intelligent grey eyes, followed closely by his kind smile.

"Thank you for your patience, Alexandra," he said. "How are you feeling?"

She opened her mouth and closed it—twice—before she settled on the truth. "Confused," she said, before hastily adding, "sir."

The man laughed. It was a pleasant sound, deep and hearty. The noise filled her with warmth. "No need to call me sir, my dear. My name is Darrius."

She smiled at him. Maybe it was the fact that she'd awoken to hear him quietly singing, or that his calm and pleasant demeanour filled her with a sense of peace, but whatever the reason, she felt relaxed in his presence.

"Confused, Darrius," she repeated.

His eyes lit with humour. "I've no doubt about that, Alexandra. You've had quite a knock on the head."

At his words, Alex realised that her head *was* throbbing slightly. But she didn't remember hitting it. In fact, she couldn't remember anything after falling through the black square.

"How did I get here?"

"You fell," Darrius answered.

She really needed to start phrasing her questions differently. Either that, or she needed to meet people who didn't feel the unnecessary desire to state the obvious.

"And how did I land?" she clarified. "Without dying?"

"As to your first question, you landed head-first, which really was unfortunate," Darrius said. "But no matter, a little bump won't cause you discomfort for too long."

Lucky me, Alex thought.

"As for your second question," he continued, "why would you have died?"

"Uh… maybe because of how far I fell?" Alex said. Darrius just looked at her so she added, "It was a *long* way! Like, *flatten-into-a-pancake* long way."

He perched his fingers together under his chin. "And yet, here you are before me in one piece."

"Yes, I can see that," she said, barely refraining from rolling her eyes. "I'm just not exactly sure how I'm *in* one piece."

"The Library is full of wonders," Darrius simply said. "No one alive knows all of its secrets."

"We're still in the library?" Alex asked, gobsmacked. "How deep down are we?"

"Come and see for yourself," he offered, motioning for her to follow him over to a curtain.

Alex rose unsteadily to her feet and walked across the room, reaching out to pull the curtain aside. "What the...?"

Clouds. That was all she could see. Fluffy white clouds in a periwinkle blue sky that stretched on forever. She looked down, but there were only more clouds beneath her.

Vertigo took a hold and Alex swayed on her feet. Before she could fall, Darrius grabbed her elbow and led her back to the couch. He walked over to the wall beside one of the bookshelves and tapped on a remote TCD. Within seconds he was pushing a bowl of soup into her hands.

"Eat," he said gently, patting her shaking hand. "Then we'll talk."

Alex nodded, too shocked to speak, and picked up the spoon. As she slurped the soup she tried to process what she'd just seen. Aside from the obvious impossibilities, she couldn't get past the fact that she'd entered the library at night with her friends, but from the view out the window it was clearly daytime again. She must have been unconscious for hours. Jordan and Bear were probably worried sick about her. She only hoped they hadn't done anything stupid—like tried to follow her down the black square.

Alex glanced around as if expecting her friends to pop out from behind a bookcase, but when they didn't appear, she decided to presume that they had made it safely out of the hopscotch room and—hopefully—begun organising a search party for her.

On that optimistic thought, she gulped down the last few mouthfuls of soup and scraped the sides of the bowl before laying it aside.

"Better?" Darrius asked.

"Much. Thank you."

He waved aside her gratitude and waited for her to speak.

She gathered her thoughts and said, "So, I fell, right? And I landed on my head?" Darrius nodded. "But where did I land *geographically* speaking? If we're still in the library, how come we're, like, hundreds of storeys up in the air?"

He smiled as if he approved of her question. "As I said, the Library has many secrets. This one, however, I believe it will allow me to share with you. Hot chocolate?"

Alex blinked. "Err—yes, please?" she said, more a question than an answer.

Only after Darrius had ordered their drinks from the TCD and sat back down again did he speak. "The Library was constructed before the beginning of time—or at least, time as we understand it. We don't know how it was built, nor do we know who it was built by or even who it was built for. We don't even know the exact date it was discovered. What we *do* know is that for hundreds of years, kingdoms and empires alike sought to lay claim to this marvellous archaeological structure."

He took a sip from his drink. "History refers to the Library as 'The Jewel of Medora'. It rose higher than the heavens and could be seen from a great distance in any direction. Its rooms held unimaginable wealth not only in the form of knowledge and wisdom, but material riches as well. For this reason, battles waged unceasingly for its ownership until even the soil was stained by blood.

"Those were dark and gloomy days. People fought for what they desired but could never truly attain. Ultimately, their greed was rewarded by death and destruction.

"The Library wasn't an object to be claimed, but a haven for all to share and use. Having witnessed so much pain and suffering, it decided that the knowledge stored within was too great for mankind to be entrusted with, since all we were capable of was seeking our own ruin. Knowledge is power, and to be human is to desire power. So the Library made a decision.

"Battle-weary and bone-tired, the newest round of combatants were nursing their injuries and burying their dead after a hard day of conflict, when suddenly the ground started trembling. Those standing were brought to their knees as the earth shook around them. Gale-force winds stripped trees of their leaves and filled the air with debris. No one could see anything in the chaos and confusion, nor could they hear anything above the deafening roar.

"But then, just as suddenly as it started, so too did it end. It was only when the dust cleared that they bore witness to a truly inexplicable sight. The magnificent Library was no more."

Alex waited impatiently while he drained the last of his drink. "Then what happened?" she prompted, sitting on the edge of her seat.

"Well, without a Library to fight over, there was no more reason for the bloodshed," Darrius told her. "The armies retreated and the soldiers were sent home. The loss of the Library was a cause for mourning—so much knowledge and treasure had been lost—but many secretly rejoiced over its disappearance. In fact, we now commemorate the event with an annual holiday, one which we'll be celebrating in only a few weeks from now, called Kaldoras. Loosely translated, it means 'peace'. Over time, most people have forgotten the true reason for the holiday, and it has become much more commercial in nature, as is the way of events such as this. Kaldoras is now hailed as an excuse for gift-giving and feasting with loved ones, but the real origin of the celebrations is because, after the Library's disappearance, peace came to the lands for the first time in generations."

Darrius let her mull over that for a moment before he continued his story.

"Now," he said, "around the time of the Library's disappearance, a young Meyarin by the name of Eanraka founded a school for what he referred to as the 'gifted'. He invited those whom he believed to have special talents to come and learn in an environment that would train them to the best of their abilities. But ultimately he was just one person, even if he was a Meyarin, and he was soon overwhelmed by challenges. He thought of abandoning his school until one day the answer to his problems literally appeared before him. Eanraka was walking towards his office when he tripped down a staircase he'd never seen before and found himself in an immense underground room."

Darrius smiled at Alex and said, "You can see where the story is going, no doubt. The room he stumbled upon was the foyer of the great Library. From that day forward the Library was once again in a place where people could share in its knowledge. No longer the Jewel of Medora, the Library now rests unseen except by those whom it considers worthy."

"But... doesn't everyone know that the library is at Akarnae?" Alex asked. "Students have come and gone for years since then."

"You're quite right that the general population understands that there is *a* library of quality at the academy, but very few realise it is *the* Library of legend. It doesn't reveal its secrets to just anyone, you know."

"And that's another thing," Alex said. "You said the library didn't like all the fighting and made the decision to disappear... But, Darrius, it's a *library*. A *building*. Why do you keep talking about it as if it's a person? I can practically hear you capitalise it."

"It is much more than a person," he answered cryptically. "I can't explain what I don't understand, but all I know is that the Library is, for lack of a better word, alive. And it seems to like you. Very few people over the course of history have been Chosen to bear its secrets. No doubt you're going to have some interesting times ahead of you, Alexandra."

Alex looked at him with wide eyes. She was already stuck in another world; she wasn't sure if she could handle her life becoming any more interesting.

"There's something else I should warn you about," Darrius continued, oblivious to her thoughts. "As you've likely gathered from the adventure which led you here, the Library isn't merely a building for storing books and resources. Knowledge and wisdom come from experiences and challenges, adversity and even failure. The rooms you may encounter won't be at all like what you'd expect to find in a normal library. But if you so desire, you'll learn more than you could possibly imagine as you explore its secrets."

If the other rooms he referred to were anything like the hopscotch room, then Alex wasn't really sure that she was up to such exploration. But at the same time, she had to admit she was a little excited about the possibilities. Jordan and Bear would love it.

"Can I tell my friends about all this?" Alex asked, knowing she would anyway.

"I think those who showed you the chequered room can share in your knowledge since they must have been trusted enough to unlock some of the Library's secrets. But that doesn't mean they'll always be able to accompany you wherever you go. Their access will likely be much more limited than your own. As for anyone else, you should hide your knowledge of the Library's existence—partly for your own safety."

"How many other people know for certain that this is the Library of legend?" Alex asked. "And are able to explore it?"

"Other than myself? Very few. From what I've heard, all current and previous headmasters of Akarnae are made aware of the Library's existence, but they don't necessarily have access to all of its secrets."

"But I'm not a headmaster!"

Darrius chuckled. "No, you're not. But the Library may choose to reveal itself to anybody who it believes worthy. You've been Chosen, Alexandra. You should feel honoured."

Alex wasn't sure what she felt, so she asked another question. "The guy who opened the academy all those years ago—Eanraka, right? As in, 'Akarnae' spelt backwards? Seriously, he couldn't think of anything more creative?"

When Darrius didn't respond, she cleared her throat awkwardly. "Anyway... You said he was a—a Meyarin? What is that?"

Darrius looked deep into her eyes and answered, "Yes, I suppose you wouldn't have heard of them yet. Their existence is not openly discussed these days."

Before she could say anything, Darrius stood and walked over to his bookcase.

"I'm familiar with some of the literature from your world," he said as he rifled through the titles, "and as best as I can compare, you would understand those from Meya to be called 'elves' or 'fair folk', though no such translation exists here. They are simply those who have existed from the beginning. They are immortal beings, often referred to as 'the graced ones'. They can be killed just like any other creature, but if left alone they'll live forever, since their bodies are immune to illness and decay.

"Their race is unlike any other. They are beautiful to behold and blessed with inhuman strength, speed, agility and intellect. They can be either your greatest ally and most trusted companion, or your worst enemy and most treacherous adversary."

It was all a bit too much for Alex. "Are you telling me that you have *elves* here? Because I don't know what 'literature' you've read, but the only books that have elves in them are works of fiction. Elves aren't real."

She paused before adding, "And for that matter, how do you know I'm from another world? Or even what my name is?"

Darrius didn't answer immediately, and she started to rise nervously from her seat. But then he let out a quiet, "Ah-ha!" and pulled a book from the shelf, turning back to her. "Sit down, Alexandra. You have no reason to fear me," he said distractedly as he flicked through the pages. "I know who you are and where you've come from because the Library told me."

He walked over to his desk and absentmindedly picked up a piece of paper which he passed to her.

Alexandra Jennings: third year transfer student, originally from Freya.

"Who wrote this?" Alex said, staring in awe at the ancient-looking calligraphy. As she watched, more words appeared on the page.

Is it so hard to believe in a sentient Library?

She gaped at the page as one final sentence appeared before it was wiped clean:

Embrace the wonder.

Darrius either didn't notice her shocked expression, or he ignored it to answer her question. "I believe it's one of the secrets of the Library that's too difficult for us mere mortals to understand. I learned long ago that some things are meant to remain a mystery."

Alex had no choice but to accept his answer, and she placed the now-blank paper to the side, where it immediately vanished. "Now, where were we?" Darrius asked. "I think you were talking about your 'elves' not being real. And yes, I'm aware that's true where you're from. But history is different here."

He handed her the book he'd found, motioning for her to take a look. The page was already open and the writing was in a language she'd never before seen, but it was the picture that he clearly intended for her to see. There were two people, one male and one female, standing in a forest clearing with the moonlight streaming down on them. Even in a two-dimensional portrait, they seemed to jump out of the page and demand her attention. They were both so hypnotically beautiful that Alex could have continued staring at them for hours.

"As you can see, they paint quite an enchanting picture," Darrius said, closing the book and moving to place it back on the shelf.

Alex felt the loss as if it was a physical detachment and she stared longingly at the bookcase. "What happened to them?"

"No one really knows," Darrius said. "One day they were amongst us, the next they weren't. Their city, Meya, and its surrounding forests just vanished into thin air, along with their entire race. It's one of our greatest mysteries, and while there are many theories, no human knows the complete truth of what happened."

"How long ago was this?" Alex asked.

Darrius thought for a moment. "History isn't so clear on that account. Thousands of years ago, at the very least. I would estimate the time to be perhaps a few hundred years after Eanraka discovered the Library. That's not so great a time considering the Meyarin lifespan."

Alex let that sink in and said, "Okay, I think I've had all the history I can take for, oh, the next five years." He chuckled and she continued, "But thanks, Darrius, for answering my questions."

"Anytime, dear child, anytime."

She smiled despite the child remark since she knew his kindness was genuine. "So, the million dollar question: what happens now?"

He tilted his head to the side. "What do you mean?"

"Well, I can't stay here forever," she said. "How do I get back to the, um, ground?"

"That's simple," Darrius answered. "The same way you arrived."

She furrowed her brow. "Didn't I fall here?"

"You did," he replied. Seeing her expression, he added, "Is there a problem?"

She stood and walked over to look out the window again. It was still the same view. If anything, it seemed like they were even higher than when she'd first looked. But since the clouds obscured her vision and the ground wasn't even in sight through them, she had no way of knowing if that was true.

"Yeah, I'd say there's a slight problem," Alex said, gesturing towards the view.

"I don't make the rules, Alexandra," Darrius said with an apologetic shrug. "You asked me how to get out, and I answered. It's your choice whether or not you follow my advice."

"How about some different advice?" she asked. "Like the kind that doesn't involve falling to certain death?"

"I'm afraid I have no other options for you."

He didn't look afraid. In fact, he seemed completely at ease. Not to mention completely serious.

"You're mad," she said without thinking.

Darrius smiled and replied, almost jovially, "You're certainly not the first to believe so."

At least he wasn't offended. He almost seemed to take her insult as a compliment, proving to her that he was, in fact, a very strange man.

Alex took a deep breath and closed her eyes. As she did so, she heard a voice like a whisper in the wind: "*Just believe.*" She snapped her eyes open and turned to look behind her, but there was no one there.

"Let's say for a moment that I believe you," she said. "Would I really have to jump?"

Darrius appeared to think about it and her hope soared until he said, "I suppose I could push you."

She groaned and banged her head against the wall.

"The laws of gravity are simple, my dear," he said. "What goes up must come down."

He wisely remained silent while she grumbled into the wall about staircases and elevators and how technically she'd never *gone* up since she'd only fallen down in the first place. There was no such thing as falling *upwards*.

"Come along, then," he said, pulling her away from the wall. "While time is of little consequence here, I do have work to be getting on with and your friends are likely anxious for your return."

Alex blew out a resigned breath and followed him across the room until they stood in front of a door she hadn't noticed before. When Darrius turned the handle, the entire door vanished, opening to nothing. Unless, of course, the sky could be considered a destination.

She scurried backwards three steps before Darrius latched onto her arm with a firm grip.

"There's really nothing to be afraid of," he said, as if commenting on something as mundane as the weather. "Remember how I told you that the Library often teaches through challenges? Well, this is merely one such obstacle."

"You also mentioned that it teaches through failure," Alex pointed out, her body shaking in fear.

"So I did," he agreed, cheerfully. "But not, perhaps, failure as you understand it. And I don't believe this particular challenge will end in failure."

He managed to gently pull her one step closer to the ledge.

"I—I don't think I can do this, Darrius," she stammered as he coaxed her forward another step.

"I, however, have no such doubts."

Alex looked up at him. She hadn't noticed earlier, but his eyes were really more silver than grey. More importantly, they were full of confidence—in her. Darrius truly believed she could do this. So she decided to trust him and—literally—take a leap of faith.

He must have noticed her sudden conviction because he smiled and released her arm. "Until we meet again, Alexandra."

She was too focused to question his parting statement, so she just nodded and—after squeezing her eyes shut—did possibly the most insane thing she'd ever done in her entire life.

She jumped.

Seventeen

The wind pummelled Alex's body and roared past her ears at a near-painful volume. She strained to open her eyes against the pressure battering her, and when she did, she wished she'd kept them closed since the ground could finally be seen through the clouds. It was still a *long* way off.

She wondered for a moment about the impossible height from which she was falling, but her thoughts scattered when her speed increased. She wasn't just freefalling anymore—it was as if she had weights tied around her, pulling her down to the ground faster and faster.

Alex had to close her eyes again to ward off her nausea. It didn't help much since she could still feel and hear the wind pushing her closer and closer to the ground. The solid, hard, ground.

But then, gradually, she started to slow down. It didn't take long before the wind began to ease, and then it died out completely, leaving Alex's ears ringing and her body tingling from the aftermath. She had no doubt that if her eyes had been open they would have been watering like crazy. But they were still closed—at least until she heard the most unexpected sound.

"ALEX!"

"NO!"

Her eyes snapped open and the first thing she noticed was a roof above her head. How on earth had she managed to fall *through* and *into* a building?

Scratch that, the *first* thing she noticed was that she was, in fact, not dead. Then she noticed the room she was lying in; a room with a familiar chequered floor.

Alex sat up too quickly and had to hold her head in her hands until the room stopped spinning. Her ears were still humming and when her vision cleared she finally noticed what was going on around her.

Jordan and Bear were standing in the middle of the room, both looking horror-stricken as they stared down into a black square on the floor.

Three squares simultaneously changed colour and they were able to jump closer to one another and yet still stay near the black square. Jordan looked as if he was about to jump straight down the square, but Bear's arm latched onto him and held him back.

"Let me go!" Jordan cried. "We have to do something!"

"I know that!" Bear yelled back. "But jumping in after her isn't going to help anyone!"

Alex watched the scene with fascination. It was as if no time had passed even though she'd been gone for hours—overnight, apparently. She hadn't understood Darrius's earlier comment about time being of little consequence, but now she marvelled over the realisation. Then she noticed that her friends looked like they were both about to do something very stupid, so she snapped out of her shock and called out to them.

"Guys! I'm over here!"

She couldn't help laughing at their incredulous expressions when they spun around to face her.

"Alex?" Jordan gasped, his eyes wide.

"Yeah, it's me," she said. "I'm okay. Really."

He didn't look like he believed her—or that he believed she was really there. Bear, too, was gaping at her.

"I'm kind of tired," she said when neither of them moved. It was true—the adrenaline from the fall was fading, taking away all of her energy. But fortunately she had landed right where the torch was that identified the safe exit, so at least she wouldn't have to cross the room again. "Any chance we can get out of here now?"

That seemed to spring them into action, and without another word they quickly—but carefully—made their way over to her, looking up every so often as if to make sure that their eyes weren't playing tricks on them.

They reached her in record time and she felt the breath leave her as first Jordan and then Bear enveloped her in a crushing hug.

"H—How—?" Bear stammered.

"It's a long story," she said. It was true, for while only seconds had passed for her friends, much more time had passed for her.

"But, you were over there," Jordan said, pointing to the centre of the room where the ominous black square had yet to change colour. "And you fell."

She laughed again, her good humour returning now that her feet were back on solid ground. "Yes, Captain Obvious, I was, and I did."

"But—But you're here now."

"So it would seem."

Both of them continued to gape at her so she decided to go easy on them. "Let's just get out of here and I'll tell you what happened, okay?"

They nodded and she huffed in frustration before adding, "But *only* if you start acting normal again. I'm perfectly fine, so stop looking at me like I'm about to disappear or something."

That was apparently what they needed to hear, since they both relaxed and grinned at her. Jordan even gave her a mocking salute, and if she hadn't been so relieved by their changed expressions, she might have kicked him. Instead she just said, "Let's get going."

"Um, about that…" Bear looked so guilty that Alex just *knew* she wasn't going to like his next words. "We might not have been completely truthful with you before about this being the exit."

She closed her eyes and counted to ten before she spoke. "Where *is* the exit, then?"

"It's sort of—uh—" Jordan hesitated, winced, and quickly finished, "—back where we started."

As one, all three of them turned to look across the room.

No. Way.

"It was supposed to be fun," Jordan added meekly.

Alex sighed. She couldn't be angry with them. They'd only wanted to show her a good time. But she really was tired, and she had absolutely no desire to cross the room again. So, without knowing why or how, just simply that she *could*, she placed her hand on the wall beside the torch and *willed* an exit to appear.

She heard Jordan's quiet *"Wicked!"* and Bear's incredulous whistle when a door appeared out of nowhere, but she'd experienced one too many surprises already that day for her to truly appreciate what she'd just done.

It was almost a relief to find that the door opened into the great foyer of the Library—only almost, because standing in their path was the grizzly librarian.

"So," he said by way of greeting. "It would appear you have indeed been Chosen."

Alex nodded cautiously but didn't say anything.

He pursed his lips and squinted at her through his glasses as if judging her worthiness. Whatever he saw must have been enough since he soon relaxed his posture. "Very well," he said, and without another word he turned and hobbled back over to his desk.

"Right, then," Alex said, breaking the strained silence as her friends continued to stare at her. "I need chocolate. Stat."

After a quick visit to the Rec Room's dining area, Alex followed the boys to their bedroom, where she ingested copious amounts of chocolate while telling them about everything that had happened to her. When she was done, silence descended.

"Wow. That's just... *wow*."

Alex looked at Jordan. "Crazy, right?"

He snatched up another chocolate bar—his sixth—and peeled back the wrapper before taking a bite. "Definitely. You're a bit of a freak, you know. Why does all the weird stuff happen to you?"

His affectionate look took the sting out of his words, but still Alex frowned. She'd been wondering the same thing.

"I for one think this is totally awesome," Bear said, leaning back on his bed. "Just think of all the possibilities!"

"Absolutely!" Jordan agreed, downing the rest of his chocolate and shoving the pile of empty wrappers off his blanket and onto the messy floor. "Imagine all the trouble we can get into!"

Alex suppressed a groan. "Don't get ahead of yourselves," she said. "We still don't have any idea what all this Library stuff means."

"What's left to know?" Jordan asked. "The legend is real, the Library likes you, and you've been Chosen to share its secrets. Bear and me too, by extension. What do you reckon, mate?"

"That's the gist I got," Bear said. "Sounds pretty sweet to me!"

"I suppose..." Alex said, albeit hesitantly. Part of her was still wary, but there was another part of her, like Jordan and Bear, that was excited by the possibilities. "I'm never going into that hopscotch room again though, you hear me?"

Both boys nodded and Bear pointed out, "It wouldn't matter anyway since you could just make another door appear."

"I have no idea how I did that, so let's not count on it happening again."

"The look on the librarian's face..." Jordan snorted, before mimicking the little man, "*Very well.*"

They burst out laughing at his impersonation and when they were calm again Bear asked, "So, when do we get to have our first Library adventure?"

Alex thought for a moment before saying, "I want to solve this Aven mystery first. Can you guys wait until the weekend? That gives me four more days. I'm sure I'll find something by then."

They hid their disappointment well—if Jordan's pout and Bear's sigh could be considered hidden expressions.

"The patience will be good for you," Alex said, yawning. "All that chocolate has made me sleepy. Or maybe it was everything else that happened. Either way, I need to crash."

She stood up and headed to the door, only turning around to say, "Don't forget, you can't tell anyone about the Library."

"You can count on us," Jordan promised, waving her out of their room.

Eighteen

It took all week, but by Saturday morning Alex had finished searching through all of the yearbooks from the previous fifteen years. She was sure Aven couldn't have been older than that, but still she'd found no trace of him anywhere.

The more she thought about it, the more Alex was convinced to just leave it alone. She might not ever see him again anyway, and for some strange reason, that made her feel oddly disappointed. There had just been *something* about him; something so... appealing. Half of her had been enamoured, and the other half... repulsed.

There was something else about him, too. Something not quite right. Alex remembered feeling the need to please him, to do whatever he asked of her. She'd never felt so compelled, so *tempted*, before in her life. Even just thinking about it made her skin crawl, so she resolutely decided to let go of the entire Aven issue. It was time to move on.

"Hey, Alex!" Jordan called out as he jogged over to her.

She was sitting underneath her favourite tree by the lake, enjoying the beautiful day and attempting to clear her head. So far, no such luck, so she was glad for the distraction. "What's up, Jordan?"

He took a seat beside her. "What are you doing for Kaldoras?"

"Kaldoras?" The foreign word triggered a memory of Darrius telling her about the Library and the upcoming annual holiday. "It's sort of like Christmas, right?" At Jordan's blank look, she mumbled, "Never mind."

Sometimes Alex found it easy to forget she was in a whole new world. And with everything else going on, she had failed to remember that there was only a week left until classes were suspended for the break. She definitely wasn't looking forward to what was sure to be a lonely holiday, since most of the other students were leaving to visit their families. Added to that, it was also the first time ever that Alex wouldn't be with her parents for Christmas, and she felt sad just thinking about that.

"I'll be staying here," she said, trying not to sound too miserable about it. "It'll be a good chance to catch up on homework." Eugh. What an awful prospect.

"How 'bout an alternative?" Bear said, appearing from behind them and sprawling onto the ground. "I was just talking to Mum and she told me to bring you home with us for the holidays. Ordered, more like. Once Mum starts insisting, you really don't get much of a say in the matter."

"I couldn't possibly," Alex said, though she was touched by Bear's offer. "Kaldoras is for family time, or so I presume."

"Don't be ridiculous," Bear said. "We always have heaps of people over to celebrate. It's not so much family time as it is a global event—especially with Gammy's cooking."

Alex still wasn't sure until Bear added, "And besides, Jordan's coming too, so it's not just my family."

"You're going?" Alex asked Jordan.

"Sure am," he answered, as if it was a silly question. "Ever since I met Bear, I've spent Kaldoras with his family."

"How come?"

"My folks are always busy around the holidays," he said, sounding slightly bitter. "Fundraisers, royal galas, charity balls... the whole socialite shebang."

Her eyes widened. "Your parents are socialites?"

"For lack of a better word," he mumbled, not meeting her eyes.

Alex was curious and she found it difficult not to ask more questions. But she could tell that it was a sore subject, so she didn't press him.

"In any case, I always meet up with them at the New Year's Eve Gala," Jordan said, as if there had been no interruption. "My parents like to parade me around like a peacock, gushing over how *talented* I am and how *proud* they are."

He paused before continuing in a quiet voice, "Three hundred and sixty-four days of the year they hardly know I exist. And then, for just one day, they act like I'm the centre of their universe."

"Jordan..." Alex didn't know what to say, so she just placed her hand on his arm.

He smiled, but it was half-hearted at best. "Don't worry, Alex. I'm used to it."

"And there are benefits," Bear said, plucking a blade of grass and shredding it between his fingers. "The Gala is the biggest New Year's event amongst the upper classes. Blackmail certainly has its perks."

Jordan saw Alex's confusion and he smiled again—a proper smile this time. "A few years ago I told my folks that if they wanted to drag me along to play the 'happy family' charade, then they had to let me bring whoever I wanted with me. Bear has come with me every year since and, unless you have any objections, I'll be dragging you along this year as well."

Kaldoras at Bear's house with her two best friends, and a New Year's Eve party. Alex's holiday was certainly looking up.

"Now," Jordan said, his eyes sparkling with anticipation, "I could be wrong, but I think someone promised us we'd check out the Library this weekend?"

"You know, where I come from, most teenage guys avoid libraries," Alex said. "If you're not careful, people might start to think you've become nerds."

"Hey, now," Bear said, feigning hurt. "We prefer the term 'library folk'. It's much less derogatory."

Alex and Jordan stared at him, before all three of them cracked up laughing.

"*Library folk?*" Jordan gasped out. "Where did you pull that one from?"

"I don't know," Bear said. "Must just be my superior wit."

Alex sent him a sidelong glance. "That's it exactly."

"Well," Jordan said, composing himself. "Let's go and be *library folk*, shall we?"

It was only when they entered the foyer that they realised they had no idea where to start.

"Can't you make another door appear or something?" Jordan asked.

"I told you," Alex said, "I have no idea how I did that the first time. It was probably just a fluke."

"You said that you just *knew* you could do it, right?" Bear asked. "Why don't we wander around and see if you feel something similar again?"

It was a logical suggestion, but Alex felt uncomfortable walking around and staring at the portraits and tapestries while waiting for something—anything—to happen.

"Miss Jennings?"

She glanced up and noticed the librarian waving at her. After exchanging perplexed looks, the three friends headed in his direction.

"Good morning, sir," Alex said.

"Yes, yes," he muttered distractedly. "Might I ask what you and your friends are doing?"

"Uh—" She hesitated, unsure what to tell him. "We're just trying to get into the Library, sir."

He raised a bushy eyebrow. "You didn't think to use the stairs? Like every other time you've been here?"

Alex shifted on her feet. "Well, we're not really trying to get to that particular part of the Library today."

"Nonetheless, I dare say it's as good a place for you to start as any. More so than walking around aimlessly in my foyer."

She nodded, understanding that perhaps they were looking in the wrong place. "Thank you, sir."

"Where are we going?" Jordan asked as Alex led the way to the staircase.

She shrugged. "He suggested we go down. He might be cryptic, but I doubt he'd give advice without reason."

Partway through their trek down the stairs, Alex noticed something strange. "Does anything seem different to you guys?"

The three of them paused and the boys looked at her questioningly.

"Nothing?" she asked. "Never mind, then."

They continued their descent until her friends finally noticed what she'd already observed.

"Why are there so many stairs?" Jordan asked.

The study level of the Library was only a short trip down from the foyer and that was where the staircase ended. For some reason, even though they were on the same stairs that *should* have taken them to that level, they had already descended much further down—at least four floors so far—without passing any kind of exit.

"Fascinating," Bear murmured, tapping his knuckles against the solid stone wall.

They continued walking down, until finally they reached a dead end.

"I wonder what—" Alex started to ask just as all three of them stepped off the stairs and onto the stone floor. Her words were cut off when the torches blew out and darkness surrounded them.

"That's just great," she said. "I don't suppose either of you brought a flashlight?"

Silence.

"Guys?"

No answer.

"Yeah, okay, you're hilarious. What do we do now?"

Still no response.

She swung her arms out, fully expecting to smack into one of them, but all she found was empty space. Her heart started to beat wildly at the thought of being all alone in the darkness.

The flames suddenly flared to life again and she felt a hand grab onto her shoulder.

"Thank goodness," Alex said as she spun around. "Why didn't you—*AHHHH!*"

She scrambled backwards to get away from the—*thing*—that had grabbed her. It looked like a man in a suit of armour, except there was no man inside. There was absolutely nothing above the shoulders, just empty space where the neck and head *should* have been. It was a headless, rust-covered suit of armour. And if that wasn't creepy enough, it was also holding an enormous battle axe in the air, as if ready to attack.

She didn't have a moment to wonder about its appearance before the axe swung towards her face.

Alex automatically threw herself out of its path, hitting the ground hard. She scrambled to her feet and gaped at the suit of armour which had just—impossibly—tried to behead her.

Regardless of how supernatural it sounded, she hadn't imagined its attack.

Proving her thoughts true, it moved a step forward while raising the axe again, prompting Alex to react instinctively. She didn't think; she just spun on her heel and ran away as fast as her legs would carry her.

The dead end had transformed into a long, torch-lit corridor, but she had no time to question the strange architectural phenomenon as she sprinted for her life down the hall. She could hear the suit of armour coming after her, its heavy metal clunking with every step it took.

In her mad dash, Alex noticed hundreds of closed doors all along the hallway, interspersed between the solid stone brickwork and flaming torches. Each door looked different from the next, with a dizzying assortment of sizes and shapes. While some were normal, like those which were wooden and simplistic in design, others were made out of brushed glass, strange glowing metals, and even—in one case—some kind of iridescent rainbow cloud.

As curious as she was, Alex was too focused on running away to think about entering any of them. But when the corridor abruptly ended in what looked like a medieval dungeon, she regretted her lack of exploration, since there were no doorways left and she was now trapped.

She spun in a circle, taking in the cobwebs that covered almost every surface of the room and the slime that dribbled down the walls from the ceiling. There was even a set of rusty manacles hanging from the roof. But the most disturbing feature was the human skeleton perched in the corner. Bony hands held the pommel of a gleaming sword, and the head was shielded by a helmet which thankfully covered the entire skull.

It was a disturbing sight and Alex couldn't help but stand and stare for a moment. Then she heard the sound of grinding metal as her pursuer caught up to her and she turned away from the skeleton to face the animated armour.

"Now listen here," Alex said, hoping it could be reasoned with. "I don't know what you think you're doing, but I want to know what you've done with my friends!"

The suit of armour stopped in front of her and she felt her confidence grow. If it hadn't been for the metallic *screech* of warning then she wouldn't have had time to duck when the massive axe whooshed towards her head again at an alarming speed.

For the second time that day, she hurled herself onto the floor and rolled out of the way. She quickly rose to her feet before ducking away again when the axe swooped a second time. Her reflexes were much improved—mostly thanks to Finn's unwavering disciplinary tactics in PE—but she was definitely not capable of fighting this thing. Still, she might be able to knock it over.

The axe swung at her again and, as she dropped to the ground, she kicked out at the knee joint of the armour. The suit wobbled slightly, but if anything, she'd done more damage to herself, since her foot was now throbbing from kicking the unyielding metal.

"This is bad..." Alex murmured and she dodged the approaching axe again. She couldn't keep throwing herself to the ground every time it came at her. It was time to try something else.

After the axe swooped towards her once more, she rolled quickly to her feet and launched herself at her attacker. Alex had hoped to catch it off guard and cause it to topple, but as she straddled the rust-covered torso, she found it to be as immovable as an oak tree.

She, however, was not so fortunate.

The armour wrapped its gauntleted arm around her waist and threw her across the room. She smacked into the rough stone wall with a sickening crunch and collapsed to the ground.

"*Oww.*" Alex made a groaning sound and pulled herself into a sitting position. She didn't think anything was broken, so she couldn't account for the crunching noise until she realised that she'd landed on the skeleton. Her natural reaction was to roll away, gagging, but when she noticed the sword again, she managed to set aside her disgust.

Alex rose painfully and reached for the weapon, shuddering as she pried the skeletal hand off the pommel. She gripped the sword tightly and turned back to face the suit of armour, raising the blade in front of her. It was heavier than she'd expected, but it was still usable.

Before she could so much as blink, the axe was once again swinging towards her head. She was trapped in the corner and had little option but to put all of her adrenaline-fuelled strength into lifting the sword to meet the axe mid-air. The two weapons collided with a horrible metallic screech, and Alex quickly deflected the blade away from her head.

The axe swung at her over and over again, and each time she met the weapon with her sword. But unlike the suit of armour, Alex was quickly running out of energy. She wouldn't be able to continue deflecting its attack for much longer.

"Somebody, please help me!" she cried out.

Her whole body trembled with the effort of maintaining her defence. Sweat beaded on her forehead from exhaustion and fear. Her weakened arms almost dropped the sword after another jarring attack, but she renewed her grip when something caught her eye. Both the sword and the axe had the same engraving etched onto their blades; it looked like a coat of arms with a decorative shield split into three parts.

The breastplate on the suit of armour had the same picture engraved where the heart should have been. Turning her head slightly, Alex found that the helmet on the skeleton was also etched with the same emblem. And from out of nowhere she had an idea.

When their blades met mid-air in the next attack, instead of deflecting the axe, Alex gave one heaving push forward, causing the armour to stumble back. Using her downward momentum, she directed her blade into the bony neck joint of the skeleton lying at her feet. It immediately turned to dust, leaving the helmet sitting amongst a pile of ashes.

Out of the corner of her eye, Alex saw the axe coming towards her head again. Dropping the sword, she scrambled to pick up the helmet, thrusting it in front of her face like a shield. The impact of the axe on the helmet sent her staggering into the wall and she gasped out a grunt, straining against the armour's strength.

The front of the helmet was facing towards her and the coat of arms pulsed slightly with light. Something about the light reminded her of the TechnoConnectivity Devices, which helped her to realise what she needed to do next.

Mustering her last reserve of strength, Alex heaved against the axe with all her might, pushing her attacker off balance and backwards a few steps again. It gave her the room she needed to move into position.

Just as the armour regained its balance, Alex leapt on top of it and held on for dear life. It stumbled again but recovered quickly, and she felt rather than saw its gauntleted arm reach out to throw her off once more. Before it could do so, she tightened her grip and jammed the helmet onto the collar of the armour, pressing her palm to its now glowing coat of arms.

A flash of blinding light filled the room and Alex was thrown into the wall—again. When the light faded and her eyes recovered from her daze, she gaped at the sight in front of her and exclaimed, "I can't *believe* that actually worked."

Nineteen

Alex was breathing heavily and shaking all over, but that didn't matter because standing before her was a full suit of armour, complete with helmet, and no longer rusting. It was gleaming, in fact. But more importantly, it was bowing to her.

When it rose from its bow it kept one gauntleted arm crossed in a formal salute. "How doth thee, fair lady?"

Alex gaped at it. Or rather, at *him*.

"What be thy title?" the armour asked.

"Err... My name is Alex."

He tilted his helmeted head as if confused. "Be not thy title somewhat... masculine?"

She stared at it. Him. Whatever. "My full name is Alexandra, if that makes a difference?"

"Salutations, Lady Alexandra," he said. "My gratitude I bestow upon thee, for ending a much grievous curse."

"You're... welcome?"

"Sir Camden be my name," he said, bowing again. "I shalt forever be in thy debt, and as such I shalt serve and protect thee always."

Alex just continued to gape at him as her heartbeat began to stabilise.

"How doth a fine maiden such as thyself cometh to be thus situated?" he asked. "These here dungeons appear unseemly for a lady. Perchance thou might consent upon a knightly escort from such unsavoury quarters?"

Translation: *I'll lead you out.* Alex was all for that, as long as he wasn't about to go ballistic on her again.

"Just to clarify," she said hesitantly, "you're not going to chop me up into little pieces, are you?"

"The lady need not fear Sir Camden," he said. "I be a Protector Knight of the Highest Order. To induce harm on one such as thyself, I would truly hath to lose my head!"

"Yeah, that sounds about right," Alex mumbled. But in the end, she figured there was nothing for it. "I really should find my friends," she told him. "Will you help me?"

"A quest!" he cried, joyous. "A noble quest to find thy loyal retainers! Fear not, fair lady, for together we shalt uncover the mysteries of thy kinsmen's whereabouts."

He reached down to pick up the sword she'd dropped and secured it into the empty scabbard at his waist. Then he offered her one of his gauntleted arms and, after glancing at it warily, she accepted his steadying grip.

Sir Camden started to lead her down the corridor but after a few steps he paused in front of one of the many doors lining the hallway. When he opened it, Alex couldn't keep from gasping. Spanning out farther than her eyes could see was a vast, grassy wasteland. If Jordan and Bear were in there, there was no way she would ever find them.

But that wouldn't stop her from trying.

When Alex moved to step through the door, Sir Camden closed it in front of her.

"Hey!" she cried.

"Thou kinsmen not be through there," he told her. "And there be naught point in wasting time on useless folly. We shalt continue onwards, fair lady."

He started walking down the corridor again, stopping in front of the next door. This one opened to a tropical rainforest, and it was so real that Alex could actually feel the humidity in the air as it blended with the cool draught in the stone hallway.

When she moved towards it, the knight blocked her path again, so she asked, "How do you know they're not in there? Or in the last one, for that matter?"

"I hath been in this here Library for many millennia," he said. "In such time, I hath discovered many secrets buried within. Thou wouldst do well to favour this knight's judgement on the matter, lest thou wander off at will and perish."

He seemed to know what he was talking about, so she decided to follow his lead. That, and she didn't want to perish.

They continued up the corridor opening doors as they went. Some opened to what Alex considered normal library rooms—the type with actual *books*. But more often than not they opened to incredible sights: a desert, a swampland, a rocky mountainside, a beach at sunset. There was even an underwater city through one of the doors, and Alex was relieved to discover that a protective barrier kept the corridor from flooding.

Unfortunately, that particular barrier wasn't included with one of the other doors that opened to a monsoonal rainstorm. The water felt like daggers from the force of the wind blowing through the doorway, and within seconds Alex and Sir Camden were drenched. The knight grumbled about rusting, but he was kind enough to wait while Alex rung out her dripping clothes.

Her favourite door by far was the one that led to outer space. Just like the underwater door, there was some kind of barrier that kept atmospheric levels balanced so they didn't float off or lose oxygen. And the view was spectacular. Alex could have gazed upon the twinkling stars and distant planets for hours, but Sir Camden pulled her away.

"Can't we have another quick look?" she begged.

He just continued to pull her further down the corridor and said, "When questing, one must be fully committed to one's task, lest one become distracted and conquered."

She actually found the words to be very wise so she let him pull her away without further argument. And she got her own back when the next door opened to an ancient-looking weapons cache that had *everything* in it. There were swords and shields, bows and arrows, and crossbows with bolts already drawn to fire. Spears, scythes, maces—even jousting poles.

Sir Camden was enraptured by the armoury and it was Alex who had the pleasure of closing the door in his face while throwing her own interpretation of his words back at him: "Someone wisely told me that when you're on a mission, you have to be fully committed to your task, otherwise you can get distracted and fail."

He bowed slightly to her. "True words, fair lady, true words."

After a few more doors—including a particularly unpleasant one that opened to a blizzard and left Alex covered in snow and shivering from the cold—she couldn't hold back her questions.

"What's the deal with this Library?" she asked. "Libraries are supposed to be filled with books. I know this one is... special... but what's with all these random doors?"

"A question I shalt use to answer thee," Sir Camden replied. "Perchance two noble knights were to engage in a duel of swordsmanship in order to win the affections of a fair maiden. One such knight hath lived life by his sword. He hath fought in many a battle and won many a challenge. The other knight hath a scholar's reputability. His esteemed intellectual knowledge of swordplay hath titled him a swords master of the highest order, however, he hath little practise with a blade, but for a few basic manoeuvres. Who doth thou believe would win the duel and capture the fair maiden's heart?"

"I feel like I'm stuck in the Middle Ages," Alex murmured. Then she said, louder, "The man with the experience would win. The other guy might know what to do in theory, but he wouldn't have the practical knowledge or experience needed to win the fight."

"Thou art correct, Lady Alexandra," Sir Camden said. "And so true it be with this here Library. Literature may increase one's depth of knowledge, but not all knowledge be found in literature. Only with practical experience can one truly learn and thus be considered knowledgeable."

Wow. He'd surprised her by actually answering her question—and making sense despite his outdated speech.

It was interesting. But it wasn't as much of a surprise as it might have been had she not already experienced the hopscotch room and the tower above the clouds. Not to mention, how she'd fallen from that tower and through those clouds and then opened a previously non-existent door and... well, pretty much every adventure that she'd had in the Library truly was an actual *experience*. She had to admit they had all been kind of exhilarating. In a horror-movie kind of way.

"Perchance thy loyal retainers art where thou last gazed upon them?" Sir Camden asked.

"Huh?"

Alex hadn't realised that they'd reached the end of the corridor. There were no more doors to enter, no more incredible and unbelievable sights to witness—just a dead end with a solid stone wall. But that should have been impossible, because when she'd run away from the headless suit of armour, she'd started at the bottom of a staircase and sprinted straight down the only corridor.

The place was a labyrinth.

As if that wasn't enough, for the second time that day all the torches extinguished, leaving them surrounded by darkness.

"Not again," Alex groaned.

Just like the last time, the light came back quickly. And just like the last time, she was shocked by what was in front of her.

"That was weird," Bear said. "It was like a blackout, but… not."

Alex couldn't believe it. Both her friends were standing at the bottom of the staircase, right where she'd last seen them. She glanced behind her and, sure enough, the room was once again closed off with a solid stone wall. There was no sign of the corridor beyond.

"There must have been some kind of draught or something that blew out the torches. But they seem okay now," Jordan said, before glancing over at Alex and doing a double-take. "Whoa! Check out the wicked-cool suit of armour behind you!"

Alex gaped at him. Was that seriously all he had to say?

"I could've sworn that wasn't there a moment ago," Bear said. "But it *is* pretty cool. And in great condition."

Bear walked towards Sir Camden and reached out to lift his visor, but the knight moved faster and locked his gauntleted hand around her friend's flesh.

"Aghh!" Bear tried unsuccessfully to jerk his arm back. "What the—"

"One doth not disturb a knight's armour without consequence, young sir. Even if one be the fair Lady Alexandra's loyal kinsman. Doth the young lord challenge Sir Camden to a duel in the most noble of contests?"

Bear stared at the knight with wide eyes and a pale face. "Err—huh?"

"He wants to know if you're challenging him to a swordfight," Alex translated.

Bear looked at her, then back to Sir Camden, taking in the lethal sword belted to the knight's waist. He finally looked back to his own arm which was still trapped in a vice-like grip. "Uh—no, thank you," he said. "I'm kind of attached to my limbs."

Jordan chuckled quietly. "No pun intended."

"As thou wish," Sir Camden said, releasing Bear's arm. "Perchance another opportunity shalt avail itself to us at a more agreeable time."

"Not likely," Bear mumbled under his breath as he massaged his wrist. Alex could already see bruises forming on his skin.

"Doth these gentlemen be thy loyal kinsmen, Lady Alexandra?" Sir Camden asked.

"Yes, these are my friends," Alex answered.

"Very good," he replied. "Another quest hath come to a victorious end. I fare thee well, loyal retainers, and I leave the lady under thy protection."

He saluted formally to Jordan and Bear and they mimicked the gesture back to him, albeit awkwardly. The knight seemed satisfied by their attempt and turned to Alex.

"I bid thee farewell, my lady," Sir Camden said, bowing again and raising her hand to where his mouth would be if not for the armour. "Whenever thou hath need of my knightly services, thy need only call for me, and I shalt come to thine aide."

"Thank you for all your help, Sir Camden," she said, gently pulling her hand from his metallic grasp.

"Until next we meet, Lady Alexandra," he said cheerily, turning around and walking straight through the solid stone wall.

Jordan sucked in a surprised breath. "How did he do that?"

Without waiting for an answer, he walked over to the wall, pressing against it. It didn't budge under his weight, and when he vanished Alex guessed he was attempting to use his transcendence gift. A second later he reappeared, apparently unsuccessful.

"I can't get through," he said. "It must be warded like our dorms."

"Where did he come from in the first place?" Bear asked, joining Jordan at the wall. "It was like he just appeared out of nowhere!"

Alex waited in silence while they continued exclaiming their shock over the knight's appearance and disappearance.

"I don't think we're going to get anywhere this way," Jordan finally said. "Let's head back upstairs and see if we can find a secret level somewhere else."

"I agree," said Bear. "There's sure to be heaps of places to find, especially since the Library likes you or whatever, Alex."

"Are you serious?" she finally snapped. "Don't you have any questions for me? Like, 'Are you all right?', 'Where have you been?' or even, 'What's with the deranged knight who tried to kill you but has now declared himself your protector?'"

They looked at her like she was crazy.

"Err... *Are* you all right?" Jordan asked.

"Let's see," she started, her exasperation obvious. "I've just spent hours searching aimlessly for you both, since I had no idea where you were or if you were okay. And that's not even mentioning the years I've had taken off my life from fear of decapitation by an enchanted, headless suit of armour hell-bent on killing me. Which, by the way, was a super fun experience." Her sarcasm may have been a little overdone, but it was justifiable in her opinion.

"So to answer your question: no, I'm *not* all right." She ended her rant. "And quit staring at me like that."

"Maybe you should start at the beginning," Jordan said tentatively.

She crossed her arms. "Oh, so *now* you want to hear about it, huh?"

"Alex," Bear said, walking over and placing a calming hand on her shoulder. "We didn't mean to seem rude, but you have to understand that, as far as we're aware, you've been with us ever since we walked down those stairs a few minutes ago."

"You thought I was with you? Why would you…" Alex took in his troubled expression and frowned. "Did you say a few minutes ago?"

He nodded. She looked over at Jordan who seemed just as confused by her outburst as Bear.

"We only just walked down the stairs," Jordan said. "When the lights went out, it was dark for about three seconds before we could see again. And your knight friend was with us then, Sir Can-Opener or whatever his name was."

"Sir Camden," she said absentmindedly.

"Last week when you fell down the black square, more time passed for you than for us," Bear pointed out. "Maybe the same thing happened again here?"

"There must be some kind of distorted space–time continuum when you actually enter the inner Library areas," Jordan mused. "That would come in handy in *so* many ways."

Alex shook her head in baffled amazement. "Once again, I feel like I've entered a sci-fi movie. And that's ignoring the fact that I'm from another world. This is insane. But there's no other explanation."

She looked at her friends and felt immediately guilty. "I'm sorry for snapping at you both. I was just worried, and then annoyed, and then confused. Not a good combination."

Bear squeezed her shoulder and smiled his acceptance of her apology.

"No sweat, babe," Jordan said with a wink.

She narrowed her gaze. "Don't call me that." He smirked despite her warning tone, so she added, "Or I'll tell Sir Camden that you called him a can-opener and challenged him to a duel."

His smirk dropped right off his face. "Fine," he mumbled, ignoring Bear's laughter. "But we want the entire story. Don't leave anything out."

The three of them sat at the bottom of the staircase while she told them everything that had happened.

When she was finished, Jordan asked, "Do you think you'll ever see him again? Sir Can—er—Camden?"

"Why? Are you worried I'll tattle on you?" she asked.

"I reckon I could take him," Jordan said, flexing his arm muscles.

Bear and Alex burst out laughing and, after mock-scowling at them, Jordan joined in.

"Seriously, though," Bear said, "he seemed pretty adamant that you'd meet again."

"After I gave him back his head—and how weird does that sound?—he said he would be forever in my service. I just have to call and he'll come, apparently."

"Stalker alert," Jordan said with a chuckle.

"I'm sorry we weren't there when you needed us," Bear said, "but it sounds like you did more than okay on your own."

"Yeah," Jordan agreed. "Still, I wish we could've come. I would've loved to have seen those doorways. Maybe the Library will let us go with you on the next adventure?"

"I hope so," Alex said. She felt proud of what she'd accomplished on her own, but she would have had more fun with Bear and Jordan by her side.

Her stomach chose that moment to interrupt their conversation by grumbling at an embarrassingly loud pitch.

"Hungry?" Bear said.

Alex snorted. "What gave me away?"

"Come on," Jordan said, pulling her to her feet. "I think you've had enough excitement for the day. Let's go get you some food."

No argument here, Alex thought, and she followed her friends back up the stairs.

Twenty

The next week of classes crawled by so slowly that it was officially dubbed the 'Never-Ending Week'. When Friday finally rolled around, Alex's first three subjects dragged on *forever*, but when the gong sounded at the end of Chemistry, she could practically see the light at the end of the tunnel. All she had to do was get through one more class and she'd be on holidays for the next two weeks.

"I can't believe Fitzy's still going on about how great your fireball was," Jordan said with a laugh as they left their Chemistry room and started down the corridor.

"I know!" Alex said, remembering how she'd accidentally blown up half the lab earlier that week. "It wasn't even that impressive—it may have looked big, but it didn't damage much. No staying power."

"Says the girl who walked around for three hours without any eyebrows," Jordan murmured.

"Yeah, well, at least Fletcher was able to fix my problem with that healing paste. He can't do anything to fix what's wrong with your face."

"Ha ha," Jordan said dryly. "You've got Combat now, haven't you? I don't even know why you bother going anymore since all you do is sit and watch."

"It's the principle," Alex said. "Karter's made it very clear he doesn't want me there, and even though I certainly don't want to be there either, my pride is at stake. I refuse to let him see me quit, even if I'm not actively participating."

She paused before quietly adding, "And maybe a little part of me is hoping that one day he'll get so sick of seeing me sitting on the sidelines that he'll start teaching me something simple, something I can handle."

"Well, good luck with that today," Jordan said. "I've got to run if I want to make it to Archery. We're meant to be out in the forest and I'm hoping Finn will be mapping out his new obstacle course so I can *accidentally* shoot an arrow through his—"

"Jordan! Hurry up!" Mel called out over the sea of students. She stood with Bear near the entrance to Gen-Sec, and when Alex and Jordan headed over to them, she bounced excitedly and chanted, "Last class, last class, last class!"

"Didn't you just have PE?" Alex asked. "How do you have so much energy?"

"Finn was easy on us Betas today," Mel said. "All we had to do was map out the new obstacle course he's planning for some of the upper levels when classes start back."

Jordan muttered unhappily under his breath, clearly disappointed that he wouldn't get a chance to try and shoot their teacher.

"I don't envy you guys," Mel continued. "Finn is a genius— an evil genius, but a genius no less. You're going to *die*!"

"I'm so glad you're finding joy in our potential demise," Alex said, unable to keep the bitterness from her tone.

Mel grinned. "You know you love my positive outlook on life."

Alex shook her head in exasperation, but her lips curved into a smile. Mel really was a lot of fun; it was a shame she and Connor were rarely around.

"Time to go, guys," Bear said, hustling everyone along.

They parted ways and Alex headed towards the Arena, resigned to waste the next two hours while her classmates beat each other up.

After she took her seat on the sidelines, Alex watched as the five boys stretched and talked amongst themselves. As far as she knew, only two of them had a close friendship outside of class—Declan Stirling, the tank of a guy who had decked her on her first day, and Kaiden James. Both were in the year above Alex, while her other three classmates were older. Sebastian Gibbs and Nick Baxter were in their fifth year, and Brendan Labinsky was a first year apprentice. Despite their age differences, they all got along well, and they were indisputably the best Akarnae had to offer when it came to physical fighting and defence.

Alex still had *no* idea whose sick idea of a joke it had been to stick her in with them.

"Jennings!" Karter bellowed when he entered the Arena.

She turned to face him, surprised he'd even acknowledged her presence. Usually he ignored her completely.

"Sir?"

He glared at her until she hesitantly stood and walked over to him.

"Yes, sir?" she tried again.

"Tell me what you've learned since joining this class," Karter ordered.

Alex gaped at him. Was he serious? Didn't he remember his orders for her to sit and be silent in every class?

She looked closely at him, trying to guess his intention. His gaze was narrowed, but there was something in his eyes—a challenge. Well, she wasn't going to back down. She might not have learned anything by her own experience, but she'd spent hours observing the others.

Alex ignored the condescending stares of her classmates

and blurted out the first thing that came to mind: "Brendan is arrogant."

Her eyes widened, but she couldn't take the words back, so she continued quickly to cover the amused and indignant noises coming from her classmates. "His technique is solid, but he's overconfident of his own ability and often relies on brute strength which makes his movements sloppy."

She sneaked a peek at the oldest boy in the group and found him scowling at her. Big surprise. She really didn't want him killing her in her sleep or anything, so she hurried to say something complimentary. "When he's not being cocky"—she heard a hiss but continued anyway—"he has a lot going for him. When he doesn't taunt his opponents and actually focuses on what he's doing, very little can get past his defences."

Alex didn't risk looking at Brendan again, but at least he wasn't hissing any more. She quickly moved on to her next victim. "Declan is a machine—I've learned that first-hand." She smiled at him tentatively and he surprised her with a friendly wolf-grin back. "His size is intimidating enough to make anyone think twice before attacking him, but if they were stupid enough to take him on, he's actually got some mad skills up his sleeve."

She went on to list the rest of her observations about Declan, and then Nick and Sebastian too, until only one classmate remained.

"Kaiden is..." she searched for the best word before settling on, "creative. He's quick on his feet and he's a master of improvisation. His actual technique makes fighting seem effortless, but it's his resourcefulness that makes him such a dangerous weapon. And if there's one thing I've learned in this class, it's that Combat isn't all about strength and power; it's about creativity and out-of-the-box thinking. That's what'll keep you standing long after your opponent has hit the ground."

Alex trailed off into silence, which continued to the point where she actually heard a cricket chirping in the background. The lack of noise was so uncomfortable that she made the mistake of looking around, and she immediately became trapped in Kaiden's curious stare. She'd never been close enough before to notice how incredibly blue his eyes were. They complimented his dark hair and tanned complexion perfectly. He was one of those naturally gorgeous guys—the kind who were automatically off-limits because they were usually too good to be true.

He raised a questioning eyebrow and she quickly averted her eyes, embarrassed to have been caught staring back.

"Right," Karter grunted, finally breaking the prolonged silence. "At least you haven't been twiddling your thumbs and thinking about shoes during my class."

Alex jerked with shock. That was about as close to a 'well done' as she'd ever heard him give anyone.

"But since you're such an *expert*," he continued, and she cringed at his inflection, "then you're wasting away on the sidelines, aren't you?"

It was clearly a statement, not a question.

"You lot, pair up and get started," he told her classmates, all of whom were still staring at her as if they'd never seen her before. "Jennings, come with me."

Alex scrambled to keep up with Karter as he led her through an archway in the side of the Arena and into a large, sheltered space.

"Suit up," Karter commanded, gesturing towards some padded armour hanging on the wall.

Alex did as ordered, and after donning a helmet, protective vest, and knee and elbow guards, she looked and felt ready for some reasonably hard-core rollerblading.

Karter, however, had other ideas.

"Do the course as many times as you need until you can complete it from start to finish without mistake," he ordered, pressing on a remote TCD terminal by the door.

Within moments the room came to life as objects around the floor started moving, forming what looked to be an obstacle course. There were dangling ropes, rock walls, ditches, slime pools, stepping stones, and even a *moving* balancing beam located underneath three heavy-looking, swinging sandbags.

It wasn't an obstacle course, Alex realised—it was a *hospital* course. Because that was surely where she would end up afterwards.

"Come find me when you're done," Karter said, walking out of the room. "But only when you can do it perfectly."

She looked at the menacing course and gulped before taking a step towards the first obstacle.

Twenty-One

Karter arrived to check on her progress at the end of their two-hour class. Unfortunately, Alex had yet to complete the course without falling, tripping, hitting or slipping, which meant she was stuck there until he was satisfied.

She was covered in scratches from the thorn-filled ditches and coated with slimy gunk from sliding off the swing-ropes— not to mention soaked to the bone and covered from head to toe with mud. But, despite all that, she'd finally figured out a strategy for getting around safely and she was confident that if Karter hadn't scared her when he'd entered the room and yelled at her to hurry up, then she just might have made it through in time to leave with everyone else.

Instead, the interruption broke her concentration and led to her being smacked in the head by a swinging sandbag. The force of the hit knocked her off the narrow balancing beam and into the muddy bog below. It wasn't the first time she'd come off the beam, but it *was* the first time she'd been hit by the heavy bag—and it *hurt*, even with her protective gear cushioning the impact. She ended up just sitting in the mud for a moment, completely dazed.

"Get up, Jennings! You're wasting my time!" Karter barked, and she had little choice but to move.

Alex's newly pounding headache and ringing ears messed with her balance so much that it took another half hour before

Karter was satisfied enough with her performance to let her go. She smiled with exhausted relief, but that wasn't how he interpreted her expression.

"Don't look so cocky, Jennings," he grunted. "You were on the easiest setting and it *still* took you longer than any student I've ever had before. When you come back after the holidays I'll be increasing the level of difficulty and I'll continue to do so every week. I doubt you'll be smiling much then."

"I wasn't—" she broke off, realising there was no point in defending herself.

"And make sure you go and visit the Med Ward before dinner," Karter ordered. "You're a mess."

As a result of the extra time she'd been stuck on the obstacle course and her unplanned visit to see Fletcher, Alex didn't have long before the food court was due to close for the night. She looked disgusting and probably smelled awful, but she was also starving. If she stopped off to have a shower first, there was no way she'd make it back in time to eat. So, after deliberating for a moment, she decided to risk it and hope that the other students had already finished and returned to their dorms to pack for the holidays.

When she entered the food court it *was* emptier than usual, but there were still a few stragglers around. She heard muffled laughter as she walked further in and saw the guys from her Combat class still eating. Clearly they'd had time to shower and clean up, unlike herself.

"Still alive?" Declan called out to her from across the room.

"Piece of cake," she called back, thankful that Fletcher's painkillers kept her from hobbling like an old woman in front of them.

They laughed again—at her, not with her—and she hurried to find a table with some kind of privacy.

Glancing around the room, she spotted D.C. sitting alone in the corner with her head buried in a book. Perfect. No one would bother her if she was with the difficult girl. Alex had learned early on that the red-head was a people-repellent. Everyone knew to stay away from her lest they face her wrath. It was exactly what Alex needed at the moment.

"Hey, Roomie." Alex took a seat at the table.

D.C. looked up in surprise. "Can I help you?" she asked, clearly annoyed by the interruption.

"Nope," Alex said, popping the 'p'.

She picked up a menu and ordered at random, so hungry that she didn't even care what she ate. Almost instantly her meal arrived—a hamburger with salad on the side—and she started eating with relish. After a few bites she felt D.C.'s eyes on her, so she looked up.

"You stink."

Alex almost choked on her mouthful. She quickly ordered a glass of water and guzzled it down to help clear her throat. "Gee, thanks."

"And you look terrible," D.C. added.

"Don't hold back now," Alex said.

D.C. didn't ask for any explanations about her appearance and Alex didn't feel inclined to enlighten her; she had already accepted the fact that D.C. didn't want anything to do with her. In fact, other than in class and sometimes just before bed, they hardly ever saw each other.

It was kind of sad. Alex could have used a close female friend, especially when she was surrounded by guys most of the time. But it was clear D.C. wasn't interested in friendship—with anyone.

Despite all that, Alex was still curious about her, so she asked, "What are you reading?"

"A book."

Right. That was helpful.

"Is it good?" Alex tried again.

"Would I be reading it if it wasn't?" came the response.

"It could be a textbook."

"It's not."

"So, it's a novel?" Alex guessed.

D.C. sighed and put the book on the table, marking her place. "No, it's not a novel," she said, her voice tight with irritation. "If I answer your question, will you shut up?"

Alex took another bite while she pretended to think about it. "Maybe."

D.C. made an annoyed sound and pushed her chair back, ready to leave.

"Hey, don't go!" Alex still needed her people-repelling buffer around until she finished eating. "I promise I'll be quiet."

The other girl eyed her warily before slowly taking her seat again. She then did something unexpected and slid her book over so that Alex could see the cover. *The Lost City: What Really Happened* by A. N. Onymous.

Alex snorted at the author's name, but then she focused on the title again. "*The Lost City?*" she asked, handing the book back. "What lost city?"

D.C. looked at her strangely. "Meya, of course. What other cities have just disappeared?"

"Oh, right," Alex said. "Meya."

Alex remembered what Darrius had told her about the missing city. She would never forget the image of the enchantingly beautiful Meyarins, but she was pretty sure he'd said they were kind of a taboo subject. She wondered how her roommate, of all people, had managed to get her hands on such a book.

"What does it say really happened?" Alex asked, curious.

"I thought we agreed you'd shut up once I told you what I was reading?" D.C. said, opening the book to start reading again.

"Right," Alex murmured. Conversation over.

She picked at her salad and gulped the rest of her water before standing and saying, "I guess I'll see you later?"

"You're deductive skills are astounding," D.C. replied, not looking up from her book.

Alex clenched her teeth and walked away before she could say anything she would regret. She headed straight for her dormitory and, after a much-needed shower, she ventured down to the Rec Room in search of Jordan and Bear.

"Finally!" Jordan greeted Alex when she found both her friends hanging out with Connor and Mel. "Where have you been?"

"Karter decided it was time for me to start pulling my weight," she said, collapsing onto a beanbag in front of the fire. "He kept me back late and I had to visit Fletcher afterwards."

"That sucks," Connor said. "I'm only Gamma for Combat, but I don't think that matters to Karter. It's almost like he can smell weakness."

Alex wasn't sure how to take his comment, so she just smiled at him and gave what she hoped was a supportive look. "Yeah," she agreed. "Listen guys, sorry to be lame, but I'm wrecked. I pretty much just came here to find out what's happening tomorrow." She addressed her comment to Bear and Jordan since she was leaving with them in the morning.

"Mum sent over a Bubbler earlier in the week so we can take off whenever we want," Bear told her, referring to the vial of liquid that, when smashed on the ground, opened a Bubbledoor. "The sooner we're out of here, the sooner our holiday starts, so I say we aim to leave early-ish."

"What about the wards?" Alex asked, confused.

"They'll be deactivated tomorrow so students can leave," Jordan explained, "and they'll be taken down again at the end of the holiday when we all come back. It happens at the beginning and end of every break so we can come and go easier."

"Oh," Alex said, seeing the logic in that.

"Do you reckon you'll be okay to leave straight after breakfast?" Bear asked, bringing the conversation back around.

She nodded. "Sounds perfect. I'm really looking forward to meeting your family and seeing somewhere outside the academy."

Alex noticed the questioning looks the cousins sent her way and realised that she hadn't been careful enough with her words. "It's been so long, I mean," she covered, "since I arrived and all. It feels like I've been here forever. It'll be nice to get away... again."

She'd never been a very good liar, but thankfully Jordan came to her rescue.

"Yeah, it does feel like forever," he said. "I think we're all pretty excited for the break. I can't wait to have some of Gammy's apple pie. Mmm." He smacked his lips and rubbed his stomach. Alex thought he might have even been drooling a little.

"We go home every weekend, so it's not such a big deal for us," Mel said. "But still, it'll be nice to not have classes and homework for a fortnight."

Alex agreed wholeheartedly. Two weeks with no PE sounded heavenly. She was about to respond but her words were cut off when she yawned.

"You should go to bed," Jordan said. "You're going to need your energy for the next two weeks."

"Holidays are meant to be relaxing," she informed him.

"You've never been on holiday with us before," Bear said, grinning. "You might even need a holiday from your holiday."

Just the idea of it made Alex feel even more tired, so she bid them goodnight and stumbled up to her room.

She was asleep before her head even hit the pillow.

Twenty-Two

"Excuse me, Alex, may I have a word before you leave?"

Alex quickly swallowed the last of her breakfast and looked up to find Administrator Jarvis standing at the head of her table.

"Sure," she said, leaving her friends and following him outside and around the corner for some privacy.

"Firstly," he began, "I'd like to apologise for not contacting you before now. It's been some time since we last discussed your transition into academy life and I should have paid more attention to you, especially considering your unique circumstances."

"Don't worry about it," she said, waving aside his words. "I'm sure you've had a lot to deal with, what with the headmaster still gone and everything else." She didn't mention the Lockdown, but she was sure it was still causing Jarvis some concern, if the bags under his eyes and his pale complexion were any indication. "And besides," she continued, "you know what they say about the whole sink-or-swim concept. Sometimes it's good to be thrown straight into the deep end."

"From what your instructors have said, you've become quite adept at treading water," he said with a smile.

Alex snorted in disbelief. "They're lying."

He chuckled before turning serious again. "There's something else I'd like to talk to you about."

She nodded, prompting him to continue.

"I understand that you're staying with the Ronnigans for the holiday, is that right?"

"Yeah. Jordan spends Kaldoras with them every year and Bear invited me along this time. They didn't want me to be left here on my own."

"Of course, of course," Jarvis said. "Very kind of them."

"Is there a problem?" she asked when he trailed off into silence.

He shook his head as if to clear his thoughts. "No, no problem. I'd just like to caution you—while I know you're a smart girl, and I'm sure your friends and the Ronnigans will take good care of you, you must stay on your guard. It's still vitally important that no one discovers where you're from, especially now that you have access to the Library and its secrets."

"You know about that?" she asked, surprised.

"Professor Marselle contacted me as soon as you were Chosen," Jarvis explained.

"*He* knows about that?" she asked, even more surprised.

"He's the headmaster—of course he knows," Jarvis said. "His position affords him the responsibility of knowing the truth about the Library, much like yourself."

"And you?" Alex asked, wondering how Jarvis fit into the picture.

"Much like your friends—who I presume you've told—I'm not Chosen, nor do I have the access granted to a headmaster. All I know is that there are some who are able to discover the Library's mysteries, and that you are one of them. Again, it is vitally important that you keep this secret."

"I know," Alex said. "I've already been given the lecture." When he looked at her sternly over his glasses she tried to take back her flippant remark. "I mean, yes, I'll be careful."

"Good," he answered, apparently satisfied. "Now, there's one last matter I need to speak with you about. I've never mentioned it before, but your enrolment here lists you as a scholarship benefactor due to your… unorthodox circumstances. As such, you're entitled to certain benefits."

Jarvis reached into his pocket and pulled out a leather pouch, handing it to her. It was heavier than expected, and something inside jingled with the movement.

"Akarnae's scholarship students receive a monetary support supplement in addition to having their educational fees waived," Jarvis said. "I've been keeping track of your allowance since there was no point in giving it to you before now, but it'll likely come in handy for you over the next couple of weeks. Especially with Kaldoras just around the corner."

Alex's eyes widened. He was giving her *money*? She'd never actually thought about how she would support herself outside of the academy. She hadn't even considered how she would afford to buy Kaldoras gifts for her friends. But now she didn't have to worry about any of that.

"The pouch is self-updating and accessible only by your DNA fingerprint," Jarvis said. "Your allowance is deposited weekly and anything you don't use will remain in a networked savings account for when you have need of it. Just be sure not to let anyone else put their hand in the pouch, as they'll find themselves without their fingers."

Medoran technology was amazing. Alex felt like she was holding her own little bank—a very secure little bank. "How much is in here?" she asked, weighing the bag between her hands.

"Enough to last you for a while, I dare say," he responded cryptically. "You'll find that we're rather generous when it comes to supporting our students."

He indicated for her to put the pouch away and when she tucked it into her pocket he asked, "Is there anything else you'd like to discuss before we return to your friends?"

Alex was going to deny it, but she figured it was better to finally get it off her chest even if she didn't think there was anything to worry about anymore. "Actually, there is," she said. "You know a few weeks ago when the academy security triggered the Lockdown?"

Jarvis froze and Alex worried if perhaps she shouldn't have brought the subject up. But there was no going back now.

"Well, after it was all clear and we were allowed out again, I ran into a man on my way to your meeting. It was actually the second time I'd seen him, the first being the day I arrived in Medora."

"A man?" Jarvis asked, his posture as tense as a brick wall. "What man?"

"He said his name was Aven."

Jarvis showed no outward reaction, but his next words sounded strained. "Did he say anything else?"

"He was kind of weird both times," she said, mentally replaying their conversations. "He mentioned that he used to be a student here, and I'm pretty sure he came to see Professor Marselle. I told him the headmaster was away but you were here if he wanted to speak with someone else."

Jarvis seemed to be concentrating on her intently, and Alex wasn't sure whether that was a good or bad sign.

"He, uh, said he didn't want to bother you and that he'd just come back another day," she told him.

"Is that all he said?"

"Yes," Alex answered, before remembering something else. "Oh, wait, both times he went on about some kind of power he expected me to have. I thought he was referring to my gift—which I still don't have, by the way—but he seemed to be talking about something else entirely."

Jarvis was so still that Alex wondered if he was even breathing.

"And how did you reply?"

"I didn't," she answered. "The first time I was disoriented and thought he was a nutcase, and the second time D.C. interrupted us and he took off before I could say anything."

Jarvis sent her a sharp look. "Your roommate saw him too?"

"No." Alex shook her head. "At least, she said she didn't."

He seemed to think about that before he relaxed slightly and asked, "Why didn't you tell me about this sooner, Alex?"

"I just didn't want to cause a fuss over nothing. I'd forgotten all about our first encounter in the forest since I was so distracted with settling in here, and as for the second meeting... well, I overheard Fletcher telling someone that alumni were always welcome on academy grounds and could get through whatever security wards the headmaster had set up, so I just presumed Aven was telling the truth and wasn't any kind of threat."

"Then why bring this to me now?" Jarvis asked.

"Because I did some research and I wasn't satisfied with the results." At his questioning look, she explained, "Aven didn't look much older than thirty and I was curious about him because he was..."

She paused, trying to find a more appropriate description than 'hot'.

"There was just something about him," she finally said. "Something that captured my attention." She shuffled her feet and hurried on to say, "I wanted to make sure his story checked out, so I went to the Archives and looked up the academy records from the past fifteen years. It took some time, but he didn't come up in any of the class lists. Since I didn't have any evidence or proof that he even existed— let alone that he was here—I let it go, not seeing a point in bothering anyone."

Jarvis appeared to be lost in thought and Alex nervously moved from foot to foot while she waited for him to speak.

"Thank you for telling me about this, Alex," he eventually said. "I'm acquainted with the man you speak of and I'll be sure to pass the message on to Professor Marselle that Aven was here to meet with him."

Alex wilted with relief. She'd worried for a moment that she'd made a huge mistake by not going to Jarvis straight away with her report. Fortunately, that didn't appear to be the case.

"If you ever have any concerns regarding strangers on campus again, please don't hesitate to bring them to my or another professor's attention. *Your* safety is paramount," Jarvis said.

Alex thought his emphasis on '*your* safety' seemed a little odd, but she presumed he'd meant it to encompass all the students— not just her—despite how it had sounded.

"Yes, sir," she agreed.

"Good," he said, nodding. "Now, let's head back before your friends come searching for you."

They retraced their steps until they stopped at the entrance to the food court.

"I hope you enjoy Kaldoras, Alex," Jarvis said. "And remember to stay on your guard."

Alex promised to do so and headed inside, thinking all the while about how strange their conversation had been.

Twenty-Three

"Are you ready for this?" Bear asked ten minutes later as he led the way out onto the grounds.

Alex fidgeted with her backpack and said, "As ready as I'll ever be."

"You'll be fine," he encouraged. "My family can't wait to meet you."

"No pressure then, huh?"

He laughed. "It's not like you're my girlfriend. You don't actually *have* to impress them, you know."

"You can be my girlfriend, if you want," Jordan said, winking at her.

She made a face at him. "In your dreams."

"Break it up, you two, or Mum'll give you both 'the talk'," Bear said. Then he cocked his head thoughtfully and added, "Actually, never mind. That'd be hilarious to watch."

"As hilarious as the time she gave *us* 'the talk'?" Jordan asked.

Alex burst out laughing. "*What?*"

"Total misunderstanding," Bear murmured, looking uncomfortable. "Jordan was giving me some pointers about how to talk to the girl I had a crush on a few years back. Mum overheard part of the conversation and jumped to the wrong conclusion."

"I couldn't look her in the eyes for a week," Jordan said with a chuckle. "But it sure gave Bear the incentive he needed to go get his girl."

Alex had to hold her stomach she was laughing so hard.

"No wonder you want me to act like your girlfriend," she said, elbowing Jordan. She then turned her attention back to Bear and told him, "I'm suddenly feeling much more confident. Let's get out of here."

Bear grinned in response and pulled a Bubbler vial out of his pocket, throwing it at the ground. As soon as the iridescent portal was large enough, he picked up his backpack and stepped through.

Alex waited for him to get clear before she approached the colourful wobbling substance. She'd seen a few Bubbledoors open up in her time at Akarnae, but she'd never used one herself. Nor had she ever been so close to one. It truly was beautiful, with the sunshine glinting off the rainbow-coloured, bubble-like substance.

"Any day now," Jordan drawled, pulling her from her observations.

"Patience is a virtue, you know," Alex said.

"I have too many virtues already. I don't think my personality could handle any more."

Alex shook her head at his arrogance and stepped forward into the Bubbledoor. She was instantly surrounded by the colourful light as her weightless body travelled across a vast distance at an impossible speed. She almost fell flat on her face when the movement stopped, and she was still trying to get her feet under her when Jordan walked straight out behind her like a pro. No jelly-legs for him, apparently.

"That was so cool!" she said, finally managing to steady herself enough to look around and note the woodland surrounding them. "I wish we had these back home."

"They're not hard to make," Bear told her. "All you need is the proper chemical equation and the right ingredients."

Alex snorted. "So says the Chemistry genius. Most of the stuff we learn about in Fitzy's class isn't even possible in Freya. Before coming here I'd never even heard of—"

"You know the great thing about holidays?" Jordan interrupted loudly. "The fact that we don't have to talk about anything academy-related. Like Chemistry."

Both Alex and Bear understood the not so subtle hint and dropped their conversation without argument.

"How far away is your house?" Alex asked Bear.

"Turn around," he said.

Alex did so and she couldn't help but smile at her first glimpse of Bear's home. The Bubbledoor had delivered them onto a little cobbled path that wound from the edge of a forest straight up to a cottage. Well, 'cottage' probably wasn't the best description, since it was quite a large house. But it was just so homey-looking, with wildflowers in the garden and a half-sized wooden picket fence. Vines grew along the walls of the house, making it look like something out of a fairytale. All in all, it was completely enchanting.

"Wow, Bear, this place is amazing," Alex said.

He shrugged, but she could see his pleased expression out of the corner of her eye. "It's home."

"Let's get inside," Jordan said. "I'm *starving*."

"You just ate breakfast!" Alex was amazed yet again at the never-ending pit that was Jordan's stomach.

"That doesn't mean I'm not hungry again," he said, nudging them forward.

Bear led the way up the winding path and pushed open a wooden gate that squeaked a little on its hinges. As they approached the house, Alex saw a curtain flutter on the other side of one of the windows. When they were just steps away from reaching the front door, it was thrown open and a blurry missile launched itself at Bear.

"BARNY!" the missile squealed.

Bear laughed and picked up the little girl who had attached herself to him. He threw her up in the air before catching her again and swinging her around in his arms while she giggled madly. When they were both so dizzy that they had to stop, he set her back on her feet and she stumbled over to give Jordan a hug.

"Jordie!" she greeted, just as enthusiastically.

"Hey, kiddo!" Jordan said as he picked the little girl up and squeezed her tightly. She started laughing when he began to tickle her mercilessly.

"Stop! Stop!" she gasped.

"Never!" he cried, cackling maliciously.

"I'll tell Mummy"—she tried to say between laughs—"that it was you"—she hiccupped—"who broke her favourite vase last year!"

Jordan stopped immediately and lowered her to the ground, raising his hands in surrender. "How do you know about that?"

"I know *everything*," she said, with the confidence only one so young could exhibit. She then turned and squealed again, throwing herself at a surprised Alex. "We're going to have *so* much fun together!" she sing-songed as she hung from Alex's waist.

Not sure what to do, Alex hesitantly put her arms around the smaller girl. "I—um—can't wait?" she said, looking to Bear for some kind of explanation.

"Evie, let go of Alex for a second," Bear said. "Do you remember how to introduce yourself properly?"

The little girl released Alex from her surprisingly strong grip and stood up as tall as she could—which meant that she reached Alex's hip.

"Hello," the girl said in her most proper voice. "My name is Evelyn Louise Ronnigan. I'm five years old and I live here with my family. It's very nice to meet you."

Alex tried not to laugh when the child who had been wrapped around her a moment ago held out a hand to shake. Instead, Alex knelt down so they were at eye level and she formally took Evelyn's hand in her own.

"Hello, Evelyn," Alex said seriously, shaking the offered hand. "I'm Alexandra. But you can call me Alex."

Evelyn beamed and bounced excitedly on her feet, causing her brown ringlets to swing wildly around her head. "You have to call me Evie! Evelyn is only for when I'm in trouble."

"Evie it is," Alex agreed, and the little girl smiled even wider. She then grabbed Alex's hand and pulled her into the house, leaving the boys to follow along behind them.

"MUMMY!" Evie called out. "THEY'RE HERE!"

A middle-aged woman with light brown hair and piercing blue eyes walked into the hallway, wiping her hands on her apron. "Evelyn, remember what we said about not yelling in the house?"

Evie hung her head. "Sorry, Mummy."

"I'll let it go this time," Mrs. Ronnigan said, "but next time you'll be given a time-out."

The little girl nodded eagerly, happy to get off with a warning. Then the older woman turned to the three newcomers.

"Sweetheart," she said, holding her arms out for Bear.

Jordan was closer and he jokingly stepped into her embrace. "Hey, Dotti!" he said, hugging her fiercely while Bear tried unsuccessfully to swat him away. "I've missed you!"

"I'm sure you have, Jordan," Bear's mother remarked dryly, but she was smiling at him. "Or, rather, you've missed my cooking."

"You're a package deal," he said cheekily, before Bear finally elbowed him out of the way.

"Hi, Mum," Bear said, wrapping his arms around his mother. She was tall, but he still dwarfed her in his embrace. "It's good to see you."

"We've missed you," she said softly.

Alex felt like she was intruding on what should have been a private moment, but no one seemed to mind her presence. Evie was happily swinging their joined hands as if they'd known each other for years.

Looking at the close-knit family, Alex's heart gave a melancholic pang as she wondered about her parents and what they were doing for their Christmas holiday. Even though her life at the academy kept her busy enough not to feel too homesick, she still missed them. But she knew that even if she was back in Freya, they would still be half a world away from her. At least this way she was with her friends. She only hoped that wherever her parents were, they were enjoying themselves.

When Mrs. Ronnigan finally let her son go, she turned to Alex with a warm smile and said, "Bear has told us so much about you, Alex. We're so pleased you could come and stay with us."

She shocked Alex by hugging her tightly, as if she too was a part of the family.

"Thank you for having me, Mrs. Ronnigan," Alex said. "I can't tell you how much it means to me that you've opened your home to a complete stranger."

"Nonsense," the other woman said, waving away her gratitude. "The more the merrier, as we Ronnigans like to say. And feel free to call me Dorothy. But *not* Dotti." She said the last while directing a frown towards Jordan, to which he just smiled innocently in response.

"Bear, why don't you take your friends upstairs and get them settled," Dorothy suggested. "Knowing you boys, you're probably hungry, so come back down when you're done and Gammy and I will have something ready for you."

"Apple pie?" Jordan asked hopefully.

"We'll see," Dorothy said, and she took Evie's hand and walked back through the door she'd entered from.

"Let's go," Jordan said, eager to speed things along.

As they walked up the hallway towards the staircase, Bear played the courteous host. "There are three levels to our house," he said. "Here on the bottom floor we have the kitchen, dining room, lounge room, and Dad's office. He tries not to bring work home with him but sometimes that can't be helped."

Alex had no idea what Bear's dad did for work, but before she could ask, he continued with the tour.

"Gammy also has a room on this floor, but it's more like a self-contained flat that joins onto the kitchen." They reached the staircase and started up it while Bear continued, "You'll be staying in Blake's room on the second floor, Alex. Mum has already set it up for you."

"Who's Blake?" Alex asked.

"My brother," Bear said. "He's going to bunk in with Johnny, my other brother, when they arrive."

"I'm fine just sleeping on a couch somewhere," Alex told him. "I don't want anyone to be put out because of me."

"They don't mind," he said. "And besides, they're not due here until Kaldoras Eve because of work, and they'll only be able to stay for a few days. You'll be much more comfortable this way."

Bear went on to explain that other than Blake's room, the second floor had the main bathroom, his parents' room, and Evie's room. After pointing out each of their bedrooms, he led her straight to where she would be staying.

Blake's room was nice. Really nice, actually. There was a big, comfortable-looking bed along with a large desk and a built-in wardrobe. Best of all were the huge double windows that looked straight out the side of the house and into the forest that surrounded Bear's home.

"Nice view," Alex said as she put down her backpack and sat on the bed. "Where are you both sleeping?"

"In the attic," Bear answered.

"The attic?"

"It's awesome," Jordan said. "They've added a wall down the middle so that Bear's room is on one side and Johnny's is on the other. Both rooms are massive, with more than enough space for me to stay up there too."

"Huh," Alex said, trying to reconcile the image she had of spider-infested attics with what she presumed was her friend's bedroom. She shook her head and moved on. "I can't believe I never asked you about your family before, Bear. I had no idea you had brothers and a sister. Is it just the four of you?"

"Yep," he said. "Just us."

"What about you, Jordan?" she asked. "Do you have any siblings?"

Jordan's body became rigid, but he cleared his throat and answered, "No, it's just me."

She knew he was sensitive when it came to his family so she turned her attention back to Bear, which prompted Jordan to visibly relax once again.

"Tell me about your brothers, Bear. What do they do?"

He shared a secret grin with Jordan before saying, "I think it'll be more interesting if you hear it from them."

Alex was even more curious now, but all she said was, "If you say so."

The boys left her to unpack and took off up into the attic, but they returned barely five minutes later with Jordan claiming starvation. Alex had to practically run after them as they led the way back downstairs into the dining room where they found an elderly lady sitting at the table. She could only be the infamous Gammy.

"Do you have a hug for an old woman, Barnold?"

She was exactly as Alex had imagined. Grey-haired, short and plump. Her wrinkly face was lit up with a smile and her entire presence exuded warmth and love.

"If you can find me an old woman, Gammy, I'll be happy to give her a hug," Bear said. "Until then, you'll have to take her place."

It was so cheesy, but Alex still smiled at her friend's response, watching as he wrapped his grandmother in his arms. She was almost the size of a child next to his bulkiness.

"Don't think you're getting away without some loving, sonny," Gammy said to Jordan after releasing her grandson. She wagged a wooden spoon at him threateningly until he engulfed her in a hug too.

"Looking good, Gammy," Jordan said when he pulled away. "You must be knocking back the blokes with that spoon of yours."

"Cheeky as always," she huffed at him, her eyes crinkling. "Now sit down and let old Gammy feed you."

Alex moved to take a seat as well, but Gammy stopped her by gently grasping her hand.

"Not you, dear," the older woman said. "You can follow me. I want to learn all about the young woman who's keeping my boys in line."

"Pity we left her back at the academy," Jordan quipped.

"Hush," Gammy silenced him. "Or there'll be no pie for you."

It was like she'd said the magic words, since he immediately closed his mouth and sat down.

Gammy led Alex by the hand into the kitchen and pulled out a stool for her to sit on.

"Can I help with anything?" Alex asked, watching the older woman flit around while stirring this, adding that, and pouring here and there.

"Thank you, dear, but I'm almost done." As she spoke, Gammy turned off the stove, rinsed her hands and put on some padded mittens. She opened the oven and pulled out the most delicious-looking dessert Alex had ever seen in her life. It was the legendary apple pie, and even though she had yet to taste it, Alex suddenly understood what Jordan had been raving about. It truly was a work of art. Beautifully golden and perfectly shaped, it looked like something from the cover of a cooking magazine. Alex's mouth watered as the aroma engulfed her senses.

"Now, we'll just let this cool for a moment before I add my special sauce," Gammy said, setting the pie down on a cooling rack.

She pulled out the stool beside Alex and reached forward to clasp their hands together. The familiarity was strangely comforting.

"Tell me about yourself, dear," Gammy said.

Alex wasn't sure where to start. "What would you like to know?"

"Whatever you want to tell me."

Alex had the strongest urge to tell the older woman everything about her crazy new life, to get it all off her chest and ask for advice from someone much older and wiser. But instead of answering, she surprised even herself by asking a question. "Are you gifted?"

Gammy laughed. It was a deep belly laugh that scrunched up her wrinkles and brightened her eyes. "Oh, you *are* a treat, aren't you?"

Alex didn't understand Gammy's reaction, nor did she know how to respond.

"And you're remarkably observant," Gammy added, patting her hand comfortingly. "That's good. You should always follow your instincts. Intuition can be the most advantageous gift one can possess."

Alex still had no idea what she was talking about.

"You're correct in your assumption," Gammy said. "I was once a student at the academy, a long time ago now. Barnold and I are the only Ronnigans who can claim to have a gift worthy of Akarnae's recruitment. As the years have progressed, many have forgotten my true gift, instead believing it to be my cooking. Food is my passion, and time and practise have led to some delicious results. But my true gifting is something you might be able to figure out on your own."

Alex responded to the unspoken question by saying, "I'm not exactly sure what it is, but all I know is that you make me feel really comfortable. It's almost like nothing can go wrong so long as you're here."

"That's the effect of my gift, dear," Gammy said. "The gift of peace."

"I like it," Alex said wistfully. "It's very relaxing."

Gammy chuckled again. "I'm glad to hear it."

"Does it work like an empath?" Alex asked, thinking about how she'd read in her Core Skills textbooks that some people have the ability to manipulate the emotions of others. "Is it something I could block if I tried? If I wanted to?"

"Peace in itself is a gift," Gammy said. "It's not something that can be manipulated or distorted. An empath can force calmness and serenity upon a person, but peace by its own nature must be *accepted* by the receiver. I'm not influencing you so much as projecting what I have and offering it to you. My gift exudes from within me, and you can choose to accept it or reject it."

"Do you project all the time?" Alex asked.

"Only when I think someone is in need of a little comforting." Gammy winked at her. "As you should know, most giftings are like light switches—they can be turned on and off at will. You seemed pretty unsure of yourself just before and I wanted to help you feel at ease."

Alex squeezed the older woman's hands. "Thanks, Gammy. I can see why everyone loves you so much."

"Pish posh. They just love my cooking."

"That too," Alex agreed.

"Now that you've heard a little about me, will you tell me about yourself?" Gammy asked again.

Alex shifted on her seat. "There's really not that much to say." Or that she was allowed to say. "I started at the academy almost two months ago and it's been pretty rough getting used to everything. The classes are hard—some of them more so than others. But Bear and Jordan have really helped me settle in. I can't imagine having better friends."

Thankfully Dorothy chose that moment to walk into the kitchen, saving Alex from having to say more.

"Bear mentioned that you had originally planned to stay at Akarnae over the holidays," Dorothy said, sitting in Gammy's vacated seat when the older woman stood up to drizzle her sugary sauce over the pie. "May I ask what your family is doing for Kaldoras?"

"My parents are away at the moment," Alex said evasively. "They're on an extended work trip and there was no way for me to meet up with them."

It was the truth, but Alex still felt bad because it wasn't the entire story.

"Well, their loss is our gain," Dorothy said kindly. "Now, let's help Gammy get this pie out to those boys before they start eating the furnishings."

"Too late!" Jordan and Bear called out from the next room.

Gammy dished out hearty servings and Alex helped carry them into the dining room where the boys were eagerly waiting.

"Gammy, you're a miracle in flesh," Jordan said, tucking into his slice before it was even settled on the table.

"Close your mouth while you're eating, sonny," she scolded him. "You'll enjoy it more."

"Not possible," he said, but at least he swallowed first. "*So* not possible."

Twenty-Four

The Ronnigans' house was located just outside a sleepy little village called Woodhaven, and Alex spent the rest of the day playing tourist with Jordan and Bear.

"Have you lived here all your life?" she asked as they walked down the cobbled streets past more enchanting cottages.

"I actually grew up in the city," Bear answered, walking comfortably with his hands in his pockets. "It was only when Dad was promoted that he and Mum decided they didn't want to raise us amongst all that craziness, so we moved here and he now commutes to work."

He kicked a stone and watched it bounce along the road before he continued, "I was ten at the time. At first it was hard—we were all used to the busy city life and it was so quiet here. But we learned to love it. Besides, the backyard forest is a pretty awesome playground."

Seeing the picturesque woodland that surrounded—and in some places, interrupted—the village, Alex figured he had a good point.

They continued walking through the quiet streets of Woodhaven, taking everything in. As they passed some of the houses, people called out greetings to Bear, and often to Jordan as well. It was all so… neighbourly.

There weren't many shops in the village, which wasn't all that surprising considering its small size, and none of them were anything like what Alex had expected. There were no grocery shops, post offices, medical centres or department stores. Instead, there were places with names like Dubble Bubble, which appeared to stock all sorts of Chemistry-related supplies—including Bubblers, if their advertising was to be believed. There was also a little candy shop called The Sweet Tooth, which had hundreds of colourfully wrapped lollies on display. Further along was a small boutique clothing store and its name caused Alex to do a double-take.

"Dorothy's Designs?" she read out loud, turning to Bear. "As in, your mum?"

"Yeah," Bear answered. "Mum designs the clothes but she mostly works from home so she can look after Evie. Her sister— Aunt Tessa—looks after the shop."

"I had no idea," Alex said. "I guess I just figured she was, well—"

"A stay-at-home mother and housewife extraordinaire?" Bear finished for her with a gentle smile. "She is. And that's what's most important to her at the end of the day. Anything else she gets to do is just a bonus, in her eyes."

Alex made an understanding noise and they kept walking. The next shop along was a puzzle store called Mind Over Matter which was bursting at the seams with all sorts of different games and activities.

"I love that shop," Jordan said. "There's just so much in there. It's wacky to the extreme."

They crossed over to the other side of the street and Alex saw that the next establishment was a bookshop. But there was something decidedly strange about Ye Olde Bookshoppe; it had an almost otherworldly feel about it. As they walked past the entryway, she snuck a glance inside, but it was too dark to see anything.

They continued on until they came to the end of the road and all that was left was a private path leading further up a hill towards another cottage in the distance.

"What do you say to a drink before we head back?" Bear asked.

Jordan's face lit up. "On the house?"

"Of course," Bear said, to Alex's surprise. She had expected him to tell Jordan to pay for himself. "There's nowhere better!"

Alex wondered if she was missing something. And then she was sure of it, when the boys started leading her up the path towards the cottage.

As they moved closer, Alex had to squint her eyes because there was something moving on the roof of the house. The closer they walked, the more clearly she could see, and her eyes grew wider in shock and amusement. When they reached the front garden, there was a short fence with a wooden sign:

ON THE HOUSE
The finest brewing establishment
in 763.8 miles

It wasn't the sign that clued Alex in to what Jordan and Bear had been talking about—it was the establishment itself. Everything was on the roof of the house. There were tables and chairs, many of which were populated with cheerful patrons, if the laughter and chatter reaching her was any indication. They were literally *on the house*.

Alex couldn't do anything but laugh at the absurd sight, and her friends smiled at her reaction.

"It's something, hey?" Bear said.

"It sure is," she agreed.

"Just wait until we're up there," said Jordan. "No one makes better drinks than Benny and Sal."

He led the way around to the back of the house where there was a narrow staircase leading up to the roof. Alex was amused by the 'Please watch your step!' sign, and she wondered at the practicality of a staircase leading to a rooftop pub. That was just asking for trouble.

At the top of the stairs, she paused to take in the view. There were more customers than she would have expected considering the time of day. But it *was* almost Kaldoras, and On The House looked like the kind of place where friends and family would meet to spend time together.

"What happens when it rains? Or snows? And what about at night? How do people see? And don't they freeze?" Alex fired out question after question.

Someone chuckled from behind her. "We've a newcomer, it seems."

She turned quickly to see an older man who had snuck up on them.

"Always a pleasure to meet a beautiful girl," the man said, taking her hand and pressing it to his lips.

"Ease up, Benny," Bear said, grinning. "You're outdoing even *my* charm."

The old man guffawed. "You learned everything you know from me, squirt. It's good for you to have a refresher course sometimes."

Alex bit her cheek to keep from laughing. Benny's rough-and-tumble appearance made him seem more likely to throw a patron off his roof than attempt to woo them with his words. She couldn't imagine him teaching Bear how to be charming—in the real sense of the word, not just using his gift.

"Good to see you, old man," Jordan said, slapping Benny's shoulder in greeting.

"Jordan Sparker," the man replied, shaking his head. "We just can't get rid of you, eh?"

"You know you missed me," Jordan said with a cocky grin. "No one else laughs at your jokes."

"Benny, this is Alex," Bear interjected. "She's staying with us for the holidays."

"As I said before, little lady, it's an absolute pleasure," Benny repeated. "I only hope these two monkeys don't give you a bad impression of the rest of us here in Woodhaven. We're not all scallywags."

"*Scallywags?*" Bear spluttered at the same time as Jordan cried, "*Monkeys?*"

"You see?" Benny said. "They even interrupt old men in conversation with beautiful young women. So discourteous."

"Father, you're not bothering our guests again, are you?"

Alex turned at the sound of the new voice and found a girl in her early twenties walking over to them.

"Look who's come home for the holidays, Sal!" Benny said.

"Well, if it isn't two of my favourite customers." The girl beamed at Jordan and Bear. "It's about time you came back from that school of yours."

"What are you talking about, Sal?" Jordan asked, sounding playful. "We all know you only have one favourite—and that's me."

Sal laughed before motioning to Alex. "Who's your friend?"

"I'm Alex," she answered for herself. "I'm staying with Bear's family for the holidays."

"Nice to meet you, Alex," Sal said. She was tall and gangly, but she had a pretty face and soft eyes. "The Ronnigans are great people. I'm sure you'll enjoy your stay."

Alex smiled and nodded her agreement.

"I was just about to explain to Alex what happens when we have bad weather," Benny said to his daughter.

"Let's show her instead!" Sal said excitedly.

Before Benny could argue, Sal pulled a remote TCD out of her apron and pressed the screen. Immediately there came a rumbling noise as the roof of the house began to tremble under their feet. Alex reached out for the guardrail, but before she could latch on, it started to move upwards. What she'd thought to be open air between the rail and the floor—or roof—was actually a kind of transparent glassy substance, which was now expanding to lift up and over their heads. When all four perimeter guardrails locked together in the middle of the newly constructed ceiling above them, an invisible dome sheltered the entire space.

"We have *got* to come back here at night," Alex said, looking up through the crystal-clear material and into the sky.

"We will," Bear promised.

Sal clicked the TCD again and the guardrails slid back down to their original places, opening up the outside atmosphere again.

"Now that the show's over, how about a drink?" Benny offered. "On the house?"

Alex wasn't sure if he was making a pun or not.

"What do you think, Alex?" Jordan asked with a gleam in his eyes. "Sal makes the best dillyberry juice you'll ever taste, and we all know how much you love it."

Bear laughed and Alex glared at the both of them.

"You like dillyberry juice?" Sal asked, her face lighting up with pleasure. "I make mine with an extra special secret ingredient. I can promise you've never tasted anything else quite like it!"

"Um—I've actually been trying to quit," Alex said. "Bad habit and all that."

Jordan snorted and she discreetly stomped on his foot, satisfied when his amusement turned into a painful grunt.

Alex didn't want to explain her real reason for avoiding the purple energy drink since it was still embarrassing to think about her first experience with the fruity liquid. But the look on Sal's face was so disappointed that Alex didn't want to upset the kind girl.

"It's been a while, so maybe I could just have *one*," she agreed. She wouldn't make the same mistake and overdose again.

Sal clapped excitedly and flitted away down the stairs to make their drinks while Benny led them over to a table and told them he'd be back shortly with their order.

"How does that work?" Alex asked her friends. "Them getting the drinks up here, I mean. Does Sal just walk up and down the stairs over and over again?"

"No, no," Jordan said. "There's usually always one of them up here serving customers while the other is in the bar downstairs mixing the drinks. Once the orders are made, the drinks are transported up here for delivery."

"How are they transported?"

"Like in the food court where you can touch the menu and your meal arrives," Bear said. "The person downstairs places the drinks on the TCD, and a networked TCD up here receives them."

He pointed to a flat mini-bar and, as she watched, three drinks appeared out of thin air. Benny picked them up and placed them on a serving tray, heading in their direction.

"So convenient," she mused out loud, and her friends nodded in agreement.

When Benny reached them he transferred the bubbly purple drinks onto their table. "Enjoy, kids," he said, before walking off to serve another customer.

Alex looked at the drink in front of her and sighed. "I *really* hope I'm not going to regret this."

Twenty-Five

It turned out that Alex had nothing to worry about. Other than a slight buzz, the dillyberry juice didn't cause her any negative side-effects. And it was true what they said about Sal's concoction—it was delicious. Even so, Alex was careful to keep to her one-glass limit.

The three friends spent the afternoon talking with Benny and Sal before they made their way back to Bear's house around sunset. It started snowing during their return walk, and while she was near-frozen, Alex still thought it was worth it to see the picturesque village dusted with the first snow of the season.

"We're home!" Bear called out as he opened the front door and stomped the ice from his shoes.

"Just in time for dinner," said a man walking down the staircase towards them.

"Dad!" Bear leapt forward to embrace his father.

"Good to see you, son," Mr. Ronnigan said, hugging him back tightly. He looked exactly like Bear, just older, with the only other difference being a dangerous-looking scar that ran down the side of his face from his temple to his ear.

When he finally released his son, Mr. Ronnigan reached over to pull Jordan in for a hug. "Good seeing you too, kid," he said, messing up Jordan's hair as he let him go.

"Kid? Really?" Jordan huffed, but Alex could hear the affection in his tone.

Mr. Ronnigan then turned her way with a big, welcoming smile. "You must be Alex," he said, holding out his hand. "I'm Bear's father, William."

"It's nice to meet you," she said, grasping his firm, calloused hand. He caught her off-guard when he yanked her forward and embraced her just as tightly as the boys.

"You three look frozen to your socks," he said as soon as he released her. "Let's get some food into you."

They followed William into the dining room just as Gammy and Dorothy walked out of the kitchen carrying steaming trays of roast chicken and vegetables. Alex felt her stomach rumble appreciatively and she heard Jordan moan with delight.

Evie skipped over to grab Alex's hand, leading her to a seat where they could sit next to each other.

"I see you've already made a friend," William noted, taking his place at the head of the table.

Alex thought he was talking to her, but it was Evie who answered.

"Yup," she said. "Lexie and I are bestest friends forever!"

Alex blinked. Lexie? When did *that* happen?

"But I thought *we* were best friends forever?" William asked. He was pouting comically and Alex had a hard time hiding her amusement.

"Silly, Daddy," Evie said. "You're my bestest *daddy* forever!"

"Oh," he said, smiling indulgently. "I guess that's okay."

Dinner with the Ronnigans was a blur of questions as the family all caught up. Soon enough the interrogation eased and Alex had the chance to ask a question of her own.

"Bear mentioned that you commute to work each day," she said to William, ignoring the fact that commuting wasn't exactly a difficult feat thanks to the convenience of Bubbledoors. "What is it that you do?"

"I'm a Warden," he said, spearing some broccoli onto his fork. "I work out of our headquarters in Tryllin. It's challenging, but rewarding at the same time."

Tryllin was the capital city, if Alex remembered correctly, and it was located on the far north-eastern coast of the continent. From what Bear had told her during their tour of the village, Woodhaven was located somewhere in between Akarnae and Tryllin. Those Bubbledoors were amazing if William could use one to travel thousands of miles and back every day.

"What's a Warden?" Alex asked.

William had been in the process of lifting the broccoli to his mouth when he paused and placed the fork back on his plate. "You don't know?" he asked, with surprise—and suspicion—in his eyes.

"I—"

"Alex has grown up with overprotective parents," Jordan jumped in before she could say anything else incriminating. "She's been kind of... sheltered."

Alex was pretty sure Jordan had just managed to imply that she was daft. Knowing that he was only trying to cover for her, she kept her mouth closed and speared a carrot on her plate a touch more aggressively than normal.

"Still, it's strange that she hasn't heard of us," William said.

"They didn't want her worrying about things that had nothing to do with her," Bear added, looking at her meaningfully. Clearly she was meant to go along with the story.

"Yeah," she said, half-heartedly. "I've learned a lot since starting at Akarnae."

"That *would* be a culture shock," William said. He was still looking at her curiously, but the suspicion was gone from his eyes. "To answer your question, a Warden is a peacekeeper. We're officers of the law, responsible for upholding justice and protecting the innocent. We act on behalf of the royal family and we're held accountable for the safety of the kingdom."

"Whoa," Alex said, impressed. "Tough break."

William laughed and nodded in agreement. "It sure has its moments."

Alex didn't ask any more questions, not wanting to sound even more naïve. Instead, she ate her food and listened to the comfortable sounds of a loving family. She found herself fighting off a wave of nostalgia as memories flooded in from meals she'd shared with her parents over the years. Her mother and father might have been caught up in their passion for work a lot of the time, but they'd always tried to spend at least one meal each day with Alex. It didn't even matter that many of their 'family dinners' had been shared around a campfire at one dig-site or another with any number of work colleagues, because they were still some of the best memories Alex had from her childhood. And now, being with the Ronnigans and experiencing their version of a family meal... well, it was extremely comforting. And Alex loved every minute of it.

After dinner, Gammy disappeared into her flat off the side of the house, William said he had some work to catch up on, and Dorothy took Evie upstairs to get her ready for bed. Jordan, Bear and Alex decided to settle in the lounge room, which had cushy couches and a large projector screen.

The three of them watched movies for the rest of the night using the Ronnigans' high definition virtual reality projector. Just like in the Rec Room, Alex again felt like she was a part of the show, and after the second movie she was so exhausted by the special effects that she had to excuse herself. She crawled her way upstairs and into Blake's bed, sighing contentedly when she realised that it was even more comfortable than it looked.

Twenty-Six

Over the course of the next week Alex spent most of her time with the Ronnigan family who embraced her as one of their own. She played games with little Evie, watched Gammy cook meal after meal, and even helped Dorothy work on a new evening dress design. Jordan and Bear spent most days with Alex too, but they also went off to do their own things. Where they went and what they did, she didn't want to know.

When Kaldoras Eve finally rolled around, Alex realised that she still hadn't bought any presents, and since Jordan and Bear were out exploring the forest, she took off into the village on her own.

It was easy enough to find something for Bear. Dubble Bubble was the perfect shop for him. The owner, Anton Grey, helped Alex pick out a vial of Liquid Light that, when unstoppered, would last for up to three hours. He even threw in a second vial for her to keep as a freebie after Alex knocked into one of his experiments and started a fire. She felt horrible, but he congratulated her on causing the chemical reaction he was after and invited her to stop by again anytime.

Jordan was trickier to find a gift for, but remembering his comment about the puzzle store Mind Over Matter, Alex purchased him a gift voucher so that he could pick something out for himself later.

She bought a packet of colourful sherbet fizzes from The Sweet Tooth for Evie, and then she tried to figure out what to get the rest of the Ronnigans. The entire family had been so nice to her and even though she'd yet to meet Johnny and Blake, she still wanted to get something for them—as well as Dorothy, William and Gammy.

Knowing that it would be too weird to buy something from Dorothy's Designs to give Dorothy's family, she bypassed that shop altogether. Which left only one store—Ye Olde Bookshoppe.

Alex crossed the street and stepped into the dark interior of the store, squealing when she accidentally walked through a thick spider's web. She shuddered as she dropped her bags and brushed the stringy web off her clothes, shaking out her hair for good measure.

When she was positive that no spiders were clinging to her, Alex finally looked up and took in the room. The sunshine from outside didn't help to illuminate the store since the windows were boarded up, so it took a few moments for her eyes to adjust to the darkness on the inside. When she could see properly, she gazed around in awe.

There were books, all right. Shelves and shelves full of them, sprawled about the room in complete disarray. There was also a glass cabinet of jewellery in one corner, directly opposite another cabinet that looked like it held antiquated weapons from before the dawn of time. All around the shop were cobwebs so strategically placed that it was almost as if they were set there for decorative purposes.

Before Alex could decide if she should enter further or back out completely, a voice directly beside her caused her to jump.

"You wish to speak to Lady Mystique?"

Alex stared at the hunched-over woman addressing her. She was *really* old. Not like Gammy old; more like 'I was alive with the dinosaurs' old. The wisdom in her gaze was at once entrancing and terrifying.

"No, thank you," Alex said hesitantly. "I'm just here to look around."

"You wish to speak to Lady Mystique?" the woman asked again, stepping even closer to Alex, who backed away instinctively.

"Err—no. Thanks. Some other time, perhaps."

"You wish to speak to Lady Mystique?" The old woman continued to step forward, and Alex continued to step away.

What was with this woman? Could she only ask the one question?

"I'm just browsing," Alex said in a firm, loud voice, hoping that the raised volume might help.

"*You wish to speak to Lady Mystique!*"

Alex actually jumped again with the force of the old woman's order. It didn't sound like she was asking a question anymore, and Alex quickly glanced back at the doorway she'd come through, hoping to make a quick exit. But the woman had backed her into one of the bookshelves and was blocking her path. Talk about a pushy salesperson.

"Fine," Alex relented. Other than shoving the woman out of the way, she didn't have many other options. "I'll speak with your lady if you promise to leave me alone after that."

The old crone's face transformed. She actually looked amused, if her crooked smile was any indication.

"You're a stubborn one, Alexandra Jennings," she said. "But Lady Mystique is pleased to make your acquaintance."

"*You're* Lady Mystique?" Alex frowned at her. "Why all the fuss?"

The woman shrugged off her behaviour as if harassing complete strangers was a regular occurrence. "I wanted to see how you'd react."

Alex let that sink in—along with the fact that the woman seemed to know who she was without asking—before she said in a dry tone, "Did I pass your expectations?"

"Well, you're remarkably polite," Lady Mystique said, and Alex wasn't sure if she was being sarcastic or not. "But otherwise, yes. Your gift is very powerful. It will serve you well when you finally understand it."

"My gift?" Alex stepped forward eagerly. "You know what my gift is?"

The old lady grinned crookedly again. "Of course I do. Lady Mystique knows all."

Alex wasn't certain if the woman was just a big fake, but there was something about her eyes that spoke of unfathomable knowledge. One moment they sparked with youthful energy, and the next they seemed to hold the weight of the ages.

"So, what is it?" Alex asked.

"It's something you'll have to discover on your own, child. And you will, when the time is right."

"I see," Alex said. She was disappointed but she also had a feeling that this Lady Mystique wasn't going to say any more, regardless of how hard she pressed. "What *can* you tell me?" Alex tried instead.

"Lady Mystique can help you with your search. For today, that is all, but it will be enough," she said. "Next time, perhaps more."

"My search?" Alex asked, uncertain as to what the woman meant.

Lady Mystique reached out to pull a book off the shelf, placing it into Alex's arms. She then beckoned for Alex to follow as she led the way around the store, grasping random objects and handing them over. Finally she stopped at the counter, motioning for Alex to place all the items on the glass top.

"What is all this?" Alex asked.

"It's what you came for," the woman replied.

Alex looked over the items, confused.

"This will be your gift for Jonathon," Lady Mystique said, pointing to the first book, *Advanced Metaphysics: A Technological Perspective.*

"I don't understand," Alex said, wrinkling her nose at the brain-numbing title. "Who's Jonathon?"

Lady Mystique looked at her as if she was slow, and something clicked in Alex's head. "You mean Bear's brother, Johnny?"

"Indeed."

It was then that Alex realised the items on the counter were Kaldoras presents, ones that the old woman had hand-picked for her.

"You'll give this to Blake," Lady Mystique said, pointing to another book in the pile. It looked old—impossibly old—and yet it was perfectly intact, with obscure-looking symbols carved into the cover.

"Dorothy will love this," the woman continued, handing over a dainty brooch. It was made out of a glowing silver-like metal that almost looked to be emanating light.

"This will be for the one you call 'Gammy'." Lady Mystique held out another book, this one tattered and falling apart. The title was handwritten, and poorly at that. From what Alex could read, it was a homemade recipe book.

The old woman passed over the last object—an antique dagger. She pulled it from its sheath and, despite its apparent age, the blade still gleamed. It seemed to be made of the same kind of silver metal as the brooch.

"This will be perfect for William's collection," she told Alex, stroking the weapon fondly. "It has no equal."

Alex looked at the items in front of her with awe. *How...?*

"Lady Mystique knows all," the old woman said.

Alex groaned. "Don't tell me, you can read my mind?"

"No." Lady Mystique wheezed slightly in what Alex presumed was a laugh. "Not even I can manage that. Perhaps when you first arrived, but not now. Your confusion is simply written all over your face."

There was so much of that explanation that Alex wanted to ask about, not the least of which was the fact that she didn't think Lady Mystique was referring to her arrival into the store. But she let it go, somehow certain that the woman wouldn't reveal her secrets.

"These are the gifts you came searching for," Lady Mystique said. "Will that be all?"

Alex looked through the glass casing on the counter and—not entirely sure why—she asked, "Can I please have that as well?" She pointed to a delicate charm bracelet made out of the same glowing metal as the dagger and the brooch. The charms on the bracelet were miniscule prancing horses, all frozen in different stages of movement. The light reflecting in and around them made it seem like they were actually moving, circling the bracelet. It was beautiful, entrancing even.

"A lovely trinket," said the old woman. "Who, may I ask, is it for?"

"My roommate," Alex said, surprising herself. At first she had wanted the bracelet for herself, but when asked the question her answer had been natural. Obvious, even. "She doesn't like me very much, but she loves horses. I think." D.C. was graded Epsilon with Alex for Equestrian Skills, so it made sense.

"I'm certain Delucia will love this," Lady Mystique agreed, pulling it out and placing it in a box.

Delucia? Was that D.C.'s real name? Alex had no idea.

She watched while Lady Mystique gift-wrapped the items and it was only when the old woman placed them into a bag that she realised she had yet to pay.

"How much do I owe you?" Alex asked, pulling out her money pouch. Looking at all the gifts—they were perfectly wrapped in shiny paper with bows *and* nametags—she hoped she had enough from her allowance.

Lady Mystique just handed her the bag and patted her gently on the hand. "It is I who will owe you, Alexandra Jennings."

What did *that* mean?

"Um—but how much for the gifts?" Alex asked again, not at all comfortable with how the other woman was looking at her. Admiration. Hope. Sorrow. Those ancient eyes showed a myriad of emotions that Alex wanted to run away from.

It felt like a lifetime before Lady Mystique looked away from her and said, "There's no charge for you."

"No," Alex protested. "That's very kind, but you have to let me pay for them. Otherwise they're not really my gifts to give."

"A gift given is a gift received," said the woman, her voice hinting at a depth of wisdom Alex couldn't begin to comprehend. "And a gift received can become a gift given. We'll meet again, Alexandra Jennings."

Alex had to blink a few times before she accepted the fact that Lady Mystique had disappeared before her eyes. She'd faded out like a mist, dissolving into nothing.

"I'll just let myself out, then?" Alex called into the empty store, and only a quiet wheezing laugh answered her as she headed to the door.

It was a testament to how much Alex had learned to accept odd events since arriving in Medora that she didn't run screaming down the street. Instead, she walked calmly back to the Ronnigans' house, replaying the woman's parting words over and over in her mind.

A gift given is a gift received. And a gift received can become a gift given.

Twenty-Seven

Alex was still deep in thought when she reached the Ronnigans' house, but the moment she walked in the front door she knew something was different. There were loud voices—*new* voices—coming from the dining room, which meant that Bear's older brothers must have arrived.

Curious to finally meet them, Alex raced upstairs to hide her presents before hurrying back down again. In her excitement, she failed to pay attention to her surroundings, and at the entrance to the dining room she tripped over one of Evie's dolls, tumbled forwards, and landed face-first on the solid floor with a loud, "*Oomph!*"

Alex rolled onto her back, completely dazed, and groaned with humiliation. Her timid voice echoed in the now silent room as she asked, "I don't suppose we can act like that didn't just happen?"

Her question broke the gaping silence, and suddenly everyone was laughing.

Alex flushed brightly as William walked over and offered his hand, pulling her to her feet. "That's one way to enter a room," he said. At least he was trying to be polite—Jordan and Bear were both hunched over, laughing so hard they were crying. Great friends, those two.

"Yeah," Alex said, pressing her fingers to the side of her face that had taken the brunt of the fall. "I've always maintained that if you're going to do something, do it well."

William chuckled in agreement and led her towards the table where the others were sitting. Dorothy was in the middle of scolding her daughter for leaving toys lying around, and Evie quickly got up to give Alex a hug and a watery apology, to which Alex hurried to reassure the younger girl that she wasn't hurt.

"Just my pride," she mumbled to herself as Evie went back to her mother.

Alex then turned to face the new family members sitting at the table. "Hi," she said awkwardly. "I'm Alex."

To their credit, they didn't laugh at her again. But their eyes were still shining with mirth.

"We've heard a lot about you," said the elder of the two young men, standing up to shake her hand. "I'm so pleased to see it's all true, if that spectacular entrance is anything to judge by. I'm Johnny, by the way, and this is Blake."

As Blake reached out to shake her hand next, Alex tried to make sense of Johnny's words. What had they heard about her? She looked to Bear for more information but he skilfully avoided eye contact. Whatever his brothers had heard must not have been overly complimentary.

Alex tapped her fingernails on the table until Bear finally glanced up at her, and she sent him a questioning look. It might have seemed more like an accusatory glare, but whatever.

"Hey!" he said. "I've seen you in PE and, let's face it, you've had your moments."

"That doesn't mean you had to *share* those moments," she said, feeling embarrassed all over again.

"I didn't share *all* of them," he said, and Alex felt some relief. Until he added, "Jordan told them about the rest."

She promptly transferred her glare towards her other friend, who just smiled and waved in response.

Alex turned back to Bear's brothers and said, as seriously as she could, "Whatever you've heard, they were lying."

Blake breathed out on another laugh. "Don't worry, Alex. I think we've just seen for ourselves how amazingly coordinated you are."

She felt as if her face was on fire, but she rallied on and said, "That was for your benefit. I didn't want either of you to be intimidated by my awesomeness—which I'm sure you've heard all about—and I chose to sacrifice my dignity to even the playing field."

"How kind of you," Johnny said, the corner of his mouth twitching.

"I'm actually still feeling a little intimidated," Blake admitted. "Do you mind going and doing that all over again? Just so I can feel a little less threatened by your—ah—*awesomeness*."

Alex had to bite back a smile of her own. It wouldn't do her any good to encourage them. "I'm sorry," she said, her voice full of false regret. "Only one show per day."

"I guess we'll just have to look forward to tomorrow, then," Blake said, giving her a sly wink.

"All right, everyone," Dorothy said. "That's enough teasing. Alex, dear, will you help me bring the food out? We'll do our part now and then we can leave the cleaning for the boys to do later."

Alex eagerly followed the other woman into the kitchen, happy for any excuse to leave the room and regain her equilibrium. As she helped dish out the meal, she thought about Johnny and Blake. While Bear and Evie took after their father with their dark hair and eyes, the two older brothers looked more like their mother. They both had light brown hair just like Dorothy, and while Johnny had inherited his father's darker eyes, Blake had the same piercing blue ones as his mother. They also both seemed to be casual and easy-going like Bear. Alex was sure that once she got over her embarrassment she would get on with them just fine.

When they all sat down for dinner, she had the chance to ask Johnny and Blake what they did for work.

"I'm a Techno," Johnny answered. At her blank look, he added, "Dad said you were sheltered, but I had no idea—"

"Johnny," William interrupted, his warning clear.

"Sorry, Alex. I've just never met anyone who hasn't heard of a Techno. Or a Warden, for that matter." Johnny shook his head as if amazed and then said, "Technos are upper-level Chemists who manipulate technology to sustain and advance communication and integration. The latter involves the transference of matter—like how stuff is transported through TCDs. I don't have much to do with that, though, since I'm in the communications sub-division. We get to work on TCD applications and software, continually generating new ideas to bring to the market."

"Sounds interesting," Alex said. She didn't know enough about TCDs to understand what he was talking about, but it was clear he enjoyed his career choice. Even so, she didn't particularly want to get caught up in a conversation that she knew would only hurt her brain, so she turned her attention to Blake and asked, "What about you?"

"I'm with the ISDS—the Inter-Species Diplomatic Service. Mostly I liaise with Shadow Walkers, but I've also spent some time working with Flips and with Jarnocks."

She tried to keep her expression neutral, not wanting to let on that she had no idea what he'd just said.

"I know what you're thinking," Blake said.

Alex seriously doubted that.

"Most people say I'm too young to be in the Service," he said, "but that's just how it worked out. The ISDS recruited me straight out of school and I continued my training in the field.

They'd never let me out there on my own if they didn't believe I could handle myself."

He trailed off and Alex realised that she was supposed to say something.

"That sounds awesome." She cringed at her lame response and tried again. "It must be really interesting work. Especially with the... Shadow Walkers."

What on earth was a Shadow Walker? Wasn't that what Jordan had called their SOSAC teacher, Caspar Lennox?

"Yeah, they're interesting all right," Blake agreed. "But they're about as easy to read as a rock, so negotiating with them is near impossible."

"I'll bet," Alex said, as if she knew what she was talking about. Jordan sniggered from beside her and she elbowed him in the ribs.

The conversation drifted to safer topics and Alex was left thinking about what she'd learned.

"How old are they?" she whispered to Jordan when everyone else was busy talking.

"Blake's four years older than us and Johnny's five years older," he whispered back.

"How did they end up with such cool jobs, since they're still so young?"

"Students who don't qualify for Akarnae pick a specialisation to focus on when they're fourteen. At eighteen they graduate and either get a job or continue studying elsewhere."

Jordan paused to take another bite of food before he continued, "Both the ISDS and ChemTech—which is the research organisation that recruits Chemists to train them into Technos—usually require four more years of study before recruitment, but both Johnny and Blake were exceptions. Johnny's so brilliant that he was hacking into secure TCD servers when he was thirteen, and Blake not only graduated at the top of his class in Languages, Politics, and Inter-Species Relations, but he also smashed through all the previous records when he took his exams."

"Wow," Alex said, impressed. "So they're both really smart?"

"The whole family is," Jordan said. "It's ridiculous."

Alex nodded as she recalled Bear's amazing potential in Chemistry. She was about to comment on it but she remembered something else and instead asked, "What's a Shadow Walker? And the other things Blake mentioned? I didn't understand anything he—"

"Who wants dessert?"

Their attention was diverted when Gammy placed a steaming chocolate pudding on the table. Alex's mouth watered at the sight and she looked up at Jordan.

"We'll talk later," he promised.

But later never came, since after dessert they were herded into the lounge room to uphold a Ronnigan family tradition. Every Kaldoras Eve the family sat together to share their memories of the year that was and talk about the things they were grateful for. When Alex's turn came, she simply said, "I'm grateful to be here."

Everyone *awwww*ed, but when she looked at Jordan and Bear she knew they understood the 'here' that her words encompassed. When she'd first arrived in Medora, all she'd wanted was to find a way back home. But now, even while still missing her parents, she couldn't imagine being anywhere else.

And that scared her more than anything.

Twenty-Eight

Alex was woken at the crack of dawn the next day to open presents with the family, and she was overwhelmed by the unexpected gifts she received.

Jordan and Bear had pooled together to get her a remote ComTCD so she could always stay in contact with them. The little holographic device was a lustrous gold colour, and she immediately fell in love with it.

"But wait, there's more," Jordan said after she thanked them. "Part of it's from Johnny, too. He's added some special apps that haven't even been released to the public yet! I'll be borrowing this baby for sure!"

"Let her have it for at least five minutes, Jordan," Johnny called from across the room.

Jordan grumbled a little, but he eventually surrendered the ComTCD to Alex, and she moved it out of his sight while she reached for her next gift. She gasped when she opened the box to find the dress she'd been helping Dorothy create over the past week.

"We wanted you to have something nice to wear to the Gala," Dorothy said, handing her another box that she said was from William. Inside was a pair of shoes that matched the dress perfectly.

Alex looked quizzically at William who just smiled back and said, "Do I really look like the type of person who knows the difference between stilettos and wedges? No. I'm just the financier. But I wanted to get you something, even if I thought it was best for you if I didn't choose them myself."

She was touched by their generosity and thanked them both profusely before reaching for her next gift, which was from Gammy. Inside was a single sheet of paper with the title: TOP SECRET. Alex's smile widened as she read the rest of the words and realised that it was the recipe for Gammy's famous apple pie, secret sauce included. When Alex looked across the room and caught the older woman's eyes, Gammy pressed a finger to her lips and winked.

"Open mine next, Lexie! Open mine!" Evie cried, shoving her gift into Alex's face.

Inside was a small bunch of wildflowers glued to a hairclip. They were beautiful, and Alex immediately clipped them into her hair, causing the little girl to clap with happiness.

"You can keep them forever!" Evie exclaimed. She was so excited that Alex didn't want to ruin the moment by telling her that the flowers would eventually die.

"She's right," Bear said. "She asked me to preserve them for you. They're frozen in time, forever looking as fresh as the day they were picked."

Alex looked at him in surprise. "More genius Chemistry stuff?"

He shrugged modestly. "Someone has to do it."

Alex thanked the little girl with a squishy hug and a raspberry kiss, before she picked up her next package, which was from Blake. She wasn't sure what to think when she opened up a small jewellery box and found a ring inside.

"Don't get the wrong idea," he joked from across the room. "Even I don't move that fast."

Alex chuckled along with everyone else, but she was distracted by the strange ring. It was unlike any kind of jewellery she'd ever seen before. The band was as black as onyx, but it was the stone secured in the centre of it that was most intriguing. It was also black, but as she looked closer she noticed that the inside was swirling with dark, inky colours as if there was a gas or something trapped inside.

"Hey! How come she gets one of those? I've wanted one *forever!*" Bear said, looking enviously at her gift.

"From what you've said, little brother, it sounds like Alex and trouble go hand-in-hand," Blake said. "I thought she might need it more than you."

Bear grumbled a little, but he reluctantly agreed.

"There's only enough Shadow in there for three Walks," Blake told Alex as she slipped the ring on her finger, "so it's for emergencies only, got it?"

She nodded even though she had no idea what she was agreeing to. She would just have to ask Bear about the ring later. In the meantime, she had one gift left, and it wasn't labelled.

"That came through our TCD earlier in the week," William told her. The Ronnigans had a much more integrated TCD than her new little Communications one. They used theirs for everything from grocery shopping to sending and receiving post. Alex had even used it to send D.C.'s gift through to the academy with a note asking Jarvis to forward it on to her roommate.

Alex opened the gift in front of her, wondering who could have possibly sent it. Inside was a book: *Overcoming Iatrophobia: How to turn your fear into your friend.* The author had a list of abbreviated titles next to their name, as if that was supposed to mean something, but Alex still had no idea if the present was actually for her.

She turned the book over and read the blurb, laughing out loud when she discovered that iatrophobia was a fear of doctors. She opened the front cover and found a note inside:

Happy Kaldoras, Alex!
I don't normally give presents to students, but I
saw this book and thought of you. Here's hoping it
will provide you with some much needed counselling.
Wishing you an enjoyable holiday,
Fletcher.

Alex laughed again as she read his scratchy note, and she wondered briefly why all doctors seemed to have nearly illegible handwriting, no matter what world they came from.

Now that everything was open, she put her pile of treasures to the side and waited while everyone else finished with their own unwrapping. They *ooooh*ed and *ahhhh*ed, and, in Evie's case, squealed with excitement. Some of the loudest exclamations came when they opened up their gifts from Alex, but their reactions weren't quite what she'd expected.

The first surprise came when Johnny opened his *Advanced Metaphysics* book, which apparently wasn't meant to be released to the public for another six months. There was an awkward silence when he asked her how she'd received a copy so early, and she ended up stammering out an uncertain answer.

"I guess the woman who gave it to me must have known the author?"

Everyone—including Alex—was sceptical about that.

The book for Blake caused her even more trouble, since she soon discovered that it was an original copy of a manuscript that was handwritten over three thousand years ago. Only two copies were ever made, and neither had been seen for hundreds of years. Even the dialect was ancient—a dead language. Meyarin, as a matter of fact.

When Blake mentioned that little piece of information the room went completely silent as everyone waited for Alex's explanation.

"Um…" she hesitated. "The woman at the bookshop must have had it for a while then, I guess?"

Even to her ears it seemed impossible.

Her predicament worsened further when William pulled out the glinting dagger. He stared at it in wonder for a moment before locking eyes with Alex. They weren't the comforting eyes of the Ronnigan patriarch she'd come to know, but instead they were hardened, suspicious eyes. Eyes that made her realise she was now facing William the Warden.

"Where did this come from, Alex?" he asked, his voice deceptively calm.

"The same place as the rest," she said, feeling a flicker of anxiety. "Lady Mystique helped me with all of your gifts, except the ones for Jordan, Bear and Evie."

"Lady Mystique?" William asked, walking over to sit beside her.

Alex furrowed her brow. Maybe they knew her by another name. "The owner of the bookshop."

"What bookshop?"

"The—The one down the road. In the village." Seeing the blank looks around her, Alex added, "Ye Olde Bookshoppe."

"Alex," Bear said, "there's no bookshop in Woodhaven."

"What?" she said, taking in their serious expressions. "Of course there is! We walked straight past it when we visited On The House."

William exchanged a glance with Bear before turning back to Alex. "So, when you went shopping yesterday you went into this bookshop?"

She nodded.

"What happened once you were inside?"

Alex told him everything, only leaving out the end part of her conversation with Lady Mystique and the fact that the old woman seemed to know much more about Alex than she should have. She finished by saying, "I figured she was a friend of your family or something. But she wouldn't let me pay for the gifts, and at the end she just…"

"She just what?" William pressed.

"Um… she just… disappeared," Alex said, wincing at how ridiculous she sounded.

"Disappeared?" he asked, frowning. "How?"

"She just sort of… faded out."

William stared into her eyes as if they would show whether she was telling the truth or not. Finally, he looked away from her and back to his dagger.

"This is a Meyarin blade," he told her. "It would have been forged thousands of years ago by their ancient warriors. It's a dagger of incomparable worth, made out of priceless metals. It's not something an old lady would give to a complete stranger so that you could gift it to another complete stranger."

"Don't forget my book, Dad," Blake added. "I believe it's worth much more even than your dagger."

"My brooch, too, seems to be made of the same metal as your blade, Will," Dorothy said, adding to the growing list.

Alex started to feel faintly nauseous.

"I don't know what you're all diddling on about," Gammy spoke up. "We've been given some wonderful gifts from a remarkable young lady who only wanted to find us something she thought we'd like and appreciate. We're not showing much gratitude with all these interrogations. We ought to count our blessings, not question them. It's Kaldoras morning, a time to receive gifts and be thankful. Now, come and help me in the kitchen, Alex dear, before they forget their manners entirely and turn into wild animals."

Alex quickly scrambled after Gammy and tried to collect her thoughts. How could there be no bookshop in town? She'd seen it across the street from the other shops every time she'd walked the little strip. But, despite her own experience, she knew the Ronnigans were telling the truth, too. Which led to the question: why could she see it when they clearly couldn't? Was Ye Olde Bookshoppe perhaps like the Library, and only certain people could access it? Alex didn't think so. She had a feeling the weirdness was influenced more by the owner of the shop than anything else. But why had Lady Mystique opened her doors for Alex? And why had she given her such remarkable gifts to give to the others?

"Now, now, dear, wipe that worried look off your face," Gammy said. "Such a pretty girl shouldn't look so confused."

"Sorry, Gammy," she said gloomily. "But I *am* confused."

"Yes, well, I don't think you're the only one, sweet pea," Gammy said. "I can't remember the last time I saw my William so flustered. But Missy wouldn't have caused this stir without reason, don't you worry."

"Missy?" Alex asked, not sure what Gammy was talking about.

"Your Lady Mystique."

"You know her?" Alex cried.

"We've met," Gammy said. "It was a long time ago, mind you, and just the once. She helped me out of a tight spot. Saved my life, in fact." Gammy paused with a thoughtful look on her face. "It's funny how the world works. That day I was carrying a book with me—a book I'd written myself, detailing all my favourite recipes and the ones I was still improving. After saving my life, Missy asked if she could borrow it for a while. It was a small price to pay, really, but it's nice to have it back in my possession again."

Alex's eyes widened as she realised that the book she'd given Gammy was actually Gammy's own recipe book.

"Why don't you take a seat, dear. You look a bit peaky."

Alex didn't argue as the older woman led her to a stool and placed a glass of water in front of her.

"Now, you just sit there and keep me company while I cook up a feast," Gammy said.

Alex sipped her water and concentrated on the melody Gammy began humming, readily receiving the peace that was flowing out of the older woman.

Eventually Alex had to move as the Ronnigan household began to fill with more and more people. Apparently Bear had been telling the truth when he'd said that Kaldoras was a community event for his family.

Benny and Sal arrived first, bringing with them a large flagon of Sal's homemade dillyberry juice to serve with lunch— much to everyone's pleasure.

Next came Dorothy's sister, Tessa, who surprised Alex by pulling her into a hug and giving her a small wrapped package, saying, "To go with your dress." Inside were two tear-drop earrings, delicate and beautiful. Alex stammered her thanks and tried to apologise for not getting Tessa a gift in return, but Tessa just laughed, saying she hadn't expected one.

A number of other guests arrived and, just before they all sat down to eat, Anton Grey hurried through the door, apologising for his tardiness. Alex was more concerned by the smoke coming off the back of his jacket than anything else, and she watched as Bear quickly spoke to the Chemist, pointing him towards the bathroom.

Anton rushed off, calling out, "So sorry! Had a little accident in the lab! Be right back!"

They all laughed and waited for him to return before they sat down to start Gammy's amazing feast, revelling in the happiness of the day and enjoying one another's company. Not for the first time, Alex felt the warmth of contentment stirring in her chest. She never would have guessed upon arriving in Medora that she could have felt anything other than alienated and isolated in this strange, new world. But sitting around a table brimming with

256 · Lynette Noni

food and merriment, she realised her presumptions couldn't have been further from the truth. She felt safe. She felt comfortable. And, most importantly, she felt *loved*.

"What are you thinking about, Alex?" Jordan asked from across the table. "You look like you're miles away."

Alex shook her head and offered him a soft smile. "I'm just having a moment."

He glanced at her quizzically but only said, "Well, when your moment's over, can you pass the potatoes? They're begging for my attention."

Alex chose not to comment on the mountain of food already covering his plate and instead handed the potatoes over. As she turned back to her own delicious but much more appropriately sized meal, she sent a silent thought back to her world: *Merry Christmas, Mum and Dad. I hope wherever you are, you're as happy as I am.*

Twenty-Nine

The days following Kaldoras passed by in a blur of food and laughter. Johnny and Blake were due to leave after lunch on New Year's Eve, so the family—which now included Jordan and Alex—crammed in as many experiences together as they could. One of those experiences included a walk into the village so that Alex could prove to them that Ye Olde Bookshoppe existed.

Unfortunately for Alex, when they entered the bookshop all they found was a half-collapsed building. No books, no weapons or jewellery, and no Lady Mystique. If not for Gammy's reassurance that she'd previously met with the lady, Alex would have questioned her own sanity. Instead, all any of them could do was shrug and try and put the strangeness out of their minds.

Woodhaven turned out to be a winter wonderland, with everything from a fantastic sledding hill to a small frozen lake that was perfect for ice-skating. They skated and sledded until the point of exhaustion, and even had a snowman-building competition which ended in a massive snowball fight.

Before she knew it, the week came to an end, and it was time to say goodbye to Johnny and Blake.

"You take care of yourself, Alex," Johnny said, pulling her into a hug.

"I'll try," she promised.

"Be good, and don't do anything I wouldn't do," Blake said, giving her a hug as well.

"That doesn't give me a lot to work with," she replied with a knowing smile. If there was one thing she'd learned about Blake in their short time together, it was that he enjoyed the thrill of a challenge.

"Exactly," he said, adding a wink for good measure.

While she was sad to see them go, Alex was also excited, because it was finally the day of the New Year's Eve Gala.

"I better go and start getting ready," she said after Johnny and Blake departed.

"Do you need any help?" Dorothy asked.

"I think I'll be fine, thanks," Alex said. "But I'll call if I need anything."

As she headed up to Blake's room, she couldn't help but chuckle when she heard Bear whispering incredulously to Jordan, "It's three o'clock! Does she seriously need two hours to put on a dress?"

Alex ended up thoroughly enjoying those two hours, despite the ridicule of her friends. Every so often it was nice to actually be girly and feel like the young woman she was.

"Ten minutes, Alex!" came Bear's voice through her door.

"Coming!" she called back.

She glanced one last time at her reflection, still surprised by what she saw. The dress Dorothy had designed for her was stunning. It was a sky-blue colour and made out of silky material that flowed softly down her body, swishing as she moved. On her feet were the silver strappy shoes William had given her, and she wore the teardrop earrings from Tessa along with Evie's wildflower clip pinned into her hair. All in all, she felt—and looked—like a princess.

"Alex! Come on!"

Hearing the impatience in Bear's voice, Alex moved away from the mirror and dropped her ComTCD into the purse

Dorothy had loaned her for the night. "You told me I had ten minutes," she said as she opened the door.

"And three have passed," Bear said. "Which only leaves us seven to get you downstairs in those heels."

Alex took in Bear's worried expression. "Are you all right?"

"I'm fine," Bear answered. "But I don't know if Jordan is."

"Why? Where is he?"

"His parents called an hour ago and said they wanted to see him before the Gala. He told me he'd meet us there."

Alex frowned. "I thought he didn't get along with his parents?"

"He doesn't," Bear said, leading the way downstairs. "I don't think they've ever hurt him or anything like that, but they're pretty negligent as far as affection goes. They're just too caught up with themselves to invest any time in him."

"Then why did he go to them?"

"They're still his parents," Bear said. "He won't admit it, but he would give almost anything for their attention, I think."

"Poor Jordan," Alex said, feeling sad for her friend.

"Don't," Bear warned. "The last thing he'd ever want is pity. He's got us, at least. And he'll need us tonight."

"So what are we still waiting here for?" Alex asked cheekily. "I've been ready for hours!"

"Yeah, right," Bear said, rolling his eyes. "But you look hot, so those hours must have been good for something."

Alex sent him a look that said more than any words could. "There's a reason you don't have a girlfriend, *Barnold*, if that's how you give a compliment."

He laughed at her expression, before bowing cordially. "I apologise, my lady. You look *beautiful*."

"That's more like it." Alex chose to ignore his over exaggerated dramatics. "You clean up all right yourself."

It was true. He was wearing a tux—something she never would have imagined him to own, let alone wear. But he looked rather dashing in it, not that Alex was surprised.

"Oh, don't you both look wonderful!" Dorothy cooed when she caught sight of them in the hallway. "My little boy's all grown up."

Alex had to cough into her hand to hide her laugh.

Bear tugged awkwardly at his collar, blushing slightly. "Mum. Please."

"I'm sorry, darling. You just look so handsome! So much like your father." Dorothy brushed some invisible lint off his jacket.

"And that's our cue to leave," Bear said, handing Alex her coat and pulling her towards the front door.

"Have a fun night!" Dorothy called after their retreating backs. "We'll probably be asleep when you get home but we'll see you in the morning!"

Bear just waved without turning and continued to drag Alex out the door.

"Are we using a Bubbledoor?" she asked when they were outside.

"Yeah, but we have to go separately for security reasons," he said. "The hosts are always paranoid about party crashers."

He handed over a bulky envelope and motioned for her to open it. Inside were two small Bubbler vials, along with a beautifully scripted invitation.

On behalf of His Royal Highness:

Alexandra Jennings

is hereby invited to attend the
New Year's Eve Gala

Alex read the words a second time and asked, "Does this mean the royal family will be there?"

Bear shrugged. "Not necessarily. All the invitations to elite events are written 'On behalf of His Royal Highness' just so they sound more impressive. I doubt the king and queen will be in attendance."

"It still sounds really exclusive," Alex said, her stomach fluttering with nerves. She smoothed a non-existent wrinkle from her dress, hoping she looked okay.

"It's not that big of a deal," Bear assured her. "I mean, it is, but everyone's always so snobby that it's easier to see it as a bit of a joke."

"Right," Alex said, not at all comforted. "What do I need to know about these security measures?"

"You just need to have your invitation with you to be able to Bubble in and out of the venue," Bear said. "Each Bubbler is formulated to work only when in range of the invitation it's linked with. It's really complex Chemistry, but all you need to know is, if I swapped one of my Bubblers with one of yours, it wouldn't work because yours is networked to link with your specific invitation. I can only get there and back by using my two Bubbler vials, provided that I have my invitation with me as well."

"What happens if I lose my invitation?" Alex asked. "Or one of my Bubblers?"

"Err—it's best if you don't," Bear said. "Of course, it happens every year to someone. But you'd have to go and talk to the hosts and that's not something we want to have to deal with tonight, if you can help it."

"Understood," Alex said, securing both the invitation and the second Bubbler in her purse.

"These Bubblers were created specifically to arrive and depart from a single place—the Gala," Bear said. "Normally the first person through a Bubbledoor has to envision where they want it to open out at, but with these the destination is already pre-set."

"That makes things easier," Alex said. It could have ended disastrously for her otherwise, since she had no idea where they were going.

Bear nodded and said, "I'll see you in a minute, okay?" Without waiting for a response, he smashed his vial on the ground and jumped into the shimmering colours, disappearing from view.

Alex followed immediately after him, stepping into her own bubble portal and landing in the middle of a rose garden lit by twinkling fairy lights. A huge marble mansion glowed in the background, and Alex felt the need to pinch herself to see if she was dreaming.

"Nice, huh?"

She spun around, relieved to find Bear behind her.

"It's incredible," she said. "Does someone actually live here?"

"The hosts of the Gala," he said. "It's called Chateau Shondelle, which translates roughly to mean: 'I have a massive house and an equally large stick shoved up my—'"

"*Bear!*" Alex hissed, looking around to see if anyone else was in hearing range.

"Anyway," he continued, ignoring her reprimand, "the Gala is held here every year. There's a massive ballroom inside which is perfect for the event."

Alex struggled to take in the size of the mansion. She couldn't even begin to imagine living in a place like this.

"Come on, we'd better get inside," Bear said, pulling gently on her arm.

They walked straight over to and then through a double-arched entryway, continuing down a brightly lit corridor. At the end of the hallway was an attendant waiting beside a set of closed doors.

"Invitations?" he asked in a bored voice.

They handed over their invites and the man looked at them closely before returning them. "Proceed," he drawled, and the doors opened automatically with his acceptance.

Alex tried to contain her amazed expression when she stepped into the ballroom, but it was challenging. Crystal—possibly diamond—chandeliers hung from the vaulted ceilings, an elevated stage held a string orchestra, and there was even a buffet feast spread along one entire wall of the room. People everywhere were dancing, laughing and eating their way into the New Year.

Bear chuckled at Alex's expression as he led her down the steps and further into the room. "Pretty fancy, huh?"

Alex nodded and continued scanning the room, keeping an eye out for Jordan. She soon spotted him standing with a group of people near the far wall. Like Bear, he was also wearing a tux—and wearing it *well*—but Jordan clearly felt uncomfortable. He was standing tall, his posture stiffer and sharper than she'd ever seen, and his face was a mask of stone. On one side of him stood a man and on the other a woman, both of them blond and beautiful. Their body language oozed confidence and self-importance.

"Are they his parents?" Alex asked, pointing out the group.

Bear tensed slightly. "Yeah, that's them. Marcus and Natasha Sparker. I've only met them a few times, but they're a real piece of work."

Alex didn't doubt his words. Even standing on the opposite side of the room she felt intimidated by them.

"Now that we're here, should we go and rescue our friend?" she asked.

Bear looked at her strangely. "Ah, no. We don't want to interrupt them. Jordan will come and find us when he can."

"What do you mean, 'when he can'?"

"Remember what he said about his parents showing him off? They'll parade him around for a while—which is what he agreed to do in order to get us here—but then they'll get sick of him and he'll be free to hang out with us for the rest of the night."

"That's horrible," Alex said. How could anyone's parents be so uncaring? "What do you normally do while you wait?"

"What do you think?" Bear tipped his head towards the buffet spread. "These people might be snobs, but they're snobs with access to the best chefs in all of Medora."

Alex laughed, feeling her anxiety dissipate, and she eagerly followed him in the direction of the food.

Thirty

"I'm *exhausted*."

Alex looked up from her chocolate mud cake to find Jordan collapsing onto the chair beside her, loosening his bow tie and stretching out his legs.

"You look it," she agreed, spooning another bite of pure heaven into her mouth.

"You're supposed to tell me how devilishly handsome I look," he said with a pout. "That no amount of tiredness could ever diminish my ruggedly perfect looks."

"My mistake," Alex said, enjoying her cake too much to pay close attention to his words—at least until he slid the dessert away from her and started devouring it. "Hey!" she cried, pulling the plate back and shielding it behind her arm. "Get your own!"

He looked at her with the saddest puppy-dog expression she'd ever seen, and she glanced from the cake to him and back again, before sighing and removing her arm.

"We'll *share* it," she said, emphasising the 'share'.

"You're the best!" he said, or at least that's what she thought he'd said, since his mouth was full of chocolate.

"Are you done for the night, mate?" Bear asked from Alex's other side.

Jordan nodded and swallowed quickly. "Yeah, I'm free. And it's a good thing too, since I think if Emily Walters continued

266 · Lynette Noni

making those goo-goo eyes at me, I might have ended up in an arranged marriage." He shuddered while Alex and Bear laughed even though they didn't know who he was talking about.

"Jordan, darling, there's one more person we'd like you to meet," came a feminine voice from behind them.

Alex looked around to see Jordan's parents standing there waiting for him.

"But, Mother——" he started.

"Come along, son," his father interrupted in a tone that allowed no room for debate. "This will only take a moment, and then you can come back to your... *friends.*"

Alex didn't like Jordan's father one bit. The cursory glance he gave her and Bear only highlighted the fact that he considered them to be beneath his notice. His wife didn't even look in their direction, but instead she ordered her son to stand up straight and fix his tie.

Jordan sent Alex and Bear an apologetic look, promising to be back soon.

"They're..." Alex failed to think of an appropriate description that could be said in public.

Thankfully, Bear understood the words she couldn't say. "Yeah, I know."

They watched as their friend was led across the room to yet another group of haughty-looking aristocrats. While he appeared to fit in with them, there was something in his stance that screamed of rebellion. Alex was amazed that Jordan could have grown up around these people and yet still turned out to be the decent—if playfully arrogant—friend that she knew.

"How did it happen?" she asked Bear, before realising that he couldn't read her mind. "How did he turn out so *normal* surrounded by all this?"

Bear looked torn, but he eventually said, "His brother died, five years ago."

Alex's eyes widened. "Jordan had a brother?"

"An older brother, Luka. There was a ten-year age gap between them, but Jordan idolised him. I never knew Luka, since I didn't meet Jordan until we started at the academy, but from what he's told me, Luka was everything anyone would want in a brother. He was smart, funny and an all-round nice guy. Jordan was a spoiled brat in comparison, having always been given everything he wanted—except maybe some quality attention from his parents. But Luka gave him that attention. They weren't just brothers, they were best friends."

"What happened?" she asked.

"Luka killed himself," Bear whispered and Alex gasped. "It was very sudden; no one even knew anything was wrong. He was so normal, so happy. It really hit Jordan hard."

"How awful," Alex said quietly.

"Yeah," agreed Bear. "But what's worse is that Luka left a note for Jordan."

"What did it say?" she asked, unable to hold back her curiosity.

"I don't know," Bear said. "Jordan never told me. But it changed him. He decided he didn't want to be the spoiled child anymore, and that's how he became the person he is today."

"That must have been difficult, to lose his brother like that and not have his parents around for support," Alex said.

"Yeah," Bear agreed. "I can't imagine having to go through that. But Jordan's made of tougher stuff than we sometimes give him credit for."

Alex murmured her agreement and they descended into silence. She looked around the room, watching the waltzing couples who shared whispered words and secretive smiles.

Bear must have followed her gaze since he stood from his seat, held out his hand, and asked, "Do you want to dance?"

"Um… I don't really know how."

"That's okay," he said, grinning widely as he pulled her to her feet. "I don't either."

Alex laughed and allowed him to lead her to the dance floor. Despite his words, it was soon clear that he at least knew the basics since he was able to keep them moving in time with the music. He was the best partner she could have imagined for her first waltz, and he even managed not to cringe every time she stood on his feet—which happened a lot.

"You're not too bad," he said after they finished their third dance. They'd decided to skip the next one to catch their breath—and in Bear's case, rest his damaged feet.

She snorted. "Liar."

"Okay," he conceded as he handed her a glass of water which she eagerly gulped down. "You're not too bad *now*. When we started, I thought I'd have to amputate my toes by the end of the night."

She chose to take his words as a compliment. "I've truly flourished under your expert guidance."

"That's what all the ladies say." He winked at her and proclaimed, "I am the dancing king!"

"Did he have some of the punch?" Jordan asked Alex as he stepped up beside them. He gestured towards their empty glasses. "You know that stuff's potent, right?"

Alex laughed and shook her head. "No, it's just him being normal."

"Ah. That explains it," Jordan said. "Well, in that case, I'm going to have to insist you sit this next one out, buddy, while I show Alex how to *really* dance."

Jordan took Alex's glass and handed it to an indignant Bear before sweeping her into his arms and back out onto the dance floor.

Alex had to admit that he was a much better dancer than Bear. He held her firmly and she didn't have to look down at her feet because he led her through the steps with such a confident assurance that she followed him without hesitation.

"You're very good at this," she said as he guided her around the room.

"I've been dancing at events like this since I was five," he said, shrugging away her praise. "I'd want to not completely suck after all that time."

"I suppose so," she agreed, imagining a cute little five-year-old Jordan trying to waltz across a ballroom.

"I'm sorry about before," Jordan said as he led her effortlessly through a complicated set of steps that she and Bear had disregarded on their previous attempts. "With my parents, I mean. I know they can be a bit... difficult."

"It's no problem," Alex said, but she didn't know what else to say after that. He looked guilty, and she wanted him to know that it wasn't his fault.

"When I was seven, my parents took me to a dinner they'd been invited to," she told him on a whim. "It was some sort of awards night to acknowledge the difference they and others around the world had made in the scientific community. It was a huge deal and they wanted to make a good impression. I'm still not sure why they let me tag along."

Jordan gave her his full attention and she wondered if perhaps she should have thought of a better story.

"What happened?" he asked.

"We were seated at a long table beside the most important people, including all the major sponsors and the potential future investors. Halfway through the main meal I reached for a bread roll and accidentally knocked over someone's wine glass. When I tried to help clean it up I slipped off my chair, and as I fell I grabbed onto the tablecloth, which caused everyone else's food and wine to end up in their laps. We were escorted from the event, despite the fact that the awards hadn't even been announced by that stage. My parents were so embarrassed that they grounded me for a month."

Jordan laughed, the first proper laugh she'd heard from him all night.

"It's kind of different to your situation," she admitted as their song wound to a close. "But if it helps, most families are dysfunctional in some way. I'm the odd one out in mine, as are you in yours. Us weirdos have to stick together."

"Thanks, Alex," he said, hugging her tightly in the middle of the dance floor. "What would I do without you?"

"You'd be a mess," she told him as he let her go. "Crying your eyes out, snotting all over your tux. Believe me, that's not something anyone wants to see. So be thankful I'm here, saving us all from that unpleasant sight."

He laughed again and then turned serious once more. "Bear told you about Luka, didn't he?"

She was startled by the unexpected change of topic. "How...?"

"I was watching you guys after my parents dragged me away. It was written all over your face. Am I right?"

In a quiet voice, Alex admitted, "Yeah, he told me."

Jordan looked into her eyes for a moment before he finally nodded. "I'm glad you know." He didn't say anything else. Instead, he reached for her hand and led her off the dance floor.

"Time for a bathroom break," she said once they were with Bear again.

Jordan gave her directions and she hurried off before she could forget them. She retraced her steps out of the ballroom and walked down the corridor until she came to a massive winding staircase. Supposedly the bathroom was on the next floor up, at the end of the hallway, but Jordan had failed to mention that the staircase was designed to spiral through the centre of the chateau, which meant that it opened out in the middle of the floor. The hallway led in both directions, so Alex did a mental eenie-meenie-miney-moe and chose to head down the left corridor.

The hallway was long, really long, and much darker than the ground floor had been. Paintings hung from the walls and hollow-eyed statues stood at attention in between closed doors.

Alex picked up her pace, wanting to finish her business and get back to her friends—or just people in general.

Finally she arrived at the end of the hallway only to find two doors, one on the right and one on the left. Not sure which one to enter—and cursing Jordan for his lack of proper directions—she decided to try the right door first. She opened it but it was too dark to see so she stepped into the room and the lights came on automatically. Instead of a bathroom, it was a storage room of some kind, so she quickly backed out and stepped across to the other door, hoping that she wouldn't have to trek back down the hallway.

Just like the first room, it was too dark to see what was inside until she walked far enough forward that the lights turned on.

Still no bathroom.

This time she'd entered a professional-looking study. She was about to retreat again when something mounted on one of the walls caught her eye and she found herself walking towards it unconsciously.

It was a sword. The weapon itself seemed normal—as far as Alex's limited knowledge went—but the blade was something else entirely. It was completely black, swirling with an inky darkness that was almost identical to whatever was inside the ring Blake had given her for Kaldoras. In all the holiday excitement she'd never had the chance to ask anyone about it, much to her annoyance now.

She was just about to grasp the hilt of the sword and pull it off the wall for a closer look when a voice startled her.

"What are you doing in here?"

Thirty-One

Alex jumped and turned around. Standing in the doorway was a burly man covered in dark tattoos—even his bald head had thorny swirls of ink ingrained into the skin. He was without a doubt the scariest-looking person Alex had ever encountered.

"I-I was looking for the bathroom," she stuttered.

"This ain't no bathroom," he said, pulling out a long, jagged knife. "And you ain't supposed to be in here."

"Whoa," she said, backing up with her hands in the air. "Take it easy. I'm just in the wrong place. And I'm leaving."

"Too right you are," he said, advancing towards her. "But we can't have you spreading lies to all your little friends now, can we?"

Alex continued to back up until she slammed into a bookshelf. The man had crazy eyes, and he didn't look like he was bluffing with that knife. She frantically looked around for a way to escape.

"What's going on in here?"

Alex heaved a sigh of relief at the sight of Jordan's father entering the room.

"This one was snooping," said the burly man.

"I was not!" Alex felt safer now that there was a witness. "I got lost on my way to the bathroom. This place is like a huge maze—they need to put up signposts."

The two men stared at her, one with a bloodthirsty expression, the other with a carefully blank mask.

"You're acquainted with my son, aren't you?" Marcus Sparker asked.

"Yeah, I'm Jordan's friend." Alex was relieved that he remembered her. "And he's probably wondering where I am."

Something flashed across Marcus's face—a dash of amusement, perhaps?—before it was blank once more. "I'm sure my son can wait a moment longer," he said, his voice as soft as silk. "He wouldn't deny me the honour of greeting one of my own guests."

She looked at him in confusion. "*Your* guests?"

The amusement stayed on his face for longer this time. "Didn't Jordan tell you? Surely he wouldn't keep you in the dark?"

Now Alex was getting annoyed. "Tell me *what?*"

"Who your hosts are," Marcus said. "My wife and I hold the Gala each year, here in our ancestral home—in *Jordan's* ancestral home—Chateau Shondelle."

"*You* live here?" Why hadn't Jordan told her? Or Bear, for that matter?

"Marcus," the tattooed man said, "I caught the girl red-handed. Let me deal with her."

"Enough, Gerald," Marcus snapped. "Can't you see I'm having a conversation with this charming young woman?"

"But, Marcus—"

"*Enough!*"

Gerald glared at Alex but kept his mouth shut. He didn't put the knife away though, and it glinted threateningly in the lamplight.

Marcus turned back to her. "What's your name?"

"It's your party," Alex said, feeling irritated and uneasy. "Shouldn't you know who your guests are?"

His expression tightened. "You'd do well to remember who you're speaking with, girl."

She shuddered at the dark look in his eyes. "Alex," she told him. "My name is Alex."

"Alex who?" he prompted.

Wondering why it mattered at all, she said, "Jennings. I'm Alexandra Jennings."

His blank features transformed, showing his surprise. "Well, well, well," he said. "I had no idea my son kept such... *interesting* company."

Alex didn't say anything. She didn't understand his comment and she *really* didn't like the calculating look on his face.

"Your mind is silent," Marcus stated. "I'd like to know why."

"I have no idea what you mean," she answered calmly, despite her racing heart. Was he a mind reader? Jordan had never told her much about his parents—she didn't know if they were gifted or not. But if his father had the ability to look into her thoughts then she needed to get away from him immediately, regardless of how 'silent' he found her mind to be.

"I don't mean to be rude," she said, "but as I mentioned earlier, Jordan is probably wondering where I am. So, if you'll excuse me?" She made to push past him but Gerald stepped into her path, raising his knife.

"And as *I* mentioned earlier, my son can wait," Marcus returned. "Why don't you have a seat so that we can become... better acquainted." He leaned casually against the desk—his desk, she presumed—and indicated for her to sit.

"I'd rather not, thank you," she told him, crossing her arms.

Apparently that was the wrong answer, because Gerald growled and took a step forward.

"Touch me and I swear I'll scream," Alex said. Her insides were fluttering with fear, but on the outside she maintained a steely resolve, determined not to let them see how freaked out she really was. She didn't even know if screaming would do any good, since they were quite a distance from the ballroom and it was unlikely anyone would hear her. But she wasn't going to stand there and be a complete pushover.

Marcus actually laughed. It was a chilling sound, and not at all comforting.

"Dear girl, we mean you no harm," he said, smiling at her. Like his laugh, the expression was unnatural, and didn't match the look in his hard blue eyes.

"Then why won't you let me leave?" she pressed. "You have a house full of guests downstairs, remember? Shouldn't you be getting back to them?"

"My wife is entertaining them," he said, unconcerned. "I would be remiss in my duties as a father if I ignored an opportunity to get to know one of my son's friends."

"Perhaps there are other fatherly duties you would do better to concentrate on," Alex said before she could stop herself. She regretted the words immediately, and she bit down on her tongue to keep from saying anything more, but the damage was already done. The effect of her statement was almost tangible; she could practically feel the room drop in temperature as the tension rocketed skywards.

Marcus pushed off from the desk and was in front of her before she could take a breath. "What did you say to me?"

She took a step back, bumping into Gerald who stood too close behind her. "I—I—"

"Do you know who I am?" he whispered, his voice soft and deadly. "How dare you speak to me in such a way?"

She couldn't say anything, mostly because she wasn't sure which question to answer first, but also because she was too distracted by Gerald's blade, which was mere inches away from her spinal cord.

When she remained silent, Marcus nodded to Gerald and she felt the tattooed man's arm snake around her stomach while his other hand moved to hold the knife at the base of her neck. The sharp blade pressed against her jugular, freezing her to the spot.

"Answer me!" Marcus ordered.

"Don't you think you're going a little overboard?" Alex managed to croak out, but even that slight movement caused the blade to prick into her skin. She couldn't keep her body from trembling in response, which only increased the pressure of the knife against her flesh.

Irrationally, she found that she was furious with her Combat teacher for failing to prepare her for such a situation. Even if Karter hadn't turned her into a kung fu master, she still might have learned enough self-defence to get out of her current predicament in one piece.

"If I apologise for insulting your parenting skills, will you let me go?" Alex finally asked. Her emotions were shot—she was afraid, but she was also angry. What they were doing to her was not cool, and she couldn't contain her natural reaction of unchecked sarcasm. "I promise to sound like I mean it."

Gerald tightened his grip and she felt a painful sting as the blade cut deeper into her skin, causing a drop of blood to dribble down her neck.

"You do realise that people are going to wonder how I got that in the bathroom?" she hissed at Marcus, strangely emboldened as a result of the cut. "I doubt they'll accept the excuse that *I fell*."

"Only two people would notice, and neither would have reason to believe you," Marcus said. "And if they did, they could be taken care of just as easily."

Alex paled at his implied threat. He wouldn't really hurt Jordan and Bear... would he?

"Neither of them will know about it at all if you don't make it back to the ballroom," Gerald whispered into her ear. He tightened his grip on the blade even more, causing another drop of warm liquid to trickle down her skin.

Fear and anger continued to brew within Alex, both emotions demanding her attention. She wasn't sure whether to rage, scream, or cry. Her body felt clammy and tense, her muscles were coiled and ready for action. But she couldn't do anything, not while she was trapped in Gerald's arms.

"Look, I don't—" Alex wasn't even sure what she was going to say, but it didn't matter since her words were interrupted.

"Ah, Alexandra, here you are."

The voice shocked her as much as it did the two men holding her captive. They both jumped away from her and turned towards the new arrival.

Alex could only gape at Darrius, who was standing in the doorway exuding an aura of safety and comfort.

"What an... *unexpected* surprise," Marcus said smoothly, hiding Gerald from view so that the tattooed man could move his knife out of sight. "However did you get in here, old man?"

"You know me, Marcus," Darrius said. "I'm always up for a good party."

"I wasn't aware that you were on the guest list." Marcus's voice was as flat as his expression.

"It was pure chance that I happened by an invitation. Your chocolate mud cake is amazing, by the way." Darrius seemed outwardly calm, but his silver eyes were as hard as steel as he took in their appearances, particularly the small cut on Alex's neck.

"I was actually hoping to have a word with Alexandra before she departed for the evening," Darrius said, turning to her. "May I have a moment of your time?"

Alex nodded frantically at him, her heart still beating wildly in her chest. She desperately wanted to get away from the two dangerous men, but she still didn't move, fearing that one of them would reach out and grab her if she made to leave.

"How kind of you." Darrius smiled at her and she felt her fear begin to fade. "If you'd like to follow me, we can speak outside. Marcus, Gerald, always a pleasure."

Judging by Marcus's expression, it was anything but a pleasure for him, but he still allowed Alex to step away. After a few careful footsteps, she raced out of the room.

"Darrius!" she cried when he closed the door behind them. Her relief was so strong that she almost hugged him. "What are you doing here?"

"Just a happy coincidence," he answered. "You haven't happened to come across the bathroom, perhaps? I must have taken a wrong turn at the top of the staircase."

Alex was certain he wasn't telling the truth but she was too grateful to demand an explanation. "I think you just saved my life."

"No, I don't believe that to be true," Darrius told her seriously. "Had I not arrived, you would have found your own way out."

Alex wished she had as much confidence in herself as he did. "Well, thank you, anyway," she told him. "I owe you one."

Halfway down the corridor she reached up to the cut on her neck.

"I can't go back down there looking like this," she said. "Jordan and Bear will freak—Jordan especially, since his father is responsible. And this is the Sparkers' *house*. Marcus could try and corner me again." She shuddered at the thought.

"I can help you get back to Akarnae from here, if you want?" Darrius said. "If I'm correct, you'd only be a day or so earlier than your fellow students. You could even visit Doctor Fletcher for a healing salve."

That was an appealing thought. And it would also mean no difficult questions from her friends.

"You have a Bubbler back to the academy?" Alex asked. "I thought they had to be specially made for the Gala?"

"No, not a Bubbler," he said, but he didn't elaborate. "Do you have a way to contact your friends so they know you're all right?"

"I have my ComTCD," Alex said, "but I don't know what I'll say to them."

"One problem at a time, Alexandra," he said. "One problem at a time."

Darrius led her back down the staircase, past the ballroom, and out the front door, stopping only when they reached the rose garden where she'd arrived hours earlier. He pulled something from his tuxedo jacket and it took her a moment to recognise what it was.

"That's a Communications Globe," Alex said, looking at the cloudy sphere. "I thought they were only used at Akarnae?"

"They are. Fortunately for us, it will override the security restrictions placed on outgoing transportations from the chateau, and it will also deliver you safely through the wards surrounding the academy."

"Convenient," she said. "But how did you get it?"

"This one belongs to your headmaster," Darrius informed her. "I'm certain he won't mind you borrowing it, so long as you return it to him."

"Oh," Alex said. "But how will you get out of here?"

"I have some business to attend to first," he said, not quite answering her question. "We'd best send you along now, before your friends decide to call out a search party."

"What should I tell them?" she asked, fresh out of ideas.

"The truth is always a good place to start," Darrius said, "but perhaps in this instance you should leave out some of the details." He then pressed the Globe into her hands. "You should land just outside of your headmaster's office. I recommend you visit Administrator Jarvis and advise him of your arrival. He'll ensure the Globe is returned to its owner."

Alex sent him a grateful look. "Thanks so much again, Darrius. For everything."

"You're most welcome, Alexandra," he said, his eyes shining silver in the moonlight. "I look forward to our next encounter."

"You know you can call me Alex, right?" she told him, ignoring his comment and the promise it seemed to hold. He had a knack for showing up whenever she was in trouble and she didn't like the idea that she might need his help again soon.

Darrius just smiled at her before saying something—a word she didn't recognise—and she felt a whooshing of air against her body as the Globe transported her away from the mansion and towards the academy.

Thirty-Two

Alex landed in the antechamber outside the headmaster's office and pulled out her ComTCD, wanting to get the conversation with Bear and Jordan over with. As she waited for her Device to connect with Bear's, she had the presence of mind to scrub away the blood that was still lightly trickling down her neck.

"Alex?" Bear said as he answered her call. Both his anxious face and Jordan's were projected in the hologram that rose out of her screen. "Are you okay? We've been looking everywhere for you!"

"I'm okay," she told them. "Sorry I worried you." She made sure to keep her free hand covering her neck, hoping that they wouldn't notice her unnatural body language.

"Where are you? We'll come to you," Jordan said, his voice strained with concern.

"Uh—I'm actually not there anymore."

"You left already?" Bear asked in surprise. "That's okay. It's kind of boring here anyway. We'll come back home now, too."

"No," Alex said. Seeing their startled looks, she quickly explained, "I'm actually at the academy. It's kind of a funny story."

She left it hanging, realising that it wasn't funny in the slightest.

"Basically, your directions suck, Jordan." Alex tried to huff a laugh but she was pretty sure it fell short. "I got a bit—um—

lost... and then I sort of ran into Darrius. You remember me telling you guys about him? The man I met in the Library? Up in the clouds?"

"The guy who made you jump out of the building?" Jordan asked. "What was he doing here?"

"It's your party, how should I know?" She hadn't meant to bring it up, but she was still annoyed that his father had been the one to tell her.

Jordan disappeared from the hologram and she worried that he was upset with her until she heard him ask Bear if he could have a moment. Bear smiled reassuringly at Alex before he too disappeared and then only Jordan came back into view.

"I should have told you," Jordan said quietly. "I don't know how you found out, but I'm sorry it wasn't from me."

Alex sighed and looked away.

"I didn't want you to think any less of me," he whispered, which caused her to turn back to him.

"Why would I think less of you?"

"Because of all this." He gestured to the opulent ballroom surrounding him. "This isn't me. I may have grown up here, with these people, but that's not who I am now. I didn't—I *don't* want you to think I'm anything like my parents."

Alex actually snorted. "That will never happen, Jordan. You're *nothing* like your parents." She didn't want to judge his mother, but she was certain he was nothing like his father.

"I try not to be," he said, still uncertain. "But I can't help that there's a little bit of them in me."

"And a whole heap of plain, old, boring you," Alex said. Perhaps quite a bit of his brother Luka too, but she kept that thought to herself. "That's the part that matters, the part we know and love."

"All right, all right." Bear elbowed his way into the projection again. "Enough of the mushy sentimentality. You never explained how you got back to the academy, Alex. That Bubbler should have taken you straight to my house. And why didn't you come and tell us that you were leaving first?"

"Um... So, like I said, I ran into Darrius. He said he was lost too, also on a mission to find the bathroom." Alex was trying to keep as close to the truth as possible. "Your house—sorry, *chateau*—is huge, by the way, Jordan. It took us forever just to reach the staircase again. Then we got so turned around that we somehow ended up out the front in the garden."

Now she would have to come up with some little white lies.

"I was desperate to go by that stage." The words were true, even if the meaning was different. "I didn't want to walk all the way back inside and ask for clearer directions, only to get lost all over again." That was less true, but not terribly deceitful. "It turned out that Darrius had the headmaster's Communications Globe with him and when he offered it to me all I could think was that it would be so much easier to find a bathroom when I knew where they were, so I used the Globe to get back here. Silly, I know, but I do feel much better now."

That was also the truth. But she was really starting to need that bathroom break again.

"What can I say?" She sent them an apologetic grin. "When you've got to go, you've got to go."

"What is it with girls and bathrooms?" Jordan asked Bear quietly, as if forgetting that Alex was right there.

"I'm kind of stuck here now, I guess." She was saddened by the thought that she wouldn't get to say a proper goodbye to the Ronnigans.

"Yeah, that sucks," Bear said. "We'd come and get you, but the academy's security wards won't allow us to Bubble in until Sunday afternoon like everyone else. If only we all had ComGlobes, hey?"

"That would be nice," she agreed. "Will you thank your family for me? And tell them how sorry I am that I didn't get to say goodbye?"

"Yeah, no problem," Bear said. "You'll see them again, Mum'll make sure of that. You're one of us now, just like Jordan here."

Alex smiled at the thought.

"And we'll make sure to bring all your stuff back with us, too," Jordan promised.

"Thanks guys, you're the best."

"We know."

"Okay, well, I guess I'll see you both the day after tomorrow," she said.

"It's already tomorrow," Jordan informed her. "Happy New Year, Alex."

She glanced down at the time displayed on her ComTCD and realised he was right. "Happy New Year," she repeated back to them.

"May this one be even more interesting than the last," Bear added and she groaned, causing them both to laugh.

"Don't even *think* that," she said, before wishing them goodnight and terminating their connection.

That went better than expected, Alex thought as she exited the room and hurried down the staircase.

It was late, already after midnight, and she wasn't sure if she should follow Darrius's advice and seek out Jarvis. She decided to try his office just in case he was still up, but if he wasn't there then she would look for him in the morning.

She couldn't remember what floor the headmaster's office was on, so she had to walk down the entire staircase before ascending it again to reach Jarvis's office on the eighth floor. She knocked on the closed door, not really expecting an answer, and was surprised when it opened.

"Alex?" Jarvis's tired eyes widened comically at the sight of her. His clothing was rumpled and he looked like he was about to drop with exhaustion. "What are you doing here? In the middle of the night, no less?"

"Hi, Jarvis," she said. "Do you have a minute?"

He ushered her into his office, motioning for her to take a seat. "What happened to you?" he asked, taking in her formal attire—and her injury.

"Oh, it's nothing, really," she said, waving away his concern. Now that she was safe and warm it didn't seem as bad. "Just one of those wrong place, wrong time things. Come to think of it, they happen to me a lot."

He looked at her seriously. "Alex, please. What are you doing here? No, *how* did you get here?"

She handed him the Communications Globe.

His brow furrowed with bafflement as he turned the misty sphere over in his hands. "Where did you get this?"

"My friend Darrius gave it to me," she answered. 'Friend' seemed as good a title as any for the man who kept popping up unexpectedly. "He said it belongs to the headmaster."

Jarvis looked surprised. "You were with Darrius tonight?"

"You know him?"

He nodded—somewhat hesitantly—so she answered, "We ran into each other at the New Year's Eve Gala." When Jarvis continued to eye her strangely, she asked, "Is there a problem?"

"No, no, not at all. It's just... I didn't realise you were on such familiar terms."

"I hardly know him, really," Alex said. "He just sort of turns up whenever I need him."

Jarvis laughed. "Yes, he does seem to have a bit of a sixth sense about him."

"Thankfully that sixth sense led him to me tonight," Alex said. "He saved me from a difficult situation at Chateau

Shondelle, and bada-bing, here I am." She then pointed to the ComGlobe. "He also mentioned you'd be able to get that back to Professor Marselle."

"I'm sure he did," Jarvis murmured. In a louder voice he asked, "Do you want to tell me what happened to your neck?"

"Just part of that difficult situation I mentioned," she said, not wanting to elaborate.

Jarvis waited to see if she would say more, and when she didn't, he pursed his lips and said, "I can see you're tired, so I'll let it go for now. But I *will* be discussing this with the headmaster."

"Discuss away," Alex said, unsure why Professor Marselle would even need to know about it. Or care, for that matter.

"You should go and get some rest, Alex," Jarvis said. "You're a bit pale."

I'm sure I am, she thought, suddenly exhausted.

Alex bid him farewell and stumbled down the staircase and out of the Tower, heading straight to her dorm building. Her visit to Fletcher would have to wait until morning since she was too tired to go anywhere but to her bed.

Bathroom first, she corrected, *then bed*.

Thirty-Three

"What are you doing here?"

"Mmmghnfffff…"

"I said, what are you doing here?"

The voice was annoyingly insistent. Alex pulled her pillow over her head, hoping to block out the sound.

"You're bleeding," the voice said again, this time not as loud, but definitely closer. "Why are you bleeding?"

Alex groaned when the questions continued to interrupt her peaceful sleep. She moved the pillow away from her face and opened bleary eyes, surprised to find her roommate standing over her.

"D.C.?" she said in a sleepy voice. "Why are you in my room?"

"It's *our* room. And what are *you* doing here? Students aren't due back until tomorrow afternoon."

Alex sat upright, remembering that she wasn't at the Ronnigans' house anymore. She rubbed her eyes, feeling the cut on her neck pull with the movement. "Ow."

"What happened to you?" D.C. asked again. If Alex didn't know any better, she would have thought that the other girl seemed concerned. But that wasn't possible.

"Nothing," Alex mumbled, dragging herself out of bed. She quickly dressed in a pair of jeans and a thick woollen coat before she looked over at her roommate. The other girl seemed almost disappointed by the lack of explanation but Alex wasn't sure why, since D.C. never usually cared about anything Alex had to say.

"And you're back early because…?" D.C. asked again.

"Why are you here early?" Alex asked, turning the question around.

"I never left," D.C. answered.

"You stayed here for Kaldoras? On your own?" Alex asked before she could stop herself. "What about your family?"

D.C.'s expression tightened and Alex regretted asking something so personal when they were barely even on speaking terms.

"My family is away on business," D.C. said. "And I wasn't alone. There were other students who stayed here."

"Right," Alex said. "Did you have fun?"

She cringed. What a stupid question. D.C. must have thought so too, judging by her expression.

"I answered your question, now why are *you* here early?" she asked for the third time.

"Does it really matter?" Alex released a frustrated breath. "I'm here now, and everyone else will be back tomorrow. What's the big deal?"

"The security wards shouldn't have let you in," D.C. said. "So that means you must have come back because of special circumstances."

The red-head's eyes flickered to Alex's wounded throat, but Alex just shrugged, neither denying nor confirming her assumption.

"I'm just concerned for my own safety," D.C. continued. "If someone's after you, they might come after me to get you. I deserve to know if I have to watch my back because I have a roommate who can't keep her nose out of other people's business."

Okay, that wasn't fair.

Not wanting to say or do something she'd later regret, Alex turned and walked straight out the doorway, ignoring D.C.'s cries for her to come back and answer her questions.

Presuming it was too late for breakfast, Alex headed directly to the Med Ward. Fletcher was there, just like she'd hoped, but he wasn't alone. With him stood another man, someone she'd never seen before. He was interesting to look at, with dark skin and a tangled mess of flaxen-coloured hair that was braided halfway down his back. Short for a man, he stood just under Alex's height, but what he lacked in length was made up for in steroid-like muscle mass. Aside from the strange contrast between his dark skin and light hair, Alex rather thought he reminded her of a Viking, with his long moustache and thick plaited beard. But her observation could have also been influenced by the horned helmet resting atop the crown of his head and the armour wrapped around his torso.

Despite his bizarre attire and weathered features, the Viking man had a kind face and directed a beaming smile towards her when she approached.

"Alex!" Fletcher greeted. "Jarvis said you might be paying me a visit today."

"I couldn't stay away," Alex said. "You know how much I love this place."

He tsked quietly as he looked at her neck. "Classes haven't even started back yet and already you're here to see me. That book must have been helpful."

She laughed with him. "Yes, thank you. I particularly liked the 'Doctor! Doctor!' jokes."

"I'm pleased to hear it," Fletcher said. "I don't believe you've met Varin yet, have you?"

"Varin?"

290 · Lynette Noni

"That's me," said the other man, his voice as large as his muscles.

Varin the Viking, Alex mused. *Seems fitting.*

"Nice to meet you," she said, feeling strangely at ease around him.

"Likewise, Alex," Varin said. "Fletch here has been regaling me with tales of your misfortune. You certainly do like his Medical Ward, don't you?"

Something clicked then and Alex realised Varin was the patient who had been in quarantine on the day of the Lockdown, the one she'd overheard Fletcher speaking with.

She covered her shock quickly with an annoyed expression. "What happened to doctor–patient confidentiality, Fletcher?"

He just grinned and motioned for her to jump up onto the closest bed.

"I better get going and leave you to it," Varin said. "But I'll see you in class on Thursday, Alex."

"Class?" she repeated, not sure what he meant.

"Species Distinction," he clarified. "I'm your professor, but I use that term lightly."

"Oh." Alex had forgotten that her spare period wasn't actually a spare period.

Varin waved goodbye to both of them and Fletcher excused himself for a moment before he returned with her file.

Alex eyed it warily. "It's getting kind of big."

Fletcher chuckled. "You're one of my best patients." He placed the clipboard onto the bed. "Now, let's have a look at you."

He poked and prodded before finally using a vanilla-scented salve to seal her skin back together. Within seconds her wound was completely healed, and Fletcher ushered her out the door, ordering her to enjoy what remained of her holidays.

The rest of Alex's day passed by uneventfully. Her Equestrian Skills instructor, Tayla, invited her on a trail ride out into the snow-covered forest, and afterwards Alex helped clean out the stables in preparation for the start of classes. When she made it back to her room after dinner that night she was exhausted, but satisfied with her hard day's work.

Determined to keep her good mood, Alex ignored D.C. who was already in bed, reading. She thought her roommate would follow her lead, but she was wrong.

"What I said this morning—" D.C. started to say.

"Don't," Alex cut in. "You don't have to worry. No one is coming after me. I was just in the wrong place at the wrong time, that's all." She kept her voice low and calm. It was easier to keep her annoyance in check that way.

"I didn't mean—"

"Seriously," Alex interrupted again. "You're perfectly safe."

"But—"

"And even if someone *was* coming after me," Alex broke in again, "I'm sure you would still be safe, since anyone with half a brain can tell that we're not friends. They would have to be pretty thick to try and get to me through you."

D.C. didn't try and talk again. She didn't do anything, in fact, except slowly raise her book once more. Her sleeves were rolled up and Alex felt her throat tighten when she noticed that the other girl was wearing the charm bracelet she'd sent her for Kaldoras. Something about the gesture brought tears to Alex's eyes, and she realised that she must be more tired than she'd thought if she was so affected by something that clearly meant nothing.

Thirty-Four

Alex was bored, and that was the only excuse she had for being in the foyer of the Library the next afternoon. Her friends weren't due back to the academy for a few more hours, and she needed something to do while she waited for their arrival. Against her better judgement, she decided that a trip to the Library could prove to be the perfect distraction. When she'd last travelled into its depths she'd almost been beheaded, but the time with Sir Camden had definitely given her a taste of adventure. A similar experience—perhaps with a touch less danger—might be exactly what she needed.

The foyer walls had all changed since her last visit, and Alex paused to admire a beautiful oil painting of a waterfall cascading down into a lake-filled valley. It was so realistic that she almost felt as if the water was trying to fall right out of the painting.

The librarian wasn't anywhere to be seen so, moving away from the painting, Alex headed across the room and started down the staircase. Just like the last time, it continued much further down than normal.

Even though it was her intention to explore, Alex still had a fluttery feeling in her stomach. She wondered if she might find Darrius again, and she could ask him more questions about what had happened at the Gala. Or maybe she would have another run-in with her knight in shining armour.

The possibilities were still running through her mind when the staircase came to an abrupt end at a solid stone wall with a single door cut into it. The simple piece of wood was closed, but Alex felt as if it was beckoning her to open it up and step inside.

After hesitating for a moment, she reached out and opened the door to find... nothing. Just a dark, empty space.

Alex stepped forward for a closer look, and the moment her head moved past the doorframe, invisible hands pulled her body through. She couldn't help but let out a surprised shriek when she discovered there was no floor beneath her feet anymore, and she plummeted through the darkness at an alarming speed until she was jerked to a halt and suspended in mid-air. Heart pounding, she waved her arms around, searching for something solid to grasp hold of, but all she found was more air.

Ever so slowly, Alex felt herself being lowered until she felt solid ground beneath her, much to her relief.

Despite there being no distinguishable source of light, the darkness began to fade as a bluish luminescence lit up the large space surrounding her. Soon enough Alex was able to see that she was in a cavern of some sort. It was a deep, rocky crevasse in the ground, with no discernible entrance or exit. She was completely underground.

There was a body of churning water not far from where Alex sat, the noise echoing loudly around the enclosed space. It was a river, roughly ten metres wide, slicing through the middle of the cave and splitting it in half. The pitch-black water flowed rapidly through semi-submerged fissures cut into the rock on opposite sides of the cavern. The two fissures were barely large enough for the raging torrent of water to pass through, and they appeared to be the only breaks in the otherwise solid walls of the underground chamber.

Alex rose and started walking carefully around the cave, wondering why she was there.

"*Why do you think?*"

Her heart skipped a beat and she whirled around, expecting to find someone behind her. But no one was there.

"Weird," she muttered to herself, figuring the noise of the river echoing around the cavern was playing tricks on her mind.

When she made it to the solid rock wall, she followed it along until she reached the river's entrance. Keeping her distance from the fast, dark water, Alex knelt to the ground and peered into the fissure. There didn't seem to be any way for her to get through the gap without entering the water. She looked down at the churning river and felt her stomach clench with dread at the thought. Even if she had some kind of inflation device, Alex would still be hesitant to use it. She was a strong swimmer—she maintained that her near-drowning in PE wasn't her fault—but the current was way too rapid. She wouldn't venture in unless she absolutely had to.

Alex followed the wall back the other way until she reached the opposite side, where the river exited the cave. Again she found that it was impossible to pass through the fissure without jumping into the water.

Frustrated, Alex turned and carefully walked along the steep bank of the river's edge, halting when she reached the middle of the cave. She looked over to the other side of her rocky prison and realised that even if she found the courage to cross the water, she could see no evidence of an exit over there.

"A little help here?" Alex called out, not even sure who she was calling to.

"*I thought you'd never ask.*"

Alex whirled around, certain she'd heard a voice this time. But there was still no one there.

"Where are you?" she asked.

"*I'm here.*"

Helpful. Not.

"Who are you?" Alex tried again.

"*I am who I am.*"

Again, not helpful in the slightest.

"*What* are you?" Alex asked, hoping for more of an idea.

"*I'm everything. Everything you hear. Everything you see. Everything you touch, taste, smell. I'm all around you, Alexandra Jennings.*"

Alex hesitated. "You're the Library?"

The voice chuckled. It was a strange sound, but full of warmth. "*That's how you know me, yes.*"

It wasn't really an answer, but Alex had a feeling it was all she was going to receive. "Why did you bring me here?"

Alex was asking about the cavern, but the Library's answer surprised her.

"*Because you are Chosen.*"

"I... don't understand."

"*Take a look around you, Alexandra. What do you see?*"

Alex decided to humour the voice. "I'm in a cavern split by a river that's preventing me from getting to the other side."

"*Is it really preventing you?*" the voice asked.

"Have you seen that water?" Alex replied. "I'd probably be swept under within a second and left to drown. That's if something didn't eat me first."

"*What else do you see?*"

Alex looked around. "That's pretty much it. Is there more?"

"*I see darkness. I see segregation. There's life here, and death too. The river ebbs and flows and the current forces the change; but in what direction? And for what purpose? What choices will be made and who will be affected by the consequences? There are many decisions and many possible outcomes. Tell me, Alexandra, if given the choice, what would you choose?*"

The noise in the cavern died out as the river stilled. One moment it was a raging torrent and the next it was as peaceful as a frozen pond. Three huge boulders rose to the surface of the water, creating a steady bridge for her to cross.

Alex was astounded by the river's sudden change, but her gaze was quickly captivated by what appeared on the other side of the water. Because now there was an open doorway resting in the middle of the cave.

And it led straight to her house at Cannon Beach.

"*You have a choice to make, Alexandra,*" the voice said.

The puzzle pieces snapped together as Alex thought about the Library's impossible doorways. "It was you who brought me through to Medora, wasn't it?" she whispered.

"*I merely presented the opportunity.*"

"Why?" Her question was part agonised, part desperate. She needed to know why everything had happened—and more, why it had happened to *her.*

"*Because you are Chosen,*" the voice said, repeating its earlier response. "*And you are needed, for such a time as this.*"

"What's that supposed to mean?" Alex asked, wondering why she wasn't already running across the river and jumping through the doorway back to her world.

"*It means what it means,*" the Library said. "*And it's up to you to decide what it means.*"

"Stop speaking in riddles!" Alex cried, frustrated.

"*I speak only the truth,*" the voice said, softening. "*It's you who must interpret that truth, otherwise I would be denying you the freedom to make your own decisions.*"

Alex let out a deep breath and said, "So, basically you're telling me you brought me here for a reason, but you won't tell me what that reason is because you don't want to influence my choices?"

The voice didn't say anything and Alex took that as a sign to continue. "And now you're saying I can go back? Just like that?"

There was still no response and Alex looked longingly at the doorway back to her world, to her *home.*

She took a step forward before she paused. "Can I come back? Once I've gone through, can I come back through the doorway?"

Again there was no response. Where had the voice gone? It seemed like it had told the truth about not telling her what to do. But there really was only one decision she could make. For all she knew, this was the only opportunity she would ever have to get back to Freya. There was no guarantee that the headmaster would be able to find a way home for her whenever he finally decided to return to the academy. This might be her only chance to get back to her normal life. Back to her parents. Back to where she actually *belonged*.

Placing one foot in front of the other, Alex carefully stepped onto the first boulder, then the second and the third. Before she knew it, she was standing in front of the doorway, staring up at her house.

One minute… Two minutes… Three minutes passed and she just stood there, looking through the doorway.

The choice was obvious—she had to go through. But still, she hesitated.

What if she couldn't come back? The Library may have brought her through to Medora once, but that didn't mean it would do so again.

And what about her friends? Jordan? Bear? The rest of the Ronnigan family? Fletcher and Jarvis and the other professors? What about Darrius? What if she never saw any of them again? She wouldn't get the chance to say goodbye, and they'd have no idea what had happened to her.

But if she didn't leave, she might never have access to a doorway like the one in front of her again. Was she willing to risk her life—her parents—her *world*—just to spend more time with a handful of people she'd known for only a few months?

As she stood in front of the doorway, Alex thought about everything that had happened to her since she'd first arrived in Medora. All the impossibilities she'd witnessed, all the amazing adventures she could never have dreamed of experiencing. Was she really willing to let all of that go? Did she even have a choice?

Alex turned and glanced behind her into the dark uncertainty of the cavern one last time. A silent tear fell down her cheek as she closed her eyes, whispered a heartfelt goodbye, and reached for the door.

Thirty-Five

A resolute *click* echoed around the cavern.

Alex looked at the closed door in front of her and another tear slipped down her cheek. She hoped she hadn't made the wrong decision, but for better or worse, she knew in her heart that she just wasn't ready to leave this world of wonder and the people in it.

Full of determination, Alex turned her back on the door and retraced her steps across the boulders to the other side of the river. The moment she stood on the cavern ground again, the rocks disappeared from view and the river roared into motion once more.

"*You've made your choice?*" the voice asked, back again.

"I have," Alex answered, feeling more and more confident of her decision.

"*I'm pleased.*"

"What happens now?" Alex asked.

"*As always, that's up to you,*" said the Library. "*But know that I am with you.*"

Alex presumed it was meant to be a comforting thought, but instead it kind of creeped her out to think that a disembodied presence would be following her around.

"I'm being stalked by a sentient Library," she said to herself. "Could my life be any weirder?"

"*Trust me, Alexandra, this is only the beginning.*"

"Awesome," Alex muttered. "So, now that we've had this bonding session and all, how do I get out of here?"

"*Through the river*," came the reply, as if it was obvious. At least she'd been given a straight answer and not another riddle this time. But still...

"I just crossed the river," she said. "Remember?"

"*I didn't say* over *the river, but* through *the river*."

Alex looked at the rapidly moving water and took a defensive step away from the edge.

"Nuh-uh, no way," she said. "You dropped me in here, so you can just fly me straight back out, thanks."

"*It doesn't work that way*," the Library told her. "*If you always re-live the same experiences, you'll never learn new skills or have opportunities to develop your character*."

"I'm pretty happy with my character as it is," Alex said, staring at the water with rising trepidation. It was as if the river was becoming more violent the longer she looked at it. Even the craziest adrenaline-seeking daredevil would think twice before taking a plunge into the fathomless depths.

"*Challenges are beneficial, Alexandra*," the voice said. "*They make life interesting. Isn't that why you came searching for me today—because you were bored?*"

"Bored, yes. But not suicidal," Alex argued. "And I wasn't looking for you. I was just... looking around."

"*For a distraction*."

"Yes," she reluctantly agreed.

"*And here you've found one*."

Alex looked at the water again. Was it just her imagination, or did it look even deeper and darker than before?

"Do I have a choice?" she asked. She wanted another option; *any* other option.

"*You always have a choice*," the voice reminded her. "*This one is just simpler than some of the others that you have faced—and have yet to face*."

"So, I can either stay stuck down here until I starve to death, or I can leave and *maybe* survive—but that's not necessarily guaranteed at this stage? Great choices I've got there."

"*And yet, they're still choices.*"

Alex huffed out a breath. "Okay, I'm sorry if this offends you, but it has to be said: you've kept me safe so far, but, well, you're a *building*. Sentient or not, I'm having a hard time accepting your guidance, especially when it comes to these die-hard trust exercises. Are you *sure* there aren't any other options?"

There was silence for a moment, and then—

"*I've enjoyed speaking with you, Alexandra,*" the voice said, and to Alex's annoyance, it sounded amused. "*I hope we have the opportunity again soon.*"

Just like that the voice left, leaving Alex alone to face the raging river in front of her. She paced a few steps up and back as she tried to convince herself that it would all turn out okay. Part of her knew she would be fine, but another part of her was terrified anyway. It was just like when she'd jumped out of Darrius's room above the clouds. She hadn't died then, so she wouldn't die now.

Or so she hoped, anyway.

"You can do this," Alex told herself, and before she could change her mind, she closed her eyes and took a running leap into the river.

The force of the current pulled her straight under the icy water, tearing at her body and tossing her around like a rag doll. Within seconds she was dragged through the exit fissure, and all traces of the cavern's glowing luminescence disappeared, leaving Alex in pitch-black darkness.

She frantically pushed against the tide, swimming with all her might to reach the surface for some much-needed air. The lack of light was terrifying, and even when she finally managed to break through the top of the water, the darkness was all around her still, along with the loud, echoing noise of the churning river.

The further Alex travelled, the more frightening the darkness became. She couldn't see anything, not even her own hand in front of her face. In fact, she was becoming so cold that she could hardly even *feel* her hands. She needed to get out of the water, and soon.

Alex felt a shift in the current as it began to pick up speed. The noise grew louder, and as the river churned and gurgled she had a sudden, horrifying idea about where it ended.

"Oh, please no," she gasped, as a faintly glowing light brought her destination in sight.

The river was about to end, all right. In a waterfall.

Alex struggled to move her frozen limbs, but it was too hard to battle the current. She barely managed to put up a fight before she was falling over the edge.

The water crashed down around her. The noise was at once both deafening and silent as together Alex and the river plummeted to the ground. She tried to look down, but all she could see was more water falling beneath her and a cloud of mist much further on where the waterfall disappeared into whatever was below.

Falling.

Falling.

Falling.

Inexplicably, the moment Alex entered the mist she started to slow down. Her speed continued to decrease as she fell through the spray, blinded by the haze. When her vision finally cleared, her eyes widened in shock for a single moment before she crashed into the watery surface below.

It wasn't the landing that had surprised her, but rather the scenery around her. She'd seen it before, only an hour or so ago, hanging in the foyer of the Library. It was as if Alex was *inside* the oil painting—as if she'd fallen down the same waterfall and into the lake that spiralled through the valley.

She didn't have the chance to wonder about the impossibility since, even though the vapour had slowed her progress, the fall had still pushed her deep into the water. Instead of stopping, Alex felt herself being pulled further down, and she tried not to panic as everything became darker all over again.

After a few seconds she noticed a light up ahead, almost as if someone had turned a lamp on underwater. Whatever was pulling her down continued to drag her closer to the light, and it became larger and larger until she was pulled straight into it… and out the other side.

Alex landed on a cold, hard floor, sucking in huge gulps of desperately needed air. She was frozen to the bone, saturated, and lying in a pool of water. But she was also alive and back in the Library's foyer, after having apparently fallen straight through the oil painting. As she lay there gasping and shivering, she stared at the picture and remembered her earlier thoughts about it being so masterfully created that it looked like the water was rushing straight out of the picture. Someone clearly had a warped sense of humour.

Alex sat up painfully, shaking feeling back into her frozen limbs. A long, hot shower and some nice warm soup would have her back to normal in no time, she hoped. Fletcher would never let her live it down if she had to visit him twice before term even started. That just wouldn't do.

Distracted by her thoughts and the uncomfortable sensation of her circulation easing back into her now tingling extremities, Alex only realised she wasn't alone when someone cleared their throat, interrupting the silence.

Oh, the librarian was going to *kill* her for the watery mess she'd accidentally caused.

"We have to stop meeting like this."

Alex frowned when she heard the smooth, melodic voice that definitely didn't belong to the grisly librarian. She looked around and, after gaping for a moment, came to her senses and forced herself up to her still-tingling feet.

Despite having just fallen out of a painting, Alex's only thought was that she must look like a drowned rat with her dripping hair and her clothes plastered to her trembling body. If there was one person in the world who she most certainly did *not* want to look like a drowned rat in front of, it was this man.

"Aven," she breathed, still panting lightly after her previous lack of air.

"Alexandra," he greeted, smiling as he leaned casually against the wall. "I'd hoped we'd meet again soon, but I must say, I never presumed the circumstances would be quite as *dramatic* as this."

"Heh," she tried to laugh but it sounded awkward. She felt like she'd just been caught with her hand in the cookie jar.

"I decided to drop by for a visit," he continued, taking a step towards her, "but I have to say, your arrival was much more spectacular. This is indeed a pleasant surprise. I had no idea you were so... *familiar*... with your Library here."

Alex swallowed nervously. He was too entrancing, too mesmerising—just like the other times they'd met. She shifted backwards, and his narrowed gaze followed her movement.

"I like to study." Alex tried to act nonchalant. "Libraries are good for that."

"This one in particular, or so I hear," he said, his golden eyes staring straight into her own.

She wondered for a horrible moment if Aven was gifted with mind-reading abilities, like Professor Marmaduke and possibly Marcus Sparker. He'd claimed to have studied at the academy, which meant he must have a gift of some description, but she had no idea what he was capable of doing.

Dancing elephants wearing pink tutus. She dredged up the bizarre mental image and watched his face for a reaction. None came. No surprise, no amusement, nothing to indicate that he could read her thoughts—much to her relief.

"I guess it's pretty good," Alex agreed. She then started rambling, hoping to distract him. "But it doesn't always help much with the practical subjects. You would know that, since you went here. Studying doesn't work for PE, hey? Or even Combat. Actually, most of the classes here are pretty hands-on, come to think of it. So, yeah, it's a great library, but not always a big help in those areas."

She really didn't like the look in his eyes. It was a calculating, knowing look that left Alex with an uncomfortable feeling in the pit of her stomach. It was definitely time for her to get out of there.

"I'm making a mess," she said, validating her excuse by gesturing to where her clothes were still dripping water onto the floor. "I should get going."

Aven moved then—much faster than she thought possible—and he clamped his fingers around her upper arm.

"I don't believe we've finished catching up yet." His grip was so firm that it was almost painful, especially considering her body was still tingling uncomfortably. "It would seem we now have much more to talk about, Alexandra Jennings. All along I'd hoped I was right about you, but I was never certain. Now, much to my pleasure, I'm confident in my belief of who you are and what you can do."

Alex tried to pull away from him, but he only tightened his grip more, enough that she was sure he would leave bruises.

"Let me go!" she ordered him. She was sick of being manhandled by bullies. It was as if someone had painted a target on her head that said 'Easy Pickings'. Well, no more.

When he didn't release her, she aimed a kick at his shin, hoping that if nothing else, surprise would make him loosen his grip. Instead, the impact on her pins-and-needles foot caused her to hiss in pain.

"Do you seriously think you can fight me? *Me?*" Aven laughed at her. It was a horrible noise, full of dark amusement. She shuddered at the sound, more chilled now than when she'd been in the icy water.

Alex winced when his fingers tightened even more around her arm, and she started to lose feeling in it—again. There was no way she could fight him in her current half-frozen state.

"Let's take a walk, shall we?" Aven said. "It's time to test what you can do."

He pulled her forward and she had no choice but to follow. Despite her annoyance—and her growing fear—she managed to amuse herself by kicking water up at him with every forced step. But when his grip increased to an almost snapping-bone level she followed along sedately, although grumbling all the way. She was tired, hungry and freezing. Not to mention, soaking wet. All she wanted was some food, a shower and her bed. Was that too much to ask?

"Why are you here, Aven?" she asked him wearily. "What can you possibly want from me?"

He laughed again. "Strangely the two are the same, as fate would have it. I've been searching for you for years, it would seem. And now here you are, perfectly situated to see to my will."

"Not likely," Alex murmured.

"You can't resist me, Alexandra," Aven said confidently. "And even if you could, you wouldn't. For who better to aid me than you? We're destined, don't you see? And together we'll change the world."

"I like the world the way it is," Alex said. "So it looks like you're on your own with that."

He just smirked knowingly and didn't respond.

She tried to yank her arm back, hoping that his concentration would have lapsed somewhat, but no such luck. "Seriously, Aven. Let. Me. Go," she said. And then for emphasis she added, "*Now.*"

"What are you going to do?" he asked, not breaking his stride. "You can't fight me, you can't escape me. There's no point in trying. You'll give in; it's inevitable. You'll see."

"Not more riddles," Alex grumbled.

"Riddles?" he asked, pausing to look into her eyes. "What riddles?"

"None of your business." She turned her face away and noticed that they were already at the top of the stairs that led down into the Library.

"Tell me of what you speak or I'll—"

"You! You're not allowed in here!"

It was the old librarian, *finally*, and Alex wilted in relief at the sight of him.

"Who's going to stop me, old man? You?" Aven laughed again, that horrible, chilling laugh.

"I don't have to stop you, Aven Dalmarta, for you know as well as I that you can't go where you wish without permission," the librarian said, shaking his wooden cane angrily.

"*Without permission,*" Aven repeated, emphasising the words and looking meaningfully at Alex before turning back to the librarian.

The little man paled, but held his ground. "She won't help you," he said. "And she can't be forced to do so, as you well know. Only through a decision made out of her own free will can you be given permission to enter. And judging by the look on her face, you won't be receiving what you've come for."

When Aven turned to look at Alex, he clearly didn't like whatever he saw in her stubborn expression. His beautiful face turned menacing, with his eyes blazing furiously and his lips twisting into a sneer. He was terrifying to behold and Alex flinched away from him, worried that he might actually take a swing at her.

Instead, he let her arm go, and in an instant his features were once again filled with light and beauty.

"I'm sorry if I hurt you," he said, his golden eyes begging her to forgive him. "I merely wanted to show you something."

Alex shook her head and forced herself to ignore everything in her that was willing to believe his apology. It was an act, she knew. He was lying. He'd been lying ever since they'd first met.

"You need to leave," she said, wishing her voice didn't sound quite so shaky.

Aven stilled, and she could see the effort it was taking for him to keep the pleasant expression on his face.

"As you wish," he said, surprising her. "But we'll meet again soon, my dear Alexandra." And then he was gone, vanishing in front of her as if he'd never been there.

"I'm not your 'dear' anything," she whispered into thin air.

She looked up and made eye contact with the librarian whose face was pinched with worry. But he wasn't looking at her, or even at the space where Aven had been standing. Instead, he was looking over at the oil painting. Or rather, he was looking at the pool of water on the floor underneath the painting.

The librarian turned back to her, took in her appearance, and then finally pointed at the watery mess on the ground. "You'll be cleaning that up, I suppose?"

It wasn't a question, but Alex nodded anyway and followed his instructions to find a mop and bucket.

By the time she'd finished wiping up all the water she was ready to collapse. She didn't even bother grilling the librarian for information about Aven before she hurried out of the Tower and up to her dorm for a steaming hot shower.

Questions, questions, questions. Her head was full of them.

Judging by the lack of light outside when she finally left her bathroom, Jordan and Bear would be due to arrive back at the academy soon. But she was too tired to do anything other than fall into bed and try to forget the events—and the choices—of the day.

The last question that flitted across her mind as she drifted off to sleep was perhaps the most important: *Did I make the right decision to stay?*

Thirty-Six

"Alex."

"Alex?"

"*Alex!*"

"Huh?" Alex looked up from where she was doodling in her notebook. "Oh, yeah. I completely agree. She's an absolute toad."

Bear looked at her for a moment before he gently said, "Alex, we stopped complaining about Luranda a full five minutes ago."

"Oh," she said sheepishly. "Sorry, guys, I'm not really with it."

"You're thinking about Aven again, aren't you?" Jordan guessed.

It was true. She'd been distracted ever since speaking with Jarvis first thing on Monday morning. He'd completely dismissed her concerns, telling her that the librarian had already met with him to discuss Aven and she didn't have to worry about anything. Despite his reassurances, he hadn't been able to meet her eyes during their entire conversation, which had made Alex believe that he was hiding the truth from her. She just couldn't figure out why he'd decided to keep her out of the loop, especially when it seemed like she *was* the loop.

When Jordan and Bear had seen Alex that first morning back at breakfast they'd known straight away that something was wrong, and not just because she'd been absent the previous night. She'd been forced to tell them every detail of her Library encounter, and while they were pleased she'd decided to stay in Medora, they were furious about the way Aven had treated her. In the few days since then they'd remained as close to her as possible, just in case he'd decided to make another surprise appearance. Their obsessive-compulsive tendencies weren't necessary, but she appreciated the support all the same.

"We can worry about him later, but for now we should get going," Bear said, breaking into Alex's thoughts. "We don't want to be late for Varin's first class back."

That was enough to motivate Alex to forget about Aven for the time being. She'd been looking forward to her first Species Distinction class ever since meeting the teacher on the weekend, and she eagerly followed Jordan and Bear as they led the way across the campus. They walked for what felt like forever until they finally approached a massive barn-like building at the border of the grounds. A huge sign labelled it as 'The Clinic'.

"Welcome students!" Varin called out once their entire class had arrived. He was again wearing the horned Viking helmet and armour, but no one else so much as blinked at his attire. "Come on in!" He opened the large doors and beckoned them to move inside.

Alex's eyes widened when she stepped through the entrance and found a massive grassy arena surrounded by a solid steel fence. Around the perimeter of the room—outside of the fence—were raised seats overlooking the enclosed space.

"I know I've been away for a while," Varin said as soon as they were all seated, "but that just means we've got a lot to catch up on. I'll be moving through the material quickly, so make sure you ask questions so you don't fall behind."

Alex was certain that no matter how many questions she asked, she would likely still be behind.

312 · Lynette Noni

"We're going to carry on where we left off last year," Varin
continued. "Who remembers what species we were learning
about?"

A tall blond girl named Kimberly raised her hand.
"Dertfoots, sir?"

"Dert*feet*," Varin corrected. "Plural, they are 'Dertfeet', on
their own they are a 'Dertfoot'. They can get rather touchy
about that, so it's important you remember."

Alex looked at Jordan. He just winked at her and motioned
to the front where Varin was typing into a TCD panel mounted
on the fence. A groaning noise rumbled throughout the arena
as the steel boundary slowly rose higher until it touched the roof
of the barn.

Alex couldn't see anything through the barrier and she
wondered what the point was until Varin clicked at the screen
again and the solid metal faded until it was transparent.

"That's *so* cool." It reminded Alex of the roof over On The
House.

"Keep watching," Jordan said, pointing to a gate on the far
side of the arena that Alex hadn't noticed.

She had to blink a few times when the gate opened, because
slowly walking through it was one of the strangest looking
creatures she'd ever seen. It was like a rock, really. A huge
animated boulder—brown and dirty, with some patches coated
in moss and lichen. As it moved closer, Alex could see a small
leafy plant growing out of the crevasse where its neck joined its
shoulder.

"What *is* that?" she asked, though not as quietly as she'd
intended.

"It's a Dertfoot, Alex," Varin answered. "He's been in the sun
all day so he's rather sleepy right now, but don't underestimate
these big fellows. Their skin is as hard as the earth itself, and
one blow will knock you out for a week."

Alex watched as the Dertfoot circled a spot in front of them—strangely enough it reminded her of a cat—and it lazily plonked itself onto the ground. Within seconds it looked like a sleeping lump of rock, and if she hadn't seen it moving with her own eyes just moments before, she would have thought it was just a normal boulder.

"They're not the most intelligent of beings," Varin continued, "but it doesn't really matter since barely anything can cause them harm."

The rest of Alex's first Species Distinction class was spent learning all about Dertfeet—what they ate (mud), how they communicated (by grunting), what they liked (sunshine) and disliked (anything cold), and where they lived (on the outskirts of the Soori Desert, just south of the Durungan Ranges). Alex was still a bit unclear about how they reproduced—let alone how to distinguish between genders—but she wasn't quite willing to ask *those* questions in front of her classmates.

All in all, it was the weirdest class Alex had ever experienced, but even so, she was already looking forward to whatever Varin might teach them next time.

As the weeks passed by, Alex slowly fell into a comfortable pattern again. Species Distinction quickly became one of her favourite subjects as she learned about all manner of creatures from Flips (human-like beings who lived in pressurised underwater cities and could breathe in both atmospheric and aquatic environments) to Goppers (toothless lizard-like reptiles) to Jarnocks (tree-dwelling little people who used poisonous darts as weapons) and even Veeyons (large flying creatures that could spit venomous green sludge).

True to Varin's teaching style, not only did she learn the theory about the different creatures, but she also got to see what they looked like and how they acted when they paraded around the arena. The Flip and the Jarnock even answered questions for the students, since both species were somewhat bilingual even if they did have strange accents. Those were particularly fascinating classes, and not just because of the differences between their races.

The Flip, named Tork, sat amongst the students and spoke with them as equals, answering their questions with confident ease. He had a diplomatic manner and after a while Alex was able to overlook his luminescent green skin with its bright yellow tribal markings. Aside from the unique colouring—and his webbed hands and feet—he otherwise looked and acted like a normal human being.

Mareek the Jarnock, however, had to be contained behind the transparent barrier for the entirety of his stay. Some moments the small dirt-covered man was as civil as could be, answering questions and providing them with anecdotes about his life in the trees. But then out of nowhere he would raise his hollowed pipe to his mouth and blow a poisonous dart straight towards them, screaming in his native language. The barrier blocked his attacks, but his unexpected change of mood always earned a squeal or two from some of the students in the class—and not just the girls.

Alex's other classes continued pretty much like normal; the only surprising development came from Professor Marmaduke who pulled Alex aside one day to comment on how proficient her mind defences had become. The teacher raved about how much studying Alex must have done to reach such an accomplished level of mental defence in such a short time. Alex had no idea what the woman was talking about and simply smiled and nodded. By the sound of it, it seemed like Marmaduke wasn't able to read her mind anymore, and ultimately Alex didn't care why that was as long as it stayed that way.

As for the rest of her classes, Finn was still the psychopath he'd been before the holidays; Karter consistently forced Alex to battle it out on his ever more challenging obstacle courses; and even Maggie increased the difficulty of the targets Alex had to aim for in Archery. Tayla, Caspar Lennox, Doc… it seemed like *everyone* had jumped on the 'go hard, or go home' bandwagon.

When it came down to it, Alex was secretly grateful for their rigorous demands. Every night she fell into an exhausted sleep where not even her dreams had the energy to dwell on her worries. She didn't forget Aven's threat, but as time progressed, she began to feel much more at ease.

January turned into February, and February turned into March. The academy suffered from a late cold snap right at the beginning of spring and with it came a surprising amount of fresh snow, but as they entered April the weather brought warm, sunny days and clear blue skies.

It was on one of these days that Alex found herself heading to Jarvis's office on an errand for Fletcher to retrieve one of his patient's administrative files.

When she ascended the Tower staircase and reached the eighth-floor antechamber, she noticed that Jarvis's door was slightly ajar. She was just about to knock and enter when she heard voices from within.

"I'm telling you, we need to warn her."

Alex was surprised to hear the voice of her Archery instructor, and she hesitated by the door.

"And I'm telling you, Magdelina, the less she knows, the safer she is. The safer we all are, in fact. She already knows too much as it is. Worse, *he* knows that she knows."

That was the librarian's grizzly tone, and Alex felt her stomach clench at his words. Was it possible they were talking about *her*? She leaned forward, anxious to hear more.

"He hasn't been back since then," came Jarvis's measured tone. "Maybe he doesn't know as much as you believe?"

"Oh, he knows," the librarian said, his voice grim. "It was written all over his face. Triumph. Victory. Like he'd already won."

"Then we need to tell her!" Maggie cried. "If she knows what he means to do, and *why*, then she won't help him!"

"I don't think Alex would help him regardless," Jarvis said.

So they *were* talking about her. Alex felt the air rush out of her lungs and she missed whatever it was he said next, something about her knowing right from wrong.

"You underestimate Aven," Maggie warned. "He'll find a way to take the choice away from her. She's the only one who can give him what he wants, and he'll stop at nothing to get his way."

"He can't enter the Library without her permission— permission that can't be taken from her. She has to give it willingly," the librarian stated, as if reading from a textbook. He'd said something similar to Aven all those months ago, and it made as much sense to Alex now as it did then.

"Do you understand what it would mean?" Maggie demanded. "If he gets through, do you know what will happen? The moment he steps through that doorway—"

"It's impolite to eavesdrop," a voice whispered in Alex's ear, causing her to jump. Thankfully, the people inside Jarvis's office didn't hear anything and they continued their heated conversation. But Alex missed what was said next because she was trapped by the dark eyes of Ghost as he locked her in his piercing gaze.

"I wasn't…" Alex started to tell Hunter, before realising that she'd been caught red-handed and lying wasn't going to do her any good. "I mean, I was. But I didn't mean to."

Lame. Even he seemed to think so, since he cocked his head as if daring her to do better.

"It wasn't my intention," she clarified, still speaking quietly. "To eavesdrop, I mean."

She winced, wondering if maybe she should have just lied after all.

"Why did you, then?" His eyes searched her face.

"Because they're talking about me," she said, defiantly. "And I think I deserve to know what they're saying."

Hunter continued to stare at her as if judging her character on the basis of what he saw in her expression. After a moment he nodded slightly and said, "I agree with you."

She gaped at him, swallowing the new defence that was already on her tongue.

"But I also believe it's now time for you to deliver your message so that you can go and think about what you've learned," Hunter added.

Alex hesitated and asked, "You're not going to tell them I was listening?"

He smiled slightly. It was the first expression she'd ever seen on his face that didn't make her want to run in the opposite direction. "If they were foolish enough to leave the door open while discussing delicate topics, then that's their problem. And for what it's worth, you did well to not give yourself away, considering the content of their conversation."

He'd complimented her. An actual compliment from Ghost, of all people. She wasn't sure how to respond, but it turned out that she didn't have to, since he raised his hand to knock loudly on the door.

The conversation ceased immediately and Hunter pushed his way into the room, not allowing those inside to realise the door had been unlatched.

"Ah, Hunter," Jarvis greeted warmly. "We were just discussing—"

"Alexandra Jennings is here with a message for you, Administrator," Hunter interrupted, causing Jarvis to pale slightly when he saw Alex moving into the room.

Despite everything else, she was curious how Hunter even knew her name. He seemed to know a lot, she realised, since it appeared that Jarvis had been about to include him in their conversation.

"Alex, I didn't see you there," Jarvis said. She'd never before seen him look so uncomfortable—or so guilty.

Maggie and the librarian were watching her closely, and so was Hunter, who was silently urging her to act normal.

"Administrator," she greeted, pasting a smile on her face. "I hope I'm not interrupting anything important?"

She saw Hunter smile ever so slightly again and knew he approved of her approach.

"Not at all, Alex," Jarvis said, a shade too quickly. "What can I do for you?"

Alex explained the reason she was there and Jarvis quickly excused himself to go and access the student's file, which was apparently held in a different office. He was only out of the room for a total of two minutes, but it felt like a lifetime while Alex waited with Maggie staring straight at her and the librarian avoiding her eyes completely. Hunter was the only one at ease; he sat on the edge of Jarvis's desk, cleaning his nails with a wicked-looking dagger.

Finally, Jarvis re-entered the room and gave Alex a copy of what Fletcher needed. "Is there anything else I can help you with?" he asked, but she could tell he was eager for her to leave.

Alex opened her mouth, but before she could say anything she caught Hunter's gaze again. He shook his head a fraction, the motion so small that no one else would have picked up on it, but his warning was clear.

"No, Administrator," she said, breaking away from Hunter's dark eyes to look back at Jarvis. "I've got all I need, thanks."

And she did have all she needed. Because as she walked down the Tower and back out into the sunshine, Maggie's final words played over in her head, clicking everything into place: *If he gets through, do you know what will happen? The moment he steps through that doorway—*

A tide of understanding washed over Alex, making her feel lightheaded. She tried to restrain her whirring thoughts, but like a jigsaw snapping itself together, all she could do was wait for the pieces of the puzzle to settle. And once they did, she finally saw the bigger picture.

Alex was from Freya. She'd been brought through to Medora by the Library because she was Chosen. Being Chosen meant she could access the secrets within the Library, including— hypothetically—the doorway back to her world. She didn't know if she could find it again, nor was she certain whether the headmaster would be able to once he returned. He was still gone for who knew how long, anyway—which was probably why Maggie had said that Alex was the only one who could give Aven what he wanted. And what Aven wanted, Alex now realised, was to find a doorway to her world: he wanted to get to Freya.

Alex still didn't understand why he needed her permission— or even what that meant—nor did she have any idea why he was so desperate to get to her world. But what she did know was that his reasons must be nefarious indeed if the stoic Maggie was so worried.

When it came down to it, Aven's purpose didn't matter, because there was no way Alex would ever let him step through that doorway. She might not have much waiting for her back in Freya, but it was still her world, her *home*—and her parents were there. If there was one thing Alex was sure of, it was that she would do whatever it took to protect the ones she loved from Aven, no matter what his plans were.

Thirty-Seven

Neither Jordan nor Bear could shed any light on why Aven might want to get to Alex's world, but they agreed that it sounded dodgy enough to be a cause for concern, so the three of them remained more vigilant than ever over the next few weeks. But despite their best efforts, it didn't take long before they all became distracted by the daunting amount of revision homework they needed to do for their end-of-year exams.

"What are you thinking about?"

"How much I can't wait to go to sleep," Alex answered, when Jordan's question pulled her from her thoughts. "I keep reading the same paragraph over and over again."

"I think you've been studying for too long. I say we get out of here for a while."

Alex looked pointedly at the pile of textbooks and study notes scattered across her table in the Rec Room. "You're not serious?"

"Of course I am!" Jordan said. "All we've been doing is study, study, study—for*ever!*"

"It's been, like, a week, mate," Bear said, joining their conversation. "Tops. We put it off as long as we could, remember?"

"A week too long," Jordan whined.

"A week *necessary*," Alex corrected. "Exams start on Monday."

"Sometimes it's good to take a break," Jordan argued. "Too much studying can make you forget everything you've learned."

Alex looked at him sceptically. "I'm not sure that's how it works."

"Maybe not where you're from," he said, "but here your brain can rot and start oozing out your ears if it's stuffed too full of information."

"Ew!" Alex wrinkled her nose. "Graphic, much?"

"Hey, if you *want* your brain to start oozing out of your ears..."

She threw a wad of paper at him and opened her Med Sci textbook. "You're going to have to try better than that."

"But Alllleeeexxxx..."

His whiny tone reminded her of a cute but annoying child, and when he started making pathetic whimpering noises, Alex found herself relenting. They had been studying for hours, a little break wouldn't do any harm.

"What exactly do you have in mind?" she asked.

"Yes!" he cried, fist-pumping the air victoriously.

Bear closed his textbook with a snap and asked, "What's the plan, Sparkie?"

"I don't know," Jordan admitted. "I didn't think you guys would actually take a break. But now that you've agreed, why don't we go for a walk? Maybe we should go and see what's happening in the Library?"

He'd said it innocently enough, but still Alex tensed slightly at his meaning. She hadn't had any more Library experiences since her journey down to the cavern, but she wasn't willing to tempt fate, especially since she'd begun to realise that it was only when she went *looking* for some kind of adventure that the Library gave it to her. When she ventured in there just to study—a frequent occurrence over the past few months—she encountered no otherworldly experiences. But she was pretty sure Jordan didn't intend to study there tonight.

"I thought you wanted a break from schoolwork?" she asked, glancing around nervously. There were too many people still in the Rec Room for them to speak freely.

"You can do all sorts of things in a Library," he retorted. "Have *all sorts* of adventures."

A quiet snort nearby stopped Alex from replying immediately, and she turned to find her roommate sitting at the next table over, buried in her books.

"Something funny?" Jordan asked the red-head.

"Just the image of you playing hide and seek around the bookshelves," D.C. said, not looking up from her notes.

"You're just jealous," Jordan said with a grin. "Hide and seek is awesome."

"Do you want to come with us?" Alex blurted out before she could stop herself. If D.C. was with them, they couldn't get into any trouble, right? Even so, she didn't know who was more shocked by her question—her roommate, her friends, or herself.

D.C. looked up from her book, unsure whether it was a real invitation or not. Alex tried to keep her expression open, but all she could think about was the fact that they hadn't spoken to each other about anything other than class projects in weeks, possibly months. D.C. must have been thinking along the same lines because she quickly dropped her gaze.

"No, thank you," she said quietly, turning back to her notes. "I have to study."

Alex wasn't sure why she felt so disappointed. Jordan and Bear didn't seem to mind either way, and they waited for her to pack up her books.

"Actually, I think I'm just going to head to bed," Alex said, not in the mood anymore. When she saw their deflated expressions, she added, "Why don't you go and play some *hopscotch?*"

Their faces lit up with excitement.

"Just don't—uh—*fall* or anything," she said, trying to subtly warn them not to deliberately get into trouble. They wouldn't necessarily make it out in one piece like she had.

"We'll be fine," Jordan assured her, his eyes shining with anticipation. "Mere child's play."

After they left, Alex collected her stuff and headed to her room. D.C. appeared a few minutes later and, as always, the silence between them was uncomfortable.

"Do you want the first shower?" D.C. asked tentatively.

Alex blinked, surprised that the other girl had spoken at all, let alone asked a polite question. "Um—no, thanks. You go ahead."

D.C. nodded and collected her pyjamas. Soon after she entered the bathroom, Alex heard the water turn on.

She stared at the wall, thinking about their almost friendly interaction. In the end she came to the conclusion that, like everyone else, D.C. must have been feeling the stress of the exams—so much so that her usual hostility was toned down.

It was a nice change, Alex thought, even if it was unlikely to last.

"I feel like I'm *dying*," Alex groaned, collapsing onto a chair in the food court.

It was Wednesday night, and she was just over halfway through her exams. They were so much harder than anything she'd ever experienced before in her life, and she was already feeling physically and mentally wrecked.

"Hear, hear," Bear agreed, slumping down next to her.

Jordan only mumbled inarticulately as he rested his head on the table, not even able to formulate proper syllables.

The three of them had just come from their PE assessment, and Finn hadn't held back. He'd tested their endurance, strength, speed and resourcefulness over a three-hour period of progressively nastier challenges in the field, forest and lake. Out of their class of sixteen, only eight had actually finished the entire examination without being carted off to the Med Ward. Alex wasn't surprised that Jordan and Bear had made it through fine, but she was beyond shocked that she had, too. Finn had actually smiled at her—slightly—once it was all over.

"I don't even think I have the energy to eat," Jordan mumbled into the table. "Can someone else feed me?"

No one answered him, too tired themselves to verbalise their thoughts.

So far Alex had completed her examinations in Medical Science, SOSAC, Archery, Equestrian Skills, and now PE. The others had also had their Core Skills exam, but Marmaduke had ended up exempting Alex from the assessment. At first Alex had been pleased to learn she had one less exam to worry about, but then she'd been told that it meant she would have to repeat the class again in her next year or until she developed her gift and passed the test. How annoying.

Alex's favourite exam by far was for her Equestrian Skills class, where she'd had to complete a cross-country course in the forest. She'd ridden a horse named Fiddle, and together they'd jumped logs, dodged low swinging branches, trudged through a muddy riverbed, swum through a creek, scaled and descended a steep hill and galloped across grassy fields. At the end of the exam Alex had been covered in mud and scratches, but she'd still had a smile on her face from the exhilarating experience.

It would have been great if all of her exams could have been so much fun—but they weren't. Alex's brain had strained so hard for the answers to her Medical Science and SOSAC exams

326 · Lynette Noni

that she'd actually wondered if Jordan had been right about it oozing out of her ears.

"Only four more to go," Bear said, moaning in pain as he reached for his menu. "Six down, four to go. We're over halfway. Just two more days left."

Alex wasn't sure if he was encouraging them or encouraging himself, but either way she was glad for it. It gave her the energy boost she needed to force down some food before following her friends to the Rec Room where they began to revise for their exams the next day—History and Species Distinction. While neither subject would be easy, at least they didn't have practical components, which would hopefully allow her body the chance to recover. She desperately needed the reprieve, especially considering that Friday was going to be terrible, with both her Chemistry written exam and lab experiment, *and* her Combat assessment.

No, she definitely wasn't looking forward to that, even if it meant the end of her exams.

Thirty-Eight

Alex stared out at the colossal Arena on Friday afternoon and tried to convince her body to take the necessary steps forward.

"Come on, Alex," she murmured to herself. "You can do this. In a few hours you'll be all done. Don't let the butthead scare you. *You can do this!*"

"Do you need a push?"

Alex whirled around, embarrassed to find Kaiden watching her with undisguised amusement.

"Uh—no, thanks. I'm good," she said, trying to stand a little taller.

"Let's get in there, then," he said, his blue eyes filled with laughter. "We wouldn't want to be late for the *butthead.*"

Alex felt her face flush and she quickly strode down the hill, hoping he wouldn't notice her embarrassment. Too late, she realised, when she heard his quiet chuckle from behind her.

She entered the Arena with her head held high, determined not to show her fear to anyone else. The rest of her classmates were already there, stretching and talking quietly amongst themselves. She sat down near them—not too close—and began her own warm-up routine.

Ten minutes later Karter walked in and the six of them stood to attention.

"Today's the day we find out how much you've learned this year," he said without preamble. "Pair up."

328 · Lynette Noni

As usual, the group split in two, a pair of boys together—Brendan and Nick—and a group of three—Sebastian, Declan and Kaiden. Alex, as always, stayed on the outside and waited for further instructions.

"Are you deaf, Jennings?" Karter barked. "I said *pair up*."

"But—" she swallowed her protest when he turned the full force of his glare on her. He wasn't really going to make her fight with them, was he? Her classmates had spent years learning how to attack and defend. She, on the other hand, had spent barely a few months learning how to duck and dodge as things flew at her face. There was simply no comparison.

Knowing she had little choice in the matter, Alex looked over at the boys, wondering who she should pair herself with. Their faces showed everything from contempt to curiosity, and it was clear that none of them wanted to be stuck with her.

She wasn't sure how it happened—perhaps they'd noticed her miserable expression—but as she watched, Declan and Kaiden looked at each other in silent conversation and then began a paper-scissors-rock contest. Kaiden's scissors cut Declan's paper, causing the big guy to sigh in disappointment before he detached himself from the group and walked over to join Alex.

"You *so* owe me for this," he told her in a whisper.

Alex nodded mutely, knowing that he was putting not just his grade on the line, but also his dignity.

And then she realised what that meant.

Alex turned to look at her partner, taking in all six feet and four inches of pure muscle. She'd gone up against him once before and ended up unconscious. She wasn't exactly excited about a repeat performance.

"Right," Karter said, interrupting her internal freak-out. "This is a three-hour exam. The first hour and a half will focus on attack and defence. You'll fight for fifteen-minute intervals with a three-minute break after each match to catch your breath and swap opponents."

Alex swallowed nervously when she realised that meant she would have to fight all of her classmates at one stage or another.

"The last hour and a half will be something different," Karter added vaguely, before further describing what they were about to do. "Your first three rounds are unarmed combat, followed by staff and finally sword. If your opponent overcomes you to the point that you admit defeat—or I admit it for you— then you're out and you have to wait for the next round. Now find a space and get ready to begin."

Alex gaped at him. Surely that wasn't it? What about rules? Safety? Were they going to get any protective padding? Or at least a helmet?

"Do you need a push now?" Kaiden whispered as he walked past her. From anyone else she might have thought it was unnecessarily cruel, but she could see the compassion in his eyes. He, at least, understood that what Karter asked of her was impossible.

"Come on," Declan murmured, indicating for her to follow him to a free space. "And don't worry. I'll go easy on you."

"Don't," Alex said firmly.

He paused and turned around to look at her questioningly.

"Don't go easy on me," she told him, not wanting him to forfeit his grade for her. "Just do what you would normally do."

"But… No offence and all, but I'll probably hurt you," he said, rubbing his neck awkwardly. His muscles flexed with the movement, hinting at the strength she already knew he commanded.

"It wouldn't be the first time," she said, mustering up a wry smile.

He laughed lightly before turning serious. "It's not a fair fight."

"Is it ever?" Alex asked, shrugging. "Please don't hold back on my account. Maybe we'll both get lucky—if you knock me out again, I'll get to skip the rest of the exam."

"I'll see what I can do," he said with a slight grin, continuing towards the far side of the Arena.

"On my count," Karter bellowed, his voice carrying around the massive area. "Three, two, one, *begin*."

Alex frowned when Declan hesitated. "You're not afraid to hit a girl, are you?" she taunted. "You never used to be."

He narrowed his gaze but still didn't come at her. Alex noticed Karter watching them and she knew that, even though *she* was destined to fail this exam, she wouldn't let Declan go down with her.

It took a lot of goading—and some low blows on her part—until Alex was able to convince Declan to fight. Even then, he still wouldn't flat-out annihilate her, but he put up a pretty good show. Alex, however, was more impressed by her own much-improved reflexes, which helped her stay on her feet far longer than expected. The last time she'd fought Declan she'd acted on pure survival instinct, whereas this time she was actually in control. And it felt *good*.

At least it did until he managed to catch her around the waist and wrestle her to the ground, trapping her in place.

"Jennings, you're out," Karter called across the Arena, as if she hadn't already realised as much.

Declan eased up off her back and she rolled over, accepting his offered hand. They walked together to the side of the Arena and watched the rest of their classmates attack each other. Alex couldn't help noticing that they were all much more violent than Declan had been.

"You're not too bad, you know," he said kindly. "Much better than last time."

Alex snorted and rubbed a tender spot where it felt like he'd almost shattered her thigh. "Yeah, right."

"I mean it," he said. "You dodged most of my attacks. Your reflexes are excellent."

"But I completely suck at attacking," she said.

"That's because you don't have any experience. With a bit of work, I reckon you could learn how to hold your own."

"Well, thanks for the vote of confidence," she said. "But we've still got over two and a half hours of this exam left and no one can learn *that* fast."

"Yeah," Declan agreed, wincing with sympathy. "Not your best afternoon."

Soon Karter blew his whistle to signal that the first interval was over. None of the others had been defeated. She had a feeling it was going to be a very repetitive—and painful—afternoon.

As Alex continued swapping through partners, she realised that Declan had been way more than easy on her. Her reflexes continued to help her during her unarmed combat with both Sebastian and Nick, but ultimately both boys brought her down hard—and with much more force than Declan.

But none of her unarmed matches were anywhere near as bad as her round with Brendan, where they attacked each other with heavy wooden staves. Again, the only thing that kept Alex in the fight was her ability to duck and dodge every time he swung the weapon at her. She probably ended up more injured from throwing herself to the ground over and over again to avoid the wooden staff than from any actual contact with it—at least until he clipped her in the stomach, forcing the air out of her lungs and winding her. She automatically doubled over into a protective ball with her arms wrapped around her abdomen, and he took the opportunity to swing the staff up at her head, smashing it into her skull.

He must have completely pulled back on his attack, since while it hurt like crazy, she was only dazed for a few seconds, as opposed to unconscious or dead—both of which could have been possible.

The hit still disoriented her enough that he was able to use the staff to trip her over and onto the ground, pressing the weapon firmly against her windpipe.

Karter's call of "Out, Jennings!" was a welcome relief. Especially since it meant she only had one more opponent to face before the first part of their examination was over.

As Alex took her place in front of Kaiden, she felt her heart thudding erratically in her chest. Of all the matches, this one was the most dangerous. The swords they were using weren't wooden practise weapons—they were the real deal and they had *very* sharp blades.

"Do you know what to do with that?" Kaiden asked.

She looked at the sword glinting dangerously in her hand and jabbed it forward in three quick, consecutive thrusts. "*Stab, stab, stab*, right?"

"There's a little more technique to it than that," Kaiden responded dryly. "Finesse. Etiquette. It's like a dance."

"And then you *stab, stab, stab*," Alex said again. "Right?"

His lip twitched as if he was holding back a smile. "Why don't you give your method a go and see how well it works for you?"

"Nah," she responded. "I wouldn't want to hurt you."

This time he did smile. His entire face lit up with the expression and she felt as if she'd been winded by the wooden staff all over again. Alex knew she had to get her head back on straight, but she was still a sixteen—nearly seventeen—year-old girl and he was way too attractive for his own good. Even covered in dirt and sweat, with his messy dark hair plastered to his head, he was still gorgeous. She'd noticed before—how could she not after observing him and the others for months?—but she hadn't had many opportunities to be up close and personal with him. And now they were about to attack each other with lethal weapons.

Sometimes, life just wasn't fair.

"Three, two, one, *begin!*" Karter called out for the final time.

Alex brought her sword up in front of her, balancing her feet and distributing her weight evenly. If ever there was a time when she needed to pay attention to a fight, it was now. Not only was Kaiden talented, but he was also fast and creative. She didn't stand a chance against him, but she wanted to at least put up a bit of a fight—hopefully without losing a limb in the process.

"Ready to dance, Alex?" he asked, his eyes sparkling with the challenge. "I'll lead."

She didn't get the chance to respond before he lunged at her, thrusting his sword towards her abdomen. She blocked him just in time, and the force of their two blades clashing caused her to back up a step in order to brace herself against his strength.

Alex stared at him in shock, certain that if she hadn't blocked his sword it would have sliced her in half. All he did was wink at her and pull his weapon back before thrusting it towards her again.

Game on, she thought as she deflected his attack and knocked his blade aside again. She didn't wait for him to come around a third time, and instead she pivoted to aim a powerful side-kick at his stomach. He was too fast, jumping out of the way with ease.

Once again he lunged at her, changing his attack at the last moment to come from above. She watched as the blade sailed in an arc towards her head and she threw herself at the ground, somersaulting out of the way. Alex continued rolling and used her forward momentum to jump back up to her feet again— remembering to keep her sword well away from her body.

Kaiden seemed surprised by her unexpected gymnastics and she took the opportunity to leap towards him while he was partially unguarded. She stabbed her sword at him but he parried it effortlessly, knocking her arm away as if she was a fly and he the flyswat.

Clearly he hadn't been as unguarded as she'd thought.

She stood back for a moment, shifting her weight from foot to foot as she waited for his next move. He seemed to be waiting too, but for what, she wasn't sure.

And then, as fast as lightning, he lunged at her, almost catching her unawares. She managed to meet his blade in time, but then she realised that the unexpected attack had only been to distract her from his real intention. It wasn't just the sword she should have been watching for.

Alex was on the ground before she even realised that he'd tripped her, and she watched in slow motion as his sword streamed once more towards her head. She knew he would pull it before actually beheading her, so she took the chance to kick out at him—her aim actually good for once. He grunted in pain as her heel landed on his ankle with much more force than she'd intended.

It was a stupid thing to do, in hindsight, since her kick broke his concentration just as he was pulling out of his attack. He jerked with surprise and his sword naturally followed the movement. At least he had enough sense to flick the blade away from her neck rather than continue its downward path, and his fast reflexes were the only thing that allowed her head to remain attached to her body. But she still hissed in pain as his blade grazed her from collarbone to shoulder.

Kaiden's eyes widened as her skin broke, his expression immediately remorseful. But this was a fight and he wasn't supposed to feel bad for hurting her, especially since she'd just injured him as well. The cut wasn't deep, and he could have easily done much worse.

His hesitation gave Alex the time she needed to spring back up to her feet with renewed determination. He must have noticed the resolve in her eyes, and not fear or pain, because his own face cleared of its concern and he was once again back in attack mode.

Alex feinted forwards, figuring that if Kaiden could do a fake move, then maybe she could too. But as she twisted her arm and spun it around, aiming to hit him with the hilt of her sword, he was one step ahead of her. At the very last second he surprised her by dropping his weapon and throwing his right hand out to intercept her swinging arm. He grabbed her wrist and pulled her forward, causing her to lose balance and stumble straight into him. Using her unsteadiness to his advantage, he quickly spun her around so that her back was pressed up against his chest. She struggled and almost managed to pull away, but his left arm wrapped around her waist, trapping her against his body.

The entire manoeuvre had been so unexpected that she was left a bit stunned. She wasn't exactly sure what had happened until she felt the cold, hard steel of her own blade pressed against her neck, with Kaiden's hand engulfing hers on the hilt of the sword.

Alex froze, remembering the night of the Gala when Gerald had held her in a similar position. She stopped breathing for an instant and shuddered as the memories washed over her.

Kaiden must have felt her distress because his arm around her waist squeezed reassuringly and then loosened a fraction.

"It's a dance, remember?" he whispered in her ear, his breath on the back of her neck raising goose bumps along her skin. "But sometimes your way works, too."

Her eyes lit up as understanding flowed through her. In one single motion she heaved his arm with the sword away from her neck—only gaining a few inches but it was enough—and she used his advice and *stabbed* her other elbow into his stomach.

Kaiden grunted and hunched forward, and she took the opportunity to spin out of his hold. But she'd forgotten that his other arm was still wrapped around her, and she ended up spinning him as well, unbalancing them both. They fell to the ground in a tangle of limbs, each trying not to impale themselves on her blade.

Alex twisted violently, trying desperately to extricate herself from his embrace, and then she was on top of him—not even knowing how—and her hands held the sword steady at the base of his throat. She was certain he could have easily pushed her aside and retaken the lead in their 'dance', but at that moment Karter blew his whistle and Alex looked up to see the rest of her classmates watching as she straddled Kaiden in the middle of the Arena.

Despite everything, she felt herself flush with embarrassment, and she looked back down to find Kaiden grinning up at her.

"Good dance," he said. "We'll have to do it again sometime."

"You cheated." She was puffing from the exertion and she quickly slid off him and stood to her feet.

"How so?" he asked, standing beside her and collecting his sword.

"You let me win. You could have easily beaten me a heap of times, but you didn't."

"Maybe," Kaiden said with an amused, one-shouldered shrug. "Maybe not. Either way, I think it's safe to say we now know why you have the potential to be in this class."

Alex didn't know how to respond to his comment, so she said nothing and just started walking back over to their classmates who were still watching them both intently. Declan was grinning, but the rest of them didn't seem to know what to think.

When they reached the group, Karter eyed the shallow cut at her neckline. "Do you need to get that looked at?"

"I'm fine to continue," she said, surprised that he'd even asked.

He nodded approvingly and motioned for them to follow as he moved to one of the chambers off to the side of the Arena. Alex hadn't been in this particular room before, but she still had an idea of what they would find there.

Sure enough, inside they discovered an obstacle course of epic proportions. Even the guys inhaled sharply at the sight of it.

Alex almost smiled. She'd been facing off against Karter's hellish imagination for months, and for the first time all afternoon she felt like she might have the advantage.

"Who can tell me why the last part of your exam is an obstacle course?" Karter asked.

"Because it'll test our reflexes and defensive skills in an unknown environment," Nick answered mechanically.

"Exactly," Karter said. "It also forces you to think under pressure, both from the challenges of the course, and also from the fifteen-minute time limit you'll be given."

Alex quickly did the maths in her head and realised that fifteen minutes each would take up the entire last hour and a half of their testing period. Piece of cake. Well, not really, but it beat having the stuffing kicked out of her for another ninety minutes.

"You'll be judged by how far along the course you get," Karter said. He clearly didn't expect many—if any—of them to

338 · Lynette Noni

actually complete it. "If you fail to make it through an obstacle, you have to start at the beginning again."

They all nodded their understanding.

"We'll work down in age, oldest to youngest, which means you're up first, Labinsky. Get ready."

One after another her classmates entered the course. Brendan first, then Nick, Sebastian, Declan and Kaiden. None of them managed to fully complete it, but Alex paid close attention to where they went wrong so she could learn from their mistakes.

"Jennings, you're up," Karter finally barked.

She stood and walked over to the starting line, jumping nervously from foot to foot while she waited for Karter's go-ahead.

"Three, two, one, *begin.*"

Alex started the course strongly, sailing through the numerous obstacles with only minor difficulties. As she approached the second last challenge, she realised just how well she was doing—better than anyone else so far. Even though she had to be nearly out of time, she was determined to see how far she could make it.

"Hello, old friend," she muttered to the obstacle in front of her. It was the moving balancing beam with the sandbags, a combination she'd tackled numerous times over the past few months. This particular beam moved erratically, not sequentially like she was used to. *Up-down-up-left-down-right-left-up-right-down.* There was no order to its movement, which meant she wouldn't know which way to lean to help keep her balance when it changed direction. And if that wasn't enough, there were *five* sandbags swinging above it, not just the three she'd dealt with in the past, all moving at different times and speeds.

Alex prepared herself and jumped up onto the beam, keeping her arms out by her sides for balance as she grew accustomed to the irregular movement. She stepped forward hesitantly and almost fell when the beam jerked to the left under her. She managed to steady herself and took another hesitant step, then another. Eyeing the first sandbag swinging dangerously close to her, she waited until her timing was perfect before stepping again, further this time. Her step coincided with the jagged movement of the beam, and she fell down on one knee as she lost her balance.

Alex waited, calming her trembling limbs and telling herself that it was just a little further until she'd be done. She rose carefully, wobbling even more but eventually managing to get back upright before stepping forward again.

Step—wobble—step—wait for sandbag—step—wobble—step.

She continued the entire way across the beam until there was just one sandbag left between her and safety. After that, only one obstacle remained in the course and she would be through. She glanced ahead to look at the finish line, but her distraction cost her when she should have been paying attention. The beam jerked to the right, before it continued in a quick *up-down-up-left* action that tilted Alex forward—right into the path of the final swinging sandbag. It smashed straight into her, throwing her off the beam and into the mud below.

The pain was instant. Since she had no protective gear on, her shoulder joint had taken the brunt of the impact, and even just flexing her hand sent daggers down her arm. She had to bite her tongue to stop from crying out in agony. Tears sprung to her eyes, but she refused to let them fall. Instead, she used her good arm—the right one, thankfully—to push herself to her feet.

Alex cradled her injured arm close to her body and jogged painfully back to the beginning of the course. She still had time left, and there was no way she was going to quit until Karter blew his whistle. She just hoped it would be soon.

She crawled on three limbs through the first challenge—a mud-drenched wriggle-tube—but once she reached the second obstacle—a fifty-foot high rope ladder—Alex knew she was in trouble. She tried to reach out with her sore arm but it was no use—the pain was too intense and there was no way she could hold her weight with it. But she couldn't just stand there and do nothing.

An idea came to her and she wasn't sure if it would work, but it was worth a try. Instead of stepping onto the first rung, Alex wrapped her left leg around the entire ladder, before reaching up with her good arm and pulling her weight off the ground. She then wrapped her right leg around it as well, locking her ankles together until she felt somewhat secure. She didn't know how high she would get, but with both her legs caught in the ladder she was much more stable.

Alex started to pull herself up with her good arm, using her legs to hold her position whenever she had to reach up for the next rung. Her muscles screamed from the strain, and even though she wasn't using her bad shoulder at all, even the slightest movement caused pain to ripple through her body.

Finally, when she was about three quarters of the way up, the whistle blew and she shuddered with relief. There was no way she could have gone any further. It was a struggle enough to loosen her cramping limbs and slide fireman-style back to the ground.

Alex swayed on her feet when the impact from landing back on the floor jarred her shoulder, and her vision blackened for a moment. But she was determined to walk out of the class just like everyone else, so she rallied the last of her strength and staggered over to the others. Her classmates were all looking at her strangely, but she was too focused on not passing out to try and figure out what they were thinking. She did, however, look at Karter, and on his face was an expression she had never seen directed at her before: respect.

"Well, that's it," he said abruptly. "Your exam is over. Off you go."

Alex wasted no time following his instructions. As she was walking—or stumbling—away, he barked out one more order: "Jennings, report to Fletcher immediately."

She didn't even have the energy to roll her eyes. As if she was going anywhere else.

Alex made it halfway up the hill towards the academy before she had to stop and rest. Collapsing into a sitting position on the ground, she bent over herself and held her injured arm close to her body.

"Ow," she whispered, unable to express herself in any other way.

Just as she was contemplating leaning back and closing her eyes for a moment, a pair of dark boots entered her vision.

"Do you need that push now?"

Alex laughed breathily before wincing at the pain it caused her. "This time? I think so," she admitted.

Kaiden knelt down and reached out to wrap his arm around her. He was careful to keep clear of her damaged shoulder as he pulled her gently to her feet. She was too exhausted and in too much pain to be embarrassed by his help—even when she realised that the rest of the guys from their Combat class were also surrounding them.

As a group they hobbled towards the Med Ward. Well, she hobbled—they walked.

"Is that what you've been doing during class?" Nick asked her. "That course?"

"Not that one," she answered weakly. "But other courses like it."

"You'd never been around that one before?" Brendan clarified.

"Nope," she murmured, leaning a little more onto Kaiden with every step. She was really hurting now as the adrenaline steadily wore off and she could barely hold herself upright.

"Wow."

Alex wearily turned her head to look at Sebastian who'd made the exclamation. She was surprised by the praise, and even more so to find the others nodding along in agreement.

"Yeah, that sure was something," Nick said.

"I wonder why Karter gave you more time?" Declan mused. "You were clearly done-in at the fifteen-minute mark."

"What do you mean?" she asked. Her vision turned hazy around the edges before clearing again.

"Your time ran out just after you were clipped by the sandbag on the beam," Declan explained. "You still got further than the rest of us by then, but it's weird that he made you continue on—especially with your shoulder like that."

Alex really didn't like the way he'd said 'like that' but she didn't question him. She didn't question anything in fact—not even Karter's added time—and instead she focused on putting one foot in front of the other in an effort to not collapse completely onto Kaiden.

"We're almost there," he whispered to her, almost as if he could feel her fading. He probably could, since he was practically carrying her entire weight.

Finally they stepped into Gen-Sec and made their way to the Med Ward. Alex was so relieved to see Fletcher that she could have cried.

"Dear, dear, dear," he tsked when he noticed the condition she and some of the others were in. "You all look like you've been in a war. On the losing side. Help her onto the bed, will you, Kaiden?"

Alex was trying so hard to remain conscious that she didn't even feel awkward when Kaiden lifted her up onto the mattress.

"What have you done to yourself this time, young lady?" Fletcher's tone was stern but there was genuine concern in his gaze as he inspected her shoulder.

Alex whimpered when his fingers made contact, the touch ripping pain all the way up her arm. He immediately dropped his hand and walked over to his medicine cabinet, returning with a vial of bright green pain reliever. She swallowed it in one go but was disappointed when it only dulled the pain.

"It didn't work," she told him. "Not as much as normal."

"I'll give you a stronger one in a moment," he promised. "But I need you to be able to tell me what you're feeling."

"A whole heap of pain," she said, "and then some more."

Someone chuckled and she looked up to find that her classmates were still in the room. Her pain had eased enough that she was capable of embarrassment now. "Um, how about a little privacy?" she asked, motioning for them to leave.

For some reason they seemed disappointed, but they surprised her by respecting her request and moving towards the door.

"Actually, I'd like to check over you all before you leave," Fletcher told them. "I'm guessing you've come from your Combat exam and Alex probably isn't the only one to have an injury or two. Please take a seat and I'll be with you all momentarily."

"Fletcher," she whined. "This is humiliating."

He reached out and closed the curtain around her bed to give her some privacy.

"Better?" he asked.

"Not much," she muttered, but at least her classmates couldn't see her anymore.

Fletcher inspected her shoulder again. His prodding was still painful, but it was dulled thanks to the medicine he'd given her. She still hissed when he touched a particularly tender spot.

"Well, it's definitely dislocated," he said, "but I'm not sure how bad it is without an X-ray. I'll just grab my Device."

He stepped out of sight and returned a moment later holding a book-sized, TCD-like object in his hands.

"What's that?" she asked.

"It's a MedTek," he told her. "It has an application for an X-ray feature which will show me a holographic image of your localised skeletal structure."

Alex kept still as he held it close to her body and pressed at the screen. He asked her to move a few times, rolling onto her side and then onto her front while he took X-rays from different angles.

"All right," he said, inspecting the hologram that rose out of the device. "It's a good, clean, dislocation. We just have to pop it back in and you'll be right to go. You might be a little tender for a few days, but there'll be no permanent damage."

"*Pop it back in?*" Alex repeated, ignoring his other remarks. "What do you mean by that?"

Fletcher didn't answer immediately, instead he stuck his head out the curtain and said something before moving back to her side. A moment later Declan and Kaiden invaded her bubble of privacy.

"Fletcher?" she growled.

"It means exactly what I said," he told her. "I have to pop your shoulder back into place."

Alex stared at him, not letting herself think about how he would do that. "What are they here for, then?" she asked, gesturing to the boys and dreading the answer.

"To keep you still, of course."

"Of course," she muttered, closing her eyes slowly before opening them again. "Fine, whatever, just get it over with."

"That's a good girl," he said, beaming at her. "Declan, you grab her legs. Kaiden, make sure you keep her upper half still."

As her two strong classmates latched onto her, she looked up at Fletcher. "This is going to hurt, isn't it?"

"Immensely," he said. At least he was honest. "But it will be over fast, and then I'll give you a stronger painkiller as promised."

"You'd better," Alex grumbled.

Kaiden squeezed her good arm reassuringly. He sent her a teasing grin and asked, "So, do you come here often?"

To her shame, she actually laughed, and Fletcher used her distraction to click her shoulder back into place.

Agony. Absolute agony. Her laugh turned into a muffled groan as she tried not to scream at the pain. She closed her eyes tightly, desperately willing away the urge to vomit.

Slowly, ever so slowly, the pain started to fade. Alex was soon able to open her eyes again, and as she blinked back tears she noticed Fletcher, Kaiden and Declan all watching her with concern. But it was the dark green vial of liquid in the doctor's hand that she was more interested in.

"Please tell me that's for me," she whispered, her voice cracking slightly.

Fletcher had to help her swallow it, lifting her up from her horizontal position on the bed so that it didn't spill. The moment it entered her system she breathed a sigh of relief. Her entire body relaxed as her senses dulled and the pain disappeared.

"Mmm," she hummed contentedly, lying back again. "I like that one *very* much."

"That's because it's a *very* strong painkiller," Fletcher said, mimicking her emphasis. "It'll keep you comfortable overnight, but you should come back in the morning and I'll give you a smaller dose again."

"Mmkay."

"I should mention that it also has sedative properties," Fletcher said. "You're going to be pretty out of it for the rest of

346 · Lynette Noni

the night, and you might not remember much from now until you wake up tomorrow."

"Mmkay," Alex said again, in a truly agreeable mood. She felt *wonderful*.

"Let's put the rest of you back together and then you can go back to your dorm and sleep it off."

"Sounds good," she said, her words slurring slightly. "I like sleep."

Alex kept her eyes closed while Fletcher cleaned the cut from her fight with Kaiden and used his healing salve to erase any evidence of the wound. When he was done he asked if she was hurt anywhere else, but she couldn't think straight in her relaxed state of mind. In the end he had to ask her classmates, and after a moment Brendan admitted to whacking her in the head with his wooden staff.

"It wasn't that bad," Alex murmured through a yawn.

Fletcher ignored her and inspected her skull, finding a bump but nothing too serious.

"All right, I think you're done," he said. "How are you feeling now?"

"Like I'm a cloud of happiness riding a rainbow of tranquillity," she said with a contented sigh.

Muffled laughter came from the boys and Fletcher seemed to be fighting a grin when he said, "Sounds like you're good to go, then." He opened the curtain and looked over her classmates with a critical eye. "Who's the least injured here?"

"Me," Alex answered, raising her hand in the air and waving it around. "I'm already fixed, remember?"

"Who *else* is the least injured?" Fletcher corrected, giving her a warning look.

The boys discussed it quietly amongst themselves before coming to a decision.

"Probably me," Kaiden said. "I've just got a bruised ankle, but it's not too bad."

"Can you walk?" Fletcher asked him, and Kaiden nodded. "Do you mind taking Alex back to her dorm? I think it's best if she has an escort."

Alex was so focused on tracing invisible patterns in the air that it took her a few moments to realise they were looking at her. "What?" she asked defensively. "The colours are pretty."

Kaiden tried—and failed—to hide his smile, and Alex definitely heard a snort from at least one other person in the room.

"Come on, let's get you out of here," Kaiden said, holding his hand out to help her off the bed.

"I'll see you in the morning, Alex," Fletcher said. "And Kaiden, come back here once you've dropped her off so I can look at your ankle."

Kaiden agreed and Alex nodded dazedly before she followed him out the door.

"Is that my fault?" she asked as they walked slowly across the grounds.

He stopped her from walking into a tree and moved her back onto the path before asking, "Is what your fault?"

"Your ankle. Is that from when I kicked you?"

"Sure is," he said, almost sounding proud.

"Sorry," she mumbled.

"Don't be," he told her, catching her easily when she tripped over a crack in the ground and setting her back on her feet. "You did well."

"But I hurt you!" she said, tripping again, this time over a rock. He caught her—again—and she wondered why she wasn't more embarrassed by her medically induced clumsiness. She guessed that the drugs messing with her coordination were also keeping her too relaxed to feel humiliated. It was nice.

"You were *meant* to hurt me," he pointed out. "You did exactly what you were supposed to do."

Alex thought about that while he steered her around a bed of flowers she'd stumbled towards. "I guess you're right," she said finally, and he smiled in agreement. She really loved his smile.

"Thanks," he said, his smile widening.

What was he thanking her for? Had she actually said that out loud?

"Yeah," he said, chuckling lightly.

"You can read my mind!" she cried, coming to such an abrupt halt that she actually managed to somehow trip over her own feet. It was so unexpected that Kaiden almost didn't catch her in time, but at the last second he managed to wrap his arms around her and steady her against his body.

"No, I can't read your mind," he said, stepping away from her but staying within range in case she fell again. "But I'd recommend that you think before you speak, or maybe you should stop thinking and speaking altogether, just to be safe."

Alex groaned, embarrassed now even despite the medicine in her system.

"Hey, don't worry about it," he said. "You're probably not going to remember any of this conversation tomorrow anyway."

"But *you* will!"

"Yep." His eyes sparkled with humour. "And one day when you least expect it, I might just have to remind you about it— and about how much you like my smile."

Alex decided that it would be best if she kept her mouth shut for the rest of the walk, and she concentrated instead on not tripping over thin air.

They made it to the dorm building without any more incidents—verbal or physical—and they paused at the entry.

"Think you can make it from here?" Kaiden asked.

Alex ignored the urge to stick her tongue out at him childishly. "It'll be tough but I reckon I'll be okay."

She started to walk inside but stopped after a moment, turning back to him. "Thanks for the push earlier."

"I'm already looking forward to the next time you need one," he said, his words sounding surprisingly genuine.

Alex didn't look back again, but she knew he was still watching and waiting to make sure she got inside okay.

As she made it up to her room and collapsed onto her bed, she realised that maybe her Combat classmates weren't as horrible as she'd originally thought.

Thirty-Nine

Ba-dum. Ba-dum. Ba-dum. Ba-dum. Ba-dum. Ba-dum.

Alex woke up the next morning to the feeling of her pulse throbbing painfully through her shoulder. She tried to remember what Fletcher had told her, something about visiting him for more pain medicine, but she couldn't fully remember his words. Her previous evening was all a bit of a haze after he'd popped her shoulder back into place.

How did I even get back to my room? she wondered, feeling slightly uneasy.

All she could recall was that Fletcher had asked Kaiden to walk her back to her dorm. She wasn't sure if they'd spoken at all along the way, but Alex *really* hoped she hadn't said or done anything to embarrass herself.

She groaned as she rolled out of bed and realised what a mess she was. Her clothes were covered in filth, which had transferred onto her bed and even around the room a little. She was surprised D.C. hadn't woken her up, shrieking at the mess she'd made.

Alex stripped her bed and stumbled to the shower, determined to clean herself up before she trudged over to see Fletcher for some pain relief.

Twenty minutes later she was clean, dressed and out the door.

"Alex, how are you feeling this morning?" Fletcher asked when she walked into his Ward.

"Much better, thanks," she said, hoisting herself up onto the bed and wincing slightly at the pain the movement brought. "I must have just crashed last night."

"Yes, I gave you quite a strong painkiller," he said. "I'm amazed you managed to walk all the way back to your room. But Kaiden said you made it without incident."

That was a relief, at least. She would have been mortified to find out that he had been forced to carry her.

"I can't really remember much," she said.

"That's a common side-effect of the sedative," Fletcher assured her. "But you'll be fine now. Let's have a look at how you're healing."

He used his MedTek to X-ray her again. After perusing the hologram he said, "Everything's looking good."

"How long until it's healed properly?" she asked. "And until it stops hurting?"

"Is it hurting much?"

"A little," she admitted.

"I'll give you something to help speed along the healing now that I know it's setting in the right position," Fletcher said. "You should be back to normal within a few days. Until then, I'll keep you on the pain meds."

"A few days?" Alex repeated, wondering if she'd heard wrong. "That's pretty fast, isn't it? What sort of 'something' are we talking about?"

Fletcher walked over to his medicine cabinet and came back with two vials—one green, the other a dusky pink.

"This is a regeneration motivator," he said, handing her the pink one first. "It's commonly referred to as Regenevator."

She peered into the glass. "What does it do?"

"It accelerates your body's natural healing process just like the healing salve that we use on minor cuts, but this one is taken orally. As it enters the bloodstream it motivates an increase in bodily functions associated with healing. This particular dose is specifically for damage to the skeletal structure. Other Regenevators can cover a range of internal and external maladies where there's a need for tissue, flesh and even organ regeneration. Some also motivate speedier white blood cell creation to aid against infection, which is necessary with some of the nastier wounds."

"So, a few days, huh?" Alex said again, impressed.

"Just in time for you to finish your final week of classes." He laughed at the face she made and then instructed, "Go on and drink that down."

It was a testament to how much she'd learned to trust the doctor that she didn't even hesitate before raising the flask to her lips and swallowing the pink liquid. Much like his other medicines, it had a nice taste to it, sweet and fruity.

"Since you haven't actually broken anything you'll only need one dose," he said when she handed him back the empty vial. "But you'll still be a little tender until it's done its work."

He handed her the green flask then, and she examined it before asking, "What's with the different shades? I'm used to having the bright green one, but last night you gave me a dark green one, and now this is somewhere in between. Are they different strengths or something?"

He nodded. "They each have a different concentration of analgesic, and the darker ones have an added sedative to help with the pain."

"Will this one knock me out again?" she asked, looking at the forest-coloured liquid warily.

"It's nowhere near as strong as last night's dose," Fletcher assured her. "You'll be a little sleepy for the rest of the day and you'll probably need an afternoon nap later on, but that should be all. There's only a minor sedative in it—just enough to help you relax—so you won't forget anything and your coordination will be fine."

Something about his coordination remark stirred a memory from the previous night, but Alex couldn't quite remember so she shrugged the thought away.

"Okay," she said, and swallowed the minty liquid. Immediately the throbbing in her shoulder disappeared again. Wonderful, wonderful painkillers.

"Now, best if you come back again tonight after dinner and I'll give you another dose to get you through until morning. We'll do the same again tomorrow, but by Monday you should be almost completely back to normal."

"That's good, since I doubt Finn will let me off in PE," she mumbled, getting to her feet and moving to the door.

Fletcher chuckled but he didn't refute her assumption.

"Thanks again, Fletcher," she said. "I'll see you tonight."

Alex headed straight for the food court, absolutely starving after having slept through dinner the night before. She was just finishing off her second helping of breakfast when Jordan arrived and sat down beside her.

"How're you feeling?" he asked, running his hands through his sleep-tussled hair.

She sipped a mouthful of water before answering. "Uh, good?"

"Your shoulder," he clarified. "How is it?"

"Oh," she said. "Much better, thanks. How do you know about that?"

Bear sat down opposite them—also looking like he'd just rolled out of bed—and jumped into the conversation. "We came looking for you last night to celebrate the end of exams, but we couldn't find you anywhere. When we finally ran into D.C., she said you were already asleep."

"Some of the guys in your Combat class told us you'd dislocated your shoulder and were high as a kite on Fletcher's pain meds," Jordan said. "They thought you'd probably be out of it for the rest of the night."

"Yeah, I was totally gone," she said. "But it's amazing what a good night's sleep will do. I'm feeling so much better now."

Her assurances were negated by the huge yawn that swallowed up the second half of her sentence.

Jordan snorted. "It looks like it did you the world of good."

"Really, I'm heaps better," she said, shaking her head to try and clear away the fuzziness. "I've just been to see Fletcher and he gave me some more medicine. I'll be a little tired today, but so what, right? We can still celebrate. No more exams! Yay!"

Jordan and Bear exchanged amused glances but they didn't say anything about how she'd slurred half her words.

"What are we going to do?" she pressed. "Something fun?"

"Why don't we take it easy?" Bear offered. "Something relaxing, like a picnic? It's been such a crazy week, it'll be nice to just have a bit of calm, you know?"

"Subtle, Bear. Real subtle."

"I kind of like the idea," Jordan said, ignoring Alex's sarcasm. "It'll be good just to chill out."

Alex didn't know if they were doing it for her or if they genuinely meant it, but either way she was thankful. She certainly wasn't up for anything energetic.

"I have to go and see Fitzy about something, but I'm free after that," Bear said. "Why don't we all meet back here in an hour and we'll head down to the lake?"

"Sounds good," Alex agreed.

It turned out that Jordan had to meet up with Jarvis for some kind of indiscretion he'd been involved in earlier in the week, so Alex returned to her dorm room, intent on cleaning it up a bit. The mess she'd brought in with her the previous night needed to be dealt with, but there was also a few weeks' worth of cleaning that neither she nor D.C. had got around to doing during their study-induced madness. It would be good to get on top of it—and it would also help to keep her awake.

"This is really nice," Alex said, reclining on a picnic blanket and looking out at the lake.

"Sometimes I have good ideas," Bear said, reaching for another sandwich.

"Mmm," Jordan agreed, his mouth too full of food to speak.

Alex and the boys had spent the last couple of hours lounging around outside, relaxing. Well, as much as they could, anyway, considering the circumstances.

"Why do they have to be so *loud?*" Alex murmured, not for the first time.

It turned out that she and her friends weren't the only ones celebrating the end of exams. Every student at the academy seemed to be rejoicing. Impromptu groups had formed all across the campus with loud gatherings of people making the most out of their freedom. Even with the painkillers in her system, Alex was still developing a headache from the noise of so many excited students.

"Only one week left, that's why," said Connor, who had decided to join them on their picnic at the last minute. "Everyone's excited for the summer break."

"Where do you live, Alex?" Mel asked, having tagged along with her cousin. "Maybe we can meet up over the holidays? Hang out?"

Alex froze, not at all prepared for the question. Where *was* she going to be over the holidays? With the stress of her exams, she hadn't had much of a chance to worry about her complicated circumstances, but the time was quickly approaching for her parents' return to the land of communication. They were bound to be concerned if she didn't arrive home from her 'boarding school' on time—and one phone call would tell them that she'd never enrolled at the International Exchange Academy to begin with. That would be... problematic.

What Alex really needed was to find a way back to her world, but she had no idea how to do that. She could only hope that the headmaster would *finally* return to the academy sometime in the next seven days before term ended. Then he would— hopefully—be able to get her back home before her parents lost their minds and contacted the FBI, Interpol and anyone else who would listen.

"Didn't you mention that you'll be travelling over the summer?" Jordan piped up when Alex was silent for too long.

"Yeah, that's right," she said, playing along. "I'm not really sure where I'll be, to be honest."

"Oh, okay," Mel said, sounding disappointed. "Well, we'll just have to stay in touch via ComTCD and if you have some spare time we'll organise something."

Alex nodded but she doubted they'd get the chance, even if she was still around. And as nice as Mel was, they really didn't have all that much in common. Alex would much prefer to spend the time with Jordan and Bear.

She noticed that all the boys were looking longingly at one of the ball games that had just started near where they were sitting.

"Why don't you guys go and join them?" she said. "It looks like fun."

Connor looked excited at the prospect and immediately headed off. Mel followed him as well, but Jordan and Bear remained seated.

"We're not going to ditch you," Jordan said when she looked at them questioningly.

"Seriously, guys," Alex said. "I won't be good company for much longer. I think I'll follow Fletcher's suggestion and have a nap, as embarrassing as that is."

She'd been fighting back the sleep even while cleaning her dorm earlier, and only through stubborn determination had she managed to force it aside to stay awake for the picnic with her friends.

Jordan and Bear still looked hesitant to leave her, so Alex stood, making the decision for them. "I'll meet up with you for dinner. Go have fun. Kick some butt. You know the drill."

Seeing that she meant it, they smiled at her and sprinted off to where the others were playing. Alex waved when they turned back to her, and then she headed up to her dorm.

Twenty minutes later she was still tossing and turning in her bed, desperately trying to drift off, but unable to because of all the noise outside. She'd even tried to close her window, but within minutes the room had become like a sauna, making it even more impossible for her to relax.

"*So* tired," she mumbled to herself as she sat up and rubbed her weary eyes.

What could she do?

It was a mark of just how tired she was that when a crazy idea came to her she didn't think it was stupid or dangerous. Instead, she got up and put some shoes on before leaving her room.

A few minutes later she was stumbling wearily into the Library's foyer. The librarian wasn't at his desk, which was probably for the best considering what she intended to do.

Instead of walking over to the staircase, Alex approached the closest wall and continued along it until she found what she was looking for.

"If I can fall out of one, why not into one?" she murmured to herself, staring at the picture in front of her. It was an oil painting that depicted a dark room with a roaring fireplace. In one corner of the room was a large four-poster bed with drapes around it, and in the other corner was a woman sitting in a rocking chair, knitting. Everything was frozen, captured in time by the artist, and Alex knew it would be perfect for what she needed.

"How do I do this?" she wondered.

When she'd come out of the waterfall into the foyer, she'd just fallen straight through the painting. Maybe it worked in reverse too.

Alex pressed her hand against the surface of the painting, and she was amazed when she didn't meet anything solid. Instead, her arm continued straight through and *into* the portrait.

She smiled in victory, and it turned into a gasp when she was jerked forward into the picture and tumbled out into the dark room.

"Good heavens! Where did you come from?"

Alex stood up and clutched her throbbing shoulder. After a moment the pain eased and she was able to look around the room that she'd landed in. The first thing she noticed was the lady in the rocking chair, who was staring at her with her knitting needles paused mid-stitch.

"Um… Hi, I'm Alex," she said. "I'm so sorry to intrude like this, but…"

She really hadn't thought about what she was going to say. It wasn't every day that she stepped through a painting and talked with someone who wasn't actually real.

"You must be Chosen," the woman said knowingly, rising from her seat. "No one else would be able to enter here."

"Yes, that's right," Alex said, swaying on her feet now. She reached out to steady herself on the wall behind her and noticed that the painting she'd come through was still hanging there, but instead of showing the dark room she was now in, it was a portrait of the Library's foyer. At least she knew how to get back out when the time came.

"I'm really sorry to disturb you," Alex told the woman. "I'm just so ti-ti-tired." She had to cover a yawn as she finished her sentence.

"Child, you look simply exhausted," the woman said, walking over to take hold of her arm. "Come and sit down."

Alex let the woman lead her over to the bed and she almost moaned when she felt how soft it was.

"I know this seems like an odd request, but do you mind if I take a nap? It's just… I'm so tired, and everywhere else is so noisy…"

"Of course, you poor dear," the woman said, surprising her. Maybe strange people arrived in her bedroom more often than Alex presumed. "Here, let me help you."

The woman bent down to help Alex with her shoes before she pulled back the covers on the bed. She was so kind and caring that Alex felt tears come to her eyes.

"Thank you so much," she whispered, her voice catching. She always became emotional when she was tired, and this woman's compassion was overwhelming.

"Don't even mention it," the lady said, tucking her in and tenderly brushing the hair away from her face. "Now, you just close your eyes and have a good rest while I sit and watch over you. You're safe here. Sleep in peace, child."

Alex tried to thank her again, but she couldn't form the words as her eyes closed of their own accord. The repetitive *click, click, click* of knitting needles and the lady's quiet humming soon pulled her straight down into the deep sleep that she so desperately needed.

Forty

"Child."

"Child?"

"Child, you need to wake up now."

Someone was shaking Alex gently.

"Come, dear, you must awaken."

The shaking increased and Alex couldn't ignore it any longer. "Hmmm?"

"That's it. Open your eyes."

Alex did as she was asked but she couldn't see much. Everything was dark except for a small light coming from a candle the woman held in her hand.

"You need to get up," the woman said urgently.

Alex forced herself to sit up, and she pulled her shoes on before standing. Despite her difficulty waking, she felt so much better now than she had earlier.

"How long have I been asleep?" she asked, her voice groggy.

"Four turns of the hourglass," the woman answered.

Four hours. That meant it was around seven o'clock. Her friends would be worried about her if she didn't turn up for dinner soon.

"I should go," Alex said. "Thank you, again—*so* much—for the peace and quiet."

She started walking over to where she'd stumbled out of the painting, looking for the exit point.

"Child, I think something is wrong," the woman said fearfully.

Alex was about to respond when she looked at the candle again, their only source of light, and realised that the woman was right—something *was* wrong. They were in a painting, a painting that captured a set of images in time forever. So why wasn't the fireplace burning brightly anymore?

Dread welled up within Alex. "May I borrow your candle for a moment, please?"

The woman handed over the little flame and Alex held it up to the wall. The painting was still there, but it no longer showed the brightly lit foyer. The picture was completely black—a deep, smothering darkness, the likes of which Alex had only seen once before.

"*No*," she gasped.

"What is it?" the woman asked in a trembling voice.

"Lockdown," Alex whispered, horrified. It wouldn't mean anything to a woman stuck in a painting, but it meant the world to Alex. *Her* world.

"I have to go. Now." She shoved the candle back into the woman's hands and reached forward into the painting, feeling her world tilt and expand as she tumbled out the other side.

Just like the last time, the darkness was overwhelming. Alex wished she had something to see with, but she hadn't had the heart to steal the woman's only light source. She couldn't believe that she'd slept through the Lockdown sirens, but maybe they hadn't penetrated into the painting.

She carefully felt her way along the walls, making sure not to press too hard against any of the other artwork. Moving as fast as she dared, she hurried towards the staircase that would lead her up into the Tower and then out onto the grounds. It would be lighter outside and she would hopefully be able to find out what was going on.

Step. Step. Step. Step. *Thump.*

"Ouch!" she hissed into the darkness after colliding with the bottom step of the staircase. She hopped on one foot and bent over just as a radiant light flared out from the top of the staircase. Stubbing her toe had actually saved her from being blinded by the light, since it burned to look at it even from the corner of her eye.

"Who's there?" she asked, shielding her gaze with her hand.

"Alex?" called a shaky voice.

"D.C.," Alex said with relief. It was just her roommate. "What's going on? Why has the Lockdown been activated?"

The other girl didn't answer, but as the light moved steadily down the staircase, Alex's eyes began to adjust. When her vision was clear enough, the sight in front of her made her wish it was still too dark to see.

"How kind of you to be ready and waiting for us, Alexandra. I was under the impression that I'd have to drag you down here, kicking and screaming."

Aven. Talk about horrible timing—she was exactly where he needed her.

"I was wondering when you were going to show up again," Alex said, trying to keep her voice steady. "It was considerate of you to wait for exams to be over."

"Education is important, Alexandra," he said with a mocking smile.

"You really should call first, next time. It's more polite," she said, wondering why she was deliberately goading him.

Aven's eyes glinted dangerously. "How careless of me. However, I did drop by your room first. Thank you for the Liquid Light—as you can see, it's rather useful."

The thought of Aven going through her stuff made Alex visibly shudder.

"Fortunately, I've brought a gift to make up for my lack of etiquette," Aven said.

Alex sucked in a breath as D.C. came into view. She was being pushed down the staircase by another man who stopped just behind Aven. The light illuminated D.C.'s terrified features, along with the jagged knife that the man held to her throat. It was a familiar knife.

"Gerald," Alex said, trying to keep her panic from showing.

"You and I have unfinished business," the tattooed man said menacingly. "We were interrupted last time."

"Trust me, I haven't forgotten," she returned. "Does Marcus Sparker know you're here? Or are you just a hired lackey with loose loyalties?"

"Gerald is one of my... associates," Aven said. "He's here to make sure you keep up your end of the bargain."

"What bargain?" she demanded, turning back to him. "I'm not helping you with anything."

"I think you'll find that I have ways of convincing you."

"You're wasting your time," Alex said. "I won't help you get where you want to go."

Aven looked at her for a moment, not saying anything, and the silence was worse than his dangerously smooth voice.

"Let's take a walk," he finally said.

Alex opened her mouth to protest, but Aven latched onto her arm so fast that it surprised her enough to keep quiet. She struggled against him, but the harder she fought, the tighter his grip became. He dragged her across the foyer and down the staircase, with Gerald forcing D.C. after them.

To Alex's relief, the stairs stopped at the main Library level and didn't go any further. Aven's light—*her* light—illuminated the closest bookshelves but nothing else.

"I have a question," Alex said as he continued to drag her forward, lighting up new shelves as they passed. She'd given up the struggle, choosing to save her strength in case she needed it later. "The second time we met, you told me you were once a student here. But if alumni are allowed onto the grounds, why did you trigger the Lockdown? Both times? It was your fault, right?"

There were certainly more pressing questions Alex could have asked, but she needed a distraction from her growing anxiety. His answer would hopefully mean one less unsolved mystery, which might help calm her nerves, at least somewhat.

"I lied." Aven's response was as simple as it was uncaring.

Alex glared sullenly into the darkness. "What else have you lied about?"

He didn't answer and she was forced to follow him in silence after that, his pincer grip cutting off her circulation.

She looked over her shoulder and saw that Gerald and D.C. were still trailing behind them. Months ago, Alex had promised D.C. that no one was after her and that there was nothing to worry about. At the time, Alex had thought it was true, but now her roommate was stuck in this mess with her, and she had no idea how to get them both out of there.

"Ouch," Alex hissed when Aven yanked her around a pile of books. "Ease up, would you? I bruise easily."

His fingers flexed even tighter and he led the way down an aisle before abruptly turning to walk between a stack of shelves. He stopped three quarters of the way along and picked out a book, handing it to Alex. It looked innocent enough but she knew the books in the Library could trigger hidden trapdoors, and she wasn't willing to make the mistake of allowing her naivety to give him what he wanted by accident.

"Open it," he ordered.

She crossed her arms, ignoring his painful grip. "No."

"*Open it.*"

"*No.*"

"Gerald."

Alex watched in horror as Gerald tightened his hold on her roommate. His blade grazed D.C.'s flesh and she whimpered as a droplet of blood dribbled down her neck.

"Open it," Aven said again, "or your friend dies."

Alex looked from D.C.'s terrified eyes to Gerald's excited ones before she turned back to Aven. His gaze was cold and uncaring; he'd have no hesitation following through on his threat.

"I—I—"

"Last chance, Alexandra," Aven said, leaning close. "*Open the book!*"

Alex couldn't just let him kill D.C., but she still didn't know what the consequences would be if Aven made it through to Freya. Why was he so desperate to get there? Would saving her roommate mean dooming her world? Was D.C.'s life really worth the risk? Alex's lack of answers both frustrated and terrified her.

"He hasn't found what he's after yet," D.C. whispered, even as Gerald pressed the knife deeper into her skin.

Alex didn't know how her roommate even understood what was going on, but she chose to trust the other girl's words. Closing her eyes, she tore the book open, hoping desperately that it wouldn't create a doorway to Freya.

"That wasn't so hard now, was it?" Aven purred.

Alex reopened her eyes and felt her stomach lurch when she saw that a doorway *had* appeared before them. The glossy black panelling was streaked with flecks of silver, and the handle itself seemed to be glowing with an invitation to reach out and discover the secrets that lay beyond.

"After you," Aven said.

Alex looked at his hand still clenching her arm. "Are you going to let go of me so I can step through?"

"That won't be necessary," he said. "I'll follow along with you."

Well, it had been worth a try.

Alex reached a trembling hand towards the glowing handle. It was warm to touch, strangely soothing, and turned easily beneath her fingers. The door sprung open without her help, and she sagged in relief to see that it led to a torch-lit corridor full of closed doors, much like the ones she'd explored months before. Her world was still safe—at least for the moment.

"What next?" she asked, looking down the corridor of endless doors. There were many more than she remembered.

"Now I find the door I'm after," Aven said, gesturing for her to move forward. Once they were in the flame-lit corridor he stoppered the Liquid Light and waited for Gerald and D.C. to join them before he finished, "And then you will open it for me."

Alex didn't waste her breath contradicting him. Instead she asked, "Why do you even want to go to Freya? What's in it for you?"

Aven tilted his head and eyed her with bemusement. "Freya?"

She nodded. "What do you plan on doing in my world?"

He laughed then, a dark, cold laugh that set her nerves on edge. He seemed genuinely amused, as if her question surprised him.

"Freya?" he repeated again. "You're from Freya?"

Alex frowned at him. "Of course I am! That's what this is all about!" His amusement seemed to increase, and in a voice full of uncertainty, she added, "Isn't it?"

He didn't answer her question. Instead, he said, "When I first saw you appear in that forest clearing, I felt the power within you. I was certain you were who I'd been seeking for so long." His voice was contemplative and he seemed lost in his memories. "You were clearly affected by my presence and because of that, when you claimed never to have heard of Akarnae, I presumed you were merely simple-minded and forgetful. It was of little consequence to me; I didn't need you for your intelligence, I needed you for your power."

Alex opened her mouth to object—to *so* much of what he'd said—but he continued before she could speak.

"When I saw you fall out of the waterfall painting, my belief in your power was confirmed. I realised then that you were indeed Chosen, but I didn't for an instant wonder if you might be Called as well." He shook his head incredulously and his eyes focused once more. "My, my, this *is* a surprise."

She took a step backward at the dark look on his face. But he was still gripping her arm and didn't allow her the distance.

"As to why you think I'd want to visit your disgusting world, I don't know. There are far too many humans in Medora as it is."

Humans? Did he say *humans*? As if he wasn't one himself?

Alex felt dizzy. She looked at Aven, really *looked* at him, until she connected the dots between what was in front of her and the unforgettable image she'd seen in a book many months before.

Suddenly, everything clicked into place.

"You're not human," she said. "You're Meyarin."

"Very good, Alexandra," Aven praised mockingly.

It explained everything. His beauty, his grace, why she found it hard to resist him—even his speed and strength. It also explained what he was after.

"You're not looking for a doorway to Freya, but a way through to Meya, aren't you?"

He didn't answer her, and she knew she was right.

"I heard the city disappeared thousands of years ago," she said as he started pulling her down the corridor and opening doors at random. She was pleased when some of the doors opened to even more corridors full of doors. His search would hopefully take time—time in which someone would surely notice that she and D.C. were missing.

Again he didn't answer her, so she continued talking. "Why do you need a doorway to go there, anyway? If you're Meyarin, you'd have to know where your own city is, right?"

Aven opened another door and smiled in triumph. "Perfect."

He stepped over the threshold, dragging her with him. Inside was a small stone cell with no exit other than the doorway they'd entered through.

"I thought I had to give you permission to walk through the doors?" Alex asked. If he could get through them on his own, why did he need her?

Aven gestured for Gerald to bring D.C. in while he pulled something out of his pocket. In the dim light Alex saw that it was some kind of shiny wire, and she started struggling again, certain she wouldn't like whatever he meant to do with it. She tried to pull away but he was too strong. She kicked out at him—which he dodged easily—and aimed a punch at his too beautiful face.

Aven's speed was astonishing and he easily caught her hand before it made contact. He pursed his lips with irritation, yanked her forward, spun her around, and drew her arms tightly behind her back. She hissed as he pulled on her sore shoulder and she realised that she was overdue for her next dose of painkillers.

Aven deftly tied her hands together with the wire before he forced her onto the grimy stone floor and bound her ankles. Then he grabbed D.C. and positioned her to sit back to back with Alex on the ground, locking their hands together behind them and trapping them in place.

"Come, Gerald," Aven commanded, starting towards the door.

"Hey, wait a minute!" Alex cried. "You're just going to leave us here?"

"I have neither the time nor the inclination to babysit you while I conduct my search," Aven said. "Don't worry; I'll be back as soon as I find what I'm after."

"But—"

"Until then," he interrupted, "I feel the need to apologise, Your Highness, since I doubt these accommodations are up to your usual standard. I'm afraid it can't be helped, considering the circumstances."

"No need to patronise me," Alex said, frowning at the unnecessary title. She felt D.C. tense behind her, pulling uncomfortably on their bound hands.

"I wasn't talking to you, Alexandra," Aven said, pausing at the doorway. "I have to admit, when I discovered your roommate was the royal princess, it came as a delightful surprise. I couldn't have picked a better hostage."

Royal princess? Alex's stomach dropped. Surely he was lying again?

Aven smirked when he noticed her expression. "Am I to understand you don't know who you've been sharing a room with all year?"

Alex refused to say anything, but he continued, "It was difficult to find her, so well hidden as she is here at your academy. But allow me to make introductions. Alexandra Jennings, I give you Her Royal Highness, Princess Delucia Cavelle."

Alex felt D.C. sag in defeat behind her.

"I'll allow the two of you some time to become better acquainted," Aven said smoothly, before he turned and walked through the doorway. The light dimmed significantly when the door closed, and with the darkness came a silence so loud it was almost deafening.

Forty-One

After Aven left them in the dark cell, neither Alex nor D.C. knew what to say, and the silence lingered uncomfortably between them. When Alex couldn't stand it anymore, she quietly asked, "Are you okay?"

D.C. released a trembling breath. "Sure. Never better."

"We're going to be fine," Alex said, not sure who she was trying more to convince. "Someone will notice we're missing and they'll come looking for us."

"They won't be able to find us down here," D.C. said with a hint of bitterness. "Not unless they're Chosen—like you apparently are."

There was a question in her tone, like she wanted to know more but wasn't willing to ask. Alex was equally unwilling to share.

"I'm not the only person who can get down here," Alex said. "The headmaster can, as well as my friend Darrius. Someone will raise the alarm once the Lockdown is over and they *will* find us. Especially since you're here."

D.C. didn't respond, ignoring the implication, and the silence grew around them again.

Alex tried to wiggle her hands out of the bonds, but it was no use. The wire was so strong and tight that even the smallest movement caused it to bite into her flesh.

"I don't suppose you have some kind of super-strength gift?" Alex asked.

"No. But even if I did it wouldn't help," D.C. answered. "It's Moxyreel, made from Myrox."

"Myrox?"

"Meyarin steel," D.C. said. "It's completely impenetrable, the strongest metal in the world. The only thing that can break through Moxyreel is something else made from Myrox. So don't bother."

"How do you know about Meyarin steel?" Alex asked.

"How do you know Aven Dalmarta?" D.C. shot back.

"I—I don't know," Alex answered, surprised by the abrupt question. "We just sort of ran into each other randomly a while back. And then it happened again the last time the Lockdown was activated. He just kind of... appears, you know?"

"You haven't seen him since the last Lockdown?" D.C. asked.

"I saw him again the day before classes started back after the Kaldoras holidays," Alex said. Then she realised something. "But the Lockdown wasn't activated that time, so I don't know how he got through without triggering the wards."

"They were deactivated so the students could Bubble back in," D.C. said.

"Oh. I'd forgotten about that."

"What happened when you met him that time? Did I hear him right when he said you fell through a painting?"

"Yeah," Alex answered, knowing how ridiculous it sounded.

"What did Aven do when he saw that? Did he say anything?"

"Not really," Alex said. "He was pleased, I guess. And from what he said earlier, it was then that he knew for sure that I was Chosen. All I know is that he tried to drag me down the stairs but the librarian interrupted him, saying he wasn't allowed to be there."

"Did the librarian tell him anything else?" D.C. probed.

Alex racked her memory, thinking back. "He just said Aven could only go where he wanted if I gave him permission to enter."

"And you thought that meant he wanted to go to Freya?" D.C. asked. "Where you're from, right?"

Alex ignored the question about her origin and answered the more important one. "I overheard a conversation between the librarian, Jarvis and Maggie. What they said made me believe that somehow I could open the door for Aven to get to Freya, and if I did, it would have terrible consequences."

Alex paused, thinking about how she'd misinterpreted the conversation. "I was completely wrong."

"Not completely wrong," D.C. murmured. "You're right about him needing you to open the door, and you're right about the terrible consequences. It was just the destination you were wrong about."

"So he really does think there's a doorway to Meya down here?"

"He must, if he's here," D.C. answered.

"What's so bad about him finding it?" Alex asked, and then she repeated her earlier question that Aven had ignored. "And why does he even need a door to get there? Shouldn't he know where his own city is?"

"Aven Dalmarta is the Rebel Prince," D.C. said, "so it's not really his city anymore."

"*Prince?*" Alex spluttered. "What's with everyone suddenly becoming royal?"

"I'm not suddenly anything, thank you very much. I've had my title since birth," D.C. said. "As for Aven, he lost his royal status when he was banished."

"So he needs the doorway because...?" Alex asked, still confused.

"Because he's *banished*," D.C. repeated. "The city disappeared after his rebellion and he has no way of finding it again. Not without your help."

"The city vanished thousands of years ago," Alex said, doubtful. "I think you have your story wrong."

"Aven is *Meyarin*, Alex," D.C. said. "He's immortal, ageless. He might look young, but he's been around for millennia. And he's been searching for a way back to Meya since its disappearance."

Immortal. Ageless. Alex's head hurt just thinking about the two words, let alone everything they implied.

"If he's banished, what does he stand to gain by going back?" Alex asked, pushing aside the idea of living forever.

"I'd say he plans to try his hand at rebellion again," D.C. said. "And if he succeeds, the consequences will be deadly for us all."

"Why?"

Alex heard D.C. sigh in the darkness, no doubt irritated by her lack of understanding.

"Medoran History 101," D.C. said. "In a nutshell, Meyarins are a peaceful race, which is fortunate since they're also very powerful. Back when Meya was still accessible, they had strict rules about their interactions with humans. There was always a divide between the two races, even if there was no animosity. We humans knew better than to arouse their anger, and the Meyarins were careful to keep their power from becoming corrupted. It was a peaceful alliance between our two races, even if it was clear that we benefited from trading more than they did. I imagine they saw us as little children to be humoured rather than an actual threat to their society. And they were right, we weren't the threat. Their threat came from within.

"Aven was the second son born to King Astophe and Queen Niida. His brother Roka was the golden child—always faster, stronger, better. Aven sought to be worthy of the attention his brother received, but he was never quite good enough.

"It's said that one day a delegation of humans entered Meya for trade purposes. Aven had never been around humans before since they rarely ventured into Meya and he'd never left the city or its surrounding forests. But that day he happened to witness their arrival and his curiosity led him to meet them.

"When he saw how primitive their trade products were he became outraged. For years Meya had provided technology and medicine to humans, helping to advance our society. In Aven's mind, his own race had received nothing of worth in return. He stormed back to the palace and demanded that his father end the alliance since the Meyarins were earning nothing and losing everything. But his father dismissed him, saying that one day he would understand.

"Now, Aven was very young then, for a Meyarin. Young, but convinced that he was right. It was a dangerous combination. He started to meet with other Meyarins in secret, forming an anti-human society of sorts that later became known as the Rebels."

D.C. paused and Alex could imagine the other girl scrunching up her nose at the unoriginal name.

"At first they were only a small group of young Meyarins intent on changing the laws, but when no one would listen to them they decided to take action. The next time a human trading delegation entered the city, they killed them. All of them."

Alex gasped. "No!"

"Right in front of the palace," D.C. confirmed. "Witnesses were so shocked by the violence that they didn't act fast enough to capture the Rebels, but the king knew his youngest son had to have been involved. He demanded Aven explain his actions. Aven again told his father to change the trade agreement and end the alliance with humans. He said we were just a waste of space and resources, completely beneath them as a race.

"King Astophe refused, of course," D.C continued, "but Aven was still a royal prince, and short of imprisoning him for the rest of his very long life, there was nothing the king could really do. Eventually Aven apologised, claiming he'd seen the error of his ways. The king fell for it, and he ended up with a knife in his back."

Alex jerked in shock.

"Before Aven could finish his father off, his brother Roka discovered him, and the two fought. Roka easily overpowered Aven and forced him to the floor, but Aven managed to stab his blade into Roka's leg, piercing his artery. The guards appeared then, and Aven was forced to flee. An edict went out banishing him from ever returning to Meya, and the city vanished to avoid being further corrupted by his taint."

Alex just sat there after D.C. finished her story, absorbing the words and collecting her thoughts.

"It's funny." D.C. breathed out a humourless laugh. "Even though he was banished, the Rebels still won. The trade agreement ended when Meya disappeared. He still got what he wanted, or at least part of it."

"But now he wants more," Alex guessed.

"Yes," D.C. confirmed. "Years of being forced to live amongst humans has left a bitterness in him so strong that he won't stop until he has his revenge."

Alex had a feeling she knew exactly what that meant, but she still forced herself to ask, "What will he do?"

"He'll kill what's left of his family and take the throne, and with it the leadership of the Meyarin people," D.C. said, confirming Alex's fears. "And then he'll destroy the race responsible for his misfortune."

"Do you mean...?"

"Humankind," D.C. said. "He'll kill us all—or at least those of us who he can't use."

"Use?" Alex repeated.

"His *associates*," D.C. said, using the same term Aven had used to describe Gerald. "The humans he collects. The gifted ones who are willing to join his cause."

Alex shuddered at the thought. "How do you know all this? I was under the impression that information about Meya is pretty scarce."

"I've had access to privileged information all my life," D.C. answered quietly, prompting Alex to remember the book the other girl had been reading before Kaldoras, the one about Meya. It made more sense now.

With neither of them knowing what to say next, silence surrounded them again—gaping silence, filled with uncertainty.

"I wanted to tell you," D.C. finally said. "About me, I mean."

Alex snorted. "No you didn't."

"I did," D.C. stated firmly. "But in case you haven't noticed, I'm not exactly close to many people. *Any* people. It comes with being who I am."

"Then why are you so talkative all of a sudden?" Alex asked.

"Because I've realised that we're probably going to die when Aven is finished with us, so I'm officially dubbing you my first and last ever friend. Best friend, in fact, since you're the only one I have. Enjoy it. You just might get a whole hour holding that title before we're dead."

"Not fair," Alex argued, choosing to ignore the presumption about their impending death. "I had to hold the most hated enemy title for months. Now I get an hour in recompense? How is that a fair ruling, Your Highness?"

Alex's tone was mocking, but she knew the banter was helping to distract them both from their circumstances.

"I'll tell you what," D.C. said. "If by some miracle we make it out of this alive, you can keep the title indefinitely."

"What if I don't want just the title?" Alex asked quietly.

"A title has responsibilities," D.C. answered, just as quietly. "Yours would be no different."

Alex smiled, understanding the other girl's implication. "So, friends?"

"Friends," D.C. agreed. "But for the record, I don't think you quite realise what you're getting yourself into. I've been told I'm high maintenance. A *royal* pain in the butt, even."

Alex laughed. "I think I can handle that."

A few moments of contemplative silence passed until Alex observed, "You know, I think this is the longest conversation we've ever had."

"Desperate times," D.C. said, but Alex could hear the humour in her voice. "You're not as annoying as I thought you were."

"Gee, thanks," Alex muttered. "What high praise that is, coming from a princess no less."

"Princess might be my title," D.C. said, sounding irritated, "but it's not who I *am*."

"Sorry. I'm still trying to get my head around it."

"It's okay," D.C. said. "I'm just not used to people knowing my real identity."

"Does anyone at the academy know?"

"Not many people," D.C. admitted. "The headmaster, Jarvis and most of the teaching staff are aware for security reasons. And there are a handful of students who grew up around the palace and have known me since I was a child. But that's it. Very few people have seen me out of the palace for years, and I've grown up a lot in that time which is why no one else would recognise me. But everyone who does know is sworn to secrecy."

"Why?"

"A number of reasons," D.C. said. "A hostage situation like this is one of them. But the main reason, for me at least, is that I didn't want to be known as Princess Delucia at Akarnae. I wanted to be treated just like everyone else." She trailed off before continuing quietly, "But it turned out that I'm too guarded. I haven't exactly made any friends in my time here. And I was okay with that, until you came along."

"Me? What did I do?"

"You were just always *there*," D.C. said. "When I went to bed, when I woke up, in my classes. Everywhere I went, there you were. You had instant friends, you were good at the subjects without even trying, and you were so obviously happy."

Alex found it interesting to hear about her life from an outside perspective.

"You're so wrong," she said. "For most of the year I've been completely out of my element. I was thrown into this world without any idea of what was happening, and I've been trying not to drown ever since. You're right about my friends, but everything else has been nearly impossible to stay on top of."

D.C. thought about that. "It's funny, isn't it? The things we've managed to hide?"

"I'm not sure if 'funny' is the word I'd use," Alex said in a dry tone, "but it's something, all right."

"You do realise that if we make it out of here, you can't tell anyone? About me being who I am?" D.C. said, her voice hesitant and uncertain.

"We're in the same boat," Alex said. "In fact, you know more about me than I do about you. No one can know that I'm Chosen, or that I'm—what did Aven say? Called?"

"I guess we have to keep each other's secrets," D.C. said, sounding pensive.

"That's what friends do," Alex said quietly, their closeness still a new concept.

"I like that," D.C. admitted. "Does anyone else know about you?"

"Jordan and Bear do," Alex told her. "The headmaster, apparently, along with Jarvis, the librarian and some of the other teachers. Also Darrius, who I mentioned before, and a weird old lady who owns a disappearing bookshop—please, don't ask. Otherwise, no one else I know of."

They descended into silence again, but it was more comfortable now, companionable even.

"You know what would be perfect right now?" D.C. asked, trying to wriggle into a more comfortable position. "A white knight riding in on his noble steed to save the day. That's what happens in all the good fairytales. Why does it never happen in real life?"

Alex froze. "Say that again."

"Say what again? The part about fairytales? You do have them in Freya, don't you?"

"Not that, the part about the knight." But Alex didn't wait for D.C. to answer. "*Sir Camden!*"

"Um… Are you feeling all right?" D.C. asked.

"Wait for it," Alex said, feeling giddy with excitement. Why hadn't she thought of the knight before?

"Wait for *what?*" D.C. asked, exasperated.

"How doth thee, fair lady?"

Forty-Two

D.C. squealed in shock and pulled against the bonds that tied her to Alex, almost tipping them both over.

Alex couldn't see the knight since she was facing the wrong way, so she called out to him. "Sir Camden! Over here!"

She beamed with relief when he walked into her line of sight and bowed to her.

"Greetings, Lady Alexandra," he said. "Why art thou so unceremoniously tethered? Doth the lady require assistance?"

"Yes, please," Alex said, urgently. "Can you untie us?"

The knight—or suit of armour, really—pulled his sword out of his scabbard and kneeled near her feet. He slipped the blade carefully through the bonds and started to saw, but nothing happened.

"These here bonds be mighty strong," he said, pulling his weapon back out. "My sword be not as sharp as it once was."

"I *told* you," D.C. whispered, still startled by the knight's sudden appearance. "You need something made out of Myrox."

Alex sighed, realising that D.C. was right. But then she had another idea. "Sir Camden, I need you to go and find someone who can help us, can you do that?"

"A quest?" he asked, sounding just as excited as the last time.

"A noble quest," she confirmed. "I need you to find Darrius and tell him where we are and that we need help."

"I hath no knowledge of this Darrius," Sir Camden told her. "I may only search for one such as thee, one Chosen by this here Library."

Alex frowned. Darrius *was* Chosen by the Library. But she didn't have time to question Sir Camden before D.C. cut in.

"What about the headmaster, Sir Knight? Can you locate Professor Marselle?"

"Aye, that I can," he said, straightening up. "Fear not, fair maidens. Sir Camden shalt lead the cavalry to aid in thy liberation."

With that, Sir Camden walked through the stone wall without looking back.

"Do I even want to know where you met him?" D.C. asked.

"Nope," Alex said. "But I wish I'd thought of him earlier."

"You've had a bit on your mind," D.C. said kindly.

Alex nodded in the darkness, appreciating her new friend's understanding. "I just hope he finds the headmaster in time. Marselle could be anywhere and I don't know if Sir Camden is restricted to the Library or not."

"He walked straight out of here just fine," D.C. said. "He can probably use the doorways just like anyone else."

"I hope so," Alex said. "Because Aven's sure to be back soon."

D.C. didn't reply, but her silence was agreement enough. Both girls were becoming more anxious by the minute. Alex tried wiggling her hands again, even if it was no use. She stared at the Moxyreel tied around her feet, glowing despite the lack of light. It was beautiful, even if it was restricting.

As Alex squinted at the metal she thought there was something vaguely familiar about it. "This Myrox stuff," she said, "can it be made into other things? Weapons? Jewellery?"

"Yes," D.C. said. "Most of the Meyarin weapons are forged from Myrox, as far as I know. And I guess that they could just as easily make jewellery out of it as well, since it's so pretty. Why?"

Pictures whirled through Alex's head. The dagger she'd given Bear's dad for Kaldoras, the shiny brooch she'd given Dorothy. William had said both were priceless, made from Meyarin metal.

And there was one other gift which she'd forgotten about as the months had passed.

"Your bracelet," Alex gasped. "Are you wearing it?"

"The one you gave me?" D.C. asked. "I haven't had the chance to thank you for it. It's beautiful."

"Never mind that now," Alex said. "Tell me that you're wearing it?"

"I never take it off."

Alex breathed out in a rush. "It's Meyarin. I didn't realise."

"Of course!" D.C. said, understanding immediately. "It was always so pretty but I never once thought that it might be made from Myrox. It's such a rare metal outside of Meya."

"Will it work?" Alex asked.

"It should," D.C. said, excited now. "Can you reach the clasp?"

It was difficult with their hands tied so tightly together, but with some uncoordinated wiggling, Alex managed to grasp the bracelet and turn it until she could undo the clip.

"Got it," she said as it opened and fell into her hands. She manoeuvred it between their bonds and used the little leverage she had to start sawing through the metal.

It was amazing how quickly the Moxyreel surrendered to the Myrox bracelet; only a few seconds passed before the bonds broke with a resolute *snap*. Both girls groaned when their hands were free, and Alex massaged out the pain as her circulation returned. Her shoulder throbbed uncomfortably and she had to grit her teeth until the aching eased.

"Hurry," D.C. urged, prompting Alex to cut the bonds around her ankles and hand the bracelet over so she could do the same.

After they stood unsteadily to their feet, D.C. reclasped the bracelet around her wrist and Alex noticed that it wasn't damaged in the slightest.

"Remarkable," she murmured.

"I'll say," D.C. agreed. "Now let's get out of here."

"A commendable effort, but I'm afraid you're too late."

Consumed by their rush to free themselves, neither Alex nor D.C. had noticed Aven and Gerald re-enter the dungeon.

"Both of you put your hands out where we can see them. We don't want any accidents, now, do we?"

"I'll give you an accident," D.C. muttered, too low for him to hear. Or, it should have been too low for him to hear, if he was human. But he wasn't.

"Now, now, Princess," Aven tsked. "From one royal to another, surely you can understand the position I'm in."

"If you think I'm going to sympathise with you, then you have another thing coming." D.C.'s voice rose in anger. "I won't allow you to kill my people."

"Nor will I," Alex agreed, crossing her arms.

"I'm not giving either of you a choice," Aven said.

"You have to give me one," Alex said. "I have to let you through that doorway out of my own free will, remember? Otherwise you can't get through."

Aven smiled at her. It was a dark, sinister look. "You're mistaken, Alexandra. Again, it would seem. I *did* need the willing permission of a Chosen one in order to pass through the doorway into the inner Library, but you gave me that when you opened the book and entered first, leading me through. Now you just have to open the last door for me, thereby allowing my entrance. That part need not be out of your own free will."

Alex felt her blood freeze as she grasped his intended meaning, but she held her ground.

"If you want to use her to get to Meya, you'll have to go through me first." D.C. crossed her arms in imitation of Alex. Side by side they stood, neither one willing to back down.

"Do you mean to intimidate me, little princess? I'm truly trembling within."

D.C. glared at him, but Aven just smiled at her as if indulging a child.

"Don't worry, Delucia. Your role in all this is not yet over. You shall be an example to your race. A royal martyr. Surely there's no higher honour than to die for your people. Your death will be the first of many, showing your pitiful human subjects exactly what is to come with my rise to power. I will rule Meya, and with it all of Medora. And your people will be rounded up and exterminated like the vermin they are."

Alex could feel the tension radiating off D.C., but she had to give the other girl credit when she didn't react. He'd just made a declaration to commit genocide, after all.

"Enough stalling," Aven said, as if they'd asked questions. "Gerald?"

As the menacing lackey started towards them, Alex looked at D.C. and yelled out, "*Now!*"

D.C. caught her meaning, and both girls jumped at Gerald, with D.C. going for his legs while Alex grabbed his tattooed arm to steady the knife. Gerald stumbled when they collided with him but he didn't go down, solid as he was. He used his free arm to backhand Alex painfully across the face, but she refused to loosen her grip on the knife even when the effort jarred her injured shoulder. He grabbed a handful of her hair and yanked her head back, causing Alex to see that D.C. wasn't faring much better with him kicking out violently at her.

Suddenly, Alex was pulled away from Gerald, her grip wrenched from his arm by one much stronger.

"*Enough*," Aven said, holding Alex still as she struggled in vain against his unnatural Meyarin strength.

In the blink of an eye he pulled a dagger from his belt, its blade the colour of blue ice. In a single motion he sliced it across his own palm and silver-coloured blood began to flow out of the wound. Alex was so shocked that she failed to stop him when he pulled her left wrist forward and ripped the bloody dagger across her open hand.

"Eugh!" she cried in disgust and pain as he forced her bleeding palm towards his own, pressing both their wounds together. She felt her stomach lurch when their bloodied hands joined with a sickeningly wet *squelch*.

Alex ripped her hand out of his grasp, surprised when he let her go.

"That. Was. *Disgusting*," she said, in a near hysterical pitch. The wound throbbed in time with her shoulder, but then the pain in her hand began to ease and she looked down in shock as it started to heal before her eyes. After only a few seconds, all that was left was a light scar across her palm which was splashed with their mixed blood—silver blending with red.

Alex watched the dripping colours with a morbid sense of horror. She opened her mouth, fully prepared to scream out her fear and anger. "*What the—*"

"Be silent!" Aven shouted, ending her rant before she could even begin.

His order caused a burning feeling to pulse through her palm until her mouth closed of its own accord, completely against her will. As she tried to open it—without success—she noticed that Gerald had overcome D.C. and was once again restraining her.

"Now, follow me," Aven ordered, and her left hand burned again with his command.

No way, she tried to say, but the words wouldn't form. Her mouth wouldn't open. She looked at her friend with terrified eyes and saw that D.C. was just as scared as she was. They were in real trouble now, and they both knew it.

Alex's fear escalated when her feet started moving, and she found herself following Aven as he walked through the doorway and back into the brightly lit corridor of doors.

Something must have happened when he'd cut her palm, because all of a sudden she was like a puppet on a string, obedient to his command. She heard D.C. struggling behind her but there was nothing she could do to help. Her body was entirely outside of her control.

"There now, that's much better," Aven said.

Alex tried to scream at him, but her mouth still wouldn't open. All she could do was trail mechanically after him, step for step.

She followed him through a doorway which led to another corridor of doors, and then through a second doorway with the same results.

It was like a maze, Alex realised, and she desperately hoped he would lose his bearings. She couldn't stand the idea that he'd only have to order her to open the right doorway and her traitorous body would comply, allowing him to step through to Meya unhindered. If Sir Camden didn't find the headmaster soon, they were all going to die.

I'm not ready to die, Alex's thoughts screamed. She was meant to have decades of life left—time enough to grow old, surrounded by loved ones. It wasn't supposed to end like this, not here, not now. What about her parents? They would never find out what happened to her. Would they think she'd run away? Would they spend the rest of their lives searching for her, wondering where she was and if she was okay? Just the thought of them, worried and grieving, pierced Alex's heart with agony. She wanted to wrap her arms around her torso to ward off the pain, but her limbs continued to ignore her commands. All she could do was place one foot in front of the other, with each step moving her closer towards her impending execution.

When Aven eventually came to a stop, Alex's body halted directly behind him.

"It's time," he said, looking at the door in front of him with longing. "I can finally end what I started all those years ago."

No, Alex tried to say. She thought she might have broken through his control when she heard the word echo out loud, but then she realised it hadn't been her voice, but D.C.'s.

Alex turned her head—she could do that at least, since she hadn't been ordered not to—and watched as her roommate sliced her nails across Gerald's face, sending the larger man staggering sideways and clutching at his torn skin. D.C. managed to leap forward and place her body between Aven and the doorway before Gerald was up and restraining her once more.

"You're beginning to annoy me, Princess," Aven hissed. "I was going to wait until we had a larger audience, but I think this will be much more satisfying. Alexandra?"

Alex's palm tingled and she was forced to step closer to him. When she was by his side, Aven held out his hand and offered her his ice-like dagger.

Alex was repulsed by the blade, which still gleamed with their mixed blood, and she could only watch as her non-scarred hand reached out and grabbed the hilt. Everything in her wanted to flinch away, but instead her fingers wrapped around the dagger and drew it close, waiting for Aven's next instructions.

"Kill her."

Alex sucked in a sharp breath at his words. Her left palm burned like fire and she stepped forward, watching as her body moved closer to its target.

Run! she thought to D.C., hoping her eyes communicated her urgency. *Get out of here! Get away from me!* But her friend just stood there and stared at her.

Then D.C. jolted out of her shock, but she didn't try and struggle in Gerald's grip. If anything, she seemed more determined to hold her position. "Stop, Alex! Don't let him control you like this! You have to stop!"

I can't! Alex wanted to scream. She watched in horror as her arm lifted into the air, raising the dagger into an attack position.

"Fight him!" D.C. yelled. She was clearly terrified but still she didn't try to break free from Gerald. "You have to fight him! *Please!*"

I CAN'T! Alex screamed in her mind. She fought desperately against Aven's control, begging her limbs to resist the kill order, but his grip on her was too strong. She felt tears roll down her face while she tried to battle her body into compliance, but it was no use. It wouldn't listen to her.

Three steps to go.

"Stop, Alex, please!" D.C. begged.

Two steps to go.

"Don't do this." D.C.'s voice shook with fear.

One step to go.

"Please," D.C. whispered, tears falling down her cheeks now. But still she didn't try to escape, even when Alex pulled the dagger back further, ready to strike. The princess had meant what she'd said before—Aven would have to go through her if he wanted to get to Meya.

In the moment before she attacked, Alex wished that D.C. was less worthy of her crown.

I'm sorry! Alex screamed in her mind as she watched her arm slash forward through the air.

Forty-Three

Time slowed down in the moment before Aven's blade pierced flesh.

Out of the corner of her eye, Alex could see the Meyarin smirking, certain of his victory. Gerald was also grinning gleefully, even with the fingernail gouges still dribbling blood down his face.

And then there was D.C., ready to surrender her life for her people, no matter how lost the cause. She was staring at Alex through watery tears as the blade moved straight towards her heart.

"Alex," D.C. mouthed, one final time. It was a plea, perhaps. Or maybe it was an offer of forgiveness. Either way, the emotion in her eyes ripped through Alex like nothing she had ever felt before.

NO! Alex screamed in her mind. *NO! NO! NO!*

She felt something inside her snap.

"NO!"

The word tore out of Alex's throat and echoed loudly in her ears. She reclaimed control of her body and wrenched her hand away from its intended path. She was too late though, and she recoiled in horror when the blade sliced effortlessly through skin.

Gerald's tortured screams filled the hallway. He released D.C. to grab hold of the blade that was now lodged deep in his bicep, dropping his own knife in the process.

D.C. wasted no time in tackling him and knocking him to the ground.

Hoping her friend could keep Gerald contained, Alex launched forward to pick up his fallen knife and turned to face Aven. She held the weapon in the air defensively, but her hand trembled when she saw the look on his face.

"I told you to *kill her*," Aven ordered, emphasising the words. Her palm burned like liquid fire, but she wasn't under his control anymore.

"And I said *no*," she returned, holding the knife tight and ignoring the burning sensation.

He snarled at her and she had to force herself to hold her ground despite the terrifying expression on his otherworldly face.

"You *will* do what I command!" he roared.

"I'm not your puppet anymore!" she yelled back. "You don't control me!"

"That's where you should be wrong," Aven said, his voice quietly simmering now. "But you seem to be *broken*."

Alex didn't care if she was 'broken' so long as she never had to bend to his will again.

"You have no power over me now, Aven." She hoped her words were true. "And I'll never let you through that door. You're out of options."

"I'll never be out of options while you still live, dear Alexandra," Aven said, causing her to shiver with trepidation. He was never going to leave her alone until he got what he wanted.

"I doth believe the fair lady hath asked thou, sir, to depart from these here premises."

"Sir Camden!" Alex cried, happier to see him than ever before. She looked around, hoping to see others, but it was just him. She wilted with despair when she realised that he must not have found any help.

"This is your backup?" Aven asked, laughing derisively. "A rusty old suit of armour?"

"Sir Camden be my name. A Protector Knight I be, sir, and thou art unwise to mock so readily."

"You're nothing more than a distraction." Aven waved a hand dismissively. "And a lousy one at that."

"Those be fighting words, sir. Draw thine weapon."

Alex watched with wide eyes as Sir Camden stepped between her and Aven and unsheathed his sword.

Aven growled—actually growled—at the interfering suit of armour, and then he held his hand out as if waiting for something. A wounded scream came from Gerald as the ice-dagger tore out of his flesh, soared through the air, and landed in Aven's scarred palm. The Meyarin raised his free hand to stroke the blade, and before Alex's eyes the dagger grew in length and transformed into a sword.

"That weapon doth not belong to thee," Sir Camden said, pointing to the ice-coloured blade.

"The previous owner had no further use for it," Aven responded, his tone full of meaning.

"Judgement will prevail upon thee for such a grievous act," the knight said. "En garde."

Aven didn't give any warning before he thrust his sword towards Sir Camden. But the knight was remarkably nimble for a suit of armour, and he easily parried the blade and began his own attack.

The two weapons blurred through the air so fast that Alex couldn't follow them. She had no idea how the knight managed to keep up with the strength and speed that Aven possessed as a Meyarin, but he was meeting him blow after blow.

A startled cry drew Alex's attention away from the fight and towards her roommate. Gerald had the upper-hand once again, despite his injury. D.C. looked dazed, as if she'd been hit in the head, and she leaned heavily on the big man as he dragged her to her feet.

There was a loud, metallic crash and Alex whirled back around to see Sir Camden on the ground. In pieces.

Aven took advantage of her shock and used his sword to dislodge Gerald's knife from her grip, sending it to the floor with a clatter. He stroked his hand down his ice-blade again, and the weapon shrunk back down to a dagger.

Alex quickly backed away. "You can't kill me," she told him shakily. "You *need* me."

"You're right," he agreed, his golden eyes glinting dangerously. "*You* I need. But your friend only ever had one purpose."

Alex watched in horror as Aven threw his arm back and flicked it forward again, releasing the dagger. It hurtled through the air, straight towards where D.C. stood.

"*NO!*" Alex cried.

Without thinking, she leapt forward and crash-tackled D.C. and Gerald to the ground, collapsing on top of them when the blade embedded deep into the flesh of her back.

She heard D.C. scream her name, but she couldn't respond as pain ripped through her torso, pain unlike anything she'd ever felt before. Even the simple act of drawing air through her lungs caused an agonising ache to tear through her body.

Seconds passed, then minutes. Finally, as the pain gave way to numbness, Alex slowly came back to awareness. Only then did she realise that the room was full of noise. The clashing of steel against steel, the yelling of several people all at once, and one silky voice that penetrated through the foggy haze of her mind.

"We'll meet again, my dear Alexandra, and when that day comes, you *will* give me what I want."

Alex raised her head just in time to see Aven push Gerald through another doorway. He made eye contact with her a second before he leapt through himself, and she knew he meant what he'd said. He would come after her again.

She didn't have the strength to hold her head up anymore, and she collapsed on top of D.C. who was still half-trapped underneath her.

"Stay still, Alex," a soothing voice told her—a voice she recognised.

"Darrius?" she asked, her words barely audible. "You're late."

"I came as fast as I could," Darrius said as someone lifted her carefully off D.C. and placed her onto a soft, flat surface. "We all did."

"Thanks," she mouthed, but she wasn't sure if the word actually formed.

"Alex, you have to stay awake now," Darrius told her, his tone urgent.

"But I'm tired," she whispered, again uncertain if the words formed.

"I know you are, but you can sleep soon. We have to get you back to the Medical Ward first. Just a little longer now. You can make it. Just keep talking to me."

Alex realised that she was moving, or rather, someone was moving her—and fast. The speed should have jostled her injuries, but she couldn't feel anything since her body was now completely numb. It was a nice change to all the pain she'd been experiencing lately.

A voice called to her from far off, but Alex was too tired to listen to it, too tired to respond, and instead she drifted off into blissful unconsciousness.

Forty-Four

"She wove him a hat made from a melody..."

Alex groaned as the steady noise hummed through her foggy mind.

"He wondered how to fix his calamity..."

She wasn't ready to wake up yet. Her body felt like a lead weight. Was she dead?

"If she'd known how to sing, he'd have worn it with a grin..."

Her eyelids fluttered as light filtered in through the dark. She knew that song. She'd heard it once before.

"But instead he preferred it a parody."

"Darrius? Is that you?" she croaked.

"Take it easy, that's it," a soothing voice told her, and she felt something press against her lips. "Drink, Alex. It'll help."

Too muddled to object, she swallowed as someone gently tipped cool liquid into her mouth. It hurt at first, but once she started, she couldn't stop. She was so thirsty that she would have continued forever if the person hadn't taken the fluid away from her.

"Can you open your eyes, Alex?"

Her eyelids fluttered again and she willed herself to open them properly, blinking rapidly until the world focused.

"Good to see you back with us," Fletcher said, smiling down at her.

Alex tried to sit up but he put a hand out to stop her. "Just stay still for a little longer," he said. "Your body is still recovering."

"What happened?" Alex asked groggily.

"What do you remember?" he asked, peering into her eyes.

Picnicking with her friends. Sleeping in the painting. The Lockdown. Darkness. Aven.

Aven.

The memories flashed through Alex's mind in fast-forward, stealing the air from her lungs. "Everything," she whispered. "I remember everything."

"You know how you came to be here?" he asked.

"Yes. No. Sort of," she said, uncertain. "I think I got… injured, but I can't remember much after that."

Someone chuckled lightly and Alex realised she and Fletcher weren't alone in the room. She tried to look behind him, but she couldn't see who was there.

"Interesting word choice," Fletcher murmured, "however, I do believe 'stabbed' is the more accurate term. The dagger slid straight through your posterior rib cage and punctured your right lung from behind. It was touch and go for a while, young lady. You almost gave me a heart attack."

Alex winced at the memory of the blade tearing into her flesh. "Fine," she said. "I was stabbed. But how did I get here?"

Darrius came into view then, his silver eyes sparkling even in the low light of the Med Ward. "I believe I can answer that."

"Darrius!" she cried, pleased to see him. "I thought I heard your weird song!"

"Weird?" he scoffed. "It's classic folk, I'll have you know. Extremely popular."

"If you say so," she said, sharing a grin with Fletcher as he began to check her vitals.

Darrius ignored her comment and pulled a chair up beside her bed. "I've spoken with your roommate, but there are still some questions I have regarding the events from Saturday evening. Would you be so kind as to share your version of the night before I enlighten your understanding of the current situation?"

Alex frowned slightly, trying to piece together what he'd said. The only thing that really stuck was his use of the words 'Saturday evening' and not 'last night'.

"How long have I been here?" she asked.

Darrius and Fletcher shared a glance before the doctor turned back to her. "It's Tuesday. You've been in and out of consciousness for three days."

Alex gaped at him. Three *days?*

She tried to get her head around that and turned back to fill Darrius in.

"Well, it all started when I got hurt in my Combat exam, I guess. Or maybe even before that, when I overheard a conversation between Jarvis, Maggie and the librarian…"

She started at the beginning and didn't leave anything out. Darrius remained silent throughout her entire tale, flinching only when she mentioned the part about Aven joining their bloodied hands and her being his puppet for a while. When she finished talking, he gently reached across for her left hand and turned her palm upwards. What he was looking for, she wasn't sure, and after a moment his eyes moved back to her face. He stared at her for a full minute before he released her arm.

"Incredible," he whispered.

Alex was too busy looking at her hand to question his statement. Her palm was now cleaned of their mixed blood but there was a thin scar left, glowing faintly with a silver sheen, much like the colour of Aven's unnatural blood.

"Is it meant to look like that?" Alex asked, turning her palm towards Fletcher.

He looked at her in sympathy. "I'm afraid I couldn't erase it completely. You'll have that scar for the rest of your life."

"It's just a scar," Alex said, shrugging. "But that's not what I meant. Is it supposed to be glowing like that?"

Fletcher cleared his throat uncomfortably. "I'll leave you two alone while I go and update your charts."

Alex watched him hurry away and then turned back to Darrius. "It's because of Aven's blood, isn't it?"

"Yes. I presume you noticed his blood is different to yours?"

"Silver," she said, shuddering at the memory of it dribbling down her hand.

Darrius nodded and began to explain, "Aven sought to Claim you through a forbidden Meyarin bonding ritual, using his blood as an anchor and yours as a sacrifice. The rest of his race considers it the worst of all possible transgressions, an act punishable by death. To bend the will of another is to take away all of their freedom. The Claiming ritual was believed to be long forgotten, but clearly that's not the case."

Alex was glad she was lying down otherwise she probably would have fainted. "Are you saying I'm *bonded* to him?"

"No, no," Darrius said, trying to calm her. "Aven *tried* to Claim you, but you eventually broke through his compulsion. An impossible feat, let me assure you, for anyone other than yourself."

"What do you mean?"

"Had Aven been truly successful, you would have been his slave for the rest of your life, completely obedient to his will. And that life would have been unnaturally long, since you would have shared some of his Meyarin traits as a result of the bonding ritual."

Alex looked at her hand again. "Please tell me that won't happen? The last thing I need is to become some kind of half-Meyarin, half-human hybrid."

"I can't be certain, of course, but I doubt you'll suffer any adverse effects aside from the colour of your scar," Darrius assured her. "Though, I'm amazed—the blood-bonding ritual is supposed to Claim a person for life."

"Then how was I able to break through it?"

Darrius smiled and said, "I believe you may have used your gift."

She blinked at him. "Huh?"

"It's not uncommon for someone to awaken their gifting under stressful circumstances," Darrius told her. "And from the sounds of it, your situation was particularly challenging."

Alex almost laughed at his description. 'Challenging' didn't even come close.

"So, I really have a gift?" she asked, excited to finally learn what it was after all this time.

"Yes, and it's a very powerful gift," Darrius said. "One that is at once much more and much less than we desire. It's a gift that every person is given but many make light of, and very few actually use to its full potential."

"And it is…?" Alex prompted.

"Can I ask a question first?" Darrius said, and she had to stifle her groan. "When you first met Aven all those months ago, how did he make you feel?"

Alex raised her eyebrows. What sort of question was that?

"I don't know," she said, thinking back and trying to answer honestly. "He was very attractive, but I guess that's the Meyarin part of him. He definitely caught my attention."

"But what did you *feel* when you were around him?" Darrius clarified.

Alex knew what he was getting at. "I wanted to please him, to do whatever he said. I think I was pretty much willing to do anything he asked. Is that something all Meyarins can do?"

"No," Darrius answered. "They're all enchanting, as you would remember from the picture I showed you months ago, but Aven Dalmarta has an unnatural amount of charisma—much more than most of his kind possess. Even under normal circumstances, it's very difficult to defy him."

Alex thought back over her interactions with Aven.

"You, however, were able to resist his allure. On more than one occasion, if I've heard correctly," Darrius said. "Such continued resistance is beyond admirable—it should have been near impossible. Which only confirms my theory about your gifting."

"And?" she pressed. "What is it?"

He smiled at her impatience and said, "I believe your gift is your strength of will, Alex. Your willpower."

She couldn't help but be disappointed. Willpower? Seriously? Most people had that, to some degree.

"Are you sure?" she asked.

"I'm positive," Darrius said. "There's no other way you could have disregarded his direct order while Claimed and broken out of his hold. I've never heard or read of anyone being able to do so. And as I already mentioned, the fact that you were able to stand against him before then shows that even when your gift wasn't fully awakened, it was still protecting you, at least to a small degree."

He took in her expression and cocked his head. "You're upset?"

"Well, it isn't what I expected," Alex admitted. "I wasn't even convinced that I'd ever develop a gift, but if I did, I was kind of hoping for something... cooler."

"Cooler?" Darrius repeated. "How so?"

"Like being able to fly, or shape-shift, or make chocolate appear out of thin air," she explained. "You know, something exciting. Everyone can have willpower—it doesn't seem like much of a gift."

"That's where you're wrong," Darrius said. "Your willpower gift means that you will always be in control of your decisions—

400 · Lynette Noni

no matter the circumstances. You can never be manipulated or controlled by *anyone*. Most people have to train their entire lives to reach the same level of mental security that you now have without even trying."

Alex thought about what he said for a moment before she realised something. "When I came back after the Kaldoras break, my Core Skills professor couldn't read my mind anymore. Could this willpower gift have something to do with that?"

"Absolutely," he said. "Having a gift of willpower means that you won't ever have to worry about your thoughts or emotions being read, stolen, or manipulated. Nor will anyone ever be able to force you to act physically without your consent. Which again brings us back to Aven and why he couldn't control you after your gift asserted itself."

Alex realised then that while her gift wasn't superhero-awesome, it also wasn't as boring as she'd first thought. Without it, she would have remained a lifeless slave, murdered the royal princess of Medora and doomed the entire human race. All in all, she decided to be thankful and to leave it at that.

"Is D.C. okay?"

Accepting the abrupt change of topic, Darrius was quick to assure her. "She's well. A little shaken up—and rather worried about her roommate—but otherwise she's fine."

Alex nodded, relieved. "She kind of knows everything now. About me, I mean."

"I think you can trust each other with your secrets," Darrius said. "And despite the circumstances upon which it was founded, I'm certain your friendship with the princess will be beneficial for you both."

Alex's eyes widened. "You know who she is?"

"I do," he said, but he didn't elaborate.

Just as she was about to ask Darrius how he always knew things without being told, Fletcher walked back into the room.

Alex gasped as she realised something. "Fletcher! You—I—you—everything we said…?"

While Fletcher was one of her favourite people at Akarnae, he wasn't supposed to know that she was anything but a normal student. But he'd been standing in the room the entire time she'd told Darrius her story. He would have heard everything about Freya, about Aven, and about the Library.

"Doctor–patient confidentiality," Fletcher said, waving her fear away. "And it's nothing I didn't already know, anyway."

"What? How?" she spluttered.

"Did you really think I wouldn't look up the administrative file for one of my most frequent patients?" he asked, his green eyes twinkling. "I've known all about you since your first visit to me."

One more person to add to the growing list. But with Aven after her, Alex felt reassured knowing she had more people watching out for her. People who she knew actually cared for her.

"I did come back in here for a reason," Fletcher said, looking to Darrius. "I have to give Alex some more medication, so visiting hours are over, I'm afraid."

Darrius stood from his seat and smiled down at her. "We'll talk again soon."

As he walked out of the room she remembered something and called out for him. "You never told me how I got back here from the Library?"

"Your Sir Camden came and found me," Darrius said.

Sir Camden! "Is he—?"

"He's fine," Darrius said. "Whole again and ready for his next quest."

Alex breathed a sigh of relief. The suit of armour had been so brave to stand up to Aven, and she truly appreciated his intervention. He'd really proved himself to be a Protector Knight.

"As I was saying," Darrius continued, "Sir Camden made me aware of your dilemma and he led me and some trusted friends straight to you. We were a few minutes behind him because, unlike his impressive ability to move through walls, we were restricted to the pathways."

"Does that mean he never found the headmaster?" Alex asked. Time was ticking down, and there were only a few days left until she needed to get back to Freya if she wanted to arrive before her parents realised she was gone. Where *was* Marselle?

"The headmaster of Akarnae played a pivotal role in your liberation, Alex," Darrius said. "I'm certain you'll meet him soon, now that he's back at the academy."

With that promise Darrius waved and headed out the door, and Alex felt something within her relax after hearing confirmation of the headmaster's return.

Alex turned to Fletcher and noticed an amused expression on his face. "What?"

"Nothing," he responded, still smiling slightly. "Now drink up and *maybe* I'll let you out of here sometime before next winter."

She drank vial after vial of different coloured liquids until she was overcome with exhaustion and Fletcher ordered her to go to sleep.

It was an order that she was more than willing to obey.

Forty-Five

"How can anyone sleep for so long?"

"No idea. Can we poke her or something?"

"Fletcher would have our hides if he found out we disturbed his patient's beauty sleep."

"He doesn't have to know…"

There was a pause and Alex cracked her eyes open just as Jordan reached towards her. "Don't even think about it," she threatened in a croaky voice.

"Alex! You're awake!" he cried, sitting back hastily.

"Finally!" Bear smiled at her.

"Sorry to inconvenience you," she said.

"That's okay," Jordan said, taking her seriously. He grabbed a glass of water off her bedside table and held it out for her.

Bear reached his arm around Alex to help support her as she carefully pulled herself into a sitting position. She was amazed that she was able to do so without any kind of pain. Fletcher's medicines were evidently doing their job.

"What's been happening?" she asked after taking a long drink of water. "It's been—what?—three days?"

"Four now," Bear told her. "It's Wednesday."

"Time flies when you're unconscious, hey?" Jordan said lightly.

"Something like that," she agreed, smiling.

"Nothing's really changed for us," Bear said, answering her question. "Classes are wrapping up for the year. Finn has been almost pleasant, believe it or not."

"Not," Alex said, and they laughed.

"Otherwise everything's pretty much the same as before our exams, if a little less stressful," he concluded.

"Same question for you, now," Jordan said. "And don't leave anything out."

Alex groaned. "Seriously? You're here to interrogate me? Some friends you are."

"You love us," Jordan replied. "Once again we missed out on the adventure, so spill." He must have caught her tense expression before she could clear it, and he placed his hand on her shoulder. "Hey, I'm sorry. I sound like a jerk, don't I? It's okay if you don't want to talk about it. I understand. *We* understand."

Bear nodded in agreement, his eyes full of concern.

"No, it's fine," Alex assured them. "I already had to go over the whole thing with Darrius anyway."

"Darrius? The cloud guy?" Jordan asked. "The same guy who brought you back to the academy from the Gala?"

Alex noticed that he didn't say 'from my house'. "Yeah, that's him. Sir Camden found him and he came with some others to rescue us."

"Weird," Jordan said. "Bear and I were waiting at the Med Ward when they brought you in—you were an absolute mess, by the way—but I didn't see anyone we didn't know. Just a heap of the professors and the headmaster."

Alex shrugged. "He probably stayed back at the Library to try and trace where Aven disappeared to. The others would have had to follow the headmaster in and back out. Who were they, by the way? The others?"

"Half the teaching staff," Jordan said. "Maggie, Karter, Finn, Varin, Caspar Lennox and Luranda."

"So much for the Library being a secret," Alex mumbled. "Now the whole world practically knows about it."

"We heard Hunter went in as well, but we didn't see him on this side," Bear said, ignoring her comment. "It just confirms what we already know about Ghost: unless he wants you to see him, you won't."

Alex looked at Bear for a moment before she burst out laughing.

"Lame?" he asked.

"Very," she confirmed, still smiling. "Like the blurb of a bad horror film."

He feigned offence and she just laughed again, pleased when the movement didn't hurt at all.

"Are you going to tell us what happened and why you arrived here covered in blood, or do we have to guess?" Bear asked, changing the subject back again.

Alex spent the next half hour bringing them up-to-date. She kept it brief, mostly because she lacked the energy for an in-depth discussion. Still, she told them everything she could, only leaving out D.C.'s royal status and claiming instead that the other girl played the role of a disposable hostage. Alex trusted Jordan and Bear with her life, but she'd also promised her roommate that she wouldn't reveal her secret.

"Have either of you seen D.C. since then?" she asked when she finished.

"Only in classes," Bear said. "And when... um..."

"When she was brought into the Med Ward with you," Jordan finished for him. "She was really protective of you, pretty much yelling at everyone to stay out of Fletcher's way so he could see to you. She was downright scary, really, and drenched from head to toe in your blood."

Alex shuddered at the image of what her friends must have seen—her collapsed on a stretcher and her bloodied roommate screaming at everyone. It must have been quite the scene.

"We were under the impression that you two didn't exactly get along?" Bear said hesitantly.

"Desperate times," Alex said, smiling when she recalled D.C. using the same excuse days earlier. "She's really not that bad."

Both Jordan and Bear looked a little incredulous at her words.

"Are we talking about the same person here?" Jordan asked.

"She saved my life, remember?" she said, and that shut them up.

In her mind it was true. Aven had ordered Alex to kill D.C., and if she hadn't been so opposed to the idea of murder, she never would have broken through his control over her—gift or no gift. Essentially, D.C. had saved her life, not to mention everyone else's by default.

"You're right," Jordan said quietly, still clearly shocked by her entire story but trying not to show it. "And in that case, any friend of yours is a friend of ours."

Alex looked at Bear and saw the same unquestioning acceptance on his face. She realised they both meant it, despite the fact that they had disliked her roommate for much longer than they'd even known Alex.

"Aww, you guys…"

"You're not going to start crying are you?" Jordan asked, leaning away from her. "Because I'll have to find an excuse to leave and it may not be believable on such short notice."

She laughed again. "No, I promise. No tears. Not even happy ones."

"Happy ones are okay," Bear told her. "It's the others that all men fear."

"I'll try to remember that," Alex said.

"Just so you're aware, our kindness towards her isn't purely out of our generous hearts, as large as they are," Jordan said, sharing a mischievous grin with Bear. "It helps that she's totally hot."

"Jordan!" Alex laughed. "I can't believe you just said that!"

He shrugged unashamedly. "It's true."

"You know, sometimes I wonder what you two say about me when I'm not around."

"Only good things," Bear said, patting her hand comfortingly.

"*Very* good things," Jordan corrected, looking her up and down and winking at her.

"Perv," she muttered, but she couldn't help laughing with them.

He opened his mouth to respond—probably to say something completely inappropriate—just as Fletcher walked in the room.

"I hope you're not bothering my patient, Jordan?"

"Of course not, Fletch," he replied, trying to pull off an innocent look.

Fletcher shook his head in exasperation and turned to Alex. "How are you feeling today?"

"Much better," she said. "Back to my old self, I'd say."

"I'll be the judge of that," he said, asking the boys to move away so he could check her over.

"It looks like everything has healed nicely," he said when he was finished. "Just so you're aware, you have a small scar on your back from where the dagger entered your flesh. Like your hand, I was unable to heal it completely, and it also has a slight... glow."

"Awesome," Alex said sarcastically. But at least she wouldn't have to look at *that* scar every day.

"It's barely noticeable," Fletcher promised. "While my Regenevators restored the internal damage caused by the weapon, they were useless at the point of entry. But the wound sealed shut on its own once the dagger was pulled out, as strange as that was to witness."

"That's what happened with my hand," Alex told him. "It healed right before my eyes."

"Fascinating," the doctor said. "I'm curious whether it was Aven's Meyarin blood or the unusual weapon itself that prompted the healing in both cases."

"I have no idea," Alex admitted. "And I hope never to have to find out again."

"I too would prefer it if you could avoid any similar situations in the future," Fletcher agreed seriously.

Alex noticed the concern deep in his eyes. He really must have been worried about her. She smiled reassuringly and said, "Good thing I've got a great doctor just in case it does happen again."

He chuckled modestly and then he was all business again. "As I was saying, all your injuries from your encounter with Aven have healed, and your shoulder has realigned perfectly from your Combat exam. All in all, I'd say you're pretty well recovered."

"You're incredible, Fletcher," Alex said, amazed that she was back to normal already.

"That's the wonder of modern medicine," he said.

"And a doctor who knows exactly what he's doing." Alex wanted him to understand how grateful she was for all his help.

He straightened his lab coat awkwardly and even blushed a little. She smiled at his embarrassment, but she knew better than to call him on it. "When can I get out of here?" she asked instead.

"Now, as a matter of fact," he answered. "You just have to take it easy for the rest of the night. It's almost curfew, so you'll be heading to bed soon, anyway. You should be fine for classes tomorrow and Friday, but do be careful. I'd rather not see you again until next term, and I mean that in the nicest possible way."

Alex laughed. "Gee, thanks, Fletcher. And here I thought you said I was your favourite patient."

"I have no idea how you got that idea in your head, but you're certainly my most frequent visitor."

He helped her stand, and after a momentary bout of dizziness, she was good to go. Bear and Jordan were called back in and given strict instructions to make sure she had a quiet night—to which they solemnly promised to take her straight to her room without supper. Fletcher wasn't as amused as Alex, if his frown was anything to judge by.

As they were walking out the door, Fletcher called out to her. "Remember, Alex. I'll see you *next term*."

"I'll do my best," she said, grinning at him and walking out with her friends.

As the three headed across the grounds, she wondered if Fletcher's parting message had simply been him banning her from injury for her last two days of classes, or if there was more to it than that. Perhaps he was confiding to her that he believed she would be coming back when term restarted.

Alex hoped he'd meant both.

True, she had no idea how she would return. As it was, she still needed to find a way back to Freya in the first place—but now that the headmaster was residing on campus again, she presumed he would be able to solve that problem for her, as promised. And maybe, just maybe, he could provide her with a way to come back to the academy for the next school year. It would mean the best of both worlds for her—literally. Because if it came down to it, if she could only pick one, she didn't know which world she would choose. Her parents were back in Freya, but there was nothing else tying her there. The rest of her life was in Medora. She couldn't deny it anymore, not even to herself.

It was an impossible decision, and Alex could only hope that she wouldn't have to make the choice. Because she had absolutely no idea what she would do.

Forty-Six

Alex awoke to the sound of a door slamming. The last thing she remembered was waiting up for D.C. after Jordan and Bear had left her dorm the night before, but her roommate hadn't arrived and Alex must have fallen asleep.

I guess nothing has changed after all, she realised sadly. She had hoped D.C. had meant what she'd said about them being friends, but the sound of her roommate leaving in the morning was just the same as it had always been.

"You're back!"

Alex snapped her eyes open, feeling disoriented because it wasn't morning and D.C. hadn't slammed the door while leaving the room, but while entering it.

Alex looked at the beaming smile on her roommate's face and she mirrored the expression. "I'm back," she confirmed.

D.C. stood there just grinning for a moment before she launched herself onto the bed, smothering Alex in a hug.

"You're so stupid!" D.C. yelled, even while hugging her. "What were you thinking? You almost *died!*"

"Need to breathe!" Alex gasped, and D.C. eased up a little but still gripped her tightly.

"I can't believe you did that," D.C. said. At least she wasn't yelling anymore.

"I didn't exactly plan it, if that makes you feel any better. It just sort of happened," Alex said. "It's not that big of a deal, really."

"You jumped in front of a dagger that was aimed for my heart," D.C. said, backing away so that Alex could see the oh so familiar sardonic look on her face. "I'd say that falls into the category of big deals. Huge deals, in fact."

Alex sat up, pulling her legs underneath her so that she was sitting cross-legged on the bed. "It was the least I could do," she said quietly. "Especially since I nearly killed you before that."

She expected an awkward silence, but D.C. just laughed and said, "I think you had that pretty well in hand."

Alex gaped at her. "Are you serious? I was about a second away from slicing you in half!"

"You would have stopped in time, even without me screaming at you," D.C. said, smirking. "You were much too afraid of killing the heir to the Medoran throne. Imagine how that would have looked on your résumé."

"I can't believe you can joke about this," Alex said, not quite sure if she wanted to laugh... or throw up.

D.C. sobered immediately. "I have to joke about it. It's the only thing that's helped me get through the last few days."

Alex looked closely at the other girl and noticed the dark shadows under her eyes.

"I came to visit you," D.C. said after a pause. "A few times. But you were always asleep."

"Thank you," Alex whispered, touched by the gesture.

"I meant what I said about us being friends." D.C.'s blue-green eyes were steady but her hands fidgeted nervously. "I think we should make it official, now that we're not under duress. If you still want to, I mean. No pressure or anything."

"Are you kidding?" Alex asked. Then she realised how her comment could be taken and hurried on to say, "Of course I still want to!"

D.C. grinned and reached out her hand. "To a new start?"

"A new start," Alex agreed, and they shook on it.

"I think introductions are necessary if we're to begin with a clean slate," D.C. said, sitting up straighter. "I'm Delucia Marsina Cavelle, royal princess and heir to the Medoran throne."

"I thought you wanted me to quit with the princess reminders?"

"It's called being *polite*," D.C. said, as if it was the most obvious thing in the world. "Something you clearly don't know much about, since you still haven't introduced yourself."

"You already know who I am, D.C.," Alex said, shaking her head at her friend's antics.

"Call me Dix."

"Huh?"

"Dix," D.C. repeated. "It's an actual nickname, not just my initials. It feels more personal."

"Dix," Alex repeated. "I like it."

D.C. snorted. "I'm so pleased I have your approval. Now hurry up and introduce yourself."

Alex groaned. "You can't be serious."

"Humour me."

"Fine. I'm Alexandra Rose Jennings. Good enough?"

"No," D.C. said, frowning. "You didn't tell me anything about yourself."

"You *already* know about me!" Alex said, but at the look on her roommate's face she huffed and elaborated. "I'm originally from Freya and I'm Chosen by the Library. Happy?"

D.C. smiled. "Immensely. And I'm very pleased to meet you."

"You're impossible," Alex said, but she was smiling too.

They talked long into the night, finally having the chance to share their secrets with someone who understood the importance of keeping them. The subject of giftings eventually came up, and D.C. was amazed when Alex explained her newfound ability and how it had saved them from Aven. For someone in D.C.'s position where power-plays and manipulations were all a part of court intrigue, Alex's gift was highly enviable.

Alex herself thought the same about D.C.'s gift.

"I dream about the future," her roommate said. "They're real dreams, of things that will actually happen."

"You're psychic?" Alex asked, slightly awed and a little sceptical.

"Not psychic. More like prophetic, I guess," D.C. replied. "Unlike most gifts, I can't turn mine on and off at will. The real dreams aren't very common, but when they happen, they almost always come true. My gift also allows me to revisit the dreams over and over again if I want. Sometimes I get more information, but more often than not I just see the same images repeated."

Alex was amazed by some of the examples D.C. gave her, and one in particular that occurred over the Kaldoras holidays where she'd dreamt of being abducted in a dark place and made to walk through a corridor of doors before being tied to Alex. That was why she'd grilled Alex on her return to the academy after the Gala, because she'd known something bad was going to happen to them. A voice in the dream had repeated the words '*I haven't found it yet!*' over and over again, which was how she'd been able to assure Alex in the Library that letting Aven through the first doorway wasn't going to do any immediate damage. She hadn't dreamt anything new after the imprisonment dream, despite trying to revisit the image on numerous occasions—all of which had only showed her the same events and nothing more.

"Incredible," Alex said, before they moved to a less serious topic.

Hours went by while they caught up on a year's worth of knowing each other, and soon they were slurring their words together. It was no surprise to Alex when she woke in the morning and found D.C. still curled up at the end of her bed, both of them having fallen asleep mid-conversation.

"Wake up, Dix," she said.

"Wha—?" D.C. mumbled as Alex nudged her with her foot.

"We've got to get up if we want breakfast before classes," Alex mumbled, yawning.

"Mmkay." D.C. curled up even tighter.

Alex kicked the other girl off her bed, much to the red-head's displeasure.

"Hey!" D.C. cried. She raised herself up from the ground and delivered her best quality glare.

"That doesn't work anymore," Alex said. "I know you don't mean it now."

"That's what you think," D.C. grumbled, but she couldn't keep the smile off her face. Their newfound friendship was still such a novelty for them both.

"Come on, I'm starving," Alex said. She hadn't eaten real food in four days.

They quickly got ready and headed to the food court. Alex half expected everyone to fall silent at the sight of them entering the room together—their enmity had been fairly obvious to everyone—but no one paid them any attention.

"Alex! D.C.! Over here!"

She smiled at Jordan, grateful that he'd included her roommate in his invitation.

"Are you ready for this?" Alex asked the other girl.

"Please," D.C. snorted. "I could go up against Sparkie and his pet Bear with my eyes closed and *still* come out on top."

"That's great and all," Alex said, "but here's another idea. Why don't you demonstrate the politeness you lectured me about last night and put on your nice-girl personality for a change? I know you have one—even if it is buried deep, *deep*, down."

D.C. scrunched her face up but nodded in resignation. "All right. But only because I know they mean so much to you. And only if they behave themselves."

Alex patted her on the shoulder. "They will."

Together they walked over to the table where the boys had saved them both seats.

"Morning!" Alex said brightly as she ordered the first thing on her menu, so hungry that she didn't care what she ate.

An uncomfortable silence surrounded them, and Alex didn't know how to change it. She nudged D.C.'s rigid frame, encouraging her to relax.

Her roommate sighed quietly and then leaned forward, placing her elbows on the table. "Did you guys watch the last Warriors' game?"

Instantly the tension around them disappeared as Jordan, Bear and D.C. launched into a passionate discussion about some kind of sporting event. Alex had no idea what they were talking about, but she couldn't keep the smile off her face as her closest friends began to bond.

Alex was on her way to her Combat class after lunch when Professor Marmaduke approached her.

"Miss Jennings, I've been made aware that you may have developed your gift, is that correct?"

Alex tried to ignore the '*finally*' that was all but screaming from the older woman and said, "Yes, Professor."

"Excellent," Marmaduke replied. "If you'll come with me, I'll give you your exam. Better late than never, and this way you won't have to repeat my class next term."

Alex looked at the woman before glancing at the Arena. Karter would kill her if he heard she'd skipped out on his class.

Marmaduke noticed her indecision and said, "I've spoken with the headmaster and he's cleared it with Karter. You're exempt from today's class."

Reassured, Alex followed Marmaduke back to her classroom where the professor tested her control. It was almost as if her gift was making up for lost time because, after an hour, Marmaduke was sweating with the effort of trying to use her own gift to break through Alex's mind and manipulate her or even just read her, but to no avail.

The only part of the exam that actually involved Alex doing anything was in the final hour when the professor asked Alex to try and *use* her gift. At first, Alex didn't understand what she meant, but then she thought about how Gammy could outwardly share her peace with others. Alex wondered if perhaps one day she would be able to do the same sort of thing. After an hour of trying, it was *she* who was sweating, with no results to show from her effort.

"Well, it's something to practise, at least," Marmaduke said as they finished up. "Something to work towards."

Alex didn't even know if it was possible, but she promised she would continue to try and develop it.

When Marmaduke finally released her, Alex had to run to her dorm so that she could get changed for her Equestrian Skills class. By the time she arrived at the stables she was almost late for her lesson, but she was saved by D.C. who had tacked up Fiddle for her already.

"You're the best," Alex panted, having sprinted the entire way.

"I know," D.C. said, handing the reins over.

It was one of the best Equestrian Skills classes yet, with Tayla leading them all out on an end-of-year trail ride through the forest. Alex and D.C. rode side by side, talking and laughing for the entire ride.

When they finally arrived back at the stables and finished seeing to their horses, Alex had one more thing she had to do before going on holidays.

"You go ahead," she told D.C. "I'll be along in a moment."

Her roommate looked at her knowingly. "What's with you and that pony?"

"He's just… adorable," Alex said. "I'll feel bad if I don't say goodbye."

"Fine, fine," D.C. said, laughing. "I'll meet you back at the dorm."

It wasn't hard for Alex to find Monster, but it *was* hard to say goodbye to the shaggy little pony. It took a while—and his entire body weight in apples—before he stopped head-butting her and allowed her to leave without following. She would miss the little guy, no matter where she was over the summer. But she promised him that one way or another, she would do her best to find her way back to him.

And Alex always kept her promises.

Forty-Seven

"Well, well, well. Look who's *finally* decided to grace us with her presence."

Alex held her annoyance in check as she walked into the Arena the next afternoon. It was her last class of the day, of the year in fact, and it just *had* to be Combat.

"I'm on time," she said, crossing her arms defiantly.

"You weren't for the rest of the week," Karter said.

Alex couldn't believe him. Was he seriously blaming her for being unconscious on one of those days, and in an exam on the other?

"I'm just pulling your leg, Jennings," he said after a tense moment. "Relax."

She gaped at him. Was that a *smile* on his face?

"Queenie!" Sebastian called. "We heard you were in the Med Ward, like, all week. What'd you do? Eat some bad chicken? That's what everyone's saying."

Alex turned around to find her classmates staring at her, waiting for an answer. She didn't know what to say and blurted out the first thing that came to mind. "Queenie?"

"It's your new nickname," Sebastian said. "Queen of the obstacle course. You totally nailed it last week."

"All right, enough chitchat," Karter interrupted, saving Alex from having to respond.

He told them to take a seat and everyone hastened to follow his order.

"It's been a big year," Karter said, pacing back and forth in front of them, "but you've all made it through. I'm the first to admit I don't go easy on my Epsilon students, and you've each proven your worth, one way or another."

Alex couldn't believe it. He was almost... encouraging. Supportive, even. Nothing at all like the drill sergeant she was used to.

"I expect even more from you in the coming year."

Yay, Alex thought sarcastically, but she was still amazed by his encouragement.

"That said, this year's not over yet. So, GET OFF YOUR BEHINDS AND GET TO WORK!"

Ah. There he was. Normal Karter was back.

The six of them scurried up from their seats. The boys headed automatically to the opposite side of the Arena where the weapons were kept, but Alex held back, awaiting further instructions.

Karter turned to her, heaving a sigh deep enough to blow storm clouds off course. "The headmaster wants to see you, Jennings."

She blinked at the unexpected words. "Err—okay. When, sir?"

His eyes narrowed. "When do you think, girl? Use your brain. He wants to see you *now*, obviously. In the administrator's office."

"Oh, right. I'll—I'll just go now, then?" she asked, uncertain if he was giving her permission to leave his class or not.

"Go," he said dismissively.

She hesitated, wondering if she should say something like 'See you next term' or 'Enjoy your summer' or 'Thanks for teaching me how to dodge things in your own stupid way'. But in the end, the moment passed and she walked away, glancing back only briefly to look at her classmates one final time. Her eyes caught Declan's and the big guy gave her an easy grin and a goodbye wave, which she returned.

Just as she began to turn away another set of eyes caught hers, and she became trapped in Kaiden's searching gaze. After a moment he nodded and gave her a slight smile before he turned back to face his opponent.

Alex walked quickly out of the Arena, ignoring the fact that her heart was beating faster than normal. It was probably just nerves because she was finally going to meet the headmaster. That was all. Nothing else.

Yeah, right.

By the time she reached the Tower she was too distracted by her upcoming meeting to think about anything—or anyone—else. She'd been waiting months to meet Marselle, and there was a lot riding on their conversation—her entire future, really.

Alex ran up the stairs and across the room before knocking on the door and waiting for the muffled invitation to enter. When it came, she straightened her spine and opened the door, fully expecting to see Jarvis with the headmaster. Instead, the only person in the room was—

"Darrius? What are you doing here?"

"Alex," he said, smiling at her. "It's good to see you up and about. Are you feeling better?"

"Good as new," Alex answered, looking around the room and wondering where Jarvis and Marselle were.

"I'm pleased to hear it," Darrius said. Noticing her distraction, he asked, "Is something wrong?"

"Huh? Oh—sorry, Darrius," Alex apologised, turning her attention back to him. "I'm just looking for someone."

Darrius made a show of glancing around. "It doesn't appear that anyone is here but me, Alex. Are you here to see me?"

She smiled and said, "I wish that was the case, since at least I *know* I like you. You haven't been AWOL all year, unlike… some people."

Darrius's eyes were full of understanding. "Come and take a walk with me."

It wasn't a question, and she frowned slightly in confusion. "I really shouldn't. I'm supposed to be meeting Headmaster Marselle here. Right now, I thought. But… well, clearly he's not here. Have you seen him by any chance?"

"I have, as a matter of fact," Darrius said. "I believe he's waiting for you in his office. Allow me to escort you there."

Alex was happy to accept, because even though she had been outside the headmaster's office twice, she still wasn't sure what floor it was located on.

"Thanks, Darrius. That'd be great."

He opened the door for her and led the way up the stairs. Up and up they stepped, until finally the staircase ended at the very top of the Tower.

Darrius led her through the somewhat familiar antechamber and stopped in front of the closed door. He pressed a code into the TCD display beside it and the door sprung open. Alex was just about to ask how he knew the password to the headmaster's office when she glanced into the room and her mouth snapped shut.

She followed Darrius inside and looked around the small space. Realisation dawned on her so hard and fast that she almost had to sit down. She covered her reaction by walking unsteadily over to the other side of the room and leaning against the wall.

"It didn't look like this last time," she said quietly, looking out the familiar window and down into the endless cloud-filled sky. "During the first Lockdown, I mean. It was more like a boardroom then, with a glass wall looking out over the entire academy. It looked like a headmaster's office. I guess you get to pick and choose what you want, huh? One of the perks of the job?"

Her throat was clogged with emotion. It took her a moment to realise that she was angry—at him, definitely, but mostly at herself. She felt stupid for not making the connection sooner. It had been so obvious, in hindsight. But she'd been so overwhelmed by everything else that she hadn't even paused to question his identity. If she'd stopped to think for just a moment, the truth would have been glaringly apparent.

"This is my private study," Darrius told her simply. "We're now back in the Library, having walked through a doorway connected by the code I used with the TCD. A password isn't necessary to reach my other office, which is always accessible to others—except in the case of a Lockdown. That office is used for my more formal duties as Headmaster of Akarnae."

"All this time?" Alex asked, her voice almost a whisper. "All this time, and you never said anything?"

"I don't suppose you'd believe me if I told you it was for the best?"

"You lied to me," she said, ignoring his question.

"I did not," he said calmly. "I merely withheld certain information."

"*Important* information," she said, her anger rising.

"I don't believe that to be the case," he returned, still completely calm despite her darkening mood. "How would knowing my identity have benefited you in any way?"

"You could have helped me get back home," she answered. "That was all I ever wanted."

"Which is precisely why I didn't reveal myself to you," he said, taking a seat on the edge of the couch that she'd once woken up on many months ago, on her first Library 'adventure'.

"You had no right to do that." She felt resentment burning in her chest. "You should have told me."

"You weren't ready to leave," Darrius said, his eyes sad. "Even if you didn't know it at the time."

"What's that supposed to mean?" she demanded.

"Think, Alex!" he cried, his suddenly loud voice startling her as it echoed around the small room. "Think about what you've learned here! All the things you've done, the experiences you've had, the people you've met! None of those things would have happened if you'd known who I was. You would have wanted me to take you straight back to your world, and your time here would have ended before it even began."

Alex wished she could deny his assumption, but he was probably right. Her anger deflated and she walked over to drop onto the opposite end of the couch. "It still wasn't your decision to make."

"Believe it or not, in the end it was entirely up to you," Darrius told her. "The moment the Library Chose you, your will reigned over mine since I only have the rights of a headmaster—given, but not Chosen. Add to that your natural gift of willpower, and there was your immediate ticket home."

"What do you mean?" Alex asked, not following.

"I spoke with the librarian after our first meeting," Darrius said. "Tell me, how did you get out of the chequered room with your friends? Did you just go back the way you'd entered?"

"No," she answered. "I opened a door in the wall."

"A door that wasn't previously there and one that led straight back into the foyer, correct?"

She nodded.

"How did you do it?" he asked.

"I just knew I could," she answered truthfully. "I was tired; I didn't want to have to cross the room again. I just wanted to get out of there."

"So you willed it to happen."

"I—I guess so," she agreed. "But I didn't know what I was doing. It wasn't deliberate. It just felt... right."

"What happened the next time you entered the Library?" Darrius asked, before clarifying, "Not for study reasons, of course."

"I went with Bear and Jordan," she said, thinking back to the day she'd met Sir Camden. "We were curious about what it meant for me to be Chosen. We wanted to know what the possibilities were, so went looking for an adventure, as weird as that sounds."

"And did you find it?"

Alex thought over her experience—the fight with the suit of armour, all the doorways leading to far-off places, befriending the knight. "Absolutely."

"The next time?" he prompted.

"It was just before term started back," Alex said, "straight after the Gala. I was bored. I wanted a distraction."

"Did you find one?"

"I found a door back to my world, so yeah, I'd say I was pretty distracted."

Judging by the look on his face, Darrius hadn't expected that answer. "You found a door to Freya? Why didn't you go through?"

"I wasn't ready to leave," she said quietly. "And—I don't know—but it felt like I was still needed here. Like I *am* still needed here. It's an inner knowledge, just like how I knew I could open that door in the wall—even if it didn't make any sense."

Darrius remained quiet for a moment as he thought over her words. But then Alex cut into the silence.

"Is that why there were so many doorways when Aven held me and D.C. hostage? Did I unconsciously will them into existence?"

"I believe so," Darrius answered. "It's also possible that the Library realised you didn't want him to find what he was searching for, and it sought to stall him."

"Then why was he able to find the right door in the end?" Alex asked.

"Because he's Meyarin, and exiled or not he still holds some sway with the Library because of his ancestor."

"Ancestor?" Alex asked. "What ancestor?"

"Eanraka. The Library's first Chosen, and Akarnae's first headmaster," Darrius said. "The Meyarin royal family are direct descendants. Eanraka's daughter, Queen Niida, is Aven's mother."

Alex opened her mouth to question how that could be possible considering how much time had passed, but then she remembered that a few thousand years was probably just a ripple in time for the Meyarins.

"Those from Eanraka's bloodline will always be granted access to the Library," Darrius said. "But when Aven was disinherited, the Library no longer recognised him as a descendant, and that's why he needed you to allow him permission to enter."

"Which I did," Alex muttered unhappily.

"You had little choice in the matter," Darrius said. "But unfortunately, it means he can now access the Library anytime he wishes."

"What?" she gasped. "But—But that means... What does that mean?"

"It's okay, Alex," Darrius soothed. "He can cause little damage without you. He's still exiled from Meya, and only one who is Chosen can open that particular doorway for him. I'm not sure if even I would be able to do so, with my Library accessibility more limited than your own. That isn't to say he hasn't tried to overpower me and force my hand, but we headmasters are covered by additional protection—including the wards around the academy and the Lockdown protocol. The safety of our students is of the highest priority, and the Library seems to agree."

"I wondered how that worked," Alex admitted. "The wards and the Lockdown, I mean."

"I couldn't tell you even if I tried," Darrius said. "I have no idea how it works, just that it does. It's some kind of security system the Library has set up. The Communication Globes are also Library-designed, which is why they work so efficiently, even during the Lockdown—or when a quick getaway is needed from, say, a New Year's Eve Gala."

Alex shook her head slightly, feeling a headache coming on.

"I do believe we've moved from our original topic," Darrius said, steering the conversation back around. "We were discussing your ability to influence your Library destination."

"I never really got to choose where I went," she protested quickly.

"But you can see now that you had some influence over the events?" Darrius asked, and she nodded, albeit reluctantly. "Then I believe we have the answer you've been searching for."

"The answer...?"

"Didn't you want to find a way home?" Darrius asked. "Isn't that why you've wanted to meet with me all year?"

"Oh." Her head felt muddled, but she eventually realised what he was getting at. "Are you saying I could have gone back to my world anytime I wanted? That I could have just... made a doorway appear?"

He nodded and sent her a smile of approval. She found herself wishing he was more irritating, or just downright unpleasant. But despite his deceit—or his 'withholding of certain information'—she still really liked Darrius. It was hard to stay mad at him, as much as she would like to.

"What are you thinking?" he asked.

"That you're too nice," she said. "It's annoying. I'd very much like to be angry at you, but I can't because it's me who I should be angry at. I can't believe how unobservant I am. Not just with you, but with the Library too. If I'd figured out that I was influencing it, then… well, let's just say I might have had a lot more fun and a whole heap less heart failure."

Darrius chuckled lightly and, as always, it was a comforting and peaceful sound.

"At the same time, I can understand what you said about everything I would have missed out on," she continued. "The things I've experienced, the challenges I've overcome, the friends I've met along the way—none of that would have happened if I hadn't been here."

Alex thought of her blossoming friendship with D.C. She thought of her amazing Kaldoras break with Jordan and Bear and the entire Ronnigan family. She thought of the things she'd learned just by being at the academy; how they'd shaped her identity and built her character.

Her memories led her to a single question, "Darrius, if I open a doorway to my world, will I be able to come back?"

"I certainly hope so," he said with a laugh, "or else I think Karter will find a way to circumnavigate distance and space to drag you back on Monday for your lesson."

Alex looked at him blankly. "My lesson?"

"He didn't tell you?" Darrius asked, his eyes still sparkling with amusement.

"Tell me what?"

"Karter has agreed to train you for three days each week over the summer to bring you up to speed in your Epsilon Combat class."

Alex almost fell off the couch. *"What?"*

"Something about you caught his attention," Darrius said. "He has—finally—admitted that you just might belong in his class. He's seen your potential and is willing to help develop it. It really is an honour, Alex, one I doubt many can claim."

"Honour, my butt," she murmured. "He's just going to use me as his own personal punching bag since he won't have any other students around for the entire summer."

"I fully believe Karter will treat you fairly," Darrius said. "And I also believe Combat is a skill you'd do well to refine, especially in light of recent events."

"Don't you mean, 'in light of the fact that you were just kidnapped by a crazy Meyarin who is bent on doing it again until he gets what he wants'?" she corrected bitterly.

He refused to acknowledge her mood and simply said, "That description works just as adequately, though mine was perhaps slightly less melodramatic."

She sighed, but let go of her annoyance to confirm. "So, you think I'll be able to come back?"

"I'm sure of it," Darrius said. "As you said yourself, your adventures here in Medora are not yet near finished."

She was torn between pleasure at being able to continue at the academy with her friends, and fear of what the future might bring since Aven was still out there with his plans for retribution. But as Alex walked out of Darrius's private study later that evening—using a doorway that she willed into the wall—and joined her three friends in the Rec Room, all she felt was gratitude. Gratitude for the time they'd already had, and gratitude for the time they would have in the future. The fear was worth it, she realised.

"What are you thinking about?" D.C. asked, noticing her distraction. "Are you still shocked that your Darrius is our Marselle?"

Alex had shared everything that she'd learned and now the four of them were lounging around on beanbags, enjoying their time together.

"No," Alex said. "I feel like an idiot for not realising sooner. But I was actually thinking about us—all of us—and just how thankful I am."

"Aww," Jordan said, faking a sniff. "Tear."

"Shut up," she said, throwing a cushion at him. "I wasn't including *you* in that."

"Sure you weren't," he said, smirking. "Face it, you're going to miss me the most."

"Whatever," she said, pushing him off his beanbag. "Your ego is truly growing by the second."

"Did you hear that?" Jordan said, turning to Bear. "I think she said she's going to die without me. Poor thing. It's sad when they get so obsessed that they can't stand it when I'm not around. But I think it's just one of those unfortunate facts of life."

Alex couldn't help smiling in spite of herself. She really *would* miss them.

"Will my ComTCD still work?" she asked, changing the subject to go with her thoughts.

"Not while you're in your world," Bear said, careful to keep his voice down. "But when you're here it will. You'll be able to contact us at any time, but we won't be able to visit or anything since the academy is closed to students over summer."

"I still can't believe you get to train with Karter," Jordan said. "Talk about awesome."

"I'd switch places in a heartbeat," she muttered.

"Yeah," D.C. agreed. "Finn might be a psychopath, but Karter is a machine. You'll be a tank of muscles the next time we see you, Alex."

Everyone paused for a moment, all of them imagining that picture before, as one, they said, "*Eww.*"

They laughed then, at one thing and then another and another, laughing their night away and enjoying their friendships—the old and the new.

Forty-Eight

"Are you ready?" Darrius asked the next morning.

Most of the students had already left the academy, but Alex and her friends had waited until the last possible moment before departing. It was a remarkable difference from when she had first arrived—back then she would have been sprinting to get to the quickest doorway through to her world. But time had changed Alex, and even though she was looking forward to being reunited with her parents soon, she still didn't want to have to say goodbye to her friends, even if it was only for the summer.

"No. But I don't think I have a choice," she answered, shifting her backpack on her shoulders. There wasn't much in it—just the clothes she'd first arrived in and the Kaldoras gifts she'd received.

"You always have a choice, Alex," Darrius said, reminding her of not only her gift, but also her right as a human being.

"Thanks for everything, Darrius," she said, smiling at him. "I mean it. You saved my life, a few times I think."

"You're most welcome," he said, returning her smile. "I should be around more often next term, which will allow me to keep a closer eye on you."

"Great," Alex said dryly. "Just what every student wants—the headmaster watching out for them."

"There goes your social life," Jordan quipped, and D.C. elbowed him to keep quiet.

Darrius chuckled but he didn't try to reassure her. "Remember," he said instead, "Monday, Wednesday and Friday at the Arena. Best to arrive a little early."

Alex didn't need the reminder, or the warning. She was already dreading her solo torture sessions with Karter. The only upside was that they would give her the opportunity to connect with her friends over the break. A ComTCD call was better than nothing.

"I'll leave you to your goodbyes, and I'll see you in a few days," Darrius said, and he walked away from them with a parting smile.

"I guess this is it," Alex said, looking at her closest friends in the world. *Worlds.* "For now, at least."

D.C. launched herself at Alex. "You had better call or so help me—"

"I promise, Dix," Alex said, hugging her in return. "Every chance I get."

"You'd better," D.C. threatened again, before she squeezed one last time and let go.

"Come here, you," Bear said, pulling Alex into a… well, into a bear hug. He wrapped his massive arms around her and she snuggled into his warm chest. "You look after yourself," he said as he released her. "No more crazy adventures without us, you hear?"

"I'll do my best," she said.

Alex turned and found Jordan already waiting for her, his arms open wide. She walked straight into them, hugging him tightly.

"Thank you," she said quietly. "For that first day. For bringing me here. For everything since then."

"You're welcome," he said back, just as quietly. And then, much louder, he called out, "Did you all hear that? She just admitted to being totally and completely in love with me! I knew it!"

Alex pulled away and punched him in the arm. "Jerk," she said, laughing.

She still had a smile on her face as she walked away from them, glancing back only once as she walked into the Tower. They were a picture of happy smiles and sad eyes. None of them wanted to part, no matter how short the time. But the joy of friendship came with difficult goodbyes, sometimes.

"See you all soon," she called out. It was a promise they could all hold on to. That they *would* all hold on to.

Alex didn't turn around again, instead she descended the steps down into the foyer of the Library. She waved to the librarian as she walked past and he nodded at her, his gaze grouchy as per usual but his eyes gleamed with newfound respect.

She continued walking until she reached the far staircase and headed down, concentrating on where she needed to go. The doorway appeared before her just like she'd expected, and she didn't hesitate to open it and step straight into the darkness, immediately falling into pitch-black nothingness.

When she landed in the cavern it was exactly as she remembered, raging river and all.

"Back again, Alexandra?"

"I'm ready to go, this time," she answered the voice.

The river stilled and the huge boulders surfaced once more to create a path over the water. A doorway appeared, already open and showing her house—just like last time.

"You've come far," the voice said. *"And you still have far to go."*

"Believe me, I know," Alex said, stepping carefully over the boulders until she reached the other side of the river. "Once I go through, how do I come back?"

"How did you get here?"

Alex presumed the voice was referring to her trip down into the cavern, and if that was the case then the answer was that she'd just willed it to happen.

"Are you saying that I can be anywhere, anytime, and I'll be able to open a doorway between our worlds?" she asked.

"*From Freya, yes,*" the voice said. "*But here in Medora, you need to be within my boundary.*"

"So, I actually have to be somewhere in the Library to open doors?" Alex clarified. "It doesn't work the other way around?"

"*You can re-enter a doorway if you've passed through it previously,*" the voice said. "*You'll discover that for yourself when you visit Meya.*"

Alex's stomach plummeted. "Come again?"

"*You're curious, aren't you?*" the voice asked. "*A time will come when your curiosity will lead you to the Lost City, and the door you step through will bring you back again. The same is true for any door you ever leave from—they will always return you should you choose to step back through.*"

"But from my world I can open a doorway from anywhere and come straight through to Medora?" Alex repeated, just to make sure she understood.

"*That's correct.*"

Something nudged at her then, a memory from what felt like a lifetime ago.

"Did I bring myself here?" she asked hesitantly. "That day—I remember dreading the idea of being stuck at that horrible boarding school for eight months. I remember wishing things could be different. Did I somehow create the doorway that led me here?"

"*You were Called,*" the voice said, repeating the word Aven had used to describe Alex. "*Many are Called, but few answer the Call. Fewer still respond to it and follow where it leads. Your Calling created the door for you, but you had to make the decision to step through it. And when you did, you found everything you were searching for, didn't you?*"

Alex didn't need any time to think. The answer was simple. "Yes."

"*And that's why you're not only Called, but also Chosen,*" the voice told her. "*Because you'll continue to walk through the doors, no matter where they lead.*"

Alex considered those words as she stared through the doorway in front of her. "I guess this is a good time to test that theory," she said, before closing her eyes and stepping forward.

As Alex was thrown through the air towards her world, she was filled with a calm reassurance that her journey was not at an end.

It was only just beginning.

Alex's journey continues in the second
instalment of

THE MEDORAN CHRONICLES
BOOK TWO

RAELIA

ACKNOWLEDGEMENTS

I always feel like rolling my eyes when authors express gratitude to God in their acknowledgements because, let's face it, it's corny. That said, I still want to say thanks, God, for giving me a love of words and an irrepressibly overactive imagination. You made all this happen, and I'm eternally grateful.

Massive hugs go to my incredible family: Mum, I couldn't have made it here without you. Thank you for always believing in me, encouraging me and convincing me that the best is yet to come. Dad, thank you for being the greatest father a girl could ever ask for, and for loving me waaaay more than I deserve. Nan, you're arguably the most generous human being in the world—or at least in my world. Thank you for always being there for me, in every possible way. Aunty Noni, thanks for sharing your wisdom—and your name—and for all your wonderfully stimulating conversations. And Steve, you've always been good at sharing, so thank you for having a dream so huge that it burst out of you and left a light bright enough for me to step into. You inspire me every single day.

Now onto my Pantera Press family: Marty, thank you, thank you, *thank you* for loving this story enough to recommend it to everyone else. If you hadn't believed in Alex, none of this would be happening. Extra special gratitude for *One Jump Ahead*—which is a moment I will never forget! Ali, there aren't enough words in any language to describe just how amazing you are. Thank you for putting up with my gazillion emails and for not thinking I'm a total weirdo for regaling you with inane (and irrelevant) stories about my life on a way too frequent basis. You've championed me for every step of this incredible journey. From the very bottom of my heart, thank you for making my dreams come true. John, I'm not sure if the psychopath discussion and the 'funeral test' were some kind of cool hazing ritual, but if that's the case, I'm glad I passed. Thank you for being the first person in the world to shake my hand and officially call me an 'author'. Elly, thanks for being a fabulous social media guru and for the unending supply of Coke Zeros when we met. And Susan, you've opened up a galaxy of opportunities for a baby author with impossible dreams. I'm in awe of your vision and dedication, and I'm so thankful to have you rooting for me. I hope we get to share many more chocolate meringues in the future!

Now to everyone else who helped make this happen:

Massive thanks go to my editor, Deonie Fiford, and my proofreader, Desanka Vukelich, for polishing my words and making them shine like Myrox. Also, huge gratitude goes to my typesetter from Kirby Jones for dealing with all my last-minute paranoid changes; to the team at Xou Creative for delivering an oh-my-gosh stunning cover; and to Lauren Barnett from Lauren Ami Photographs for a magical photoshoot and an author pic that absolutely rocks.

To all my colleagues at YOUnique, especially Gem-Gem, Jacqui-Bro and Harnell, thanks for keeping me relatively sane by reminding me that there is a real world outside of fiction. Special mention goes to Melanie Summer for letting me keep my job when half my work hours are spent daydreaming and the other half are spent singing. Huge respect also goes to Ben Markey, who deserves a medal for putting up with my unending, often meaningless chatter. (Admit it, my mascara stories are the best!)

I'm blessed to have a number of other wonderful people in my life, and I'd especially like to thank the following: Letitia Peffer, for being the most loyal and supportive friend I could ever ask for; Jodie Llewellyn, for all the 'tranquil time' and for introducing me to the world of fanfiction; Reesha Radford, for ignoring my advice to "run while you still can"; Rachel Griffiths, for being the bravest person I've ever encountered; Bobbie-Jo Davis, for never doubting this would happen; and Jackie Davison, for re-entering my life at the perfect time to experience the wonder of this journey with me. You guys are all amazing and I'm honoured to know you.

Ginormous amounts of gratitude go to all my early 'test subjects' who winced their way through rough drafts, especially Dana Summer for loving my characters almost as much as I do and spending hours telling me why.

To everyone who follows my blog, thank you for your overwhelming enthusiasm and for sending frequent warm-and-fuzzies my way. Virtual cookies for all of you!

And finally, to you, my readers: thank you for taking a chance on Alex and her friends, and for taking a chance on me. I can't wait to step through the next doorway with you and see where it leads!

Lynette Noni grew up on a farm in outback Australia until she moved to the beautiful Sunshine Coast and swapped her mud-stained boots for sand-splashed flip-flops. She has always been an avid reader and most of her childhood was spent lost in daydreams of far-off places and magical worlds. She was devastated when her Hogwarts letter didn't arrive, but she consoled herself by looking inside every wardrobe she could find, and she's still determined to find her way to Narnia one day. While waiting for that to happen, she creates her own fantasy worlds and enjoys spending time with the characters she meets along the way.

Arkarnae is the first of five books in Lynette's YA fantasy series, *The Medoran Chronicles*.

Lynette loves to chat with her readers. For pronunciation guides and more, connect with her online:

www.LynetteNoni.com
Facebook.com/Lynette.Noni
Twitter.com/LynetteNoni
Instagram.com/LynetteNoni